CONSPIRACY
in
EMILIA ROMAGNA
A SANTINI/DEROSA NOVEL

ERIN MOIRA O'HARA

Conspiracy in Emilia Romagna
Copyright © 2016 by Erin Moira O'Hara

ISBN: 978-0-9942469-8-1

Conspiracy in Emilia Romagna is dedicated to my relatives in Northern Italy, and my good friend, Serena Tatti. Her passionate belief in my writing has been inspiring.

BOOKS BY ERIN MOIRA O'HARA

The Knight of Castle Kildare

Conspiracy in Emilia Romagna

Beat of the Jungle

Steele Ops Series

The Kalista Diamond

Precious Gems

Jewel of the Kimberley

The Amethyst Code

Bindarra Creek

Tempting Fate

Date with Destiny

A Twist of Fate

SOPHIA DEROSA becomes entangled in a deadly web of deception when she sets out to prove the Santinis, a wealthy Italian family, were behind a conspiracy to destroy her father. Her plans come undone when she encounters Ricardo Santini, a man determined to guard his family name at all costs. After several attempts are made on her life, Sofia must trust in the very people she's certain were behind the conspiracy.

RICARDO SANTINI is a tough negotiator and an intimidating adversary. He's worked hard to restore the family vineyard after Giuseppe DeRosa almost destroyed it. The Santini's are about to launch a chain of luxury hotels throughout Emilia Romagna when Sofia DeRosa arrives in Bologna. She is beautiful, strong-willed, and set on proving her father's innocence. Ricardo finds her dangerously irresistible, yet to protect his family, he must keep her close.

ACKNOWLEDGMENTS

Special thanks to my wonderful critique partners S.E. Gilchrist and Suzanne Bellamy. Two ladies, who continually drive, incite and encourage me to be a better writer.

My beta reader Michelle Stefani, who catches everything we miss.

Cover Artist – Fiona Jayde Media, Editor – Deadra Krieger, and my formatting team at Author E.M.S. These lovely people help me produce beautiful books.

My particular thanks must go to Serena Tatti who edited this story several years ago. Her knowledge of the Italian language was invaluable.

CONSPIRACY
in
EMILIA ROMAGNA

The DeRosa Vineyard—Victoria, Australia

Autumn in Victoria so far had been mostly dismal and wet. It didn't say a lot for the upcoming winter. Sofia DeRosa glanced out the office window as the weak rays of sun sank beyond the grapevines, cloaking the desk in eerie shadows—an omen perhaps. She turned back to her computer and twisted a spiral of red hair around her finger as she scanned the latest version of the email to *Papà*. No matter how many times she rewrote it, he wouldn't be happy she was taking a holiday while he and Dante were in America. At least he'd never suspect her true destination or the reason behind it.

Taking a deep breath, she pressed send. Normally by this hour she would have locked the vineyard office and walked the short distance to the house, but not tonight. Tonight she'd processed the wine orders, cleared her desk, and now there was no turning back. The email was on its way to *Papà*.

Sofia placed her personal phone in the drawer and closed it, then shut down the computer. Her assistant could handle things in the office, and if anything important cropped up, *Papà* and Dante were only a phone call away. She would be unreachable. Sofia cringed at what lay ahead, but somebody had to clear *Papà's* name, even if it meant taking on the whole Santini family and losing her friend, Carolina, in the process.

It's time the truth came out.

Hotel Emilia Romagna—Bologna, Italy

Riccardo Santini, chief executive of Santini Holdings, signed his name to their latest hotel acquisition with a deep sense of satisfaction. *Now we only need that grand old hotel in Venezia and we will have an exclusive hotel in every major city of Italia.*

His brother strode through the doorway and threw himself into a leather armchair.

"Is something wrong, Giovanni?"

"We have a situation."

Riccardo laid down his pen and leaned back in his chair. "Oh?"

"*Papà* requires us to deal with a potential troublemaker."

"Who?"

Drumming his fingers on the armrest, Giovanni glanced beyond Riccardo to the view of the Piazza beyond. "Sofia DeRosa is arriving in *Milano* tomorrow."

"Why would that be of concern to us?"

Uncrossing his ankles, Giovanni stood and placed his hands on the mahogany desk. "According to our sister, Giuseppe DeRosa's daughter is coming to Italy to prove there was a conspiracy to frame her father. *Papà* is worried the old rumors regarding the Santini-DeRosa feud will start again. It's the last thing we need with our new hotels opening next month."

Riccardo's eyes narrowed. "How would Carolina know this?"

"Against *Papà's* wishes, our sister and Sofia DeRosa have been corresponding over the last five years. Carolina has been asking questions about the feud and the fires. *Papà* insisted she tell him why."

Riccardo rubbed his chin. "I agree with *Papà*. We do not want the old scandal resurfacing. Perhaps we can intercept Sofia DeRosa in *Milano* and change her mind. Everyone has a price."

"Do you know what she looks like or how old she is?"

"I have no idea, but I met her brother five years ago when he came to Ravenna to beat the shit out of our cousin, Nico, and drag his sister back to Australia."

Giovanni's head shot up. "What did Nico do, and why don't I know about this?"

"You were at university. Sofia DeRosa came to Ravenna to stay with her grandparents and somehow became friends with our sister, who then introduced her to Nico. When Giuseppe DeRosa found out his daughter was consorting with the enemy, he sent his son to escort Sofia back to Australia."

"What happened?"

"Nico disappeared then Carolina and Sofia fled to *Venezia*. When *Papà* caught up with Carolina, the DeRosas had already departed."

Giovanni pulled out his phone. "I think it's time we had a chat with our little sister. Is she in her shop today?"

"Si, I passed her in the hotel's foyer earlier."

"Good, once we've spoken to her, we'll go to *Milano* and deal with Sofia DeRosa."

"Agreed. Let me know when Carolina arrives. We need to know which flight *Signorina* DeRosa will be on."

"Of course."

Riccardo waited until Giovanni left the office then turned to the large window, his earlier satisfaction shot to pieces. They could not afford bad publicity. *I will stop you, Sofia DeRosa, one-way or another.*

Chapter One

Flying straight through from Melbourne to Milan without a stopover had been a bad decision. Sofia hadn't slept a wink. A shower and a comfortable bed would be very welcome once she arrived at her hotel in Bologna. First though, she needed a bottle of water. She headed to a small café alongside the departure lounge of her connecting flight. She waited in line behind two well-dressed Italian men, their rich accents floating over her.

The men turned to leave and Sofia, moving back to give them room, tripped over a briefcase. The taller of the two men reached out and grasped her arms, hauling her against him. She found herself flattened against a hard chest. Looking up, she discovered an amused pair of gorgeous, dark chocolaty-brown eyes. "Oh my God."

An easy smile spread across lips that promised sensual delights and a hint of wickedness. "Not God, *cara mia*, but I'm willing to believe you are a sprite who has been sent to bewitch me."

A thrill ran down Sofia's body to the very tip of her toes. Her breathing quickened at the intimacy of this tall, handsome, stranger's hold. His black hair, thick and wavy, fell to just above his collar. Her fingers itched to reach up and touch his smooth, strong jawline as her imagination ran wild.

Sofia, what the hell? "Oh, I didn't mean you're a god. Not that you're not, well...what I mean is...I'm sorry." She groaned.

The man's smile widened. "I'm not sorry. It's not every day I save a pretty redhead with eyes the color of deep-green emeralds."

Sofia's heart skipped a couple of beats. This man was the epitome of hot with his broad shoulders, height, and sensual dark eyes. Her gaze fell to his lips as they curved into another to die for smile and she realized he'd spoken. "I'm sorry, what did you say?"

He laughed. "I asked if you speak Italian, *Signorina?*"

"No. My father's Italian but my mother was Irish, hence the red hair." Trying to regain her composure, she glanced at the other man. He shared the same eyes, features, and wicked smile as the one holding her. "I should go. Thank you for catching me." She smoothed his jacket where she'd been clutching it as if it were a lifeline.

"As you wish, *cara mia*. It was a pleasure *catching you. Arrivederci.*"

The men strolled to a table in the cafe, leaving Sofia as ruffled as a hen facing a hungry fox. Her skin tingled where his hands had touched her. "How bizarre."

After buying a bottle of water, she found a seat and pulled out the letter she'd received last week. It was written to Giuseppe DeRosa from his sister, Renzina, almost thirty years ago, yet never posted...until now.

Curiosity getting the better of her, Sofia had taken it to a trusted Italian employee for translation. She had been stunned by its contents, then determined to see justice done.

She took a deep breath and read it yet again.

> *My dear Giuseppe, I know you refuse to speak to Papà or come home to Italia, but you must. I know who framed you, and I've hidden evidence of this shameful conspiracy to discredit you. I am too scared to do this on my own or share it with our parents, but it is only right that you reclaim your heritage and reputation. If something happens to me, take the evidence and clear your name. Then find Ariana, as she has something belonging to you. You can trust Salvatore Bondini, but be vigilant.*

Sofia shifted in her seat. Renzina DeRosa had died in a horrific car accident, coincidentally the same day she'd written this letter. But why had it not been posted until now? Sofia had met Salvatore Bondini five years ago. He was her grandparents' solicitor and the man who introduced her to Carolina. But who was Ariana?

Sofia's thoughts drifted to her grandparents, Lorenzo and Elena

DeRosa. The holiday five years ago had only eventuated after her mother's death. *Papà* had agreed to Sofia's pleas to visit them with one stipulation.

Stay away from the Santini family.

Sofia folded the letter and opened a disturbing note that had been written in English and tucked inside the envelope with Renzina's letter.

> *Giuseppe,*
> *I don't know if Renzina died because of the letter I have enclosed or she really did lose control of her car, but we all deserve to know the truth.*

A moment's guilt tugged at Sofia's heart for the five years she and Carolina Santini had kept their friendship a secret from their parents. Yet it was the only way to learn the truth behind their families' bitter feud. Murder was an entirely different matter.

Sofia slid the letter and note into an envelope, then dropped it into her carry-bag with the two copies she'd brought with her. It was a blessing business had taken her father to America. He would have a fit if he knew what she planned, or that an Italian Adonis had held her intimately.

Riccardo and Giovanni crossed the small departure lounge and found a couple of vacant seats to await the unsuspecting Sofia DeRosa.

"How will we recognize her?" asked Giovanni.

Riccardo glanced around the lounge. "Carolina said Sofia DeRosa is travelling alone and this is her flight. I'm surprised she's coming back, after her last visit."

Giovanni opened his paper. "What happened five years ago when her brother arrived?"

Riccardo kept his eyes on the entrance. "He came to our *villa*, demanding to know where his sister was and the nature of her relationship with Nico. He became hostile toward *Papà*, who refused to tell him anything. In the meantime, Carolina and Sofia DeRosa ran away to *Venezia*."

Giovanni shrugged. "So why would Giuseppe DeRosa allow his daughter to come here alone knowing she intended to prove his innocence?"

"I have no idea." His gaze wandered over the other passengers, pausing when he noticed the attractive redhead enter the lounge.

"You don't think it's her, do you?" asked Giovanni. "She's Australian, appears to be on her own, and a beauty who would definitely attract Nico."

"No, she's too fair. I've learned Giuseppe DeRosa married a Sicilian woman before immigrating to Australia. And, I met his son who has dark hair and olive skin. One would assume the daughter is of similar appearance."

Their gazes followed the attractive Australian across the lounge to an empty seat. She glanced over and a soft blush bloomed in her cheeks.

Leaning closer, Giovanni murmured, "You should introduce yourself properly and arrange to meet her in Bologna. Who knows, it might lead to the altar."

Keeping his voice lowered, Riccardo replied, "There isn't a woman alive who could tempt me into marriage. Not even one as lovely as her." Riccardo nodded toward the redheaded beauty. She looked to be in her early twenties, five foot-six or seven, and very shapely. She'd certainly stirred his blood while pressed against him. Then she'd smiled at him with those lovely emerald eyes, so alive and vibrant, and her lips had parted.

Riccardo stretched out his legs. "A woman like that will be spoken for already."

Giovanni pursed his lips. "She's not wearing any rings."

Their discussion was interrupted by the high-pitched screams of a baby and small children. Both men glanced at a flushed young woman approaching. She carried a bulging bag on one arm and a tiny baby in the other. Two little twin girls clung to her skirts, their cries irritatingly high-pitched, as if to outdo each other.

"Oh no." Giovanni groaned.

Riccardo watched the mother and her children cross the lounge, clearly searching for somewhere to sit. Almost every seat had been taken. The young mother knelt on the carpet with her back to them and attempted to calm her children. Riccardo and Giovanni stood and were about to offer their seats when the stunning redhead beat them to it. The woman thanked her in French and sank gratefully onto the chair, exhaustion clear on her flustered face.

Riccardo's eyes widened when the woman he couldn't take his eyes off held out her arms for the baby, directing the French woman to comfort her little girls. The young mother hesitated for several seconds, then handed the baby over and pulled her daughters onto her lap. The beauty then gently rocked the baby and spoke soothingly.

The baby's wailing eased then stopped as the infant stared at the young woman's face. Another moment passed then the baby gurgled and reached for a long, red curl with little fat fingers.

Turning an amused face to Riccardo, Giovanni chuckled. "Watch out big brother, she's compassionate and good with children."

Riccardo didn't bother answering, although his gaze stayed riveted on the beauty as she rocked the baby gently against her breast. *I wonder if it's possible to be jealous of a baby.*

Closing his paper, Giovanni stood. "If you're not interested in the lovely *signorina*, I certainly am."

Riccardo's jaw clenched as Giovanni strolled toward the young Australian, intent on charming her into his bed. *Damn.*

Sofia watched the Italian stroll toward her. She immediately thought of Carolina's cousin, Nicolas Lombardi, with his dark eyes and charming smile. He'd reminded Sofia of her brother when he laughed.

Sofia sneaked a look at the man who'd held her in his arms and she almost stopped breathing. He was staring at her as if he wanted to devour her. "Oh God." Her pulse quickened. The brother was almost to her.

"*Buongiorno, signorina.* My name is Giovanni. You are good with the *bambino.* Do you have one of your own perhaps?"

Sofia laughed. "No, *signore*, I don't have one of my own."

His smile and deep, rich voice was similar to his brother's. "Could this truly be my lucky day and you're not married or engaged either?"

"I'm not, but I don't know that it's your lucky day."

He gave a genuine laugh. "Will you be staying in Bologna long?"

"A couple of weeks."

"Perhaps I could persuade you to join me for dinner one night?"

Sofia looked at him thoughtfully. He was certainly good looking, but she had a mission to accomplish and men like Giovanni and his brother were way out of her league and much too distracting. "I'm sorry, I won't have time."

"Then let me show you some of Bologna's beautiful treasures."

"Thank you, but I already know my way around Bologna and I'm familiar with most of the churches and basilicas there."

"Perhaps a drive into the mountains?"

"I'm sorry, but I have plans."

"Arh, *signorina*, won't you change your mind?"

Sofia smiled. "No."

He gave her a wink. "*None problema.* Enjoy your stay in Bologna, *signorina.*"

Sofia watched him walk back to his brother then cooed at the baby. *He is nice, but he doesn't make my pulse fly like his brother did.* "What do you think, sweet little boy? Should I have gone out with him?"

Sofia wondered if the other brother might make a play for her. And if he did, what would she do? There was something dangerously tempting about him and she couldn't help but imagine what it would be like to share a kiss or three. Sofia realized the heartthrob was watching her with amusement. She quickly bent her head to the baby.

Riccardo met Giovanni's gaze as he returned to his seat and picked up the paper.

"Well?"

Giovanni scowled. "She's busy."

"She refused you, didn't she?" Riccardo laughed.

"I told you, she's busy."

"You're losing your touch, Giovanni."

"She's not married and she'll be in Bologna for a couple of weeks. Why don't you ask her out?"

"I have more important things on my mind at the moment and she's a little too innocent for my palate or yours. I suggest we forget her and concentrate on Sofia DeRosa."

An older woman carrying duty free shopping bags bustled into their lounge and stopped in front of the young mother and two little girls. After a brief conversation in French the woman turned toward the redhead and held out her hands. "*Merci, mademoiselle. Je suis la grand-mere.*"

Riccardo's breath hitched at the bewitching smile the redhead bestowed on the baby before she handed it to the woman. *How I would like her to smile at me like that. Perhaps I will introduce myself and invite her to lunch.*

"Attention passenger, Sofia DeRosa. Please see Airline staff at departure gate eight."

The redhead picked up her bag and made her way to the counter.

Chapter Two

"It can't be her, not with that creamy skin and red hair." Stunned, Riccardo stared at the redhead's retreating back. "She said her father's Italian, but her mother was Irish, and we know Giuseppe DeRosa married a Sicilian woman."

"We should check."

"I intend to." Riccardo strode after her, coming up behind the redhead as she spoke to the attendant at the gate counter.

"*Scusa, mi chiamo* Sofia DeRosa." She spoke carefully as if unsure of the words.

Irritation rose within Riccardo, not only as she was Sofia DeRosa, but also because of the leer in the male attendant's eyes as he ogled her.

"*Signorina* DeRosa, your seat has been reported as faulty and safety regulations demand we cannot put a passenger in it."

"Does that mean I can't catch the flight?"

"No, *signorina*. As we have no available seats in economy, we are upgrading you to business class."

"Business class. Wow…thanks."

"It is our pleasure, *Signorina*. I will print out a new boarding pass for you."

Riccardo glowered at the male attendant whose eyes kept dropping to Sofia DeRosa's breasts. The attendant caught Riccardo's warning glare and his face reddened. "I'm s…sorry, *signorina*, here is your new boarding pass." He darted a quick glance at Riccardo then fumbled with some papers.

Sofia DeRosa thanked the attendant as an elderly man shuffled to her left side.

Riccardo silently cursed.

"You're a lucky young lady," said the man with a British accent. "I'm eighty and have never travelled business class. Never will I suppose." He leaned heavily on his walking stick then slowly turned away.

The man didn't look a day over seventy or short of cash, if his clothes were anything to go by. Riccardo's eyes narrowed as Sofia DeRosa took a step after the man. Surely she wouldn't fall for his act.

"Wait," she called. "Sir, you can have my seat."

Crossing his arms, Riccardo shook his head in disbelief and waited.

The attendant came round the counter. "You don't have to do that, *signorina.*"

"I want to. Please, give this gentleman my seat and I will swap to his seat."

The elderly man grasped Sofia's hand. "I couldn't possibly."

She smiled at the con artist. "I want you to have it. Please."

Oh this is priceless. Riccardo placed his hands on his hips and observed as the man and Sofia DeRosa were given new boarding passes, then the old man kissed her cheek before he tottered off at a much quicker gait than when he'd approached her.

Sofia DeRosa swung around and slammed into Riccardo's chest. He automatically reached out to steady her.

She gasped. "You're making a habit of saving me, *signore,*" she said breathlessly.

Riccardo searched for words. He couldn't think of any other woman who would voluntarily give up a premium seat to a stranger. Yet, here she stood. Sofa DeRosa, a potential problem he had to deal with, smiling at him with those beautiful green eyes. He didn't smile back.

"I know who you are, *signorina.* I am Riccardo Santini. After the commotion you caused the last time you were in Italy, I'm surprised you have the nerve to come back."

Her smile faded, her face paled. She regarded him warily. "You're Riccardo Santini?" She pulled out of his arms.

The loss of her soft curves had him closing his fingers to stop reaching for her, despite her heritage and intent. He nodded curtly. "I am."

She stared at him seemingly lost for words then straightened her shoulders and drew breath. "So are you here to get rid of me like my aunt, or just warn me off?"

Riccardo blinked. "What the hell are you talking about?" He took a step closer, towering over her.

She didn't shrink or cower as he'd expected. "I'll try to be clearer, *signore*. If someone threatens the Santinis, you get rid of them, don't you? Or in the case of your cousin, Nico, disappear into thin air rather than stand up for his friends. I know your family tried to destroy my father, but are they also behind my aunt Renzina's death?"

Riccardo stilled. She hadn't raised her voice, but the little spitfire could pack a punch. He encircled her slim wrist with his fingers then lowered his voice in an attempt to keep their conversation private. "Your father deserved everything he got, *signorina*, and the Santinis are not cowards or murderers, although the way I'm feeling at the moment, murder is a real possibility."

"Your family made my father out to be a thief, a gambler, and an arsonist." She dropped her small carry-bag and poked him in the chest as tears welled in her eyes. "The Santini's accusations tore my father's family apart. He loved Italy, but it's because of your family that he immigrated to Australia." She tried to poke him again but he grabbed her free hand.

"That's absurd. What evidence do you have to support this?"

She wriggled her wrists. "My aunt had evidence that would have cleared my father, but she died before she was able to do anything about it. I'm going to use that evidence to expose those responsible."

Narrowing his eyes, Riccardo tightened his grip. Not enough to hurt her, but enough to ensure she didn't escape. "Why wasn't this evidence produced before, and why are you here and not your father or brother?"

Her gaze skittered left then right as if to ensure she wasn't alone with him, or was it because she was playing for time as she considered what to say? "My father and brother have business to attend to, but will join me soon."

"So you've come to Italy with the sole intention of blackening the Santini name?"

"I'm here to clear my father and look into my aunt's death."

Riccardo stared into her furious green eyes. *Can she be so naïve that she believes she can take on my family by herself?* "Why did you give that man your seat?"

"What? Why are you changing the subject?"

"I would like to know why you gave a premium seat to a man you don't know?"

"He's old and might never get another chance."

"He played you, *signorina.* Big time."

"Does it matter?" She wriggled her wrists again. "Please let go of me or I will call for assistance."

Riccardo grudgingly released her, stepping back when she picked up her carry-bag and swung around. He watched her stalk off, her stunning red hair swinging wildly behind her. His gaze dropped to her taut bottom as she flounced across the lounge. An unexpected and unwelcome hunger stirred low in his belly, and it wasn't for food. Of all women, why did he react to this one so readily?

She stopped at a window overlooking the runways, her posture stiff and unyielding.

Riccardo turned on his heel and approached the female attendant.

"Can I help you, s*ignore*?" she asked, her voice purring seductively.

"I want *Signorina* DeRosa moved to first class and the seat beside me."

Her eyes widened. "I'm sorry, signore, I can't do that."

"Of course you can. Just move her and I will pay the difference."

"It doesn't work that way." The attendant made a hasty retreat behind the counter.

Riccardo nodded curtly, pulled out his phone and scrolled through his contacts until he found the one he wanted.

"*Ciao,* Giancarlo, it's Riccardo Santini, I need a favor and I need it fast." He briefly explained what he wanted then finished the call and returned to Giovanni.

"Let's go."

"What happened? What did she say?"

"Come," called Riccardo, striding off.

Once in the business lounge, Riccardo repeated the conversation he'd had with Sofia DeRosa.

"So...she knowingly gave the con man her seat?" Giovanni clarified.

Riccardo sighed in exasperation. "Yes, then she dropped this conspiracy bombshell on me."

Giovanni rubbed his forehead. "We need to get a look at the evidence to see if it's legitimate."

"Of course it's not legitimate," snapped Riccardo. "There is no evidence. She is clutching at straws."

Sitting back, Giovanni surveyed Riccardo. "All right, but I think we should at least find out what evidence she's talking about before she makes these accusations public."

"I'm working on it, Giovanni. I've arranged to have her moved to the seat beside me."

"How did you manage that?"

"Giancarlo is on the airline's board of directors. I called in a favor."

"We need to keep this out of the papers. We could try buying her silence and if that fails...make her disappear."

Riccardo scowled at him. "That isn't an option, Giovanni."

The female attendant approached smiling. "*Signori*, we are boarding now. Would you please make your way to the departure gate?"

As they walked toward the gate, Riccardo glanced at the woman occupying his thoughts. She watched him, a frown marring her lovely face. Riccardo had the distinct feeling Sofia DeRosa was going to prove a much bigger problem than he'd anticipated. Never had a woman stood up to him like that, her body trembling with anger and emotion as she poked him in the chest. He almost laughed at the thought, then sobered, surprised and intrigued to find he respected her bravery. He had to remind himself she was a DeRosa and threatening to drag his family through the mud. Still, none of his adversaries had ever had such sparkling eyes or attractive curves.

Sofia fumed as Riccardo Santini and his brother crossed the lounge. *Who does he think he is?* He looked annoyed. *Good, it serves the arrogant beast right.* She joined the other passengers waiting to board the plane, surprised when the attendant took her boarding pass, dropped it in the bin then handed her a new one.

"*Mi scusi, signorina.* You have been upgraded. Have a nice flight."

"Oh...*grazie.*" Sofia proceeded down the passageway, elated when the stewardess on the plane directed her to a window seat in first class. Once seated she glanced across the aisle and was disconcerted to find Giovanni Santini sitting there reading a newspaper. She spied the empty space beside her with sudden dread.

"This must be my seat," proclaimed a deep, drawling voice.

"Oh no." Sofia looked up into Riccardo Santini's dark eyes, then watched as he handed his jacket to the stewardess and slid into the seat beside her, stretching out his long legs.

"It appears we are destined to spend time together, *signorina.*" His lips almost formed a smile.

Sofia glared. "If I thought it possible, I'd swear you had something to do with my seat change."

"Don't be like that, *signorina.* I believe there was a time you enjoyed a close relationship with a member of my family, or have you forgotten your brief affair with my cousin, Nico?"

A hiss escaped Sofia's lips. "You know nothing. Nico and I were not...we didn't. It's none of your business what we were."

"What about my sister? How did you convince Carolina to run away with you?"

"I didn't." Sofia fought to keep her temper. "We ran away together."

Riccardo lowered his voice. "I know you're still friends with Carolina. Won't she be hurt by this vindictive plan of yours?"

"I'm not being vindictive. I want to expose the truth and mend the rift between my grandparents and *Papà.*" She crossed her arms and met his gaze. Why should she feel defensive? The Santinis were to the ones who'd done the wrong thing by her father, but were they murderers? Was she in danger?

Riccardo watched fascinated as her eyes glistened with tears and her chest rose and fell as she struggled for composure. She didn't fit the bill of cold and calculating, yet what she planned to do would cause a lot of negative publicity. She picked up a magazine and flicked through it, far too quickly to see anything but a blur of color. He reached out and stilled her hand.

"Without proof, all you're going to do is cause unnecessary gossip and innuendo."

Her jaw clenched. "There is proof."

"I would like to see it for myself."

"I haven't got the evidence on me and I wouldn't show you if I did, but I do have a letter from my aunt, proving it exists." She kept her eyes locked with his.

"May I see the letter? If I'm to believe your theory, then at least let me read the letter. I promise to give it back."

She chewed her lip, then sighed and reached for her bag. "I will let you read one of my copies of the letter and a note that came with it, but only on the condition your family won't stop me from seeing Carolina."

"You have my promise." He accepted the envelope she handed him. "*Grazie.*" Riccardo withdrew two pieces of paper and read them, aware she was sneaking occasional glances at him. Perturbed, he read them again then turned to her.

"Do you mind if I show these to my brother?"

She glanced across the aisle. Giovanni was deep in conversation with the man beside him. "Okay...but you'd better not be up to anything sly, Riccardo."

Riccardo experienced an unexpected twinge of pleasure at the sound of his name on her lips, even if accompanied by those magnificent eyes glaring at him. He leaned across the aisle and passed the two sheets to Giovanni. "Read these."

As Riccardo sat back he met Sofia's wary eyes.

"Do you believe me now?" she asked solemnly.

He stared straight ahead and inhaled deeply before answering. "You are making serious allegations." He scratched his chin while he considered his next words. "You think the Santinis were behind a conspiracy to discredit your father. We believe your father brought on his own ruin. I would like to see the evidence if it exists."

She hesitated as a steward stopped to offer them refreshment towels. Riccardo waited patiently as she wiped her face and hands, then handed the towel back to the steward, who didn't seem in any hurry to move on. Riccardo raised an eyebrow at the man, who gave Sofia another smile before turning to Giovanni.

"Oh, it exists," said Sofia. "I intend to meet with my aunt's solicitor, Salvatore Bondini and then I will speak to my grandparents. I'll know more then."

Riccardo tapped his fingers on his knee. "Can I borrow a copy? My grandfather is not well and these allegations will seriously damage my family's reputation, and most likely end your friendship with Carolina. I would like to do my own investigation."

She hesitated. Her eyes were one of her best features, warm and inviting, although her hair was spectacular and he'd swear the color was natural. His gaze dropped to her top lip, which she was nibbling, something he'd like to do himself. His gut clenched.

"You seriously think I would give you a copy of the letters?" She shook her head.

Riccardo placed his hand over hers, pleased when he felt her quiver. "Salvatore is retired now and his son Michele runs the law firm. I need a couple of days before you speak with Michele."

She frowned warily. "You know the Bondinis?"

"*Sì*. They are neighbors and have been associated with my family for many years. It's no surprise they represented your aunt. Please give me two days before you make this public? And I won't impede your investigation."

"I suppose a couple of days can't hurt, but I'm doing it for Carolina, not you."

Riccardo watched her closely. It would be so easy to take those letters and destroy them. After all, it was his family's honor at stake—his grandfather's health.

The plane roared into life.

Riccardo waited until they were in the air before continuing his interrogation. "Why are these allegations only being made now?"

She picked a piece of fluff off her jeans, "It's a long story."

"It's a long way to Bologna," Riccardo replied.

"Okay... My aunt was killed in a car accident thirty years ago. Her car went over the edge of a ravine and until recently it was thought to have been an accident. Now I know she was in fear for her life and wanted my father to come and help her unveil the person who framed him. Do you remember the fire that almost destroyed my grandfather's vineyard?"

Riccardo's lips twitched. "I'm only twenty-nine, Sofia, so no, I don't remember, although I have heard stories."

"Well, before the fire started, the safe was cleaned out and the thief took bonds worth a small fortune. I believe the fire was started to cover the robbery. Unfortunately, the fire destroyed sheds, equipment, and a lot of the vineyard. My father said a witness claimed to have seen him running from the scene, and then there were gambling rumors." Her hand clenched in her lap, drawing Riccardo's attention.

Her voice shook. "My father has never gambled in his life." She blinked quickly and Riccardo sensed she was close to tears. "My grandfather and *Papà* had a massive row and then my grandfather suffered a heart attack, which was blamed on my father, so he moved to Sicily and then Australia."

Riccardo shrugged. "So what changed, who sent those letters, and why now?"

"I'm not at liberty to answer that, but it's lucky *Papà* is away and I opened the letter or..." She stopped mid sentence, her eyes flaring as if she'd said too much.

"Why come alone?" He frowned at her. "Why not wait for your father or brother?" A flash bulb went off in his brain. "Of course. They don't know you're here, do they? No one does."

She worried her lip again then sighed. "*Papà* doesn't speak to his parents, and I'm afraid he'll go berserk if he discovers his sister was murdered. So I decided to take care of it myself. But don't get any ideas. If anything happens to me, my office assistant has instructions to tell *Papà* and the Italian police everything."

"I see." Riccardo looked at her intently. "Would you leave things alone and go back to Australia, if I were to offer you a large incentive?"

"I don't want your money." She glowered at him.

"You haven't my offer yet, Sofia."

"Are you always so cynical? I have everything I need, and I certainly don't want anything of yours. Now, if you'll excuse me, I'm going to catch up on some sleep. You may borrow that copy. I have another and the original in a safe place." She turned away from him and pulled the blind down.

Glancing across the aisle, Riccardo found his brother watching with raised eyebrows.

"So she's not mercenary," Giovanni murmured in Italian before passing the letters back. "You remember what I said about making her disappear?"

Riccardo stared at him. "You're serious?" He reverted to Italian too.

"We need to keep a lid on this."

"I will not sink to kidnapping," muttered Riccardo.

"Relax," Giovanni smiled. "We encourage her friendship with Carolina and invite her to the vineyard, where as our guest, we can keep an eye on her."

"She isn't a fool, Giovanni and there is no way she will come home with us."

"No, but her friendship with Carolina is obviously important, and this way we can use their friendship to our advantage."

Riccardo leaned back in his seat and glanced at Sofia. She'd curled up on her side. A curtain of luscious red hair lay across half her face and she'd tucked her small hands under her chin. Riccardo glanced down at his own large hands. Hands very capable of dealing with anyone foolish enough to cross him, but at the moment all they wanted to do was sweep the silky strands off her face and see if her skin felt as soft as it looked.

Chapter Three

Sofia woke to the aroma of coffee and the smell of something light, fresh, and zesty. She blinked as her gaze focused on her own hand resting on a pale blue shirt, a man's shirt with a man's chest under it. Instantly she knew exactly whom she lay against.

"Oh my God." She pushed herself away.

"I keep telling you, *cara mia*, I'm not a god."

Sofia looked at Riccardo Santini and for the life of her she couldn't think of a thing to say. His dark eyes bore into her and Sofia silently cursed her big mouth, wishing she hadn't mentioned the letters. For all she knew, he could be neck deep in the conspiracy. "Why are you looking at me like that?"

"I wonder what your father would say if he knew you'd slept in my arms."

"What?"

He smiled and held out a cup. "Coffee?"

Sofia looked from his face to the cup and back again. "I don't want coffee and I don't want you telling anyone I slept with you."

A choking noise had her glancing across the aisle. Giovanni stared at her questioningly.

"No, no... I didn't mean that the way it sounded." She pointed at Riccardo. "He wanted to know what my father would say if he knew I'd slept in Riccardo's arms."

"Quando? I mean when?"

"Here, today." She rolled her eyes. "I slept against Riccardo and he's making out that we slept together." Sofia looked from one face to the other. Both men were grinning. "You're as bad as each other."

Riccardo laughed softly. "Have some coffee, Sofia, while it's hot."

She gave him a withering glare before grudgingly accepting the cup. "*Grazie.*"

He leaned closer. "I'm having a piece of *Torta al Cacao*. Would you like some?"

Sofia's eyes locked with his. "I don't like chocolate."

"Are you sure you're *Italiano?*"

She sipped her coffee and wondered why he unnerved her so. It wasn't just the fact he was related to the people who'd conspired to frame her father, and may have murdered her aunt. She carefully placed the cup on her table. It was easier to deal with him when he was being arrogant and beastly. She didn't like him smiling; it flustered her.

"I'm only half Italian, remember."

His eyes seemed to see too much and Sofia was sure he was aware of her discomfort.

"So what would your brother do if he knew you were consorting with me?"

"What do you mean consorting with you?" Sofia gasped. "Riccardo, don't joke about something like this."

"It was wrong for Nico not to stick around to face your brother, but it was probably for the best. Hot tempered men do stupid things."

Sofia took a deep breath. "I suppose my brother can be intimidating. He's as big as you and he's inherited *Papà's* temperament, but I was disappointed Nico disappeared rather than face Dante."

"So what was between you and Nico?"

"He reminded me of my brother, Dante, without being bossy. Nico was good fun and he treated me like I was special."

Riccardo seemed to consider that. "Nico isn't a boy anymore, Sofia. When he finds out you're back, well…"

"I have no interest in Nico."

"You're a beautiful woman, Sofia, and Nico is many things, but he's not stupid. He will definitely want to renew your…friendship."

Sofia glanced down, hiding her heated face behind a curtain of hair. "Excuse me, I need to use the ladies."

Pulling in his legs, he allowed her to pass. "I find it refreshing to meet a woman who blushes so easily, Sofia."

Escaping to the toilet, Sofia closed the door and leaned against it, her heart pounding. "What is wrong with me?" She splashed cool water on her flushed face and wrists. "He may be a walking, breathing Adonis, but he's still a Santini." Sofia shook her finger at her reflection. "You be very careful around Riccardo Santini. He's far too dangerous, and his joking around about sleeping with you…my God, if that got back to *Papà* it would be disastrous." She took a couple more deep breaths to calm herself, determined not to let him see the effect he was having on her. *What a joke.*

She had almost reached her seat when Riccardo glanced up. Their gazes locked and Sofia faltered. His eyes promised untold delights. *Don't go there, Sofia.*

He stood and stepped into the aisle, allowing her to pass.

"When do you plan to meet with Michele Bondini?" he asked quietly.

Dragging her gaze away, Sofia brushed past him, shivered, and sat. "I'll make an appointment as soon as I arrive at my hotel."

He sat. "But you will defer your meeting so I can make my own enquiries into your aunt's accident?"

Staring into his serious dark eyes, Sofia's heartbeat quickened. She dropped her gaze to his lips and fought an overwhelming urge to lean into him. *A Santini, he's a Santini,* she reminded herself. "I said I would wait and I will, for now."

"Thank you. Here is my card. Ring me once you're settled. We can talk over dinner."

"No, I'll meet you somewhere tomorrow, and not for dinner. If you try to trick me, then I will do this my way."

"Very well." He held out his hand to shake on it.

Sofia reluctantly gave him her hand. His touch sent her pulse racing again. By the way his eyebrow shot up, she knew he'd noticed. Pulling her hand away, she turned to the window. Moments later, they started their descent into Bologna and Sofia became distracted as she eagerly scanned the view below.

"I take it you're happy to be back in Emilia Romagna."

"Yes." She shrugged. "I never wanted to leave."

When the seat belt lights went out, Riccardo stood and moved into the aisle. "If you love it so much, then maybe this is where you belong?" Their eyes locked in a connection neither seemed able to break.

"Let's get out of here," called Giovanni, pulling on his suit jacket.

Sofia picked up her carry-bag, then stood to move into the aisle. As she brushed past Riccardo he put out his hand.

"Is anyone meeting you?"

Sofia glanced up. "No, I plan to take a taxi to my hotel."

"Why are you not staying in Ravenna with your grandparents?"

"I'd rather stay in Bologna for now."

"Then we will drop you at your hotel. Which one are you staying at?"

"I'll be fine. Riccardo."

"I'm a lot more discreet than Nico."

Sofia bit her lip until she realized Riccardo was staring at it. "Okay, *grazie.*"

In no time they were through customs, had collected their luggage, and were exiting the arrival gate, and there'd been no chance to ring Carolina. Sofia was maneuvering around happy reunions when she heard her name.

"*Ciao,* Sofia...*bella* over here."

Sofia looked across the arrival lounge to see Carolina waving madly and jumping up and down. She left her suitcase and ran straight into the arms of her friend. "Carolina, you look fantastic."

"Sofia, your hair is so long."

They were still hugging when Sofia felt Carolina stiffen. "We have to get out of here quick. It's my brother Riccardo...oh no, he's seen me. Oh saints preserve us, Giovanni's here too. We have to pretend you're someone else."

Sofia laughed. "Carolina, it's okay."

"No, Sofia, it's not. They know you're coming. We must avoid them."

"*Ciao,* Carolina," called Riccardo.

"*Ciao,* Riccardo, *ciao,* Giovanni. This is my friend...Matilda."

"Matilda," exclaimed Sofia. "Surely you can think of something better."

Carolina glared at her. "Not now."

"They already know who I am."

Carolina looked from her brothers to Sofia, her expression blank. "Oh."

"It's all right they're not going to stop us seeing each other. Are you?" Sofia regarded each of the brothers in turn.

Riccardo raised an eyebrow. "Not as long as you allow me to drop you at your hotel and give me time to do my own investigation."

Carolina's eyes widened. "You are not the same meek and shy Sofia from five years ago. What's Riccardo investigating?"

Sofia linked arms with her friend and turned her toward the exit "I will tell you later. Are you staying in Bologna? Can we meet tonight?"

Carolina lowered her voice. "Sofia, I was hoping we could avoid my brothers completely."

"Why?" She looked toward Riccardo.

"Because they're not going to make things easy for us, especially Riccardo."

Shaking her head, Sofia laughed. "Don't worry about, Riccardo. I can handle him."

Carolina squeezed Sofia's hand. "You don't understand. He's..." She rubbed her forehead. "Nobody handles Riccardo. He does the handling and you need to know Nico's mother is—"

Riccardo stepped between them. "Enough, Carolina. Give your car keys to Giovanni and you can come with Sofia and me."

Carolina groaned. "Of all the people you had to run into, Sofia."

"We met at the airport in *Milano*." Sofia had no intention of sitting on her backside while Riccardo Santini did his own investigation. She needed to stay alert, find that evidence quickly, and proceed with her own plan. "Everything is fine."

Carolina didn't appear convinced. "Famous last words." She took Sofia's carry-bag and passed Giovanni her keys. "*Ciao,* Giovanni. My car is in P1, take care of it."

"*Ciao, tutti.*" He gave them a wave and strolled off.

Ciao, tutti. Sofia couldn't help but smile. It was a favorite saying of her father's and translated, could be hello or goodbye, everyone.

The drive to Sofia's hotel was done in extreme comfort thanks to a sleek Alfa Romeo that Sofia discovered belonged to Giovanni. She sat in the back with Carolina who talked non-stop the whole way, allowing Sofia time to study Riccardo's profile. He drove well, which didn't surprise her. She doubted he did anything badly.

When they arrived at the hotel, Riccardo lifted her suitcase out of the boot, then strode toward the hotel lobby, stopping when Sofia didn't immediately follow.

Carolina gave Sofia a quick hug. "Riccardo's determined not to give us a chance to plan anything, but don't worry, we'll catch up later. I'm staying at the Hotel Emilia Romagna on Via Montebello. Ask any taxi driver and come about eight. We can have a glass of wine in the bar before dinner." She gave Sofia a conspiratorial wink. "Then we will talk."

"Via Montebello, okay got it. I'll see you then."

Sofia thanked Riccardo for the lift and waved to Carolina. As she walked up to reception she grimaced. She hadn't even made it through one day without running into a bunch of Santinis. What would tomorrow bring?

Chapter Four

Sofia woke to darkness, fully dressed on top of the bed, and her suitcase still unpacked. "Oh no." She checked the bedside clock. "Seven thirty, you've got to be joking." She tore into the bathroom, then stripped as she adjusted the shower nozzle.

She left the hotel refreshed and wearing her favorite dress, an emerald halter neck, high black heels, and her hair out. Amazingly she walked into the Hotel Emilia Romagna right on eight. A large oval bar dominated the center of the restaurant. Carolina sat on a tall stool facing the entrance and looking gorgeous in a crimson dress. Her dark, wavy hair, brown eyes, and soft olive complexion a complete contrast to Sofia's green eyes, auburn hair and fairness.

Sofia wondered if Riccardo was out socializing tonight or tied up in his office trying to find a way to hinder her investigation. She liked the idea of tying him up, then…

Carolina passed her a glass of white wine. "*Ciao,* Sofia. You have a lot of explaining to do. I can't believe you got my brothers to agree to our friendship."

Sitting on the stool beside Carolina, Sofia stuck her chin out defiantly. "I refuse to be intimidated by any of your male relatives, especially your eldest brother."

"Don't underestimate Riccardo. He will do almost anything to protect our name. He knew you were on that flight, that's why he was at the airport. If he thinks you're a threat, he will take steps to stop you."

Sofia smiled. "Don't worry. I know how to handle him. You forget I've dealt with my father and brother for years. I think it's time Riccardo met his match."

"Sofia, you are so not his match. Riccardo is nothing like Nico, or should I say, the Nico you used to know."

Sofia took the bait. "Okay, so what does that mean?"

"Nico is just like my brothers now. He clicks his fingers and women fall over themselves to run after him. When you knew him he was unpretentious, now he's *stupido*."

Sofia burst out laughing. "I've missed you so much."

"But you don't miss Nico?"

"No."

"That's good because he's in Bologna and he knows you're here."

"What? How does he know?"

"It's my fault. I was trying to find out what happened thirty years ago and my father made me tell him everything. Now they all know you are here."

"We are okay as long as *Papã* and Dante don't find out."

"I'm sorry. Riccardo and Giovanni made me tell them when you were arriving, but I didn't expect them to intercept you."

Sofia shrugged. "I told Riccardo he could do his own investigation and he promised me he wouldn't interfere in our friendship."

"Ah ha." Carolina placed her glass on the bar. "He said I could see you as long as I tell him everything you're up to."

Sipping her wine, Sofia considered her friend. They had formed a firm bond of trust over the last five years. The truth could destroy that. Riccardo was an intimidating force and obviously used to getting his own way, but she had no intention of stopping her own investigations. "We expected as much if they found out we were friends. Does Nico know about tonight?"

"*Sì.*"

"Do you think he'll show up?"

"He already has." Carolina nodded toward the restaurant's entrance.

Sofia made a teasing face of frustration before turning. She glanced toward the door and sucked in her breath. "Shit, Dante's here."

Carolina's eyes searched wildly. "Where, I don't see him?"

"In the doorway. Turn around, he'll see you."

Carolina frowned. "That's Nico in the doorway."

"What?" Sofia's gaze shot to the door again. It *was* Nico and he was smiling at her, his eyes shining with delight, but the resemblance to her brother was uncanny. Sofia could only stare as he walked toward her with an air of confidence he hadn't had five years ago. He'd filled out in the chest and shoulders, and his long scraggy hair had been replaced by a stylish short cut. He'd also shaved off his beard.

"My God, I thought it was Dante."

"Here we go," muttered Carolina. "You won't believe how smooth he is now."

Grasping Sofia's hands in his, Nico kissed her on each cheek. "Sofia, *bella*. I am so glad you have come back to *Italia*."

"*Ciao*, Nico, it's nice to see you too, but I'm only here for a short visit."

He gave her a bear hug. "I've missed you, *bella*."

Carolina rolled her eyes again before turning to the bar attendant. "*Un bicchiere di vino bianco, per favore*. I'm going to need another glass of wine to get through this."

Easing out of Nico's arms, Sofia regarded him calmly. *No racing pulse, no excited shivers. He doesn't affect me like Riccardo, but then no one ever has.* "Would you like a drink, Nico, before Carolina and I leave?"

"You can't leave, Sofia. We have so much to catch up on. It is fate that you are back. I need to talk to you about something important."

Carolina had taken a sip of wine and almost choked on it.

Sofia tried not to laugh. "Sorry, Nico, Carolina and I have plans tonight and I don't believe fate has brought us together."

"Not true. What are you doing tomorrow night? You will have dinner with me, *sì*?"

"No, I have plans for tomorrow night and Friday night and Saturday night."

"*Sì, sì* of course. I will give you my number and you can call me any time of the day or night. I will send a car for you. *Sì*?"

Carolina huffed. "Nico, you had your chance with Sofia and you blew it, now leave so we can catch up."

Nico gave Carolina a look of exasperation then smiled at Sofia. "You have fire in your eyes now, *bella*."

Willing herself to be polite, Sofia smiled. "It is nice to see you again, Nico, but as I said, I'm only here for a short visit." She was about to say more when she realized a hush had fallen over the entire room. Glancing across at a table of women, she noticed their eyes were trained on the door and she had to lean sideways around Nico to see who or what was drawing their attention. Riccardo and Giovanni stood just inside the entrance looking her way. "Oh my God."

Nico and Carolina turned at her reaction and watched as Riccardo and Giovanni made their way across the room. Sofia couldn't take her eyes off Riccardo. He had changed into fawn trousers and a plum colored silk shirt. The top two buttons were undone, exposing a touch of dark fuzz. His wavy hair looked damp, as if he'd just stepped out of the shower and he was freshly shaven and looked... *Divine.*

"*Buonasera*, Nico, Carolina, Sofia. I see you're still referring to me as your god?" Riccardo's gaze quickly swept her from head to toe. "You look very beautiful. That dress emphasizes your...eyes perfectly."

Sofia's face heated uncomfortably as Nico and Carolina looked from Riccardo to her.

Giovanni shook his head. "Don't pay any attention to Riccardo, Sofia, he enjoys making you blush." He turned to her two companions. "*Ciao,* Carolina, *ciao,* Nico."

Nico stared at Riccardo. "I didn't realize you knew Sofia?"

"We have quite a history, don't we Sofia." Riccardo drawled.

Sofia choked on her wine. "What?" She placed the glass on the bar.

"What history?" snapped Nico.

Riccardo raised an eyebrow. "Sofia has slept—"

"No." Sofia jumped off her stool and slammed into his chest. "Don't you dare say it, or I'll...I'll punch you very hard."

"You'll punch me?" he asked, placing his hands lightly on her hips.

"It's not funny, Riccardo. We didn't sleep together and we never will." She scowled.

Carolina cleared her throat. "Not so loud, Sofia, they'll hear you in *Roma.*"

Riccardo trapped her gaze and held it. "Never?" His seductive drawl so hypnotic she wanted to melt against him, taste the forbidden delights he alluded to.

Trembling, Sofia pushed his hands away. "Never. I'm completely immune to you. Come, Carolina, let's go. It's way too crowded here. *Ciao,* Giovanni, *ciao,* Nico."

Sliding off her stool, Carolina hurried after Sofia.

Riccardo waited until Sofia and his sister exited the restaurant then smiled triumphantly. *Not completely immune, cara mia. Your eyes give you away.* He turned back to Giovanni and Nico.

"What was that about?" demanded Nico.

Riccardo was still thinking about the feel of Sofia's hips under his hands and how the emerald dress clung to her body, showing shapely legs and enough cleavage to wet his appetite. She had glorious hair, a superb body, and with those radiant green eyes glittering in anger, she was enough to tempt the devil. She hadn't slept with Nico. Perhaps she hadn't slept with any man. That should have him running for the hills. Virgins definitely didn't interest him, which would normally make it easier to keep her at arm's length.

"I said, what was that about?"

Riccardo turned to Nico. "So you never slept with Sofia?"

"Stay away from her, Riccardo. She's not your type and obviously doesn't like you."

Amused, Riccardo stood his ground. "I think you'll find Sofia likes me a lot more than she's willing to admit, and as for not being my type..." He shrugged. "Perhaps she's just what I've been looking for."

Leaving Nico glowering, he turned and strolled out of the restaurant.

Catching Riccardo in the foyer, Giovanni clamped a hand on his shoulder. "What's going on? Why did you embarrass Sofia like that? It's not like you."

"It's not, is it?" Riccardo rubbed his neck. "I assumed they'd slept together and I..." *I was jealous.* He dropped his hand and met Giovanni's gaze. "I couldn't help myself."

Giovanni stared at him. *"Santé Maria."* He ran a hand through his hair. "I know you and Nico like to turn everything into a contest, but you do realize he will now make it a priority to sleep with her before you do."

Riccardo shot a quick glance back toward the restaurant. *"Merda."*

"So you do like Sofia," countered Giovanni, raising an eyebrow.

Inhaling deeply, Riccardo grimaced. "I admit she's beautiful, but as I said in *Milano*, she's not my type and she's a DeRosa. We must never forget that."

"No, we must not," agreed Giovanni. "Let's go and have some dinner."

Slamming the door of the taxi, Sofia threw herself back against the seat. "I can't believe he sabotaged me like that."

Carolina huffed. "I tried to warn you. They are going to keep a close eye on us, especially Riccardo."

"That man's impossible. He's so arrogant and full of himself and he thinks he's so funny, going on about sleeping with me. How could I have possibly thought him hot?"

Carolina stared at her with eyebrows raised. "You thought Riccardo was hot. Please tell me you're not serious?"

"That was before I knew who he was," muttered Sofia. "He's bossy, arrogant, and a beast. Why are you shaking your head at me?"

The taxi pulled up in front of a nightclub and after paying the driver, Carolina glanced at Sofia. "For your own sake, don't fall for Riccardo. He will break your heart."

Sofia looked at Carolina aghast. "How can you even suggest that? Let's just forget about him and have some fun."

They walked into the crowded cocktail lounge, alive with music and conversation. Sofia resolved not to think about Riccardo or the feel of his hands on her hips. Nor would she think about his eyes as he'd looked at her with what... Desire? Or his quietly spoken "Never?" after she declared she would never sleep with him. She groaned inwardly. Surely he didn't take that as a challenge. It was bad enough the way her body reacted to his slightest touch. *Good Lord, what would happen if he intentionally set out to seduce me?*

Sergio, the owner of the cocktail lounge, knew Carolina and seated them on a corner lounge then sent over a platter of assorted hors d'oeuvres and a cocktail each. The place had an energized atmosphere and the music was upbeat without being too loud. Sofia and Carolina spent the first hour catching up. It surprised Sofia how interested Carolina was in Dante, especially as they'd only met briefly five years ago.

As the night advanced, several men approached Sofia and Carolina, but soon moved on when they realized they were wasting their time, except for one guy. He made several attempts to buy them drinks or lure Sofia into conversation until Carolina gave him a taste of her sharp tongue. He retreated to the bar, where he sat on a stool nearby drinking and watching the crowd.

"Come on, let's dance," called Sofia.

It was like being nineteen again. They sang, laughed and danced until their throats were scratchy and their feet ached. Carolina ordered fresh drinks then Sofia led the way to their booth, her skin glistening with perspiration, her dress clinging in all the wrong places. It was a relief to collapse onto the lounge, kick off her heels and wiggle her toes.

She returned Carolina's grin as a waiter delivered their order. They were sidetracked momentarily by a couple performing a Salsa dance. After cheering and clapping, Sofia reached for her drink, an icy cold, non-alcoholic, fruity cocktail. Adrenaline still pumping, She raised the glass to her lips, relishing the zesty liquid as it cooled her parched throat.

Within minutes dizziness consumed Sofia. She began to see double and struggled to make sense of what Carolina was saying. Their persistent admirer ambled over and suggested Sofia needed air. Her tongue got in the way of her words. Her willpower deserted her as he pulled her to her feet, then began towing her to the exit. She looked to Carolina for help but found her friend staring fixedly at the ceiling. Panic hit Sofia as fogginess engulfed her brain. Then her legs buckled in the middle of the dance floor.

After a satisfying meal, Riccardo and Giovanni were leaving their favorite Thai restaurant in Bologna when Riccardo's phone rang. He answered it, listened briefly then swore.

"Some bastard spiked Carolina and Sofia's drinks then attempted to take Sofia out of the club. Sergio stopped him and one of the bouncers got the man's wallet before he escaped."

"Are the girls all right?" Giovanni's eyes held the promise of retribution, a view Riccardo shared.

"Sergio said Carolina's quite confused, but Sofia passed out. He didn't take them to the hospital, as they'd only be observed until the effects wore off and then released anyway. Sergio's certain Sofia was the man's target, and he only drugged Carolina to stop her interfering."

"*Bastardo!*" Giovanni pulled out his keys and opened the Alfa.

They drove to the rear of the nightclub and entered Sergio's private residence to find Carolina dazed but able to walk. Sofia lay on a couch as if in a deep sleep.

After speaking to Sergio, Riccardo scooped Sofia up into his arms, a surge of intense anger hitting him at the thought of what could have happened to her. He would find the person responsible and make him wish he'd never been born.

Giovanni helped Carolina into the front passenger seat of the car then held the back door open for Riccardo, who folded himself in still supporting Sofia in his arms. He held her cradled against him all the way to her hotel.

"Don't wait for me," Riccardo said as he climbed out of the car. "Take Carolina back to the hotel. I'll see to Sofia and talk to you in the morning."

"Fine, then we deal with the low life who did this," said Giovanni.

Riccardo gave a nod and carried Sofia into the hotel. No one was at reception, so he headed straight up the stairs, jiggling her a little to get her room key out of his pocket. She groaned then settled back against him. Once in the room, Riccardo dropped her stilettos and glanced around. The room wasn't large and the bed took up most of it. Balancing Sofia, Riccardo pulled the covers back then laid her on the edge. He was attempting to cover her when she groaned and started heaving.

Riccardo dragged her off the bed and into the bathroom where she vomited over his shirt and the front of her dress.

"Fuck, Sofia. I like this shirt."

Hanging limply against him, Sofia moaned.

"What am I supposed to do now? Fuck."

Scooping her up again, Riccardo placed her in the shower. He couldn't handle the smell of vomit. They needed to get out of their clothes before he gagged. He sat Sofia on the shower floor, leaning against the wall, then pulled his shirt off. There was a face washer on the vanity so he soaked it in warm water and washed Sofia's face and his chest. Then he squatted down beside her and thought for a minute.

"I don't have a choice, Sofia. You can't stay like this." He pulled her gently forward and undid the clasp at the back of her neck then pulled the zip down until he came to black panties. His groin tightened. "It's just a bit of lace."

As he leaned Sofia against the wall, the dress collapsed to her waist, exposing a black lace bra. Her breasts were perfect as was the rest of her and suddenly he was rock hard.

"Sofia, *bella*. You're going to be the death of me." Riccardo rinsed the face washer and wiped her face again, then her upper chest where vomit had soaked through and run down between her breasts. He unclipped her bra and gently wiped her breasts. Sofia moaned and moved away from the wall and into his arms. She was definitely going to kill him.

Riccardo dried her then lifted her into a standing position, letting the dress fall to the tiles. He picked her up, carried her back to the bed, then covered her and went into the bathroom to soak their clothes and have a shower. It was going to be a long night. He would have to stay and keep an eye on her, which meant lying next to an incredibly desirable, virtually naked woman he couldn't touch. He shook his head wryly as he stepped into the shower. "That's a first."

CHAPTER FIVE

Sofia yawned then flinched at the soreness in her head. Light streamed in through the slats of the shutters and hurt her eyes. Was this what it felt like to have a hangover? Groaning, she pulled the sheet over her head and attempted to retrace her night. Meeting Carolina at the hotel bar, their confrontation with Riccardo, then dancing at the cocktail lounge. Then what? A hazy memory of Riccardo cradling her in his arms. *No, that can't be right.*

Forcing her eyes open, Sofia glanced at her open suitcase and the oil painting of Venice above. *Definitely my room.* Glancing down, she realized she was only wearing her panties. Something spicy, fresh, and familiar caught her attention.

Where have I smelt that before?

Sofia focused on her surrounds and the steady breathing behind her. Swallowing, she slid her foot across the bed behind her until she came into contact with a hard, hairy leg.

"Oh God!" Sofia clamped her hand over her mouth and froze. *Please don't let that be Riccardo Santini. Wait, what if it's not Riccardo? What if it's someone else?* Sofia slowly turned, her hand still clasped over her mouth.

Riccardo Santini slept soundly in her bed, and he was naked, or at least what she could see was. Sofia cringed, horrified, then relieved it was Riccardo and not some stranger. A quiver ran through her as she lay staring at him. Reality hit. *How the hell did we end up in bed?*

Sofia threw herself on Riccardo, grabbed his shoulders, and shook him. "Wake up. What have you done to me?"

Riccardo's eyelids flew open then his gaze dropped to her naked breasts. "This can't be a dream as you're screaming like a banshee, your eyes are glittering with fire, and your nails are digging into me painfully."

"Dream?" Sofia screeched, thumping his chest hard. "I'm going to kill you."

Riccardo moved so fast, Sofia only had time to gasp before she was thrown onto her back and imprisoned by his large, hard body. He grasped her wrists and forced them above her head. Fear and fury gave her strength. She tried to bite his chin and knee him in the groin as she fought to get free.

"Sofia, listen to me. Nothing happened between us. You and Carolina were drugged last night. Sergio called me and I brought you here." He held her completely captive.

Her breathing was erratic as she stared at him in disbelief. "You expect me to believe that. I'm almost naked." She had to get away.

"I carried you to your room then you threw up over both of us. That's why you're undressed. I couldn't leave you alone in case you vomited again and choked. Please calm down. I do not want hotel staff barging in here because you are hysterical and throwing wild accusations around. I was worried about you."

His eyes spoke the truth and even though he held her completely caged, he wasn't hurting her. Sofia stared at him, her thoughts in turmoil. All she could think about was the feel of his rigid body against hers. The hair on his chest tickling her breasts, making them tingle. His legs held the bottom half of her captive. His strength surrounded her. There was also something hard pressing against her hip. She moved to relieve the pressure and Riccardo hissed, then he pushed her legs apart and settled between them.

Sofia's eyes widened with the realization of what was pressing against her. "Riccardo..." She gulped in air.

He released her wrists, but covered her mouth with his hand. "Don't scream."

Sofia stilled. That hadn't been her intention. She'd been about to demand to know what the hell he thought he was doing, but the feel of his body against hers was so shockingly intimate that she doubted she could raise even a croak.

His jaw might be clenched, but the raw lust in his eyes certainly should have her screaming and running for the nearest airport instead of quivering in anticipation.

His eyes didn't leave hers as he lifted his hand from her mouth.

Sofia's hands hovered then came to rest on his huge shoulders. She traced the tip of her tongue over her bottom lip, enthralled when his gaze tracked the movement. Taking her newfound power, she ran her fingers down his biceps and back up again.

His muscles rippled under her fingers. "Nothing happened between us, *cara mia*. I suggest you stop this little game now, or that will change rapidly."

"I don't know what you're talking about." This time she touched her top lip with the tip of her tongue.

He muttered something unintelligible, then lowered his head to trace firm lips across her cheek and down her neck, leaving a trail of shooting sparks in his wake.

Sofia shivered, her fingers curling over his hot, smooth skin.

He drew back and exhaled, his warm breath tickling her throat. The desire she saw in his eyes had a bud of wanton need blooming between her thighs. Sofia shifted restlessly, wanting to explore this new sense of power and temptation.

He held unnaturally still, watching her then his features hardened. "I will not satisfy your curiosity, *cara mia*. You are a DeRosa. I am a Santini, and never the twine shall meet." He lifted away from her. "I need to leave. Now."

Sofia had never felt such conflicting emotions in her life. The touch of Riccardo's lips was like an electrical current, running from each place he feathered a kiss to her very core, paralyzing her. His lips had been so gentle, yet his body so hard. His weight sent thrilling sensations she'd never experienced racing through her. "Riccardo?"

He didn't answer. Instead he left the bed and paced into the bathroom. Sofia let out a groan and pulled the sheet over her head. She knew the beast was right. There were enough problems between the DeRosas and Santinis without this attraction. She cringed, unable to believe she'd wanted him to touch her intimately. *What is wrong with me?*

The bathroom door opened. Sofia held her breath then released it as the room's door opened and closed. He'd left, taking his wonderful lips and magnificent chest with him. It could be worse. He could have stayed. She pushed back the covers and stood. Her balance was shaky, her throat sore and dry. She felt weak and hungry. "It could be worse."

After her shower, Sofia washed out her dress then picked up the phone and rang Carolina. She needed some answers. Little things were coming back, but they didn't make sense. She remembered being held protectively in a pair of strong arms, then someone washing her breasts with a warm cloth. Sofia groaned into the phone. "Riccardo."

"*Pronto*," came Carolina's voice.

"*Ciao*, Carolina, it's me."

"How are you feeling this morning? I was so out of it last night."

"Riccardo brought me back to the hotel."

"*Sì*, I know. You're lucky Sergio stopped that man before he disappeared with you."

Closing her eyes, Sofia leaned against the wall. "Carolina, Riccardo brought me back to my hotel and he...he slept with me."

"He what!"

Sofia bit her lip. "I vomited, so he cleaned me up, then was afraid to leave in case I was sick again."

"Did...did you and Riccardo..."

"No. He said he stayed to make sure I was okay."

"That's all right then. He rang me a while ago to tell me he has people searching for the man who drugged us. Do you want to get away? We could go to Verona for a couple of days to recover?"

"That sounds wonderful. I've always wanted to see Juliet's balcony."

"I'll meet you out the front of your hotel at ten thirty."

Sofia ended the call then rang the Bondini law firm. She was put through to Michele who immediately agreed to see her. She told him she was going away for a couple of days and made an appointment for when she'd be back. Hopefully by then she'd feel better.

Sofia and Carolina spent the next two days leisurely exploring the city of Verona. They ate at outdoor restaurants in Piazza delle Erbe and Piazza Bra. Visited Romeo and Juliet's balcony on via Capello, then Castelvecchio, a thirteenth century castle built beside the Adige

River. On their last afternoon, they rambled through Giardini di Giusti, the famous sixteenth century gardens. It was heavenly and just what Sofia needed.

They arrived back at her Bologna hotel at six, agreeing to meet the following morning for coffee. Sofia climbed the stairs, rubbing her eyes. She planned to have a shower then fall into bed. After the huge lunch they'd eaten, she wouldn't need dinner. She opened the door and turned the light on, her eyes widening in horror at the state of her room. Drawers were hanging open and her clothes were thrown over the floor. Even the sheets had been pulled off the bed. Leaving the door wide open, Sofia ran back down the stairs calling for help.

The receptionist met her at the bottom of the stairs. "*C`e` qualche problema, signorina?*"

"My room has been ransacked."

"Ransacked?"

"Upstairs…my room. Someone has trashed my room." Sofia ran back upstairs.

The receptionist followed and gasped at the state of the room. "Is anything missing, *signorina*?"

Sofia shrugged. "I had my camera and iPod with me." She pulled open her suitcase and searched its pockets then rummaged through her drawers and the clothes scattered over the floor.

"What are you searching for, *signorina*?"

"I had a spare copy of a letter, it's gone."

"Letter?"

"*Sì.* A very important letter."

The receptionist looked at Sofia in confusion. "That's all they took?"

"*Sì.*"

"I will ring the police, *signorina*." The receptionist disappeared leaving Sofia numb. She'd been such an idiot. The Santinis would go to any length to stop a scandal and thanks to her big mouth, they knew about the letter and copies. *How could Riccardo do this to me? Well, he's not going to get away with it.*

Sofia folded the original letter and stuck it in her purse, then flew down the stairs to the lobby. "I need to see someone. I'll be back later," she called to the receptionist.

Sofia hailed a taxi. "Hotel *Emilia Romagna, via Montebello, per favore*," she called, jumping in and slamming the door.

A couple of minutes later the taxi drew up outside the elegant, luxury hotel. Sofia paid the driver and stormed straight through the front doors and up to the reception desk.

"*Mi chiamo,* Sofia DeRosa." Sofia's temper flared. Her Italian was terrible and the words she needed slipped from her grasp. She raised her voice. "I want to see Riccardo Santini and I want to see him now."

A big burly security guard approached. "You have a problem, *signorina*?"

"You better believe it."

Strolling into the hotel after a meeting with his father and uncles, Riccardo glanced across the foyer to see a security guard gripping Sofia DeRosa's arm. The guard was attempting to escort her from the hotel and she was complaining loudly about being manhandled by an ape, which made Riccardo smile until he saw tears in her eyes.

"Paolo, release *Signorina* DeRosa immediately."

The guard spun around, recognized Riccardo, and let go of Sofia.

Riccardo strode over and took Sofia's hand. "Did he hurt you?"

"I'm fine." She didn't look fine. Her eyes were glittering with fire *again.*

"Did you have a nice time in Verona? Are you recovered from your ordeal?"

"Don't try and sugar coat me. You are a swine."

Riccardo towed her into the lift, then hit the button for the tenth floor, which housed his and Giovanni's private suites, and the main hub of Santini Holdings. Once the door closed he turned his attention to Sofia. "What are you talking about?"

"As if you don't know," she accused, pulling her hand free and rubbing her arm.

Taking a deep, calming breath, Riccardo tried again. "Sofia, why are you here?"

"My hotel room was broken into, but you know that, don't you?"

"No, I didn't know that. Is anything missing?"

She rolled her eyes. "The only thing missing is my second copy of the letter."

"I see."

"You see... What do you see?"

The lift doors opened and Riccardo stepped out. He acknowledged his and Giovanni's secretaries then guided Sofia toward the shattered doorframe of his office.

"What happened here?" asked Sofia. She followed him around splintered fragments of wood and into his office.

"We were broken into." Riccardo strolled behind his desk and stood in front of the chair.

"Why would someone break in here?" She walked to the window beside him.

Reaching for her hand, Riccardo turned her toward him. "They broke in to take something of yours."

She looked at him in confusion. Riccardo remained silent as comprehension hit her.

"The letter I gave you. It's gone, isn't it?"

"*Sì*." He ran a hand through his hair. "And the note. I had them in my desk."

Sofia's eyes narrowed. "How convenient?" She shoved Riccardo hard, obviously forgetting he still held her other hand. Riccardo let himself fall back onto his chair, taking her with him. She landed on his lap with a squeal and such a look of horror that Riccardo burst out laughing. The sound of a phone ringing in the reception area brought Riccardo to his senses and he reluctantly relaxed his hold on her. When she didn't pull away, he was reminded of how he'd woken two days ago. The thought of her straddling him in nothing but a bit of lace had him hardening in seconds and without another thought, he kissed her.

It was meant to be quick. Hard. Unemotional. A stolen kiss that would get her out of his system, but the instant their lips touched he knew he'd made a vital error. Her lips were soft and responsive and fitted him perfectly. He would have deepened the kiss, if not for the sound of Giovanni clearing his throat. Riccardo pulled back to find Sofia staring up at him with large luminous eyes, a soft pink tinge in each cheek, and her lips softly swollen. He drew in a deep breath.

"I'm sorry, Sofia. I shouldn't have done that."

Sofia's lips were tingling from the brief but potent kiss. It wasn't something she would easily forget. Nor would she forget the sensation of his body against hers in the hotel room. She felt her face heating and pushed away from him.

"Why did you kiss me?"

"I couldn't help myself, especially after the way you woke me."

"You're impossible, absolutely impossible." She scrambled off his lap and noticed Giovanni standing near the door. Smoothing down her dress, she ignored him and glared at Riccardo. "Do you know who broke into my room?"

"No, I don't, and I am concerned for your safety."

"Why?"

"Someone has gone to a lot of trouble to get those letters. The fact they knew I had a copy concerns me. I think you should give me the original and I'll lock it in my safe."

"I am not giving you the original." She clutched her purse tightly and backed away.

"What about the evidence then?" Riccardo stood.

"It's safe for now."

Giovanni strolled across to the desk and held out a sheet of paper to Riccardo. "Here's the address of the man who drugged Carolina and Sofia. I've got his house under surveillance and as soon as he comes home, we'll pay him a visit."

Sofia flinched. "Why would you pay him a visit?" When neither man answered, a cold shiver ran down her spine. "Let the police deal with him. What he did was bad, but I don't want you going after him on my behalf."

Riccardo's expression hardened. "Men who drug women intend to rape them, Sofia. He should be castrated."

"Not by you." Sofia clutched his suit jacket. "Let the police handle it."

Riccardo's arms came around her and he stroked her back. She knew his aim was to soothe her, but he also meant every word. He wasn't changing his mind. She had to do something.

A pretty brunette came into the office. "*Signori,* the police are on their way up and would like to speak to you about a *Signorina* DeRosa. They said it is about a recent drugging and a robbery in *Signorina* DeRosa's hotel room."

Sofia blinked in surprise. The woman spoke perfect English with a British accent.

"*Grazie*, Hannah." Riccardo returned his gaze to Sofia and raised an eyebrow. "How do the police know about your drugging, Sofia?"

"I don't know. My hotel's receptionist was going to ring the police, but I never mentioned anything about the nightclub, and I certainly didn't tell anyone I was coming here." She glanced at the door. "Riccardo, promise me you will let the police handle this or...or I'll tell them everything."

Riccardo didn't look the least bit concerned. If anything he looked amused. "I think *Signorina* DeRosa is attempting to blackmail us?"

Giovanni chuckled. "I think you are right. Isn't it lucky, she doesn't speak *Italiano*?"

Sofia huffed and shrugged Riccardo's arms away as the police entered the office with the pretty brunette named Hannah. *Who cares if he's got a pretty secretary?*

The police began speaking in rapid Italian, which she had no chance of understanding. Frustration ate at her then she glanced at the secretary. "Hi, I'm Sofia. Would you mind translating for me?"

"If you like. My Italian is not fantastic though." She concentrated on the conversation. "The police say they received a phone call informing them of the incident at the night-club two nights ago. They interviewed the owner who gave them the name of a man he suspects was responsible. The police went to a house and found your name, hotel, and room number on the back of Riccardo's business card."

Sofia frowned at Hannah. "But why would my details be on a business card of Riccardo's, and why was the card in that man's house." She narrowed her eyes. "What is Riccardo saying now?"

Hannah listened. "He says you are a personal friend and he gave you his business card, so maybe you wrote your hotel details on it and the man stole it from your purse."

Sofia stilled. "I didn't. What else is he saying?"

Hannah looked uncertain. "He says, he came to your rescue two nights ago and took you back to your hotel where he..."

"Where he what?" urged Sofia, her temper flaring.

Hannah blushed. "He says he stayed with you all night."

"Why that underhanded, arrogant..." Sofia gritted her teeth. "What's that policeman saying?"

"That they went to your hotel and were told you were out and that your room had been broken into and..."

"And?" pressed Sofia.

"I think he said the only thing stolen was a letter."

"That's right. What's Riccardo telling them?"

"He is suggesting the man who drugged you must have taken the card and when he failed to abduct you, decided to go to your hotel and search it."

Sofia stared at her. "But what about the letter stolen from this office?"

Hannah looked blank. "What letter? We had a break in, but Riccardo told the police the thief was probably after money."

Sofia's gaze locked with Riccardo's and he shook his head slightly. Why didn't he want the police to know about the letters? *And why would a stranger have my name and hotel on a business card of Riccardo's?*

Sofia watched as Riccardo smoothly guided the policemen toward the door. Hiding her inner turmoil, she smiled at Hannah. "You're English?"

"Yes, I handle the English correspondence for the Santinis."

"I see. Thank you for interpreting for me, Hannah, and it was nice to meet you."

Hannah smiled. "You too."

Strolling to a couch, Sofia sat and waited until Giovanni and Hannah had escorted the policemen from the office.

"You are a beast, Riccardo Santini. Now everyone thinks we've slept together."

His lips twitched. "We have."

"You know what I mean. They think we're...we're lovers. And I didn't write my details on your card, so how did that man get them?"

"I have absolutely no idea. What I can say is the police have more important things to do than search for missing letters. And I don't want to draw unnecessary attention to you or your conspiracy theory."

"You swear you don't know who took my letters?"

"Yes, but I intend to find out who is responsible." Taking her hand, Riccardo pulled her up and led her out of the office and into the lift. "I'm driving you back to your hotel to pack. You'll be safer in the penthouse of this hotel."

"Safer from what?" asked Sofia, rolling her eyes. "You?"

Riccardo ran his hands roughly through his hair and looked up at the ceiling. Sofia was wondering if he was going to answer her when he brought his gaze back to hers.

"Sofia, the police think you've misplaced your letter and that the man who drugged you, went to your hotel with the intention of robbing and probably raping you. They've also accepted my explanation regarding the card."

"But that's a lie. I still have the card you gave me."

"Only you and I know that, and for now I would like to keep it that way until I speak with the bast...man who drugged you. I want to know how he got my card and what your details were doing on it. I also want to know how he knew about the letters, why he wants them, and how he got past our security. That's if he's the person behind the break-ins. Until I know more, I want you somewhere safe."

"I get that, but why here in your hotel?"

Riccardo sighed. "Firstly if anything happens to you, who do you think will be blamed? We are about to launch an exclusive chain of luxury hotels and I don't need any bad publicity. That's why I didn't inform the police about the stolen letter. Secondly, your hotel has no security guards, ours does, and I will make sure they are on high alert."

Sofia opened her mouth to protest, but Riccardo placed a finger on her lips.

"You can stay with Carolina in the penthouse."

"Fine, but only if you promise to let the police handle things."

Riccardo nodded but Sofia had the feeling he was placating her and that he had no intention of leaving it to the police. What was he really up to?

Chapter Six

Riccardo drove Sofia to her hotel in Giovanni's Alfa, waited while she packed, then drove her to the Hotel Emilia Romagna. "How long have you owned this hotel?"

"Four years." He pulled into a private parking bay, collected her suitcase from the boot then led her through the foyer of the elegant hotel. As they walked past the reception counter he caught her hand drawing the curious stares of the reception staff.

She discreetly tugged her hand free. "You're doing it again, Riccardo. Your staff will think we're together."

"Good. If someone undesirable approaches you, my staff will come to your assistance. I don't want anything to happen to you."

She glanced at him sharply. "Do you know something about my aunt's accident?"

"No. I have people discreetly making inquiries. We will soon know whether the crash was an accident or not."

They stopped at the lifts and Riccardo pressed the call button. Sofia studied him closely. His shirt was evenly rolled to his elbows, exposing strong forearms. The shirt's top two buttons were open, displaying a glimpse of bronzed chest and that light dusting of dark fuzzy hair she was all too familiar with. She dragged her gaze from his chest to his strong jaw, which was darkened by the shadow of whiskers, giving him a sexy laid-back appeal.

You swear you know nothing about my aunt's death? This is not an act to lull me into a false sense of security?"

Riccardo sighed. "I've told you everything I know. If I find out anything of concern, you will be told." The lift doors opened and Riccardo placed her suitcase inside. "Here is your key card. Go to the top floor and you'll find Carolina waiting for you. *Buona notte, cara mia*, sleep well."

Sofia stepped inside the lift and the doors closed. She inserted the key card and pressed the top floor button then stared at her reflection. *What the hell is going on?*

The lift came to a stop and the doors opened.

"Finally you are here." Carolina grabbed Sofia's arm and hurried her out of the lift and across a marble foyer to a set of open double doors. "Riccardo rang me to say you were on your way up. Tell me everything."

"Wow, so this is what a luxury hotel penthouse looks like."

"Don't worry about that. You can look around later. Tell me what's going on. Why did Riccardo have you moved here? Is it true your hotel room was broken into? And did Riccardo really kiss you in his office?"

"How do you know about that?"

Carolina's eyes widened. "So it's true? Hannah told me, but I was skeptical. I can't believe Riccardo kissed you."

Collapsing onto a deep, comfortable lounge, Sophia sighed. "You and me both. I don't know what he's up to. It's as if he wants people to think we're together."

"Hmm, maybe. Tell me everything from when I dropped you off."

When Sofia finished her story, Carolina slumped on the couch, her expression flabbergasted. "Don't worry, my brothers won't kill the man who drugged us, but they can be very intimidating. They will find out what they want before handing him over to the police." Carolina frowned. "You're sure the police think this man is responsible for the break-in as well?"

"Yes, but only after Riccardo convinced them it was the most likely scenario. He neglected to inform the police about his own break-in. What if it's a set-up and someone in your family is behind the drugging and break-ins?"

"No, I don't believe they'd—"

"Caro, you said he would do anything to stop me. He told me your grandfather isn't well and Riccardo doesn't want any negative publicity."

"He was worried about you the other night, and when we got back from Verona, he was furious that I hadn't told him where we were. You still have the original letter don't you?"

"Yes, right here in my purse."

"What about the evidence? Where is it?"

Sofia clenched her hands in her lap and considered Carolina. To reveal the truth was a huge risk, but they'd been confidants for the last five years. Their goal was the same. "You can't tell anyone what I'm about to tell you, Caro."

"I promise."

Sofia took a deep breath. "My aunt hid the evidence, but I don't know where."

"But I thought… How do we find it?"

"I'm not sure." Sofia opened her purse, pulled out the letter and note, then handed them over. "It is possible someone purposely ran my aunt off the road, and that person or persons are most likely also responsible for discrediting my father."

Carolina nodded, reading and listening at the same time. When she finished, she placed the two sheets of paper on the coffee table. "I wonder who sent these, and where do we start looking for the evidence?"

Sofia shrugged. "I need to talk to the solicitor, and I think we should do it before we meet Riccardo tomorrow. This solicitor, Michele Bondini, he might know where to start."

"You could be right. Michele has known our fathers since they were boys. They grew up together. I guess we will have to…" Carolina's phone buzzed and she jumped. "*Pronto. Oh, ciao,* Riccardo, *Sì, sì, va bene.*"

Sofia watched her friend as she listened to what Riccardo had to say, but when Carolina held out the phone for her, Sofia shook her head, refusing to speak to him.

A frown crossed Carolina's face. "No, she's gone to bed. What? No, she's not beside me. She went to bed because she's tired and I'm speaking English because I feel like it. Yes, we are staying in tonight. *Sì*, okay, *ciao,* Riccardo."

"What?" asked Sofia.

"He wants to see you in the morning."

"No, I've decided to see Michele Bondini first."

"Riccardo has something important to tell you, so I've agreed to meet him for coffee."

"It's probably just a ploy to delay me seeing Michele Bondini."

"I think you should speak to Riccardo. He sounded serious."

Sofia stared out the window over a city of lights. "You really don't believe Riccardo or Giovanni had anything to do with my missing letters?"

"No, but I do think they will have us followed from now on."

"All right, I'll meet Riccardo for coffee before we call on Michele Bondini."

Carolina grinned. "Okay, *va bene.*"

They spent the rest of the evening watching a movie, painting their toenails, eating pastries, and drinking tea. Sofia's last thoughts before falling asleep were of Riccardo and their meeting tomorrow. Her stomach clenched and her pulse quickened.

Will he touch me again? Do I want him to touch me?

Her mind floated back to their brief encounter in the hotel room, her mind savoring each touch, each look. The strength in his hands as he held her captive. His muscled body surrounding her, sending electric currents racing through her. The sensual way he pronounced *So...fi...ya.* The desire she'd felt when he stole that kiss.

Yes, I want him to touch me again.

Her body trembled. *You can't have everything you want, Sofia.* She would need to stay away from Riccardo Santini and his magnificent naked chest. She squeezed her eyes shut and willed herself to relax. *Don't think about him. Think about Aunt Renzina's killer and Papà. Think about what Dante will do if you get involved with Riccardo.*

The next morning Sofia and Carolina were sitting at an outdoor café when Giovanni's black Alfa pulled into the curb beside them. Riccardo and Giovanni climbed out looking very attractive in their stylish grey suits.

Giovanni leaned down and kissed both girls on each cheek. "*Buongiorno*, Sofia, Caro."

Riccardo also kissed their cheeks then dropped to his haunches beside her chair. "How are you today, Sofia?"

She had no choice but to look at him. When Giovanni had kissed her, it had been pleasant but nothing like the reaction that raced through her when Riccardo's lips touched her skin. She stared down into his dark sexy eyes and almost leaned forward. *You fool.*

She cleared her throat. "I'm not happy everyone knows we slept together."

Giovanni's gaze lifted from his phone. "What? You really did sleep together?"

Riccardo scowled at his brother. "I don't make love to unconscious women, Giovanni. When I got Sofia back to her room she was in a bad way. I had no choice but to put her to bed and stay with her."

Giovanni stared at Riccardo. "Perhaps we should have taken Sofia to the hospital."

He shrugged. "Sergio knows what he's talking about. The girls only needed observation. If they'd gone to hospital the police would have been called and it would have drawn unnecessary attention. I did try to ring you late last night to see how Carolina was. Where were you?"

Giovanni's lips twitched. "I met up with that flight attendant."

Riccardo grinned and turned back to Sofia. "So, other than being mad at me for seeing to your comfort, is there anything else upsetting you?"

"Yes," snapped Sofia. "I regret telling you about the letters and that I trusted you." She poked him in the chest.

He caught her fingers. "I have spoken to my father, uncles, and grandfather. None had any knowledge of the drugging or break-ins."

Sofia held her hands wide. "In other words all the Santinis know I'm here and it's just a coincidence that my hotel room and your office were broken into.

His fingers grazed over her wrist sending her pulse flying again. One of his eyebrows rose. *He knows what his touch does to me.* She yanked her hand free and glared at him.

Giovanni dropped into a seat beside Carolina and rubbed his forehead. "Nothing makes sense. First the girls are drugged, then Sofia's room and your office are broken into. Are they connected or is it a coincidence?"

Sofia studied Riccardo and Giovanni. They were either extremely good actors or they really weren't responsible for the break-ins. She couldn't think when Riccardo was so close.

He grimaced. "I don't believe in coincidences and neither do you, Giovanni. As soon as we catch up with that bastard, I intend to find out the truth and then teach him a lesson he'll never..." Riccardo put a finger against Sofia's lips. "Before you bite my head off, let me make one thing clear. He intended to rape you. That aside he had your name and hotel room on my card. I need to know if you were a random target or if he's working for someone else."

"You promised to let the police deal with him." She glanced at her watch. "Oh my goodness, we have to go. I rang Michele Bondini this morning and changed the appointment."

He frowned. "I need more time to investigate your allegations. Can you give me a couple more days before you take this further?"

Be strong, Sofia. "No. I need to speak to Michele Bondini today." She stood.

"I'm going with Sofia," announced Carolina.

Riccardo inclined his head. "All right. Go and see Michele then meet us in the piazza opposite. You can tell us if he knows anything about your aunt's accusations."

Sofia found it hard to concentrate on anything but the warm fingers enclosing her arm and his magnificent eyes. She glanced quickly at Carolina who was silently pleading with her to agree. "I must have rocks in my head. All right."

Riccardo smiled. "Giovanni will drop you at Michele's office now, and we will wait in the piazza."

Sofia allowed him to kiss her cheeks and tried to ignore the tremor that raced through her. Turning away, she clenched her fingers so as not to touch where his lips had imprinted her skin. They climbed into Giovanni's sleek Alfa and he drove the short distance to Michele Bondini's office where Sofia and Carolina alighted. Hopefully, *Signor* Bondini would have information that would help them.

The solicitor's office was on the second floor of a beautiful old building. A stylishly dressed receptionist showed them into a small room with three armchairs surrounded a low table. "*Signor* Bondini will join you shortly."

As the door closed, Sofia glanced around the elegant room. "Business must be good."

Carolina nodded. "Salvatore Bondini is highly regarded and worked hard to set this law firm up. Now Michele runs it. He's not as charming as Salvatore and he's got a thing for my aunt, which annoys her."

The door opened and a well dressed balding man entered.

"*Buongiorno, Signor* Bondini, this is Sofia DeRosa," Carolina said.

The solicitor smiled at Carolina. "*Buongiorno,* Carolina." He turned to Sofia. "*Buongiorno, Signorina* DeRosa. Welcome to Bologna. I trust you are enjoying our city?"

"Well, my first night here a man spiked my drink, then someone broke into my hotel room while I was in Verona. The police think it is the same man and they have his name and address. Other than that, all is well."

Michele Bondini seemed lost for words. "I am shocked, *signorina.* I hope this man is found and dealt with quickly." He indicated they should sit, then placed a file on the low table and opened it. "Let us attend to business."

Glancing at the folder, Sofia frowned. "*Signore,* I'm not sure what business you're referring to. I'm here about my aunt's death. I think she may have been forced off the road on purpose, and I'm hoping you might know something."

Michele Bondini stared at her, shock clear on his round face. "*Signorina,* your aunt's death was a tragic accident."

Sofia looked at Carolina who gave her a nod to continue.

"Did my aunt tell you or your father about some documents she hid proving there was a conspiracy to frame my father. Or perhaps seek your advice concerning something that was troubling her just before the accident?"

"I know of no documents. You will have to be a little more specific. If you know something, then please tell me."

Sofia drew in a deep breath then exhaled. "I received a letter and the person who sent it suggested my aunt was murdered because of what she knew."

Michele paled. "Your aunt never said anything to us, but there have been rumors concerning your father and the Santinis for many years. I'm afraid I can't help you with that, but I do have some documents here for you to sign."

"Documents?" asked Sofia, leaning forward.

"Your grandfather liquidated a number of assets and wants to gift each of his grandchildren with a large amount of money before he and your grandmother leave Italy."

Sofia looked at Carolina. "Leave Italy? That can't be right." She turned back to the solicitor. "Are you sure?"

"Of course. I thought that was the reason for your visit?"

Sofia shook her head. "I don't understand. I came to see you because of a letter my aunt wrote thirty years ago. She said she wanted my father to come home and clear his name."

Michele Bondini frowned. "I know nothing about a letter written thirty years ago. What I have here is a legal document gifting money to you and your two brothers."

Sofia blinked. "I only have one brother, *Signor* Bondini."

Michele read the document again. "This definitely says two brothers, but I will look into it." He looked at her over the top of his glasses. "Your grandfather has installed a clause attached to your inheritance. The money he has left you is to be for everyday expenses and repairs to the Villa DeRosa and what remains of the vineyard."

"Villa DeRosa?" chorused Sofia and Carolina.

"*Sì.*"

Sofia stared at him, unable to believe her ears. "I was under the impression Villa DeRosa was sold years ago, and the grapevines were worthless after the fire?"

Michele Bondini wagged his finger at her. "Your grandfather's grapes were by far the most superior in all Emilia Romagna. So when he decided to sell off most of the vineyard, it was snapped up. However, he kept fifty acres and the Villa DeRosa, which now belongs to you. It is your grandfather's wish that you restore the old casa to its original state."

Sofia clasped her hands together. "I didn't know. *Papà* frequently told me stories about his home, and how much he loved it, but I thought it had been sold." She turned to Carolina. "Did you know?"

"No, although I remember different families living there over the years. They must have been renting it."

Michele Bondini cleared his throat. "Villa DeRosa is yours now, *signorina*. You just need to sign here." He pointed at a line and handed her the pen.

Glancing at the document, Sofia was relieved to see it was in English. She quickly read through it and signed on the black line. This was unbelievable. She needed to speak to her grandparents, but first things first. She handed the pen to Carolina who signed on the witness line. Then Michele Bondini added his signature.

Carolina sat back in her chair. "Villa DeRosa needs a huge amount of work. It's going to take time and a lot money."

"Maybe I could take in holiday makers. You know, turn it into a Bed and Breakfast." Sofia turned to the solicitor. "How much money has my grandfather given me for the renovations, *signore*?"

The solicitor smiled. "Please, call me Michele, after all I have been a friend of your fathers' since boyhood. As to the money." He flicked through some pages. "Your grandfather has gifted each of his grandchildren one million euros. Another five hundred, if there are only two of you."

Sofia gasped. "One and a half million euros?"

"*Si, signorina*. I don't joke about money. It is yours to be spent on improvements to the Villa DeRosa and your living expenses for a period of one year. After that time you are free to do what you want with it. I have a set of keys here for you."

Sofia automatically held out her hand. The bunch of keys jingled as Michele placed them in her palm. She didn't know what to say; her mouth had gone dry. Living in Villa DeRosa was a dream come true, and she had one and a half million euros to restore it. *Papà* thought she was on a two-week holiday in Australia. A year in Italy was going to be a lot harder to explain.

Sofia took a deep breath and stood. Her legs shook. Once she knew more about her aunt's death and had proven *Papà's* innocence, everything would be okay. Sofia smiled at the solicitor. "*Grazie*, Michele."

He stood and shook her hand. "*Ciao*, Sofia. Let me know if I can help you in any way, especially in respect to clearing your father's name. Do you have your aunt's letter?"

"I do." Sofia picked up her purse. "But I promised Riccardo Santini time to look into the whole affair before I go to the authorities. Thank you for your offer, Michele, I may take you up on it."

He hesitated. "Please wait here. I will have my secretary make you a coffee while I check your aunt's file and speak with my father. He may remember something, but it is thirty years ago and he is an old man."

"Thank you, Michele. That's very kind of you."

He left the room and several minutes later his secretary brought them coffee and pastries. Fifteen minutes passed before Michele came back shaking his head. "It is as I thought. There is nothing of importance in your aunt's file and my father knows nothing."

Sofia nodded. "Thank you anyway."

"*Ciao, signorina.* If there is anything else I can help you with, please let me know."

"I will." Sofia descended the stairs behind Carolina, deep in thought. She'd dreamed of living in an Italian villa. It was fantastic. It was terrifying. *What is Papà going to say?*

They reached the ground floor and Carolina stopped. "You know what this means?"

"A lot of work and fireworks when my father and Dante hear. And we're no closer to finding the evidence or solving anything."

"It means you get to stay here. We will deal with your family when and if we have to, but for now you have your own villa. I bet your aunt hid the evidence there."

Sofia stopped and clutched Carolina's arm. "Yes, that's exactly where she would have hidden it. You are a genius, Caro."

Carolina held the door open and Sofia stepped out and strolled to the edge of the curb, ready to cross into the piazza. Her heart lurched when she saw Riccardo and Giovanni sitting at a table with Nico. He really did remind her of Dante.

A powerful engine revved into life and Sofia glanced to her left as a huge motorcycle bore toward them. She heard Riccardo yell from across the street but she couldn't make out what he was saying for the noise of the bike. Carolina screamed then Sofia's arm was nearly wrenched out of its socket. She felt herself being lifted and propelled through the air before slamming into the ground so hard the wind was knocked out of her.

Intense pain seared through her head, then everything started to spin. She saw Riccardo's face but it seemed different, almost stricken as he gently lifted her into his arms, cradling her against his chest. A sense of safety washed over her as she slid into oblivion.

CHAPTER SEVEN

Sofia's head pounded, nausea still threatened, her shoulder ached. She fought off fatigue and assimilated her surroundings. An uncomfortable bed, so she was still in the hospital. Her nose detected spicy sandalwood, which meant Riccardo was close by, but what was that weight across her hip. Sofia's opened her eyes and her gaze fell on a head of black wavy hair.

Riccardo?

He'd taken off his jacket and rolled up the sleeves of his shirt, revealing muscular brown arms, one of which lay across her hip. His hand wrapped around her own. Sofia wondered how he could possibly sleep sitting on a chair while leaning across the bed so awkwardly. She glanced toward the window and realized darkness had fallen.

Reaching up with her free hand, Sofia touched the bandage at the base of her skull, where she now had three stitches and a bald patch. She touched Riccardo's cheek, smiling when his eyes instantly opened.

Relief flared in his eyes and his fingers tightened around hers as he sat up. "*Bella*, you're awake. How do you feel?"

"I feel like I've been through a wringer. Did the police catch the bike rider?"

"No sign of the rider, but your purse was found and handed in to the police."

"Oh, thank goodness. Are my cards still in it?"

"*Sì.*"

"So he knocked me down for a small amount of cash?"

"No, there is money in your purse."

"If he didn't steal my money than why did he knock me down?"

"We believe he knocked you down for the letter that Carolina insists was in your purse."

"Was?" Sofia clutched his hand.

Riccardo's jaw clenched. "We must assume these incidents are connected and he now has the original and copies. You were lucky you only hurt your head and shoulder," he muttered angrily.

"You call this lucky?" Sofia touched the bandage again. "Who's doing this, Riccardo?"

"I don't know, but I promise you, I will find out." He stood and paced the room. "Where is the evidence hidden?"

Sofia looked at him warily. His family had the most to lose if she proved they were part of the conspiracy to set up her father. Since she'd run into the Santinis, she had been drugged, robbed, and nearly killed. Her father's words echoed round her head. *Never trust the Santinis.*

"I can't tell you."

"Don't play games with me, Sofia. Somebody is out to stop you."

Sofia bit her lip. Her gut instinct was to trust him and Carolina swore he wasn't behind the robberies. It wasn't enough. She needed to tread carefully. "If I told you where the evidence is, you or someone in your family might get rid of it. I can tell you my aunt didn't confide in Salvatore or Michele Bondini, which is strange as she indicated we could trust Salvatore. Maybe she didn't have time to speak to him before she died. Did you hear I've been given Villa DeRosa?"

"*Sì*, Carolina told me."

Riccardo stretched his arms up and back then moved his head from side to side, as if easing kinks. Sofia watched, fascinated, as his muscles flexed and his chest expanded revealing the solid planes under his shirt. Her eyes were drawn to where the top two buttons were undone. She told herself he was forbidden fruit, but that didn't stop an overwhelming desire to see him without his shirt again, or to have those strong arms around her as he kissed his way down her neck.

"What are you thinking, Sofia," he asked, breaking into her daydream.

"What? Oh nothing, nothing at all. Why?"

"You are blushing."

She closed her eyes to avoid his gaze and relieve the pain in her head.

Riccardo was instantly beside her. "What is it, Sofia?"

Opening her eyes, Sofia grimaced. "I have a headache."

A nurse came bustling into the room. "You are awake, *signorina*. Do you need something for pain?"

"*Si, grazie.*" Sofia glanced at the nurse's nametag. "Harriet. That's not very Italian."

"No," replied the nurse. "My mamma was a fan of an actress called Harriet Nelson." She handed Sofia two tablets and a glass of water. "These will make you drowsy, but they'll get rid of your headache."

"*Grazie*, Harriet." Sofia swallowed the tablets and handed the glass back.

Riccardo's mobile rang. He answered it then opened the external door onto a small balcony. Sofia watched him through the window pacing back and forth, a look of intense concentration on his face.

Nurse Harriet sighed loudly, her gaze riveted on Riccardo. "I am envious," she confided. "He is hot. You are a lucky lady."

Sofia rolled her eyes. "Harriet, please don't let him hear you. Riccardo's head is big enough as it is and we're not togeth—" A loud buzzer sounded in the corridor and nurse Harriett jumped.

"Those call buttons have been going off for hours. All false alarms and they're driving me crazy." She rushed out of the room before Sofia could correct the nurse's mistake.

Riccardo entered Sofia's room to find she'd drifted off to sleep again, so he resumed his seat and worked on his computer until Giovanni arrived.

"We need to talk."

Riccardo closed his computer. "Have you discovered something?"

"I've been talking to Carolina and she thinks the bike rider was the same man who tried to take Sofia out of the club. A tall, skinny guy."

Riccardo glanced at Sofia. "If that's the case and he's behind the break-ins too, then we have a problem."

Giovanni also glanced at Sofia. "What do you suggest? There is a chance someone will inform Giuseppe DeRosa about the attacks?"

"For the moment we should be fine as the hospital and police think Sofia is my fiancée and it was a random bag snatching." He rubbed his chin and thought for a minute. "I think we are obligated to inform her father of these attacks."

"Can we wait a few days? The police have had a confirmed sighting of our man."

"I suppose so. In the meantime we should move her out to the vineyard. I will go and clear it with *Mamma* and *Papà*. You stay and watch over Sofia."

Giovanni grimaced. "*Papà* won't be happy having Giuseppe DeRosa's daughter under his roof."

"If anything happens to Sofia, it is our family who will be held responsible. We don't have a choice." Riccardo strode toward the lift, his mind already going over what he would tell his parents.

The next time Sofia awoke, it was to see Giovanni sitting in the chair, working on his computer. He smiled. "*Ciao, bella, comè stai?*"

"I'm okay. How long have you been here?"

"A couple of hours. How's your head?"

"It hurts. I hit the road very hard."

"Are you hungry? I can get you—" His phone rang. "Excuse me, Sofia, it is Riccardo."

Sofia closed her eyes as he strolled around the room speaking in Italian. She enjoyed the sound of his voice, so deep and sensual, like Riccardo's. When he finished and returned to the chair beside her, she managed a smile. "Where's Riccardo?"

"He went to see our parents. He'll be back soon. In the meantime I am your date."

She chuckled. "Don't let Nurse Harriet hear you. She thinks Riccardo and I are together. I must tell her the truth."

"Better you don't, Sofia. Otherwise the hospital might contact your father and I think you'll agree that's the last thing we need."

"You're right. Can you imagine what would happen if my grandparents, or God forbid, my father and brother thought I was dating Riccardo? It was bad enough with your cousin Nico and he isn't a Santini."

Giovanni gave her a cheeky smile. "If they did turn up then things would get very lively. You must be hungry. I will tell the nurse you're awake."

Closing her eyes, Sofia listened to his deep drawl as he approached the nurse's station. After a few minutes and a lot of giggling from Nurse Harriet, Sofia wondered if Giovanni would remember he was supposed to be getting her something to eat.

A rustle beside the bed had Sofia opening her eyes. "Shit." Above her stood a man in a balaclava and black clothing. He held a pillow clutched in his tattoo covered fingers. She froze, stunned by the coldness in his dark eyes and the realization he meant to kill her.

"Riccardo." Sofia pushed away and groped for the buzzer as she tried to scream, but only managed a garble before the pillow covered her face.

Terror seized her. She fought for leverage, her lungs screaming for air, her head ready to explode, helpless to do anything to attract help. She felt for and found the buzzer then pressed with her last bit of strength. *Please don't let me die.*

Riccardo stepped out of the lift and frowned at the call light above Sofia's door. An annoying buzzing echoed off the walls. Running feet had him glancing towards the nurse's station from which Giovanni and a nurse were headed his way.

"What's going on?"

Before Giovanni could answer, a man in black ran out of Sofia's room, dashed across the hall, then crashed into the fire-door exit, and hurtled down the stairs. Riccardo moved to give chase when he heard the nurse yell for help, pulling him up cold.

He swung round to see the nurse rushing to Sofia's bedside.

Dread filled Riccardo's veins as he sprinted into the room. His blood chilled at the sight of the pillow covering Sofia's face and her utter stillness. "*Merde.*" He tore the pillow away and shook her.

Giovanni hit the emergency button. "I'm going after that bastard."

The nurse was shaking as she picked up Sofia's limp wrist. "She has a pulse."

"*Grazie,* Santa Maria." Riccardo bent over Sofia, clasped her head between his hands, and covered her mouth with his lips. He'd given Sofia three breaths when she gasped and began struggling. In her panic she didn't recognize him and began clawing and scratching.

"It's okay, Sofia, you're safe now."

She was shaking violently as she pushed him away, scrambled out of the bed, and pressed her body against the wall. "Stay away from me."

Alarms were screaming and hospital staff in and out of the room were yelling as Riccardo tried to calm her. "Your attacker is gone, Sofia."

Her terror-filled gaze darted erratically around the room as she backed into a corner.

Riccardo moved toward her and her eyes flared. Gone was the trust he'd worked so hard to gain. He turned to the doctor and nurses. "Is the balcony door locked?"

"*Sì,*" they all replied.

"Good, please turn off the damn alarm and wait in the hall. I would like to speak to Sofia alone. It may calm her."

A doctor pressed the emergency button, killing the alarm. "She needs a sedative."

"Please leave the room and let me talk to her."

They filed out.

Riccardo turned back to Sofia. She had the thin hospital gown clenched tightly, drawing his attention to her breasts, hips, and thighs. This was not the time to be noticing her body. He moved closer. "*Bella.*"

"Go away. I won't get into bed and I won't let them give me a sedative. My father was right; I can't trust you."

"Sofia, I didn't have anything to do with these attacks and it was me who saved your life tonight. You have to let me protect you. I can take you somewhere safe. I'll ring your father if you give me his number?"

Sofia twisted away then cried out, clutching her head.

"Please…help…me." She sobbed and began to slide down the wall.

Riccardo swore and caught her. He lifted her into his arms, swiveled, and sat on the chair, lowering her across his thighs. After a couple of minutes stroking her back, she relaxed enough to breathe normally.

"Sofia, is your head hurting?"

"Yes."

"Then let the doctor give you something to help. I promise I won't leave you."

She opened her eyes and looked up at him. "I'm too afraid to sleep, and I don't know who to trust. That man might come back."

Riccardo could see he was fighting an uphill battle, so decided to change tactics. "Will you let the doctor give you a sedative if I take you home with me tonight?"

"What about my things?"

"I organized for Carolina to pack your suitcase. Let the doctor give you something for the pain and I'll wrap you in a blanket and carry you to the car. I promise no one will get near you. I will protect you myself."

She stared at him for a moment then took a shaky breath. "Maybe. I don't know."

"I will keep you safe, *bella*." He called the doctor in, who gave Sofia a quick examination and a couple of strong sleeping tablets.

"The police will want to interview her," said the doctor.

Riccardo raised an eyebrow. "She isn't safe here and you just gave her heavy sedatives. Tell them they can speak to her tomorrow." He wrapped Sofia in a soft woolen blanket and picked her up in his arms. He was cocooning her against his chest when Giovanni staggered in breathing heavily.

"I lost him. Is Sofia okay?"

Riccardo nodded. "She is now. Did you get a look at the man?"

"No, he jumped on a motorcycle and took off. But I'd swear it was the same motorcycle used to snatch Sofia's purse."

Sofia clasped Riccardo's shirt and whimpered before burying her face in his shoulder.

He looked at Giovanni then switched to Italian. "This is getting out of hand."

"You think one of our relatives is behind this?"

"I don't know what to think, but I sure as hell intend to find out."

Chapter Eight

Giovanni steered his car up the driveway of their family home then slowed and scowled at Riccardo. "Sofia is going to be livid when she wakes and discovers what you have done."

"*Sì.*"

Giovanni yawned. "I think I'll stay here the night and go back to Bologna tomorrow." He brought his car to a stop in front of the villa.

Their parents stood in the middle of the portico, waiting.

Riccardo wrapped the blanket tightly around Sofia, eased himself out of the car, and carried her up the steps. Giovanni followed with her suitcase.

As he reached his father, Angelo Santini put his hand on Riccardo's shoulder. "This is a mistake. You should not have brought her here. It will end badly."

"Sofia nearly died tonight, *Papà*. If something happens to her, who do you think will get the blame? I am protecting her and our name."

His mother spoke. "You both look exhausted."

Easing past Riccardo, Giovanni kissed their mother. "*Sì, Mamma.* It has been a long night and one I never wish to repeat."

As Riccardo strode up the stairs, his mother ran after him. "Your father is right. When Giuseppe finds out his daughter is here under our roof and you're—"

"I can handle it, *Mamma*. For now we need to keep an eye on Sofia. I'm sure Giuseppe DeRosa would prefer his daughter alive than dead."

"But, Riccardo, how on Earth did you convince her to come here, after everything that's happened? It can only bring trouble and how is Ariana going to react when she discovers Giuseppe's daughter is here in the same house?"

"It will sort itself out, *Mamma*. I want Sofia here."

Ignoring the guest room that his mother indicated, Riccardo walked down the hall to his own room. Pushing the door wide, he paced across to the four-poster bed and waited for his mother to turn down the covers.

Caterina Santini stopped beside him, her face questioning. "Why here? Why not one of the guest rooms, Riccardo?"

"*Mamma*, I promised Sofia I would watch over her tonight and she may well have nightmares after what happened at the hospital. To do that, I would prefer her in here with me. Would you please pull the covers back?"

She did as he asked, although Riccardo could see she wasn't finished voicing her disapproval. He removed the blanket and gave his mother her first real look at Sofia.

"Saints preserve us." She stepped closer. "Where did she get that lovely red hair and fair skin? We heard Giuseppe took up with a Sicilian woman."

After pulling the comforter over Sofia, Riccardo turned to his mother.

"He did and she died in childbirth leaving him with a baby boy. According to Carolina, Sofia's mother was an Irish girl who married Giuseppe several years after he moved to Australia. Sofia is six years younger than her brother."

"I see. Giuseppe has certainly had his share of tragedy. Does she know who Ariana is?"

Riccardo sighed. "Her name is Sofia, *Mamma* and no, I will tell her tomorrow."

"Hopefully Giuseppe won't hear what you've done, or that his daughter is here in the same house as Ariana," whispered his mother.

Riccardo looked at Sofia. "These attacks must stop, *Mamma*. I want whoever is behind them to know Sofia has my protection."

"I understand that, but was it necessary to take such drastic steps? You haven't fallen for this young woman have you, Riccardo? You're acting unlike yourself. I'm surprised, no, I'm astounded by what you have done."

Grimacing, Riccardo took a deep breath. It was going to be harder than he thought to convince his family Sofia needed to be here. It would help if he had his mother's support.

"I've spent some time with Sofia over the last few days, *Mamma*. She is compassionate, loyal, and naïve. She desperately wants to clear her father's name and restore his reputation, and while I accept her need to do this, I will not let it be at the expense of damaging our name. If she stays here, I can keep an eye on her, and at the same time keep her safe. I want to know who's behind these attacks. I need you and *Papà* to go along with my plan, and I need to know exactly what happened, thirty years ago."

His mother sighed. "I'm not sure. I was an exchange student from England when I first met your father and Giuseppe DeRosa. They were as close as brothers. We had a lot of fun together. Giuseppe was a very passionate man and would do anything for his family. I don't know what went wrong, but please think carefully before becoming involved with his daughter. If Giuseppe discovers she's here with you, he will move heaven and earth to get her back and out of your reach."

"Everything will be fine, *Mamma*. I only want to discover what's going on and try to prevent any negative publicity."

"I don't understand your thinking at all, but I can see you are determined, and there is no swaying you once you've made up your mind." She glanced down at Sofia. "I still don't understand how you got her to agree to come here."

Riccardo made no reply.

"She does know you were bringing her here?"

Sofia stirred restlessly mumbling in her sleep. "Riccardo."

His mother frowned at him. "I would prefer she was in one of the guest rooms, but if you insist on watching over her then nothing I say will stop you. Just remember, too many people have already been hurt by this feud. This plan of yours could hurt Sofia badly."

"*Buona notte, Mamma.*"

"Goodnight, Riccardo."

More tired than he could ever remember, Riccardo unbuttoned his shirt, then drew it off and tossed it over a chair. He sat heavily on the bed to remove his shoes and socks. Stood again to undo his belt, zipper, and stepped out of his trousers. He needed a shower and at least a little sleep before Sofia went berserk.

Sofia awoke slowly, still a little sore round the stitches, but her headache was gone and her shoulder pain had faded to a dull ache. She stretched carefully, opening her eyes. Above was an ornate ceiling rose and an elegant wrought iron light. The bed was massive and the sheets crisp and fresh beneath her. As she lay there she became aware of birdcalls, the smell of lavender, and a female voice singing somewhere close by. The room was furnished elegantly, if a little masculine. She was safe. Everything looked so normal, her racing heart began to calm.

She frowned at the rumpled sheets and indented pillow beside her.

A knock drew her attention and Carolina bounced through the door. "You're awake at last. I was beginning to wonder if you were going to sleep all day."

"Where are we, Carolina? I remember leaving the hospital, but not much else."

"You're in...a *villa* about an hour from Bologna. Riccardo and Giovanni brought you here last night. I was already asleep when you arrived."

"Oh, so it was you who slept with me?"

"*Scusa?*"

Sofia sat up wincing slightly and pointed to the other side of the bed.

"Ah no...I slept in my own... I slept down the hall," mumbled Carolina.

Sofia frowned. "Where are we?"

"I just remembered, I was sent up to see if you were ready for breakfast. I'll go and say yes, shall I?"

"Wait, Carolina, where are we?"

"I'll be back in a minute," called Carolina from the hall. "I need to speak to someone."

Climbing out of bed, Sofia made use of the ensuite bathroom then returned to the bedroom and crossed to the French doors. She glanced out over well-maintained gardens, a sweeping driveway, and rolling hills covered in lush grape vines. *Wherever I am, it's beautiful.* A sharp knock sounded, then the door opened and Riccardo walked in.

"*Buongiorno, cara mia.*"

Sofia quickly wrenched the curtain around her. "Riccardo, what are you doing here?"

"Carolina said you were awake, so I've brought you some breakfast. Come back to bed and tell me how you feel."

Sofia glared at him. "I'm fine, but I can't come over there. This hospital gown doesn't do up properly."

He chuckled. "It's only open at the back and I've seen you in a lot less, remember?"

Sofia opened her mouth then shut it. Clutching the gown's back, she crossed to the bed with as much dignity as she could muster and climbed between the sheets. "Where are we?"

Riccardo settled the tray across her lap. "My home. Villa Santini."

"What?" Sofia almost upended the tray. "You brought me to the home of the people who ruined my father?"

"We must agree to disagree on that point, Sofia. This is the safest place for you at the moment."

"You've kidnapped me?"

"Don't be ridiculous. Last night you agreed to let me take you to my home."

She shivered. "I was confused and scared. I thought you meant your suite at the hotel. Not here amongst the very people who set up my father."

"That is yet to be proven. By the way, the police assume the man who attacked you last night is the same man who drugged you, ransacked your room, and knocked you down on the motorcycle. They feel he is unbalanced and you were a victim chosen at random. I don't agree, which is why you are here."

"Don't the police want to speak to me?"

"No. Giovanni and the hospital staff have spoken to police and given them a description of the man running from your room. You saw nothing, so will not be bothered."

Tamping down her annoyance, Sofia glared at him. "I did see the man, but he was wearing a balaclava."

Riccardo rubbed his forehead. "It's possible he was caught on video surveillance entering the hospital. Do you remember anything about him?"

Closing her eyes, Sofia concentrated. "He was a lot shorter than you, solid, and his eyes were grey and cold. I didn't have time to notice anything else." She shivered. "I opened my eyes to see a pillow coming at me..." A memory stirred. "Wait...his fingers were tattooed."

Riccardo sat on the bed beside her and looked out through the French doors. Eventually he turned back to her, his expression serious.

"The description we have of the man who drugged you matches the man who knocked you down and the image we caught on our video surveillance in the hotel lobby. He is dark-haired, thin, and tall. Are you sure the man in the hospital was solid and short?"

"Yes."

Riccardo rubbed his hand across his chin. "Very well, I will inform the police. There is also another matter I need to discuss with you."

Filling her mouth with a mixture of diced fruit and yoghurt, Sofia nodded for him to go on.

"I came here yesterday to advise my family you'd be staying for a while. Except for my parents and siblings, I have led the rest of my relatives to believe that—"

A knock interrupted him, then Carolina and a woman Sofia didn't know entered the bedroom.

Riccardo groaned. "Is there no privacy in this home?"

Sofia glanced at the woman curiously. She was immaculately groomed, her dark hair caught up in a clip at the back of her head.

"Hello, Sofia, I have waited a long time to meet you."

"You have?" Sofia watched the woman walk across the room and then sit on the bed. Her English was impeccable with only a hint of accent. "Who are you?"

"I am Riccardo and Carolina's aunt. My name is Ariana."

"Ariana, that's my middle name."

"That's because you were named after me, my dear."

"I don't think so. I was born in Australia and I assume you're a Santini?"

"You don't know who I am?" Ariana glanced quickly at Riccardo.

Sofia shook her head. "Should I?"

Ariana turned to her niece and nephew. "Leave us, please."

"I don't think that's a good idea," said Carolina.

"Neither do I," agreed Riccardo.

"Please. Sofia and I have some things to discuss."

Sofia looked questioningly at Carolina and Riccardo then back at Ariana. "What's going on?"

Ariana exhaled. "It's okay, I don't intend to abuse her."

"It wasn't Sofia I was worried about," murmured Carolina.

Sofia gasped. "Carolina, what a terrible thing to say. Go away, both of you."

When the door had closed, Ariana picked at a thread on her skirt. "This is a long story and it may upset you. Will you hear me out before you make a judgment?"

Sofia's curiosity barometer would be her downfall. She was wary of Riccardo's motives for bringing her into his home. Did he think to pry information from her, or arrange her disappearance? It seemed unlikely with Carolina here, yet she needed to play along if she were to discover the truth. "Okay."

"My maiden name was Ariana Sofia Santini and I grew up here on this vineyard with my brother Angelo. Our two best friends lived on the adjoining vineyard, Giuseppe and Renzina DeRosa."

"My father and aunt were your best friends?" asked Sofia, confused.

"*Sì*. Please let me tell you the story."

Sofia nodded and Ariana continued, "When we were little our parents were also best friends even though they were competitors when it came to their wine and crops. As we grew older, our families hoped that one day Giuseppe and I would marry and Angelo and Renzina would marry, and although that didn't happen for Renzina and Angelo, it almost did for your father and I."

A suspicion began to grow within Sofia as she clenched her fingers. "But…"

"Let me explain, please," said Ariana softly. "I had always loved Renzina like a sister, but Giuseppe, I loved him more than life itself.

As I said, Angelo and Giuseppe were best friends from the age of five until the trouble started. When my brother married Caterina Andretti, she also became part of our group, and then your father asked me to marry him and I didn't think life could get any better."

Reeling, Sofia shrank against the bed's headboard. This beautiful, elegant, and softly spoken woman had been engaged to her father. Ariana was the one who had broken his heart by running off and marrying someone else. Sofia blanched. If *Papà* knew she was staying in the same *villa* as this woman and the family who tried to destroy him, he'd go ballistic.

"Why did you run off with another man, Ariana?"

"I didn't. I was told your father betrayed me. My brother caught him in a hotel with two prostitutes. I was so upset I let my family send me away and by the time I had calmed down enough to hear Giuseppe's side, he'd left. I discovered my father had told him I'd married someone else and that Giuseppe then made terrible threats against my family."

Ariana wiped her eyes. "A deliberately lit fire destroyed one of our processing plants and several acres of vines. Then another fire burnt out a large portion of the DeRosa vines and their main processing plant. I heard your grandfather suffered a heart attack after confronting Giuseppe over gambling rumors and the fires. Our families stopped talking and two generations of friendships came to an end." Tears trickled down Ariana's face, but she shook her head when Sofia tried to speak.

"I discovered your grandfather had banished Giuseppe and no one knew or cared where he'd gone. I was still upset about the prostitutes, but I loved Giuseppe and even with the overwhelming evidence against him, I couldn't believe he would do those things. I hired a private investigator to find him. It took months and when he did, the investigator discovered Giuseppe had taken up with a woman from the south of Italy and they were expecting a baby. I was so angry with my family for lying to Giuseppe that I ran off to Lucca where I met and married my husband. I didn't speak to my family for years."

"Why would my father name me after you," asked Sofia. "You broke his heart."

Ariana bit her lip. "After several years I hired another private investigator who discovered Giuseppe had moved to Australia. I wrote asking him to forgive me, but he never wrote back. That is, not until after you were born. I received a letter signed with a G, which is how he always ended letters to me."

"What was in the letter?" asked Sofia, curiosity getting the better of her.

"He wrote that the woman he'd been living with in Italy had died in childbirth, so he'd immigrated to Australia with his son. Several years later he'd married an Irish girl who had recently given him a beautiful daughter with a smile to melt the coldest heart. He told me he'd forgiven me for marrying another man, but would never forgive my father and brother for destroying the life we could have had together. He also told me he'd named you Sofia Ariana. I have the letter if you'd like to see it."

Sofia shook her head. "No I don't need to see it. My father might have loved you once, but my parents were happy together, right up until my mother died. *Papà* is an honest man, and I don't know how you could have believed those things."

"That's just it. I didn't."

Sofia picked up Ariana's hand. If her father could forgive this woman, than so could she. After all, she was as much a victim in this as *Papà*. Enrico and Angelo Santini had a lot to answer for.

"Thank you for coming to see me, Ariana. I'm sorry for what you went through."

Ariana wiped a tear away and stood. "Eat your breakfast now and rest." She smiled. "And welcome to the family."

Sofia nodded. "Recovering is the easy bit. I don't know how long I'll be here. If my father finds out, there's going to be big trouble."

"Maybe it might bring things to a head and clear the air," suggested Ariana. "Now I will let those two back in."

She opened the door. "Carolina, you can come in now. Where is Riccardo?"

Carolina squeezed past her aunt. "Nico's baled him up in the study and is ranting and raving because he's heard Riccardo and Sofia..." She stopped mid sentence and blushed.

Sofia raised an eyebrow. The last person she wanted to deal with at the moment was Nico. Yet he wasn't the type to rant and rave. "What did Nico hear?"

"Oh, just that...that you are...both here, in the villa...together. Oh, I must catch him before he leaves." Carolina backed out of the room. "Rest."

Ariana followed her. "I must go too. We have a party to organize." She smiled and closed the door softly behind her.

Sofia stared at the door, confused by Carolina's strange behavior. Shrugging, she set about finishing her breakfast then pushed the tray aside. She was climbing out of bed when a short, plump woman breezed into the bedroom.

"*Mi scusi, signorina*, I am Maria, the housekeeper. I have brought the clothes you had on yesterday. They have been washed and ironed because they were covered in blood."

"*Grazie,* Maria. You didn't have to do that."

Maria laid Sofia's jeans, blue blouse, and underwear on the dresser.

"It is no trouble, *signorina. Signor* Santini told me, you were hit by a motorcycle."

"Yes, but I'm fine. I'll be even better once I've had a shower."

"*Sì, sì* that is good, it will relax your sore muscles. I must get back to my kitchen, *signorina.* I am very happy for you and Riccardo."

Walking through to the bathroom, Sofia wondered what she and Riccardo had done to make Maria so happy. She flicked the shower spigot on, pulled the hospital gown off, and caught sight of her body in the mirror.

"Bloody hell." Parts of her hair were matted with dry blood. Ugly bruises mottled her right side. No wonder she was stiff and sore. She had cuts and gravel rash on her knees and elbows. "Who could hate *Papà* this much?"

CHAPTER NINE

Sofia adjusted her blouse, smoothed her hands down the sides of her jeans, and inhaled deeply. Time to meet the enemy. She hesitated at the bottom of the stairs, then breathed a sigh of relief when Carolina walked through a door at the back of the hall.

"I shouldn't be here, Caro."

Carolina hugged her. "I guess you're feeling like a lamb about to enter the den of wolves. Don't worry, they're far more curious than hungry. Why don't you go out on the terrace and I'll bring you a coffee?"

"All right."

Following Carolina's directions, Sofia found an elderly man sitting in one of the chairs, reading a newspaper. As soon as their eyes met, he set it aside.

"So you are Sofia, only granddaughter of Elena and Lorenzo DeRosa"

"*Sì.* I guess you are Carolina's grandfather?"

"*Sì*, I am Enrico Santini. How are your *grandpapà* and *grandmamma*? They don't speak to me now for thirty years. They break my heart."

Sofia stared at him. "Maybe if you hadn't set their son up and humiliated him, you would still be talking to each other."

"What is this nonsense you speak? Thirty years. Do you know your *grandpapà* and I were friends for forty years before that, best friends?" he shouted.

"No, I didn't know that." Sofia stepped closer. "Why didn't you treat his son better, if you were such good friends?"

"Why? Because he accused my family of bribing witnesses to

testify he was a gambler, and he accused us of setting him up with those women to ruin his reputation. So I tell Lorenzo, 'Your son is no good and will ruin you.' I tell him, 'There is no way I will allow my Ariana to marry such a man.' Lorenzo, he gets mad and we no speak again. Thirty years." He stared off into space.

A French door opened and Giovanni stepped onto the terrace. "*Buongiorno, Nonno*, Sofia. What's all the yelling about?" Amusement lurked in his deep voice.

"I am not yelling. Giuseppe's daughter and I are talking," yelled Enrico.

Sofia smiled at Giovanni then remembered he'd chased after her attacker.

"Thank you for trying to catch that man last night. I'm sorry for the way I reacted. I panicked."

Giovanni came over and kissed her on each cheek, his eyes twinkling. "I am glad you are well, Sofia, but you do go to extremes to get Riccardo to give you the kiss of life. Next time just ask him, okay?"

Sofia huffed. "I'm thankful Riccardo was there to save me." She lowered her voice, "But he is the last person I'll be asking to kiss me."

She walked to the edge of the terrace to admire the rolling hills, lined with grape vines. Thinking of Riccardo brought back other thoughts of being held and comforted, or was that a dream? A deep sense of foreboding hit Sofia. She looked around to question Giovanni to find he'd disappeared.

"Where did he go?"

Enrico shrugged. "How would I know? People come and go here all the time and nobody tells me anything," he yelled.

Carolina stepped through a set of French doors carrying two coffees. "Here we are. *Nonno*, would you like a coffee too?"

"*Sì, grazie*, Carolina."

"Caro?" asked Sofia frowning.

Carolina gave Sofia a too bright smile. "I have to get *Nonno's* coffee."

Sofia narrowed her eyes. What was her friend up to?

Enrico let out a snort of disgust. "Nobody tells me Lorenzo DeRosa's granddaughter is coming to stay. Nobody tells me Riccardo is engaged."

Sofia whirled to face him. "Riccardo's engaged?"

"*Sì*, to some *bella donna* from Austria."

Fumbling for a chair, Sofia sank onto the soft cushion. *Engaged.* She looked back at the view, its beauty lost on her. Riccardo was engaged to a beautiful woman from Austria. So what—it was no concern of hers. *Then why do I feel gutted?*

"Sofia?"

She turned to find Riccardo crouched beside her chair. Carolina and Giovanni stood behind him frowning at their grandfather.

Riccardo placed his hand on her knee. "Did Nonno say something to upset you?"

Enrico Santini grunted. "No, I say, nobody tells me she is here, or that my eldest grandson is engaged." His voice grew louder. "That is all I said."

Riccardo smiled. "Ah."

Sofia crossed her arms. "You should have told me," she whispered.

"I was going to speak to you first thing this morning, but when I woke, you looked so peaceful that I didn't disturb you. Then my aunt interrupted us."

Sofia stared at him incredulously. She hadn't dreamed it. Riccardo really had held her in his arms last night. What man does that when he's engaged to another woman?

Aware the old man was watching them, she lowered her voice and glowered at Riccardo. "How could you hold me like that last night? You're engaged."

"It was a kind of spur of the moment thing," he told her quietly.

Sofia shook her head. "Maybe I'm old fashioned, but I believe a man who is engaged to be married, doesn't sleep with other women. He sleeps with the woman he's engaged to?"

"And what makes you think I didn't." He lips quirked.

What does that mean? Sofia registered the tense atmosphere. Her heart raced and perspiration broke out on her forehead as she looked at each of them, replaying Riccardo's words. *No, not in my worst nightmare.*

She straightened her shoulders and met his gaze. "Your grandfather said you were engaged to a beautiful woman from Austria."

"A beauty yes, but from Australia, not Austria." Riccardo squeezed her knee softly. "You, *cara mia*. That's what I need to talk to you about."

Brushing his hand away, Sofia lurched out of her chair. "You can't seriously believe..." Stars danced across her vision. She put her hand out to grab something as dizziness hit.

Riccardo caught her in his arms and picked her up. Lots of voices started speaking at once. Sofia heard a woman's voice call from across the terrace.

"I knew this was a mistake, Riccardo. Give her some air and a glass of water."

Enrico Santini started yelling again. "Why did she faint? She isn't pregnant is she? Is that why you're getting married?"

"Stop shouting, *Nonno*," called Carolina.

Taking deep breaths, Sofia clung to Riccardo as he carried her toward a sun lounge. Nothing made sense. What was his real agenda?

An older man she hadn't seen before chose that moment to step out onto the terrace. Sofia blinked. The likeness to Riccardo and Giovanni was unmistakable. He had to be their father, Angelo Santini. He turned to a striking woman at his side.

"What's going on, Caterina? Why is everyone yelling and who's pregnant?"

Enrico Santini climbed to his feet and picked up his walking stick.

"Lorenzo DeRosa's granddaughter fainted, and now I find out she's pregnant. I'm the last to know anything in my own home," he roared. "Once upon a time my family used to talk to me, now I have to find things out for myself."

The striking woman signaled Riccardo's father to take Enrico Santini inside then turned, crossed her arms under her chest, and frowned toward Sofia and Riccardo.

As Riccardo laid Sofia on a sun lounge, she tried to make sense of the chaos around her. Impossible. She focused on Riccardo who had crouched down beside her.

"You and me...engaged?"

"Yes, Sofia. I decided it's the best way to keep you safe and it's only—"

"We got engaged last night? Was I unconscious, or delirious, or high on medication, because I have no memory of you asking me to marry you, or agreeing?"

Riccardo gave a short laugh. "I didn't ask you, Sofia. I decided this would be the best way to protect you. My parents and siblings know it isn't a real engagement, but for now, we want everyone else to believe it is."

Sofia stared at him, then at the faces around her. She chewed her lip then swallowed the lump in her throat as the enormity of it hit her. "How did this happen? How could you do this to me? Oh my God, Riccardo."

"There you go again, calling me a god," he teased lightly.

"This isn't funny What if my father finds out and never speaks to me again, or he makes me go back to Australia? I won't discover who killed my aunt, or clear my father, and I'll lose the villa. Or is that what this is about? You're using me for your own ends." She started trembling. "How could you do this, Riccardo? It will ruin everything. I refuse to be engaged to you and I don't want to go home."

"Nobody's taking you anywhere. You're staying here while I investigate your aunt's accident and find out who's behind the attacks."

Sofia looked into his eyes. "I want to believe you're being honest with me, and that you would face my brother, but even if you did, what would happen then?" She took a shaky breath. "I couldn't stand it if *Papà* and Dante never spoke to me again."

An elderly woman using a cane walked across and sat on the chair closest to Sofia. "I am Louisa Santini, Riccardo's *nonna*. This feud ends today. Enrico told me about the baby. He is ringing your grandparents now to inform them you and Riccardo will be married as soon as possible. It will come as a shock, especially for your *papà*, whom I suspect will finally break his vow of never setting foot back in this country."

Sofia stared at the elderly woman and blinked. "Baby?" Things were going from bad to worse. Her heart hurt at the thought of *Papà* finding out. It was almost a relief when Riccardo picked her up and headed back into the villa.

"Where are you taking her, Riccardo?" called Carolina.

"I'm taking her back to bed. You should have let me break it to her gently. Nobody is to do anything or inform anyone of anything in future without a family consultation."

"I will bring Sofia some hot milk," called the striking woman.

Sofia rested her head against Riccardo's chest.

"This will crush *Papà*."

"It was the only thing I could think of to keep you safe, *cara mia*."

Sofia looked up into his face, feeling oddly unsure of herself. "Maybe it isn't too late. Your grandfather can ring my grandparents back and tell him he was mistaken."

"Sofia, I've put an announcement in the paper here and in Bologna, which means it's available online as well. I did it to warn off your attacker or perhaps draw him out. If your father was setup and your aunt murdered, then I want to know why and by whom. I'm convinced it wasn't my father or grandfather, but someone is determined to stop you."

"What happens when we figure out who's responsible?" she asked softly. "What if it's someone you know and trust, someone in your family?

"It isn't."

Sofia suddenly felt vulnerable and out of her depth. "All right. What about us?"

"We break off the engagement. I'll tell people you have a terrible temper and the morals of an alley cat." His lips twitched.

Sofia gasped. "What?"

"I am joking, Sofia. Don't worry we will cross that bridge when we come to it. It could be worse. I could have married you."

"You wouldn't dare," she whispered as Riccardo laid her gently on the bed.

"No, *bella*. Marriage is something I wouldn't do lightly." He looked into her eyes.

Sofia stared back, unable to break the contact. "What about the baby?"

"Baby," queried Riccardo, one eyebrow rising.

"Your grandparents think I'm pregnant and that's why we're getting married."

Riccardo lowered his head and lightly kissed her cheek. "Then I must be careful not to get you pregnant, or I definitely will marry you," he murmured against her earlobe.

Sofia sucked in a breath and clutched his shoulders as he feathered kisses down her neck to her collarbone. Thrilling little tremors ran up and down her spine. Maybe her morals were slipping. She liked his lips on her skin and being in his arms, like last night when she'd woken and... She jerked back as if stung by a bee.

"Riccardo, you have to stop kissing me, and you can't sleep with me."

He gave a soft growl. "I'm your fiancé, Sofia, and we have to keep up appearances."

She stared at him as he lowered his mouth to hers, brushing light little kisses from one side of her mouth to the other. She was so enthralled she forgot her resolve to keep him at a distance. Her fingers tightened on his shoulders. She moved closer and hesitantly returned his kisses.

He groaned then increased the pressure, gently parting her lips with his tongue. Her body melted against his as a shiver ran through her entire body. She had never experienced anything like the ache deep inside her belly. Goosebumps raced through her as his fingers stroked her arm, then her neck and collarbone.

Riccardo broke the kiss and pulled back to stare into her wide passion-filled eyes. When she attempted to drag him back, he nearly succumbed. It took a supreme effort to ignore her inviting lips and soft body, but he had to remember, Sofia was vulnerable and a DeRosa. He couldn't take advantage of the situation, no matter how much he wanted her.

"My mother will be here in a minute with your hot milk, and I don't think you want to be caught in a compromising position."

"No, I...of course not," she mumbled, blushing profusely.

"Plus, if we don't stop now, you might end up with that baby, so you'd better behave yourself."

Sofia gave him a look of indignation. "I'd better behave... You're the one who kissed me, and you're the one who decided we should be engaged. You're the one who—"

Riccardo stopped her rampage with another deep kiss, and when he finally lifted his head, he couldn't help but smile.

"As I said, you'd better behave yourself...in private anyway. In public and in front of my family and our acquaintances we need to present a picture of a loving couple, while we get to the bottom of this mystery."

Sofia drew away from him. "Do you really think our engagement is wise?"

"Yes. I'm hoping whoever is responsible will stop the attacks now that he thinks we're engaged, and he has the letters."

She didn't look convinced. "What about my father and brother? I don't think you realize what's going to happen. They won't accept our engagement. What happens when my brother turns up here?"

"I will talk to him and explain why we are pretending to be engaged. I think he will agree your safety is more important than a feud."

She slowly shook her head at him. "I can't agree, in fact I suspect my father and brother's reaction is more likely to resemble a nuclear explosion. The fallout is going to be catastrophic. What about our um...our sleeping arrangements? Where will you sleep?"

"I intend to sleep where I slept last night."

Her beautiful eyes flared. "You can't do that. What if we, you know, what if we um..."

Riccardo laughed "You must control yourself, Sofia, and keep your hands to yourself."

She glared at him. "I'm not sleeping with you again, and I will have you know..."

A light knock sounded at the door. "Riccardo, I have warm milk for Sofia."

He winked. "*Si,* come in *Mamma.* I'm not ravishing Sofia at the moment."

Sofia threw him a warning look as the striking woman from the terrace walked in carrying a large cup.

"I am Caterina, and for my sins I am the mother of this rogue, who I insist leaves you alone now to rest." She handed the warm mug and a pill to Sofia. "These will help you sleep."

Riccardo suspected Sofia had the pill in her hand and only pretended to swallow it, as she took a sip of warm milk. If he'd wanted to drug her, he'd have chosen the milk. Still, he couldn't blame her for being suspicious.

He stood. "All right. I will see you tonight, *cara mia.*" He leaned over and kissed her lightly on the lips.

"Stop doing that." croaked Sofia, her cheeks glowing.

"We have to act like an engaged couple. I was practicing. Now I must go. I have something important to take care of."

"What?" asked his mother.

"I'm going to Bologna to speak to the police about Sofia's attacker."

"Did anyone get the motorcycle registration?" asked Sofia.

"Yes they did, and we are following that up with the police."

Sofia watched him stroll leisurely from the room as if he didn't have a care in the world. *Oh, Riccardo, when Papà finds out about this engagement, he's going to have a coronary.* She needed to fight this infatuation before her heart got broken and Dante throttled Riccardo.

She waited until he was out of earshot before turning to Caterina. "I realize you can't be happy with me staying here. I will leave first thing tomorrow."

Caterina inhaled deeply. "Sofia, I don't know what happened with your *papà*. We were friends one moment, and then everything went wrong. People were making terrible accusations against Giuseppe. My husband refused to believe them until he saw something with his own eyes that he couldn't ignore. When Angelo and his father refused to let Giuseppe see Ariana he went crazy and made threats against us. Then a deliberately lit fire did enormous damage to our vineyard. That was followed by the robbery and fire at the DeRosa vineyard, and your grandfather's heart attack."

Sofia clenched her fists. "You said you were close. Did any of you ever see my father gambling or have any reason to believe he was seeing prostitutes? Isn't it true he worked every day in the vineyard and his spare time was spent with Angelo, Ariana, and you?"

Holding out her hands, Catarina shrugged. "As I said at the time everything happened so fast, and nobody really had time to think. But you are right. I don't know when he could have had time to do those things. We never saw him gamble or show interest in any other woman after he started dating Ariana. That is, until Angelo caught him with two prostitutes."

Ignoring that last remark, Sofia chewed on a fingernail. "My father seemed more hurt by the fact that the people closest to him didn't believe him than the actual allegations."

Caterina nodded. "If Giuseppe is innocent then a terrible injustice has been done, and not just to him but to his family and friends. I think perhaps Riccardo is right and you should stay here with us while you search for your answers, but I do not believe my husband was involved. Now drink up your milk and take that tablet. I will send Carolina up to check on you around lunch time."

Sofia was about to do as she was told when another thought struck her.

"You speak English without any accent. You're not Italian?"

"No, I was raised in England. My father came to Bologna to lecture at the university so I decided to do a language degree there, which is how I met Angelo. That is also why my children speak perfect English. I insist we speak English at home. Now you must rest."

Sofia nodded and curled up into a comfortable position.

"*Grazie.*"

Caterina left the room, quietly shutting the door behind her and Sofia's gaze fell on a framed picture sitting on the chest of drawers. It was of Riccardo, Giovanni, Carolina, and their parents. They wore ski suits and stood in front of a magnificent backdrop of snow-covered mountains. Caterina had her head on Angelo's chest, his chin rested on her head.

Looks could be deceiving. The Santini men were known as tough negotiators, but were they capable of conspiracy and murder?

Sofia sighed. They didn't strike her as people who would destroy a friend, or suffocate a defenseless woman. She closed her eyes. *Don't fall for him, Sofia.*

Chapter Ten

Standing on the balcony, Sofia was admiring the villa's gardens when Carolina entered the bedroom. She turned and smiled. "Do you know what we should do this afternoon, Caro?"

"No, and I am almost afraid to ask. I've been given orders where you're concerned, but I'm curious. What should we do this afternoon?"

"We should go to Villa DeRosa and explore it." We can search for the evidence Aunt Renzina hid at the same time.

"Oh no, Riccardo left specific instructions you were to take it easy, here at this villa. I am also supposed to discourage you from doing any investigating."

"Oh please, Caro. We have to solve this thing and quickly before my brother arrives. You promised to help me."

Carolina threw an exasperated look skywards. "Maybe we could take a little look after lunch. I'll tell my mother you want to get some ideas for the renovations."

"Thanks, Carolina, you're the best, although I'm not sure I should forgive you for your part in this engagement fiasco."

"Don't blame me. Riccardo and Giovanni said it was for the best. Just don't get intimate with Riccardo. I don't need your brother exacting revenge on me, which is what Dante promised when he thought you and Nico were involved."

"You never told me that."

Carolina sighed. "I caught the late train to Venezia and Dante must have followed me. I freaked out when he grabbed me from behind and pulled me into an empty carriage."

"I bet you did."

"He explained who he was and demanded to know where you were, but I refused to tell him. I tried all sorts of things to put him off your trail. I even flirted, and he…he…"

Sofia stared at Carolina. Dante was the most self-possessed person she knew. He never willingly drew attention to himself. The fact he'd forcibly restrained Carolina proved how much he cared, and how determined he could be.

"He what?" asked Sofia, transfixed.

"He kissed me and said, if Nico touched you in any way, he would be back to exact revenge, and he'd do more than kiss me."

"He didn't?" Sofia gasped. "Why didn't you tell me?"

"Because I knew you and Nico were just friends. But Dante meant every word."

Sofia drew a deep breath. "Well, you can relax, nothing is going to happen between me and Riccardo. You have nothing to fear from Dante."

"Oh really, I've seen the way you look at Riccardo and I've caught him watching you. Whenever you're near each other, there's an undercurrent in the air."

Sofia scoffed. "Rubbish, I'm probably looking at him oddly because I can't believe his audacity. I'm not a fool, Carolina. I know the sort of women your brothers prefer and they're the complete opposite of me. Come on, let's go search my villa and you can tell me what else you did to put Dante off my trail."

Carolina threw her a suspicious look. "Okay, but if either Riccardo or Dante come after me, it's on your head."

They borrowed her mother's Mercedes and drove along a scenic route of winding, tree lined roads and rolling hills covered in grape vines. Sofia enjoyed the drive, squinting against the afternoon sun to admire the occasional farmhouse and the autumn colors of the leaves. They rolled to a stop in front of massive rust-coated gates, held shut by large chain looped around and through the bars.

Sofia climbed out of the Mercedes and stood peering through the gates along a weed-infested drive at Villa DeRosa. Her gaze swept over broken shutters, barely attached or lying on the ground amongst the weeds, crumbling and cracked render. So neglected she didn't know where to start.

Fitting a key, she unlocked the padlock and let the chain fall to the ground, then pushed one gate wide so Carolina could drive throùgh.

They stopped in front of the steps, then Sophia climbed out and stared at the villa. "Wow. It's going to take a lot of work and money to fix this. At the very least it needs patching, painting, a new roof, new guttering, and that's just the outside."

Carolina nodded. "New windows, shutters, plumbing, and wiring. It's a good thing you've been given a fortune to fix it."

Their eyes met and they burst into laughter.

Mounting the steps, Sofia held up the keys. "Come on, let's see what the inside is like." She waited for Carolina to join her before unlocking the front door. It creaked loudly as they both pushed it open.

"It smells musty." Carolina wrinkled her nose as she stepped into the dark foyer. They moved through the empty downstairs rooms, opening dusty curtains to let the sunlight in. They did the same to the second floor rooms, sneezing each time they were covered in dust motes.

"It's a lovely old villa." Sofia murmured. "We could make it beautiful again with a bit of elbow grease, and that money. Would you consider moving in with me?"

Carolina held her hand over her heart and fluttered her eyelids. "Why I'd love to, Sofia, but this is so sudden, and what about your fiancée?"

Sofia playfully swiped at her friend. "Funny haha. Can you imagine Riccardo and me living here in wedded bliss with our four bambini, two cats, and a dog? I don't think so. He is the most obnoxious, arrogant..."

"How hard have you fallen, Sofia?" asked Carolina softly.

Sofia blinked. "What, I haven't...I'm not...for goodness sake." She opened an empty linen cupboard, the shelves layered in dust. "I still can't believe the nerve of the man, announcing our engagement, without even asking me. He's lucky I'm not a man or I would have punched his lights out."

"If you were a man, you wouldn't be engaged to him." Carolina giggled.

Sofia sneezed. "I just hope my grandparents don't contact Papà."

Carolina gave her a quick hug. "I hate to tell you this, but your engagement is big news around here, and even if your grandparents can't contact your father, Salvatore Bondini probably will. I give it a couple of days before Dante arrives and all hell breaks loose."

Sofia hunched her shoulders then winced. "I've been in Italy six days, and in that time I've been drugged, robbed, mugged, suffocated, and engaged. That's got to be some kind of record. At least last time I was here it was four months before Papà found out I was involved with you Santinis. Maybe we should take off now, before Dante gets here?"

"Let's see what happens. Nothing frightens my brothers, and I know they will stand up to Dante. There's something else I think you should know though."

"What?"

"Giovanni agrees with Riccardo about the engagement, but not because it's a good way of protecting you. He thinks if you two are engaged, even though it's not real, you might actually fall for each other, and well, to be honest, none of us has ever seen Riccardo act the way he does around you. Giovanni thinks you're exactly what Riccardo needs."

"You're kidding?" Sofia blinked at Carolina. She rubbed her forehead to ward off the return of her headache. "It would break my father's heart if I fell in love with Riccardo, and anyway I want marriage and children with a man who loves only me. Riccardo has no interest in settling down with one woman for the rest of his life."

Carolina squeezed Sofia's hand. "I just thought you should know."

Sofia said nothing as they moved along a wide hall and descended the stairs. If she believed Riccardo cared for her, than she'd be leaving herself open to disappointment.

"How about the cellar?" suggested Carolina as they reached the bottom step. "All old villas have wine cellars and it's a good place to hide the evidence."

"Okay, lead the way," called Sofia in an attempt to regain their earlier light heartedness. They shone the torch in every nook and cranny then climbed the narrow steps again.

"Nothing but dust," complained Carolina in disgust as they returned to the hall.

Sitting on the bottom step, Sofia balanced her elbows on her knees and cradled her face. "Where else could it be?"

Carolina put her arm around Sofia. "Come on, let's lock up and go home before Riccardo finds out we're missing."

"All right. Thanks for bringing me here, Caro."

Acres and acres of grape vines separated the two villas, leaving Sofia wondering how many of them used to belong to her family.

As Carolina turned into her own driveway she glanced at Sofia. "Don't worry, we will figure it out and…oh no, that's Nico's car. He and Riccardo had a huge argument over you this morning."

"Me?"

"Yes. Nico accused Riccardo of taking advantage of you, and only becoming engaged to thwart him. Nico doesn't know it's a fake engagement by the way. I think he's jealous."

Sofia laughed. "I've never had any interest in dating Nico, and I can't believe he thinks Riccardo would get engaged just to thwart him." She frowned. "He kissed me."

"Who, Nico?"

"No. Riccardo. He carried me upstairs this morning and then kissed me."

Carolina stared at Sofia. "And you didn't think to tell me. I knew he was attracted to you." They pulled up in front of the villa, right behind Nico's car. He stood at the front door, waiting.

As Sofia climbed the steps, her eyes locked with Nico's furious gaze. He blocked her path. "What are you doing engaged to Riccardo?"

Carolina gave him a warning look. "Nico, leave it. Sofia's safer here and when news gets out that she's engaged to Riccardo, we're hoping the attacks will stop."

"Is that what this engagement's about, to protect you from whoever is behind the attacks? What about clearing your father or have you forgotten about that?"

Sofia glared at him. "Nico, that man tried to kill me. I need him caught so I can continue with my plans to clear Papà. I found out this morning that Ariana is the woman my father was engaged to. I intend to clear my father, if it's the last thing I ever do."

Nico visibly paled. "Are you in love with Riccardo?"

Sofia lifted her chin. "I don't think we should be having this conversation, Nico. I'm engaged to him aren't I?"

His eyes narrowed. "What happens when your father finds out?"

She swallowed. "Riccardo promised me he would face Dante."

Nico snorted. "I would like to be a fly on the wall when they have that conversation." He stalked off down the hall.

Carolina put her arm around Sofia. "Forget it. Nico's nose is out of joint. I don't know what's come over him lately. Come on, let's find Mamma and assure her we're fine."

Sofia followed Carolina through the villa to the terrace where Caterina and Ariana were sitting at a table having coffee. Nico leaned against the railing, brooding. Sofia caught Carolina's eye and tried not to laugh.

Ariana waved them to two seats at the table. "Nico, darling, why don't you bring more coffee for the girls? They look like they need it."

Nico grunted but disappeared inside to do as she'd asked.

Ariana turned to Sofia. "He's put out because you and Riccardo are engaged. He is a wonderful son, but sometimes he drives me batty."

Sofia's mouth dropped open. "Nico is your son?" She stared at Ariana.

"Yes, my dear. I thought you knew?"

Sofia looked from Ariana to Carolina to Caterina and back to Ariana again. Nico was the image of Dante, but he couldn't possibly be her brother. Papà would have left Italy before Nico had been conceived. Yet the likeness to Dante was astounding.

When Nico came back out, Sofia studied him closely as he placed a fresh coffee pot in front of them. He was as tall and broad as Dante and shared the same thick wavy hair. His eyes were brown and his jaw square with a little dimple on one side of his mouth that became visible when he smiled. He wasn't smiling now; he was watching Sofia as intently as she was watching him. His mother reached for the coffee pot.

"Grazie, darling. Sofia didn't know I am your mother."

Nico's eyebrows rose. "No, she wouldn't."

Ariana glanced between Nico and Sofia a couple of times. "It's turning warm, I may need to go to...to Lucca for more clothes. Or...or, perhaps a shopping day is called for. We could take Sofia to Milano."

Sofia wondered why Ariana was flustered. *Is it possible?*

"How old are you, Nico?" she asked as innocently as she could.

He smiled and the dimple instantly appeared. "Twenty-eight...according to my birth certificate."

Doing the math, Sofia realized he couldn't possibly be her brother. Yet. "It's strange but you're so much like my brother, Dante, it's scary."

There was a gasp and Sofia looked across to see Ariana gripping the tablecloth.

"Are you all right, Mamma?" asked Nico.

Ariana was staring at Sofia. "You have a brother named Dante?"

"Yes."

Nico rushed to his mother's side. "What is it?"

There was an uncomfortable silence as Ariana stared at Sofia. Caterina pushed a glass of water into Ariana's hand and made her drink it.

Ariana placed the glass on the table and looked at Sofia. "I'm sorry, it's just that when your father asked me to marry him, we were standing in front of Dante's statue, and we joked that our first son would be named Dante."

Sofia chewed her lip. So much for that theory. All she'd done was drag up the past and upset Ariana, but Nico's dimple and frown were so like Dante's.

She pretended to glance away at the view, but closed her eyes and listened to Nico's voice as he spoke to Caterina. He even sounded like Dante and Papà. It was unsettling, but if he really were Giuseppe and Ariana's son, then he'd have to be twenty-nine. Sofia was about to dismiss the whole idea when she glanced back at Ariana. Her eyes held pain and apprehension.

Sofia pretended to let the matter drop and turned to Carolina. "I should visit my grandparents. There are things I need to ask them."

Carolina passed her a coffee. "We can, but not tomorrow. I have a delivery of rings arriving. How's Sunday or Monday?"

"That's fine." Sofia sat back in her seat and pretended to relax, letting the conversation flow around her. In reality she was wondering what had Ariana running scared and what did Nico mean, that he was twenty-eight according to his birth certificate? Birth certificates didn't lie. Was it possible to avoid registering a birth until much later, and how did one go about finding out?

Sofia added it to her list and resolved to get hold of a picture of Nico's father. She would see for herself if they were alike.

Loud voices brought Sofia out of her daydream. She glanced across the terrace to see Ariana and Catarina had wandered into the garden. Nico and Carolina were standing face to face a couple of feet away.

"This engagement is a charade," accused Nico. "A couple of days ago Sofia swore she'd never have anything to do with Ricardo and now she's engaged to him, and I for one don't believe it."

Carolina looked quickly toward their mothers. "Keep your voice down, Nico. Riccardo came up with the engagement as a way to protect Sofia."

"So I'm right, this engagement is a charade?"

Sofia bit her lip. "Nico, whoever is behind the robberies and attacks wants me dead. I would be if it hadn't been for Riccardo. I'm not even sure who I can trust."

Nico put his arm around her shoulders. "You can trust me, Sofia. I care about you, and I'd never let anyone hurt you. You can think of me as...family."

She smiled. "I guess you could be my stand-in brother, if you like?"

Nico didn't say anything for so long that Sofia started to feel uncomfortable, then he took a deep breath and nodded. "I'm at your disposal. All I ask is that you don't take any risks."

Sofia hugged him, careful not to bump her still tender shoulder. "It's a deal, Nico."

He wrapped his arms around her gently just as Riccardo stepped onto the terrace.

"What the—" Riccardo strode over and wrenched Nico away, then whirled on Sofia. "I left instructions you were not to leave this villa then I ring to check on you and Maria tells me you've gone to Villa DeRosa. I had to leave an important meeting to come home and when I do, I find you in his arms."

"Ciao, Riccardo, it's nice to see you too." Sofia reached for his tie, adjusting it as tight as she could. "Carolina and I went to do a little exploring. And I was hugging Nico because he's consented to act as my protector while you're off doing whatever you do."

She smirked and because she couldn't help herself, she reached up and kissed Riccardo's cheek. "But it is lovely that you made it home in time for dinner."

Loosening his tie, Riccardo scowled at her. "Do not think you can flirt your way out of this, Sofia. It's a serious matter. I don't want you leaving this villa, and I would also prefer you refrained from throwing yourself at Nico."

"Anyone would think you were jealous, Riccardo."

His eyes narrowed. "You're my fiancée, remember. If you want to go somewhere, you can wait for me to take you."

Sofia stretched up and kissed him on the cheek again. "There's no need for you to take time off from your busy schedule. Nico has offered to be at my disposal."

Riccardo stepped closer. "Be careful, Sofia, you don't want to play games with me. I'm far too experienced."

An excited tremor ran through her. They were standing so close his spicy cologne swirled around her. Maybe it was the devil in her, or maybe it was his arrogant challenge, or even Carolina's alarmed expression. Whatever it was, Sofia found herself meeting his challenge and setting one of her own.

"You don't faze me, Riccardo. I'm not afraid to take you on, any time, any place."

Riccardo pulled her so close she could see tiny flecks of gold in his rich brown eyes. It was obvious by his clenched jaw that he wanted to throttle her, but they had too many witnesses.

She leaned up and whispered in his ear. "Round one to me." Laughing, she turned away and had only taken one step when she found herself swept off her feet.

"What are you doing?" cried Carolina, grabbing his arm. "Sofia isn't challenging you."

"Yes, I am," scoffed Sofia. She watched him carefully. Would he show his true colors if she made him mad enough? "I'm not afraid of you."

Nico laughed. "Sofia, you should quit while you're ahead. Riccardo's not used to having his orders ignored, especially by a woman."

Sofia's eyes locked with Riccardo's. It wasn't anger she saw, but desire. Her pulse leapt. The threat of retribution rang loud and clear. She probably shouldn't have pushed him so far.

"You'd better put me down, Riccardo. I need to go upstairs and...unpack my things, since I've decided to stay."

A lazy smile spread over Riccardo's face. "Would you like me to help you...unpack?" he whispered, close to her ear.

A thrill raced through her at his blatant innuendo. "No, I'm fine, thank you."

Riccardo stroked her upper arm softly with his thumb, a look of satisfaction appearing when she shivered. Sofia blinked, disconcerted to find she was so affected by his touch.

Ignoring her, Riccardo turned to Carolina and Nico. "Instead of unpacking, Sofia should lie down. She looks a little flushed."

Sofia opened her mouth to argue but he was already striding into the house and then up the stairs. Keep your mouth shut, Sofia, you'll only make matters worse.

When they reached his bedroom he laid her on the bed, "Are you sure you want to take me on, cara mia?" His smile screamed predator. "Men twice your size have tried and failed."

Don't push him, Sofia. Don't do it. She gritted her teeth. Hell, she couldn't let him get away with that. "I'm not afraid of you, and if you think you can intimidate..." Her voice deserted her as he leaned down and kissed her fleetingly on her neck.

Her breath caught. "Don't do that."

Straightening, he gazed down at her. "I'm leaving, but think carefully before you challenge me, tesoro." He strode to the door.

Clenching her fists, Sofia fought to hold her tongue, but it was a battle she'd never win. "Don't call me tesoro. I am not your treasure."

He hesitated at the door, his rich, dark gaze gliding leisurely along her body before coming to rest on her face. "So you do understand a little Italiano?"

Her body ignited under his intense gaze. "A little."

"I will teach you much more, tesoro." His lips curved into a slow, sexy smile. "I promise." He pulled the door closed behind him, leaving her heated and rattled.

"Oh my God."

Chapter Eleven

Sofia awoke to find the curtains had been closed and a cooling fan placed beside the bed. She glanced at her watch and blinked. *Six*. Since arriving in Italy her body clock was all over the place. She swung her legs over the side of the bed, hissing as the scab on her elbow pulled. Her emerald dress had been laid out over the chair with a note in a clean, confident, masculine scrawl.

Wear this to the party tonight, cara mia. Please.

"Party?" Her gaze flitted around Riccardo's bedroom. It wasn't right she sleep with him in here. And she hadn't spent her whole life trying to outwit her brother just to have Riccardo Santini manipulate her. He was a Santini, and *I am Sofia DeRosa*.

As she came down the stairs, numerous voices from the drawing room reached her. Sofia hovered at the doorway, surprised to see the room full of people. A sudden hush fell over the room as its occupants noticed her.

"Hi."

Riccardo strolled over, pulled her into his arms, and kissed her full on the lips. "You look stunning, *cara mia*."

She dug her fingernails into his arm and whispered, "What are you doing?"

"Kissing my fiancée. Are you feeling better, *tesoro?*"

"Why do you keep calling me that? I am not your treasure."

He bent to her ear. "We have guests, Sofia. People who knew your father."

Sofia glanced around him. The Santini family was there and the solicitor, Michele Bondini, but who were the others? She would play along with Riccardo's scheme for now. This was too good an opportunity to miss.

Caterina came forward and took Sofia's hand. "My dear, are you feeling better? I was about to send Carolina to wake you. Come, I will introduce you to some of our extended family and friends before dinner."

Throwing a brief glance at Riccardo, Sofia let Caterina lead her across the room.

"This is Michele Bondini and his father, Salvatore. They have been our solicitors and friends for years."

Sofia smiled at Michele. "It's nice to see you again, Michele." She turned to his father. "*Buona sera, Signor* Bondini. You might not remember me, but we met five years ago and my father has always spoken highly of you."

He took her hand. "*Buona sera*, Sofia. Welcome to *Italia*. I do remember you and I have always been very fond of your *papà*. I don't know if you know, but he was a magician when it came to growing grapes. Under his care, the DeRosa wines were well on their way to being amongst the best in the world."

Smiling, Sofia squeezed his hand. "Yes, he told me. He's having the same effect on our grapes at home in Australia."

Caterina led her around the spacious living room, introducing Sofia to neighbors and relatives. There were so many people, Sofia wouldn't remember Marcello from Mauro or Andrea from Antonio. Their wives names were just as confusing."

Nodding politely, Sofia studied the men's eyes, looking for either of the men who attacked her. None looked familiar.

Caterina handed Sofia a glass of white wine. "Everyone is curious, but don't let them overwhelm you."

Letting her gaze drift over the entire room, Sofia smiled. "I won't."

Michele Bondini stepped forward. "We are surprised to find you and Riccardo engaged, *signorina*. It was a well-kept secret. Have you known each other long?"

Sofia darted a quick glance at Riccardo. "A little while."

Michele smiled. "Before you entered the room, *signorina*, we were discussing the attacks, and the body they found in Bologna. Do you have any idea who he was or why he wanted to hurt you?"

"Body, what body?" Sofia turned to Riccardo who had come to stand on her left.

He put his arm around her waist. "We had a phone call from the police earlier. They found a body matching the description of the man who drugged you. He also matches the video footage of the man who broke into my office, and snatched your purse."

Sofia gasped. *Body.* "How did he die?" She willed herself to meet Riccardo's eyes, terrified of what she might see there. Had the Santinis dealt with the man?

Riccardo raised an eyebrow. "Don't even think it, *cara mia*. We had his apartment under surveillance, but he never returned. His body was found in one of the industrial areas. It appears he died from a drug overdose."

"Oh really, and what do you think?"

"I think we should enjoy our engagement party."

"Engagement party!"

Caterina Santini gave a subtle cough. "*Sì*, Sofia, we thought to give you and Riccardo an engagement party to introduce you to our closest family and friends. These people have known us and your family since...your father was young."

Sofia glanced at Riccardo. He gave the appearance of being extremely relaxed, and handsome in his open necked shirt and dark tailored pants. He wasn't the least bit bothered that these people thought they were here to celebrate a real engagement. Did he suspect someone here?

A deep chill raced through her. *Which one of you is the viper who wants me dead?* Perhaps she should get the hell out of here, but that wouldn't clear her father.

Sofia linked her arm through Riccardo's. "What a lovely surprise, and now I know that man can't hurt me, I intend to enjoy myself."

Pulling her close, Riccardo gave her a dazzling smile then dropped a kiss on her lips.

Sofia's cheeks heated. She glanced across the room to see Carolina giving her the thumbs up. Standing beside her was Giovanni, looking as relaxed as Riccardo. Ariana sat on the couch talking to Louisa, and standing behind them was Nico, staring moodily at her.

Carolina handed each person a glass of champagne, then turned and smiled. "I'd like to propose two toasts. First to Riccardo and Sofia, that they have a long and happy life together."

Everyone raised their glasses toward Sofia and Riccardo, making appropriate responses. Carolina tapped a crystal bowl with a spoon.

"I would also like to propose a toast to the end of this feud between our two families. Two families who were once very good friends and can be again."

There was an awkward silence then Nico stepped forward and raised his glass. "*Sì, sì.* To the Santinis and DeRosas," he called loudly.

Everyone in the room hesitantly raised their glasses, gazes flitting from one to another, shock, astonishment, and wonder clearly written on their faces.

Sofia met Nico's eyes across the room. He had one eyebrow raised sardonically, reminding her of Dante. It was just the sort of thing her brother would do. Was this Nico's way of declaring he would play along with their charade for now?

Everyone had either gone home or retired for the night by the time Riccardo entered his own bedroom. Expecting to find Sofia sleeping soundly, he glanced at the bed and found it was empty and her suitcase gone. He snatched up a sheet of paper from the middle of the bed.

I've moved to the guest room as is proper.

He snorted. "Proper, I'll give her proper." He marched out the door and down the hall, opening the doors of three guestrooms before he found her curled up in bed.

She rolled over and blinked at him drowsily. "Is something wrong?"

"What do you think you're doing?"

Sofia yawned. "I would have thought that was obvious to someone with your degree of intelligence. I was sleeping."

Riccardo strode across the room. "You're supposed to be in my bed, where I can keep you safe. You will move your things back tomorrow."

"I will not."

Riccardo ripped the sheet away and scooped her into his arms.

She gasped and swiped at him. "Riccardo, no. We can't sleep in the same bed."

"If you feel so strongly, you can put a pillow between us. Now keep your voice down or you'll wake everyone."

She punched his shoulder. "You're a beast and a bully."

Returning to his room, Riccardo shut the door with his hip, walked across to his bed, and deposited Sofia in the middle. She was absolutely delectable in a pale green nightie that barely covered her lovely breasts and thighs. Her look of indignant outrage had him fighting to keep a straight face.

"I'm in need of a cool shower, so make yourself comfortable. Oh, and I like the right side." He grinned as she picked up a pillow and hurled it at him. Another pillow hit the bathroom door as he closed it, then he did laugh, unable to hold it in any longer.

When he came out, she was tucked up in the middle of his king size bed, arms crossed under her clearly defined breasts and glaring at him. He glanced at the blanket and pillow lying on the floor and hid his smile. *You won't get rid of me that easily, cara mia.*

He crossed to the dresser, taking his time selecting a pair of boxers. "Did you enjoy yourself tonight? You were very popular with my relatives." He watched her in the mirror.

"Yes." Her gaze had fixed on his naked back.

He shrugged. "I don't normally sleep in anything, but I have some boxers here somewhere. Ah, here they are." He turned displaying a pair of colorful silk boxers. "Now, if you don't want to see me in all my glory, I suggest you shut your eyes."

"Hmm." Sofia's gaze was fixed on his chest.

He waved the boxers at her. "Sofia."

Her gaze dropped to his towel and she blushed. "Sorry." She turned away quickly.

Glancing down, he saw his low-slung towel wasn't doing a very good job of hiding his bulging interest. He dropped the towel then pulled on his boxers.

Riccardo picked up the blanket and pillow, walked over to a

lounge chair and dumped the blanket, then walked back to the bed and threw the pillow.

Sofia caught it and placed it beside her. "Don't you want a pillow?"

He couldn't help the smile that tugged at his lips. "Of course. I also want to sleep in *my* bed, beside *my* fiancée." He pulled the comforter back.

Bolting out of bed, Sofia swung to face him. "If you insist on sharing a room, you'll have to sleep on the floor, then I can tell my father you never laid a finger on me."

He didn't doubt her for a second. "But that would be a lie, wouldn't it, Sofia?"

"Well they don't need to know we kissed, and we haven't actually…"

Riccardo's eyes slid over her as she stood in front of him, her nightie clinging to every exquisite curve. His body instantly responded.

"You would tempt the devil, Sofia, and I'm only human." He leapt over the bed, picked her up, and placed her in the middle, careful not to hurt her shoulder.

"How dare you…" She scrambled as he leaned over her. "Riccardo, what are you doing?"

"I am laying a finger on you, and my lips." He kissed her, gently to start with and then more deeply.

She twisted her mouth away. "Don't you have any concern for your own safety? My brother will want your head on a platter."

Riccardo held her firmly and drew her chin back then set to exploring her mouth. He liked the touch of her hands against his chest as she made a half-hearted attempt to push him away. He kissed his way down her slender neck and across her collarbone.

Her body stilled.

He retraced his path back to her earlobe, gratification filling him when she tentatively caressed his back. "Do you want me, *tesoro*?"

"No, I'm just…" His hand closed over her breast and Sofia lost her train of thought. She felt a hard, solid length pressing against her hip. "I can feel your…your…"

His shoulders shook as his deep laugh filled the room.

Sofia slapped his shoulder. "What are you laughing at?"

Riccardo continued laughing and rolled off her. "I'm going to enjoy being engaged to you, *cara mia*."

Sofia glared at him. "You are the most despicable, egotistical, arrogant man, I have ever met and if you don't behave yourself, I'm going to pack my bags and leave."

He pulled her against his chest. "Are you really, Sofia? Is that what you want?"

Sofia put her hands against his chest, realizing too late her big mistake. She could feel his nipples harden under her touch and was again aware of a hard pressure against her thigh. "I...I don't do this sort of thing and we aren't really engaged."

Smiling, Riccardo kissed her forehead, nose and lips. "But we need to pretend we are."

"I don't do one night stands."

"All right, Sofia. I do not force myself on unwilling women, but be warned, I'm only human and you're not making it easy by wearing flimsy things like that." He glanced down at her finely covered breasts. "I might not stop next time."

Sofia glared at him. "I will wear whatever I like and you're the one who came in to my room and kidnapped me. If you have a problem controlling yourself and your equipment, than I suggest you go sleep at one of your hotels, preferably the one furthest away."

Riccardo chuckled. "Oh, Sofia, where have you been all my life? I've never met a woman who speaks her mind like you, or tempts me to do things I know are unwise."

Sofia huffed. "You've had everything your way far too long and it's time someone stood up to you. Now may I please go back to my room?"

"No, go to sleep. I promise I won't tempt you to seduce me."

"You couldn't tempt me if you tried." She went to pull away, only to have his arms tighten around her. "What now?"

"I am considering your challenge. But no. Go to sleep and dream about me."

"You wish." Sofia moved her shoulder into a more comfortable position. She tried to ignore his arm and his soft chuckle as she concentrated on calming her breathing. What was she going to do with him? He was asking for trouble if he thought he could flaunt this sort of behavior in front of Dante.

Her thoughts drifted over the events of the last few days. It was too much of a coincidence that the man who drugged her was dead. She shivered, remembering the coldness in the eyes of the other man who tried to suffocate her.

That was no random attack.

Who was he? She curled her fingers into fists. She needed to clear her father, discover if Nico was her brother, and find her aunt's killer before Dante arrived, or she succumbed to this intense attraction for a man she wanted to trust and liked too much.

Please don't let him be involved.

Her thoughts swung to Riccardo's magnificent physique. Those muscles rippling across his back. Unable to help it, her eyes had devoured his beautifully carved chest, the toned muscles of his stomach, then followed the fine hairline to the low-slung towel.

I'm in big trouble.

Chapter Twelve

Where is that noise coming from? Sofia stirred and let her senses engage. Birds chirped outside. Voices rose and fell somewhere within the villa. She could smell flowers and sexy cologne. She slid her toes against the crisp sheets and a warm leg.

Sofia's eyes flew open. She was sprawled over Riccardo. Before she could move the door flew open and a mob of people burst into the room in a frenzy of raised voices and exclamations.

Riccardo jerked then pulled her tight against him. "*Santa* Maria." He began shouting in Italian.

The sheet was twisted around them leaving Riccardo's naked upper body uncovered. Sofia couldn't comprehend what was happening or understand a word.

"Riccardo?" She squirmed.

"Don't move," he muttered before launching back into an Italian verbal match with his family.

Sofia glanced from one face to the next as they shouted at each other. Carolina, Nico, Enrico, Louisa, Caterina, Angelo and Giovanni, even Michele Bondini and two policemen. It would be comical if she were a fly on the wall.

"This is embarrassing." Sofia tried to wriggle further under the sheet.

Riccardo cursed and held her tighter.

Marching to the side of the bed, Carolina yelled at Riccardo then looked to Sofia and reverted to English. "Did he take advantage of you? If he did, I will never forgive him."

Sofia's mouth dropped. "No. What's going on?"

Carolina threw her an incredulous look. "You're in each other's arms, naked."

"We're not naked and Riccardo didn't touch me. We must have rolled together through the night. Nothing happened."

Carolina looked pointedly at Riccardo's bare chest as he continued a vocal tirade with Nico. "You certainly looked very cozy when we came in," she exclaimed loudly over the commotion behind her.

"Why are the police here, and why is everyone in Riccardo's bedroom? Have the police found my attacker?"

"No." Carolina dashed out of the bedroom then re-appeared carrying a soft-blue robe, which once Riccardo released her, Sofia was able to slide into discreetly.

"We can talk in the bathroom." Carolina herded her away from the din.

Sofia glanced back at Riccardo on the bed, the sheet around his hips as he yelled at the intruders. To anyone with eyes, he looked naked.

When Carolina had the door safely shut, she turned to Sofia. "My family is yelling at Riccardo because your engagement isn't real and it looks like he's taken advantage of you. Nico is yelling because he's *sure* Riccardo took advantage of you. "This is a fine mess my brother has got you into."

"What are the police doing here and why are they and Michele yelling?"

"Somebody contacted the police and told them we are holding you here against your will. Luckily, Michele Bondini was passing and saw the police car so he came in to see what had happened and is attempting to assure them you are here of your own free will."

"Surely they can see that everything's fine."

Carolina let out a shriek. "No, not fine. Everyone witnessed you in Riccardo's arms, in his bed, naked."

"We weren't. Riccardo has boxers on," argued Sofia.

Carolina scoffed. "He made no attempt to get out from under the sheets, Sofia. It certainly looks like he seduced you. Word will get out and Dante is going to turn up, and he'll—"

Unable to help herself, Sofia laughed. Her conspiracy was turning into a circus.

"I am glad you think this is funny," snapped Carolina. "You won't be laughing when Dante turns up to make minced fish of Riccardo, and ruin me."

"It's mincemeat. Dante will make mincemeat of Riccardo." Sofia laughed harder as tears ran down her face. Perhaps this was hysteria.

"Fine, laugh, but I seriously think we should make a run for it. Have a shower. I will sneak some clothes into you and then we'll escape. I'm serious, Sofia."

"I'm sorry, it's just that someone, probably a member of your family wants me dead, yet here I am in your family villa. Dante is going to go off like a bomb and drag me home in disgrace. Then, I'll lose Villa DeRosa. My aunt's killer will never be found. I'll never clear my father, or discover if Nico's my brother. I'm supposed to be pregnant and having an affair with Riccardo." She collapsed into another fit of giggles.

Carolina frowned. "Maybe you're having a nervous breakdown. I know Nico looks like Dante, but he's not your brother."

Sofia stilled, her laughter vanquished. "I think he is, Caro. I know his age doesn't fit but—" She touched her heart. "In here, I know, and I think Nico does too."

Eyes wide, Carolina stared at her. "He does look like Dante, but that would mean… We are opening a can of ants. Think of the repercussions."

"Can of worms. I know."

"Okay, first things first. Have your shower while I figure out what to do." Carolina slipped out the door.

Sofia took off her chemise and stepped into the shower. There was no way she'd leave Riccardo to face the music alone. She would explain things to Dante once he calmed down. He loved her; surely he would hear her out.

When she finished showering, Sofia wrapped a towel around her body and peeped out the door. The room was empty of people. Her gypsy skirt and white tank top had been laid out on the bed. Carolina had also thrown a few things in an overnight bag, which Sofia ignored. "Time to face the music."

As Sofia stepped out onto the terrace a policeman moved in front of her. "*Scusi, Signorina* DeRosa, my English is not so good. I sorry for intruding to you, but I must make sure you are here of your own free will?"

Sofia stiffened. "*Sì, signore.* I am engaged to Riccardo Santini. Whoever rang you is out to make trouble."

The policemen nodded. "*Sì*. We are sorry for intruding on your privacy."

"That's all right. I know you're only doing your job. Have you tracked down the man who attacked me in the hospital, or do you have any new information on the dead man?"

"No." The policeman gave a polite nod then signaled to his partner they were leaving.

As soon as they were out of sight, Carolina swooped. "Come sit at the table. Once you've eaten, we'll make our getaway."

"What getaway?" asked Nico stepping through the French doors. "What are you up to, Caro?"

She passed a bowl of fruit salad across the table. "I driving Sofia into the mountains for a picnic and to show her my new car."

As Sofia poured a glass of orange juice Michele Bondini joined Nico by the table. "An excellent idea and it's a perfect day, though I'm surprised Riccardo is not escorting his lovely fiancée into the mountains himself?"

Nico glanced over his shoulder toward French doors further along the terrace. "Riccardo and Giovanni are busy with their hotel launch. They'll be working for most of the day. I think you two ladies should stay home as I won't be here to chaperone you."

"You don't need to come with us, Nico." Carolina said. "It will be a leisurely drive up, then we'll stop at the lookout near the monastery for lunch before coming back."

Michele frowned. "Why do they need a chaperone? The man who attacked Sofia is dead? No harm will come to her here on a picnic with Carolina."

Nico sighed. "You're right, but Riccardo was pretty clear on this."

"He's over reacting." Carolina threw up her hands. "Okay, I'll get his approval."

"Enjoy your day, ladies." Michele gave them a wave.

"*Ciao.*"

"I will see you to your car," offered Nico, following Michele down the steps of the terrace. He looked over his shoulder, raising a sardonic eyebrow, reminding Sofia of Dante.

She blew him a kiss. "Straight up to the lookout and back, we promise." Sofia looked across the table at Carolina. "I thought you had to work today?"

"I will ring my assistant. He can handle things for a few weeks."

"I'm not running this time." Sofia's gaze returned to the solicitor, talking to Nico as they followed a path to the side of the villa. "Michele is a nice man."

"I don't know him that well, "replied Carolina. "But his father, Salvatore, is lovely. He often comes over to play chess with my grandfather."

Sofia chewed her lip. "I get the impression Michele knows more about my father and the allegations than he's saying, but doesn't want to offend me."

"Michele is the same age as our fathers, but it would have been his father, Salvatore, who handled the legal stuff back then. We should stop by his *villa* and ask?"

"All right, but we are not running away. Let's do a little poking instead."

"Fine, have it your way. I was only thinking of you." Carolina gave her a huffy scowl and crossed her arms. "I'll get Maria to pack a picnic while you finish your breakfast."

Sofia ladled her plate with a variety of bite size pieces of fruit, then ate as she looked over the vista of rolling hills and grapevines.

The French doors further along the terrace opened. Sofia pursed her lips as Riccardo stepped out. She'd wondered when he was going to appear.

"Ah, Sofia, how are you after our rude awakening?"

"Embarrassed. I can't help wondering why you intentionally let everyone believe we were naked or that we had...you know...?"

Riccardo dropped a light kiss on the top of her head. "It was an opportunity not to be missed. The fact you share my bed, under this roof, shows how serious we are. And, as my future wife you should be safe from the person responsible for your attacks."

"Unless someone in your family has cause to prevent me marrying you."

"They don't. Do you have any other worries?"

"It takes me forever to decide what flavor gelato I want. *Papà* and Dante will never accept we're engaged, especially after meeting only six days ago."

"Then we must convince them it was absolute love at first sight."

"I'm a terrible actress, Riccardo. Everyone always knows what I'm thinking."

He gave her an odd look then smiled. "I'm counting on that, Sofia."

"What is that supposed to mean?"

Riccardo winked at her. "I don't expect your brother until at least tomorrow night, so for now I'd prefer you stay here, out of trouble, and where I can keep you safe."

Or, is this an attempt to delay me finding the evidence? Sofia smiled up at him as innocently as she could. "Carolina and I want to go on a picnic. I don't think we can get into too much trouble, do you?" She lightly touched his sleeve.

"I'm not available today and neither is Giovanni. We need to finalize a couple of things for bid on the hotel in *Venezia*."

"Please," Sofia implored, stroking his arm. "I promise we'll be watchful."

Riccardo's eyes narrowed and Sofia hastily withdrew her hand. He was far too clever to be manipulated.

"All right, up to the lookout and straight back, no side-tracking, no searching Villa DeRosa, and take Nico with you. But remember, you are my fiancée, don't let him take liberties. I don't trust him where you're concerned." Before she realized his intention, he kissed her swiftly on the lips.

Sofia sent him a warning look. "I'm being good. It's you who's playing with fire."

"You never know who is watching." Chuckling, he turned and left the terrace.

"*Idiota stupido*," she muttered after him.

"I hope that was Riccardo you were calling a stupid idiot," asked Nico from behind her.

Sofia jumped. "Yes, it was. The fool is setting himself up for a fall."

"Oh, and how is he doing that?"

"He wants people to think this pretend engagement is real."

Nico rubbed his jaw. "What we witnessed this morning looked very real to me."

"Well it wasn't. You were all so busy yelling that no one took the time to see I had a chemise on, or Riccardo wore boxers. And nobody asked me."

He slid onto the seat opposite. "So, what was going on? I would be interested to hear your side of the story."

Sofia clenched her fists. "Nothing. Riccardo insists on sharing a room to keep me safe. I woke up that way, one second before everyone burst through the door. Riccardo wasn't even awake. We weren't making love," she added indignantly.

Nico smiled. "That sounds more like the Sofia I know. I didn't think you'd fall for someone as smooth as Riccardo, especially after only knowing him for such a short time."

Sofia's mouth fell open. "You're so full of yourself."

"Yes, so Carolina keeps telling me."

Sofia met his eyes. "Where are you off to, that you can't chaperone us?"

"I inherited my father's exporting business. I run offices in Bologna, Lucca, and Ancona. Today I have a staff meeting in Bologna, but I will be back tonight. It's much more interesting here at the moment. I will see you later, Sofia, take care."

"*Ciao,* Nico.

As soon as Sofia finished breakfast, she strolled into the kitchen where Caterina and Ariana had packed a basket with fruit, fresh rolls, prosciutto, cheese, and a bottle of homemade cider.

Carolina picked up the basket. "I thought we might go via the old monastery; it's the prettiest route."

"And the steepest, so be careful," Ariana warned.

"*Ciao.*" Carolina's heels clattered as she paced across the foyer and out the front door.

Sofia stopped to adjust the strap on her sandals and heard Caterina sigh deeply.

"I dread the next few days, Ariana. Riccardo is so determined and Sofia is such a sweet young woman. She is in over her head and it isn't going to end well."

Sofia froze then quietly tiptoed closer to the kitchen.

Ariana stood at the window looking out. "I fear to think what Giuseppe will do if he ever finds out the truth. He has had so much to deal with."

Truth? What truth? Sofia watched as Caterina went to Ariana and hugged her.

"So have you, Ariana. Maybe Sofia has been sent to us. She may be the one person who can bring peace to us all. Look at the impact she has had on Riccardo."

"I hope you're right, for all our sakes. Shall we have our coffee on the terrace?"

Frowning, Sofia turned and tiptoed to the front door. *What was that about?*

She stepped out into the sunshine and walked toward Carolina and the sports car she was leaning against.

"I've my own car today." Carolina pranced around the flashy red convertible. "Giovanni drove it here last night."

"Wow, what is it?"

Carolina climbed into the driver's seat, smiling delightedly. "It's a BMW. *Mamma* and *Papà* bought it for my birthday."

Sofia settled herself in the passenger seat and stretched out. "I like it very much. You are one spoilt girl."

Leaving the villa, they drove along the winding tree-lined road up into the mountains with Carolina pointing out everything of interest until they came to the Bondini's villa.

They spent an hour with Salvatore Bondini, whom Sofia found to be as lovely as Carolina had promised. He entertained them with funny stories about their grandfathers and fathers, although he couldn't help them with any information regarding the feud or the allegations. According to him, when the vineyard burnt down and Giuseppe left in disgrace, Lorenzo and Elena moved into Ravenna and sold off most of their land. Salvatore had organized the sale, interestingly enough to the Santini family. Was that a factor in all this?

Despondent and no closer to reaching her goal, Sofia thanked Salvatore for his time. Then she and Carolina continued on to the old monastery where they stopped for a short tour, then coffee and sweet pastries before continuing up the mountain. They eventually reached a scenic lookout where Sofia was delighted to find a three hundred and sixty degree view of mountains and valleys. She climbed out of the car and walked across to the safety rail where she stood speechless. The sky was an incredible iridescent blue with only an occasional wispy cloud floating across it, and the mountainside was covered in thousands of yellow sunflowers. Further out and down lay a network of rivers, farms, towns and mountains.

"This is fantastic, Caro. I feel like I'm on top of the world."

Laughing, Carolina threw a rug down on the thick grass. "You are on top of the world. Now come and help yourself to some of this delicious food and a glass of my grandmother's apple cider. You can also tell me what makes you think Nico is your brother."

Sofia walked over and threw herself down on the rug. "I have no proof yet, but he and Dante are so alike, and his mother and my father were once engaged."

"I admit he's like Dante, but Nico is only twenty-eight." She scrunched her eyes and tilted her head back. "He would have to be twenty nine to be your father's son."

"Does Nico look like Ariana's late husband?"

"I can't remember. The last time I met him I would have been ten and they didn't have a lot to do with us back then."

Sofia took a bite of her roll and chewed thoughtfully for a moment. "What we need is a photo of Nico's father."

"Fine, but we still have the age problem. Surely if Nico was born earlier, his birth certificate would show that?"

"You would think so."

They spent the next hour eating, laughing and lying on their backs staring up at the sky. By the time they were ready to head back down the mountain, Sofia had compiled a list. She would refuse to go back to Australia until she found her aunt's killer and cleared her father's name. She would fulfill the terms of her grandparents' gift, by spending the year in Villa DeRosa, thus bringing it back to its former glory, and finally do a little digging to find out more about Nico's heritage.

They left the mountaintop a little more optimistic than they'd started out and were enjoying their return trip down the mountain when Carolina suddenly gripped the steering wheel hard and yelled. "Sofia! Hold on!"

"Why, what's wrong? Why are you going so fast?"

"My brakes... I've got no...brakes. Shit...we're going too fast." Carolina pumped the brakes and battled to keep control of the car as they squealed around the downward bends.

Sofia tried pulling on the hand brake. It didn't make any difference. They continued squealing down the narrow mountain road, shadowed on one side by rock and on the other by a terrifying drop. All that lay between them and the sheer drop was a two-foot high rail. Sofia held her breath, her heart pounding as time and time again Carolina managed to somehow stop them plummeting over the edge or smashing into the rock wall.

"Shit," screamed Carolina.

Her heart in her mouth, Sofia, prayed.

Carolina pressed down on the horn as they came up fast behind four vehicles, which thankfully all moved closer to the rock wall. Rocketing past, Sofia glimpsed the occupants shaking angry fists out their windows.

Several long minutes later, they approached a picnic spot where Sofia realized they couldn't possibly attempt a crash stop. Family groups were scattered all over the grass. Ahead stood a narrow bridge with a small truck blocking their way. "Mother of God."

"Hold on," yelled Carolina. "I'm going to try something."

Terrified beyond words, Sofia turned to Carolina, unable to fathom what she intended.

Carolina swung the car as hard as she could toward the rock wall then almost immediately swung hard the other way. Sofia saw flashes of rock wall, then blue sky, then rock wall again before they mounted a grassy knob on the left side of the bridge and plunged down a rough bank, through small shrubby trees and into a shallow river.

The airbags exploded with a bang, hitting Sofia in the face and arm like she'd been punched. Fine powder covered her and an acrid smell filled the air.

They came to a dead stop, both girls coughing from the powder in their throats.

"We made it," whispered Carolina.

"Yes." Sofia undid her seat belt and threw her arms around Carolina.

Sobbing, Carolina hugged her back.

They were still crying and hugging each other when two men hauled the car doors open. Sofia didn't understand a word they were saying. She was numbly aware of voices as more people arrived, eager to help them out of the car and onto the bank.

Sofia could barely breathe. Had the brakes been sabotaged? And if so, who wanted her out of the way so badly they'd risk Carolina's life? Would they come after Riccardo too?

She couldn't let that happen.

Carolina did the explaining to their rescuers, who included the angry drivers they'd passed. The police arrived and organized for a tow truck and ambulance. After they'd been briefly examined. Carolina rang home, then they were bundled into the ambulance and taken to the local hospital for a more thorough examination.

Chapter Thirteen

Sofia winced as she limped after Carolina through the exit doors into the waiting area of the hospital's emergency lounge. A loud commotion drew her attention to the right where the Santinis clustered round a flustered looking reception clerk.

"*Mamma, Papà*," called Carolina. "*Noi stiamo bene.* We are fine."

The Santinis turned then Carolina's parents rushed to their daughter and hugged her.

Sofia limped around them, stopping as her gaze locked on Riccardo.

He strode across the room and wrapped his arms around her. "Sofia, what happened?"

Safe in his embrace, it took her a minute to respond. "We were coming down the mountain and the brakes failed." She shuddered. "The wheels were squealing. We almost hit the rock wall, and other cars."

Sofia knew she was blubbering and people were staring, but she couldn't stop. "We spun and spun. I thought we'd go over the edge."

"It's a miracle you didn't." Riccardo's arms tightened. "You are hurt, I saw you limping."

"My knee is bruised and my face is sore, but Carolina's beautiful car is a total wreck."

"The car can be replaced, *caro mia.* You cannot." He grimaced. "*Papà* and I spoke to the police and examined the car before it was towed away." His voice caught. "The brake lines had been slit by someone who intended to kill the two of you."

Silence reigned for several seconds then pandemonium broke loose. The Santinis shouted over each other until Riccardo put up a hand for quiet. When they calmed down, he continued. "Whoever did this must have followed the girls up the mountain, then while they were having their picnic, cut the lines, leaving only enough brake fluid to get them started down the mountain."

Carolina stepped away from her parents, her lips trembling. "Who is behind these attacks? Who tried to kill us?"

Her father put his arms around her. "We don't know, Caro, but we will find out. In the meantime you don't leave the villa, and if you do, it is only with one of us. Our vehicles are to be kept in the locked garages and everyone is to be vigilant at all times. Is that understood?"

Everyone nodded in agreement—everyone except Sofia, who shook her head. "This is my fault. If I hadn't tried to solve this mystery… If I hadn't tried to prove someone set my father up, none of this would be happening. I can't endanger your lives. I'm moving back to the hotel in Bologna."

"No," snapped Riccardo.

Sofia couldn't make head or tail of what was being said as everyone spoke at once. Some in English, some in Italian, but all seemed opposed to her decision. Enrico banged his walking stick on the floor. His gaze settled on Sofia and his family fell silent.

"My English is not good, Sofia, but I tell you anyway. I want to know who would hurt you and my granddaughter." He looked at Riccardo. "How you say in English, *Scoprire il colpevole e portarlo alla giustizia?*"

Riccardo translated. "Uncover the culprit and bring him to justice." He squeezed Sofia's hand. "The police informed us that the dead man has an unsavory reputation as a hired thug."

"But who hired him?" asked Sofia. "And why?"

"We don't know. A large amount of cash was found hidden in his house, but no evidence of who hired him."

Carolina shivered. "So…we are no closer to finding out who is behind these attacks." A statement, not a question.

No one answered her.

Frowning, Giovanni turned to Riccardo. "Do the police now believe the person who hired this thug could be the man who tried to suffocate Sofia, and cut Caro's brake lines, or do they think he is another hired thug?"

"They wouldn't comment," muttered Riccardo.

Angelo Santini let out a deep sigh. "There is something else you should know." He looked directly at Sofia. "I'm sorry, but when I realized the brake lines had been cut, I decided it is time your father knew what is going on. I rang your vineyard in Australia and discovered Guiseppe is in America on business. Your assistant refused to give me his number until I told her you'd been in an accident. She also gave me your brother's number.

Sofia clenched her fingers. She needed to stay calm, losing it was not going to help. "You've spoken to my father?"

"I tried, but Guiseppe refused to speak to me, so I rang your brother. I told Dante there had been attempts on your life and I feared for your safety. At first he thought I was lying as you are supposed to be on holiday in Australia." Angelo sighed. "I'm sorry, Sofia. Your brother is flying to *Italia* as soon as arrangements can be made."

"Dante is coming here." Sofia began to shake. *I've run out of time.*

Riccardo hugged her. "It will be all right. When your brother arrives, we will talk."

Sofia looked into his eyes. "You don't know Dante. I need to move back to Bologna, so no one else gets hurt because of me."

"Shush." Riccardo put his finger to her lips. "You are coming home with us and there will be no more talk of leaving." He lifted her into his arms and walked toward the exit doors.

Over his shoulder, Sofia observed his family's worried frowns.

Once they arrived back at the Villa Santini, a family conference was called, to which Carolina and Sofia were not invited. They were instead told to take it easy and rest while everyone else adjourned to the library.

The sound of the doorbell drew Sofia's attention and, a moment later, the housekeeper, Maria, could clearly be heard arguing with another woman in Italian.

Sofia limped to the door, surprised to see her grandparents' housekeeper, a plump woman with greying hair and pleasant features.

Signora Rinaldi appeared a little overwhelmed by the security guard and housekeeper, but when she saw Sofia, she pushed past them and rushed toward her. "Sofia, your grandparents and I didn't know what to think when we heard you were engaged, but—" she glanced at Carolina "—the announcement in the paper verified it. Then today when we were told about the accident, it was decided I should come and speak with you."

Sofia stepped forward. "*Ciao, Signora* Rinaldi. I was planning to visit my grandparents in the next few days to tell them myself."

Signora Rinaldi grasped Sofia's hand. "Is it true then, you are engaged to a Santini?"

"*Si.*" Sofia introduced *Signora* Rinaldi to Carolina then offered her a seat on the couch.

"Maria, please bring us come coffee and cake," requested Carolina.

Signora Rinaldi took a deep breath. "Your grandparents love you, Sofia, and they are worried about you. When they heard about the accident, they sent me."

Carolina cleared her throat. "How did you hear about the accident so quickly, *signora*?"

"Salvatore Bondini rang. He's been a source of comfort to your grandparents since Renzina died. Your *papà* rang this morning from America. He is very anxious. You must reconsider this engagement. There is bad blood between the two families and this will only make things worse." She twisted her skirt in her fingers. "A lot of people think Renzina's car accident was…suspicious, and when we heard your accident was on the same road, it brought it all back to your grandparents."

Sofia glanced at Carolina then back to *Signora* Rinaldi. "On the same road? Did you send me the letters, *signora*?"

Signora Rinaldi gave her a blank look. "Letters, what letters?"

"I recently received a letter that was written by Renzina before she died, but it was never posted. Do you know anything about that?"

"No, but the day before Renzina's accident we found her sitting staring out the window and when your grandmother asked her what is wrong, Renzina said she found out something terrible and was trying to decide what to do about it.'"

Signora Rinaldi sighed. "Your grandmother didn't know what Renzina was talking about and your aunt refused to say more. She gave your grandmother a heavy envelope and a photo album and told her to give them to Giuseppe if he ever came home."

Sofia tried to stem her excitement. "Does my grandmother still have them, *signora*?"

"*Sì*, she gave them to me to pass on to you, but I was in such a hurry I left the envelope at home." She opened a carry bag and withdrew an album.

Sofia accepted it and started turning the pages as Maria arrived with refreshments. The album was crammed with pictures of Renzina and Giuseppe as children, teenagers, and young adults. They looked so happy surrounded by friends and family that Sofia's heart clenched.

Signora Rinaldi refused to speak until Maria had left the room. "News of your accident is spreading fast, as are the rumors. There are people saying you are being targeted. Others say Giuseppe DeRosa will finish what he started if the—" She looked at Carolina apologetically. "*Mi scusi, signorina.*"

Carolina shook her head. "Go on, *signora*, please."

"There are people who think Giuseppe will come to finish what he started...if anything happens to Sofia. There are others saying he never did what he was accused of, and it was the Santinis behind the fires and robbery, so that they could get their hands on the DeRosa's fertile land. The only thing they agree on is—" she met Sofia's gaze "—you are in danger."

"Wow," gasped Sofia and Carolina together.

Signora Rinaldi stood. "I must leave now. Please come and collect the envelope tomorrow. I have told no one about it, but you."

Signora Rinaldi refused to have anything to eat or drink. After she left, Sofia continued to look through the album and when she turned the last page she discovered an envelope taped to the back cover. "What's this?"

Carolina leaned over. "Open it."

Peeling the tape off, Sofia opened the envelope then pulled out a single sheet of paper. "It's a poem."

"Well read it," cried Carolina impatiently.

"Okay, Okay."

"*I once had a garden, where flowers and a wishing well held center stage.*

As I grew older my garden became my secret place where I could sit and dream.

Only those closest know the key will lead them to my heart and the treasure within.'"

Sofia looked at Carolina. "Is there a well in the garden of Villa DeRosa?"

"Not that I noticed, but we can check. What are you thinking?"

"It could be a clue."

"Maybe. She talks about her garden, flowers, a well, her secret place, and a treasure. Do you think she's referring to the hidden evidence?"

"Yes," cried Sofia. "The treasure must be the hidden evidence."

"Okay, but what does she mean by '*Only those closest know the key will lead them to my heart and the treasure within'?*"

Carolina shrugged. "I have no idea. Have you noticed the phone hasn't stopped ringing? I think *Signora* Rinaldi is right. News of our crash is spreading quickly."

Over the next couple of hours they had a steady stream of relatives, neighbors, and friends arriving to personally check on Carolina and Sofia, which meant Caterina, Ariana, and Louisa had to leave the family meeting to deal with the callers. Sofia quietly slipped out into the gardens for some peace and quiet. She was wondering if things could get any worse when she came across Angelo Santini pruning roses.

"*Ciao,* Angelo, I thought you were inside talking security."

He gave a huff in reply and kept pruning.

Sofia bit her lip. *What have you got to lose?* "Angelo, may I ask you some questions about my father?"

"What do you wish to know?"

"I was wondering when you first became friends with my father?"

"We were five years old."

"So you were best friends from five to..."

"Twenty-five."

"Hmm, you spent a lot of time together I take it?"

"Every spare minute, until I married Caterina and even then we still spent a lot of time together."

Sofia took a deep breath. "Would you say you knew my father better than anyone, Angelo?"

"*Sì*."

"So you and my father gambled and regularly visited prostitutes?"

Angelo swung around, threw down the clippers, and started ripping his gloves off. "I've never gambled or been with a prostitute in my life."

Sofia stepped back at the fierceness in his tone. *Keep going. Angry people say things without thinking and he is very angry.* "But you just said the two of you spent every spare minute together. If my father was gambling and seeing prostitutes, as he was accused of, then why didn't you know?"

"He never did those things when we were together and I would never have believed it, had I not seen him with the prostitutes myself." He bent and picked up the clippers.

Sofia chewed on her lip again. She couldn't let him escape, as she might not get another chance to interrogate him. "How did you find out he was seeing prostitutes?"

Angelo rubbed his chin, and Sofia was afraid he wouldn't answer her, but then he indicated a seat, sat beside her, and stared at the ground for a minute.

"I heard rumors of the gambling and prostitutes from other friends. Sometimes I was with Giuseppe when these things were said. Your father laughed them off at first. Later he got angry as the rumors persisted, and he was forced to deny them.

"I was becoming concerned as Giuseppe was engaged to my sister, and I'd noticed women calling out greetings to him. He said he didn't know them. One day I received a call from a woman who claimed she'd loaned Giuseppe money to pay off a gambling debt, and he also owed her money for...services rendered. I said I didn't believe her and she told me I should go to a particular hotel that afternoon as Guiseppe was meeting two prostitutes there."

Remain calm, Sofia. Papà wouldn't do that. She clenched her fists. "Did you go?"

"Yes. I asked at the reception desk if they had a Giuseppe DeRosa registered. They did and they directed me to a room on the second floor."

"Wait," called Sofia. "If the woman was after money my father owed her, why didn't she go to the hotel and get it herself, or ring him? Why ring you?"

"I have no idea. When I reached the room, the door was unlocked, so I walked in and found Giuseppe with—"

"With what?"

"He was on a bed with two almost naked women on top of him."

She stiffened. *Keep it together, Sofia, you need answers.* She took a deep breath, her fingernails biting into her palms. "What did he say when he saw you?"

"He yelled it wasn't what I thought and he'd been set up or something like that."

"What happened next?"

"We got into a fight and nearly knocked each other senseless. The police arrived and hauled us into custody. Salvatore Bondini organized for us to be released without charges."

Sofia frowned. "What about the two women? What did they say?"

"They disappeared as soon as we started fighting."

"Is there any possibility he was set up?"

Looking down, Angelo fidgeted with the clippers. "I don't see how. I thought about nothing else for months. The fact many women acknowledged him by name, the rumors, and what I saw with my own eyes. I am sorry, Sofia. What can I say?"

You can tell me the truth. "What about Ariana? Could he have gone there to meet her and those women came into the wrong room?"

His head snapped up. "My sister would never meet Giuseppe in a hotel like that."

"Do you remember the name of the hotel and where it was, Angelo?"

He nodded sadly. "It was in Bologna and was called La Luna Verde, the green moon. I have no idea if it's still there." He stood and walked away, leaving Sofia to wander back to the house, deep in thought.

Dinner that night included the Santinis plus Salvatore and Michele Bondini who had come to discuss ways to suppress the mounting gossip now that Dante DeRosa was on his way. Sofia wasn't surprised that the main topics during dinner were the accident, the feud, and *Signora* Rinaldi's visit.

After dinner they retired to the drawing room and Salvatore Bondini came to sit beside Sofia. "I have offered my services as mediator between your brother and the Santinis."

"That's very kind of you?"

"Not at all. Your father phoned me today and asked that I keep an eye on you. He said due to extreme bad weather, planes in New York are grounded. It will be a couple of days yet before Dante arrives.

Great. Sofia looked around to make sure no one was within hearing. Renzina's letter said Salvatore Bondini could be trusted and she knew *Papà* liked him. "*Signore*, have you heard that Renzina found out who set up my father?"

"It has been mentioned, *si*."

"I came to Italy because I recently received a letter written by my aunt thirty years ago. She had evidence my father was set up and wanted him to come home and clear his name. I believe that evidence led to my aunt's death."

"If that is so then you must give this evidence to the police immediately."

"It's in the care of my grandparents' housekeeper. I will pick it up tomorrow."

Salvatore stared out the terrace doors into the darkened gardens. "If you are correct, Sofia, and these attacks make it appear that way, then I think you should give this evidence to the police and leave *Italia* as soon as possible."

Sofia shook her head. "No, *signore*. My brother will be here in a couple of days and there are several things I need to attend to."

"Then please don't go anywhere alone, and promise me you won't investigate this matter further until your brother arrives."

Sofia promised, but crossed her fingers behind her back then stood and strolled over to Carolina who was sitting in the corner, talking to Nico. They jerked guiltily when she stopped in front of them.

"What are you two up to?"

"Nothing. We aren't up to anything." Carolina blushed.

"Oh yes you are." Sofia pointed her finger at them.

"Okay." Nico grabbed Sofia's hand and pulled her down between them. "Carolina has been telling me about your theory and she wants me to show you a photo of my father."

Sofia sighed. "I wanted to be sure before we said anything, but I rather think you've been having similar thoughts. It's a pity you and Dante didn't meet properly five years ago, because then you would have seen the likeness for yourself."

Sofia glanced around the room; everyone was busy talking. She turned back to Nico and Carolina. "Don't say anything, just listen, okay?"

They both nodded.

"This is what I know. Ariana ran away to Lucca when she discovered my father had left his home and taken up with another woman. Why Lucca? And, if she was pregnant, how did she support herself? Where did she live? I think we need to research if there were any homes in Lucca for unmarried women back then, and I think we should go to Lucca tomorrow after we call to see *Signora* Rinaldi and pick up the envelope."

"What?" Carolina stared at her incredulously.

"Do you know how far Lucca is from here, Sofia?" asked Nico. He held up three fingers. "Three hours."

Sofia gently knocked his hand aside. "In Australia I travel those distances often, so don't be a wimp. If you're my brother, I want to prove it before Dante arrives."

Nico glanced across at his mother who was shooting concerned looks their way. "Once everyone leaves, I will show you a photo of my father. Then we will check on the Internet for maternity homes in Lucca that existed thirty years ago. Will that make you happy?"

Sofia smiled and hugged him. "*Sì, grazie*, Nico."

"You're welcome, but I don't want my mother hurt. If you're right, I will speak to her."

Sofia nodded. "Of course, and I will speak to my father. Now I'm going to say goodbye to *Signor* Bondini as I think he's leaving."

She wandered over to Salvatore Bondini who was waiting for his son to finish speaking to Angelo. "It's nice that Michele has followed in your footsteps and become a lawyer. You must be happy to be able to pass the business on to him?"

Salvatore nodded. "Indeed, Michele has taken much of the load. However, we are not close. I regret to say work took much of my time when he was growing up."

Sofia glanced across the room to where Michele still spoke to Angelo. She turned back to Salvatore and frowned. "Before everything went wrong, you were good friends with my grandfather and Enrico Santini weren't you?"

"*Sì*, Lorenzo, Enrico and I had been friends for over forty years before the trouble, and Giuseppe and Angelo had been friends from babies. My son Michele is the same age as Giuseppe and Angelo. In fact they went to school together." He straightened. "Michele is ready to leave. *Buonanotte*, Sofia, take care."

"*Buonanotte, Signor* Bondini." She looked around the room and spied Riccardo and Nico deep in conversation. Riccardo glanced at her, smiled, and then stepped through the French doors.

Sofia strolled over to the Santini women relaxing on the lounges. "I'm off to bed," she said, raising an eyebrow at Carolina. "Didn't you want to talk about restoring Villa DeRosa?"

Carolina's lips curved. "*Sì*. I will be up shortly."

"*Buonanotte*, ladies." Sofia waved and headed toward the door.

"*Buonanotte*, Sofia," they all called after her.

Five minutes later Nico and Carolina joined Sofia in Riccardo's bedroom. "These are the only photos we could find," said Nico. "I have more at our home in Lucca."

Sofia accepted the photos. "I didn't know you had a home in Lucca?"

Nico shrugged. "It's my father's ancestral home. After he died, my mother patched things up with her family and we spent the holidays here. Now she spends her time between here and Lucca."

Sofia studied the photos. "Your father is quite old in these photos, Nico?"

He smiled. "Yes, and bald."

"This doesn't help," she grumbled. "I need to see a photo of him as a young man."

"I have more photos in Lucca; meanwhile you can check the Internet for unmarried mothers' homes. Riccardo and I need to go to Bologna, so don't wait up for us."

Carolina was already opening her laptop. "*Sì, buonanotte*, Nico."

Sofia smiled at Nico as he left the bedroom, then she joined Carolina on the bed. They trawled through ten websites before they found one referring to a maternity home for unmarried women that existed in Lucca twenty-nine years ago.

"It says here it's a retirement home for nuns now." Carolina showed the information to Sofia. "I wonder if they know where the records would have been sent."

"It's worth asking, and what have we got to lose. I'll talk to—" She was interrupted by a knock at the door. "*Avanti,*" called Carolina closing her laptop quickly.

Caterina poked her head around the door. "Sofia, I just had a call from your grandmother. *Signora* Rinaldi had a fall when she got home today and broke her arm. They are keeping her in the hospital for a couple of days. She asked if you could visit her the day after tomorrow at your grandparents' home in Ravenna?"

Sofia's stomach clenched. "Was it an accident?"

"*Sì.* She slipped on her back step when she went to feed the cats."

After Caterina shut the door, Sofia let out a sigh of relief. "For a minute there I thought someone might have hurt *Signora* Rinaldi. Can we leave early tomorrow for Lucca?"

"*Sì,*" agreed Carolina. Sleep well."

"Sofia grinned. "I'll see you in the morning. *Buonanotte.*"

Chapter Fourteen

Sofia settled herself in the middle of the king size bed feeling oddly disturbed. Why did Riccardo and Nico go to Bologna tonight? Surely they weren't avoiding Dante. She frowned at the ceiling. Riccardo wasn't a scaredy-cat. He'd be back.

She tossed and turned for what seemed like hours, wondering where he was, and what he was up to. It wasn't like they were really engaged. Maybe he'd decided to spend the night somewhere else, with someone else. So be it, she didn't care.

But she did care. She liked being held by him and the feel of his warm body next to her. She liked the sound of his deep, wicked laugh, and his teasing smile. Sofia threw herself back on the pillows. "Where is he?"

She was still brooding half an hour later when the bedroom door quietly opened and Riccardo shambled in. Raising the sheet to cover most of her face, she peeped through her eyelashes, watching as he gingerly struggled out of his jacket. He groaned then cautiously sat on the bed to remove his shoes.

Sitting up, she glared at his back. "Are you drunk?"

"Shush, *mi hai spaventato*," he whispered.

"I don't care if I startled you, and I don't care if you're drunk, or where you've been. If you want to go drinking and...cavorting around Bologna, I couldn't care less, but you're the one who said we have to make everyone believe our engagement is real. How do you think it feels not to know where your fiancé is, and then for you to turn up like this?"

Riccardo let out another groan and fell backwards onto the bed. "I am not drunk and I have not been cavorting," he muttered then winced as he turned to face her. "Salvatore Bondini pulled some strings and arranged for me to see the police report from your aunt's car accident. Nico wanted to come with me. We didn't say anything in case it got back to whoever is targeting you. Now if you don't mind, I'm going to have a long hot shower."

Sofia watched as he awkwardly got to his feet and undid his shirt, shrugging out of it stiffly. "What's wrong with you, Riccardo? Are you hurt?"

"I'm fine, Sofia, go back to sleep." He undid his belt and pulled it through the loops.

Sofia threw back the covers, slid out of bed, and raced around to stand in front of him.

"Something is wrong with you." She flicked on the lamp. When she turned back to face him she gasped, shocked to see his bottom lip swollen and a bruise on his cheek.

"What happened? Who did this to you?" she whispered, gently touching his face.

Covering her hand with his, Riccardo smiled. "It's nothing, Sofia, go back to bed."

"Did my brother do this to you? Is Dante here?"

"It wasn't Dante. We'd left the police station and were approaching my car when two men in balaclavas pulled guns on us. They wanted the police report I'd copied."

Dumbfounded, Sofia stared at him as he undid the clasp on his trousers. "They had guns," she swallowed her rising panic. "They were waiting for you and Nico. Oh, Riccardo what are we going to do? They could have killed you." Sofia threw her arms around him.

Riccardo engulfed her in his arms, drawing her against his big warm chest. "Except for a few bruises and ache or two, Nico and I are fine. After the thugs ran off, we went straight back into the police station, reported the attack and recopied the statement. I want to contact the witnesses as there seems to be some confusion to what they saw."

Sofia sniffled against his chest. "I didn't mean what I said before... I do care about you, and I was worried when you didn't come home."

Riccardo kept one arm around her and with his other hand found her chin and raised it until she was looking at him through tear-filled eyes. "I care about you too, Sofia." He gently wiped away her tears with his thumb.

They were standing so close Sofia could feel his heart pounding against her shoulder. She looked up into his face to find his eyes had darkened. He had that predatory look again as if he wanted to devour her bit by bit. She pressed a little closer to the hard ridge of his erection pushing against her tummy.

She shifted restlessly as heat pooled between her thighs. Her skin prickled like a severe case of hives. They were in dangerous territory. Drawing back, she let go of his waist. "Go have a shower. It will make you feel better."

Riccardo chuckled. "I'm feeling much better already. In fact, I'm feeling so good I think I might forgo that shower and let you take care of me."

"I beg your pardon?"

He smiled. "My face hurts. You could start by kissing me there."

Sofia put her hands on his chest. She might want to kiss him, but that would be a big mistake for so many reasons. He was a playboy. What if he wanted more than a kiss? Did she have the willpower to stop him?

She pushed firmly. "I'm not kissing any part of you, Riccardo. You're the last man in the world I should be kissing."

He turned her and her knees backed up against the side of the bed. Slowly, he lowered his head until his lips lightly touched hers. Her breath hitched as he feathered light kisses across her cheek, all the way to her ear lobe and back. The thin chemise she was wearing could not hide her reaction as her breasts rubbed against his chest. He leaned into her until she lost her balance and toppled onto the bed, a small shriek escaping when he landed on top of her.

Sofia shuddered as he nibbled her earlobe then feathered kisses down her neck, and across her shoulder. Tingles spread over her skin, and a gnawing need clawed low in her belly.

"I don't think this is a good...a good idea," she whispered breathlessly.

He groaned. "You're right, *cara mia*, but you are such a temptation."

Wiggling, Sofia brought her hands up between them in an attempt to push him away only to have him clasp her wrists and pull them to either side of her hips. He lowered his lips to her neck again and kissed his way down to her collarbone and up the other side of her neck. She couldn't help the moan that escaped or the way her body responded to being pinned beneath his hard body or his erection pressed into her belly.

Quivering with anticipation, she turned her face to meet his lips. He released her wrists and rolled, pulling her with him until they were lying, facing each other.

His lips curved. "You look disappointed, *cara mia*?"

"Why have you stopped? I thought you were enjoying kissing me."

Hugging her to him, Riccardo groaned. "I was enjoying it too much and if I don't stop now, I won't be able to stop."

Reaching up, Sofia brushed a lock of hair off his forehead then ran her finger down his nose and across his cheek.

He caught her fingers and drew them to his lips to kiss her palm.

"Sofia, our kissing will ultimately end in love-making. Is that what you want?"

She shook her head, not taking her eyes off him. "No, but couldn't you just hold me and kiss me? We don't have to actually make love."

"If only it was that simple, *bella*." Riccardo buried his face in her hair.

"It is." She wrapped her arms around his shoulders and pressed closer.

The contact made Riccardo's already aroused state more uncomfortable. If his body weren't so sore, he would have enjoyed a little wrestling match, especially since his opponent's negligée was stretched tightly across her enticing breasts, leaving him longing to rip it from her body.

He fought once more as his body tried to overrule his head, driving him to seek out the pleasure he knew she would give him. In a last ditch effort he lightly ran his fingers down her spine and around her rib cage, letting them pass evocatively across one breast, hoping it might jolt some sense back into her, but instead of deterring her it seemed to delight her. She pressed her breast into his hand, the nipple hardening under his thumb.

She moaned and wrapped one of her legs around his thigh.

Riccardo tried to rein in his carnal desires, but he was only human and she was a temptress made for seduction. Her silky hair slid softly over his arm and the thin bit of satin slipped to reveal her cleavage.

Just a taste.

He rolled her onto her back, swiftly drawing the tiny straps off her shoulders and down her arms, exposing her beautiful breasts. He closed a hand possessively over one, claiming her other nipple greedily with his mouth, ignoring the aches in his body.

Riccardo was losing his ability to avoid emotional involvement. From their first meeting at the airport he'd wanted Sofia naked in his arms, his to do what he pleased with. Now here she was, her ripe luscious breasts fully revealed. She was his for the taking and he couldn't remember ever wanting a woman so badly.

She shuddered, bringing a smile to his lips. He increased the pressure of his lips and fingers, holding his demons in check. Her gasps and jolts to his touch screamed an innocence that had him groaning. She was new to this and he needed to move slowly.

She pulled her arms free of her chemise straps and ran her fingers through his hair, gamely returning his kisses. Her soft curves molded to him, scattering his wits as only she could. He should have gone with the shower. Again, he squashed his urgent need. This was about satisfying her curiosity. As long as he kept her hands above his waist he might succeed. Riccardo rubbed his thumb across one pert nipple as he laved the other.

She moaned, her fingers digging into his scalp.

He ran his hand down her silken clad waist to her smooth thigh. She shifted restlessly against him, scuttling his good intentions. He raised his body on one elbow then captured her lips, nipping and teasing as he deepened the kiss, gradually coaxing her lips apart until his tongue entered her mouth and gently explored it. With his hand, he traced up and down her thigh, pushing her negligée higher each time.

A familiar yearning stirred low in his gut, leaving him frustrated with her inexperience, yet her obvious desire to be closer had her wantonly pressing her hips to him, not caring where it led. He had to get some control back or she'd kill him.

"You like this, *cara mia*? You like me kissing you?"

"Yes." Her voice sounded husky. "I like it very much."

Riccardo deepened the kiss as his fingers trailed lower across her belly, panties and down her inner thigh. She trembled under his fingertips, her legs parting to give him access. He was still in control. Just. He slid his finger between the lace and her skin. She shuddered, digging her fingernails into his shoulder then gasped as he slid a finger inside her. *Santa Maria.* She was wet, tightly wound and on fire.

So was he. Riccardo shifted lower then took her nipple in his mouth, suckling deeply then licking and rolling the taut bud with his tongue.

All coherent thought left him as she moaned then thrust her pelvis against his probing finger, wanting, needing more. "Ri...car...do..."

He ached for succor. "Do you want me to stop," he mumbled against her breast.

"No, no don't stop," she whispered. "Not yet."

Riccardo felt his own groan rumble through him. So be it. He withdrew his finger, and placed his hands on her hips, looping his fingers around the bunched negligée and the band of her panties. He kissed and licked his way down to her belly again, then with one quick movement, whisked her clothing down her legs and rose from the bed, tossing them over his shoulder.

Her passion-hazed eyes widen but not in fear.

A bolt of lust lanced through him. In a matter of seconds he had his trousers and jocks off and stood naked, his gaze riveted on the siren in his bed.

She watched wide-eyed as he slowly climbed on the bed, her eyes darting between his face, chest, and erection. He was well endowed, which probably accounted for her fast breathing and sudden tension. Riccardo took his time, letting her grow used to his nakedness. He was proud of his physique, aware women were captivated by his looks and ability to satisfy them. They'd told him often enough.

But what seemed to have Sofia spellbound in both fascination and panic was his unmistakable declaration of manhood standing proud and erect. She shivered and swallowed nervously as he lowered himself beside her and reclaimed her lips.

He battled to control his lust as he ran his hand over Sofia's full breasts and down her exquisite body. It would be a long time, if ever, that he'd forget the image of her naked on his bed. His gaze drifted from her long tousled hair to the tip of her dainty toes. Her stunning green eyes passion-filled yet apprehensive, her swollen breasts rising and falling in unison with her fast breathing. He wanted to possess her body, mind and soul, but what he wanted most, he recognized with a jolt, was for her to be his and his alone, and not just short term. He wanted her forever.

Panting, she rocked against his fingers as he stroked and circled the sensitive nub between her thighs. She gasped as he pushed two fingers inside her and rubbed them back and forth, inciting her hips to move in motion with them. He could feel her body tightening, the craving building deep within her, yearning for more. Her legs fell wantonly wider and she moaned. He continued stroking, caressing, enticing her further and further toward the pinnacle of orgasmic release.

He traced his lips over her swollen breasts.

Her breath hitched. "Riccardo..." Her voice sounded strangled. "Riccardo, please..."

"I know what you want, Sofia." He lightly nipped as he thrust his fingers in and out.

Her body tensed, an almighty shudder ran through her, then she went rigid and shattered violently, her body clamping tightly around his fingers. He only just managed to muffle her scream.

It was so intense, so consuming, so overwhelming. Riccardo's mind blanked. She lay limp in his arms as he gently ran his hand up and down her thigh, watching her closely.

"How do you feel?" he whispered.

She drew a deep breath and beamed at him. "Fantastic... Amazing."

"Good, but I think it would be wise to stop now before we do something you might regret in the morning."

She looked thoroughly sated, cuddled against his chest, her fingers splaying as she moved her hand over his tense abdomen. "I'd like to reciprocate."

He groaned and grasped her hand as her fingers brushed fleetingly against his erection. "Not tonight, *tesoro*. It's been a long day and I want to take this slowly." He kept her hand in his and moved it to his chest.

"But I want to thank you."

"Not tonight, *cara mia*."

She grumbled then relaxed against him.

Riccardo exhaled his relief. If she'd persisted in touching him, he'd have caved to his carnal desire to possess her. It would have been a big mistake. He wanted more, much more.

He watched her fall asleep in his arms and continued watching her until his arm went numb. He felt torn between his duty to protect his family against her accusations and his longing to possess her. Eventually he eased her out of his arms and left the bed to have a long cool shower, then went down to the study.

He planned to work into the early hours of the morning, rather than tempt fate by sleeping with her. Then he'd catch a bit of sleep on the study couch before ringing the phone number on the accident report. He could only hope the couple who witnessed Renzina DeRosa's accident still resided at the same address.

CHAPTER FIFTEEN

Sofia and Carolina crept down the stairs as quietly as they could, intending to make their escape before anyone was up. They tiptoed past the drawing room.

"Now where would you two be off to at this hour of the morning?" asked Nico, who sat at the dining room table, a newspaper open in front of him.

Sofia nearly jumped out of her skin. "Nowhere."

Nico shook his head. "You didn't think I'd let you go to Lucca on your own, did you?" He slowly replaced his cup on its saucer.

Sofia narrowed her eyes. "You knew we were planning to go, that's why you're up so early, isn't it? Where is the trust?" Nico's eyebrows shot up and Sofia was struck again by the likeness between him and Dante. She also noticed Nico sported a swollen lip.

He folded his paper. "I take it you two discovered a maternity home and plan to see if my mother was registered there. It might help if I came with you, as they are more likely to give me the information. If we find nothing then we come straight back and you two can come up with an explanation for going to Lucca, okay?"

Carolina clapped her hands silently. "Thank you, Nico. This works out brilliantly. You can take Sofia to Lucca and I will go into work and sort out my new delivery." She hugged Sofia. "Now off you go before anyone else wakes up, and don't worry, I'll tell them Nico wants to show you his home. That will placate even Riccardo."

Three hours later, Nico and Sofia arrived at the nun's retirement home. They were shown into a large office looking over gardens and joined by a Sister Augusta.

"Please, sit down," she spoke in English for Sofia's benefit. "I believe you are enquiring about a woman who may have stayed here twenty-nine years ago."

"Yes, Sister," Sofia replied, sitting on the edge of her chair. "My father and Nico's mother were engaged and due to problems between their families, the engagement was broken. We know Nico's mother ran away to Lucca and we would like to know if she came here and gave birth to him."

Sister Augusta placed her elbows on the desk and linked her fingers under her chin as she surveyed each of them carefully.

"Do you have documentation proving your identity?"

Sofia and Nico handed over their passports, which Sister Augusta ignored, instead studying Nico carefully. "I was told you think your year of birth may have been recorded wrongly. Why?"

Nico shifted in his chair. "There is a chance my birth may not have been registered until the year after. It is the only explanation that works, if what we suspect is true."

"I see," replied Sister Augusta. "If your mother gave birth to you here, then your birth would have been recorded correctly by the nuns, so that will not help you. Also there are privacy laws. However, I am prepared to check our records to see if she was one of our girls during the time you have requested. I will need any names she may have used and a few days, as our records are archived in the basement."

Sofia looked at Nico. "Ariana Santini, obviously, but also write down DeRosa and Lombardi."

Sister Augusta suddenly stiffened. "Did you say, Lombardi?"

"Yes," they chorused then Nico explained, "My mother married Luciano Lombardi and we have a *villa* here in Lucca, although my father has been deceased for many years."

Sister Augusta took a deep breath. "You are not the first to enquire about a woman with those names, which is why I can give you the details. A young lady came to us by the name of Ariana Barassi, and it would have been around that time. She was four months pregnant when she arrived. She later married Luciano Lombardi."

Sofia turned to Nico excitedly. "Barassi is my grandmother's maiden name."

Sister Augusta smiled. "It was Renzina Barassi who brought

Ariana here and paid a generous amount of money toward her upkeep. Renzina came regularly to visit until she was killed in a car accident."

Nico picked up Sofia's hand. "You were right. Your aunt and my mother must have pretended to be sisters to keep her pregnancy a secret. It appears we are brother and sister, but...what about the birth certificate?" He turned back to Sister Augusta.

She pursed her lips. "*Signore*, I wasn't much older than Ariana when she arrived and from the beginning she insisted she would be keeping the baby. Ariana and I spent a lot of time together in the garden after Renzina's death. *Signor* Lombardi, a lovely older gentleman who was on the board of our maternity home and a generous benefactor, often joined us. He befriended Ariana and would sit with her in the garden most days. He eventually convinced her to marry him and let him give her child a good home."

Sister Augusta took another sip of water. "*Signor* Lombardi took Ariana away and they were married quietly before the baby was born. I believe she delivered her son in the Lombardi family home. I know this because Ariana used to visit me regularly with her baby until he started school. After *Signor* Lombardi died, Ariana remained a generous benefactor to our home until it closed."

There was stunned silence as Sofia and Nico stared at her.

Nico finally stood and paced to the window. "Luciano Lombardi was a kind man and I never suspected he wasn't my father until I overheard my grandparents questioning my mother. They seemed to think I resembled Guiseppe DeRosa. Mamma denied it and showed them my birth certificate. Then five years ago I met Sofia, through my cousin, Carolina, and I felt a connection. At first I thought it desire." He smiled at Sofia. "You are beautiful."

Turning back to Sister Augusta, he frowned. "When I discovered Sofia was Giuseppe's daughter, I opted for caution and mentioned our meeting to my mother. Her shocked, almost hysterical reaction was enlightening. She begged me not to become romantically involved with Sofia and told me about the feud between our two families."

Sister Augusta nodded. "Confidentiality laws prohibited me from giving anyone this information, however, after Luciano Lombardi died, Ariana asked me to tell you the truth, if you ever asked. I believe it was also Luciano's wish."

Sofia stood and joined Nico by the window, where she linked arms with him and leant her head against his shoulder. "That's why you never kissed me, isn't it? You suspected."

Nico put his arm around her and nodded. "*Si.*"

"My grandparents have bequeathed me and my two brothers equal shares from the sale of their assets. I thought it a mistake, but maybe they knew. What do you want to do?"

Nico turned to her. "I suggest we go to my home here in Lucca and have some lunch. I will introduce you to Roberta, our housekeeper, then we can decide our next move."

"Let's stay the night," suggested Sofia. "It will give us time to come to terms with this before we have to face everyone."

They thanked Sister Augusta and left the home, both a little subdued. By the time they reached Nico's *villa* the shock had worn off and Sofia brimmed with excitement.

The Lombardi *villa* turned out to be an impressive home surrounded by high walls and lush gardens. Sofia turned to Nico. "Your home is lovely. How can you or your mother bear to leave it?"

"It's impressive, isn't it? We moved to Villa Santini initially because my mother was lonely and missed her family. I was only a young teenager and she thought it important to have my cousins around me."

He pulled up in front of the steps and they alighted to find the front door had been opened and a plump, smiling woman was descending on them.

"*Ciao,* Nico, *come stai?*"

Nico jogged up the steps and hugged the woman. "*Ciao,* Roberta, bene, e` tu?"

"*Così, così,*" she replied glancing curiously at Sofia.

Nico released her and indicated for Sofia to join him.

"This is my…sister, Sofia. She is Australian and doesn't speak Italian, so you must speak in English." He laughed at the perplexed expression on Roberta's face. "It's a long story and if you will give us some lunch, we will explain."

Roberta nodded. "I knew this might happen one day. Come, Sofia and welcome to *la villa di tranquillità.* It means the villa of tranquility. You will understand when you see the gardens."

During lunch, Sofia and Nico told Roberta what they'd discovered, most of which she knew as she had been with the Lombardi family since before Ariana had come to live there. Roberta was very loyal to Ariana and worried how she would react. Nico reassured her all would be well. After lunch they rang Carolina with their news, then Nico gave Sofia a tour of extensive gardens, their peace and harmony due to the fountains and high surrounding walls.

After a sightseeing tour of Lucca, Nico took Sofia to dinner at a local restaurant where they spent an enjoyable few hours describing their upbringings and discovering their common likes and dislikes. By the time they got back to the *villa* it was late so Nico showed Sofia to a pretty guestroom where Roberta had laid out a nightgown and toiletries.

Sofia took a leisurely shower, climbed into bed, and drifted off almost as soon as her head hit the soft pillow, her thoughts of Riccardo and the sensual things he'd done to her.

Gravel flew as Riccardo accelerated through the gates of the Lombardi Villa. He brought his sports car to an abrupt stop under the portico, threw his door open, then leapt out and raced up the steps to hammer on the door.

"Riccardo, wait," called Ariana, closing the passenger door. "You're jumping to conclusions."

"I am not jumping to conclusions." He hammered on the door again. "You forget Nico, Giovanni, and I have a long history. I know exactly how he operates."

"Stand aside, Riccardo. I have a key." Ariana pulled out her keys as the door opened.

"A plump woman wrapped in a thick dressing gown glanced at Riccardo then Ariana. "*Signora*, what is all the noise?"

Riccardo shouldered past the woman, striding into the foyer. "Where are they?" he demanded heading for the stairs.

"Who?" asked the woman, her eyes wide as she glanced between him and Ariana.

Ariana patted the woman's arm. "*Ciao*, Roberta. Is my son and a young lady here?"

"*Si*, they arrived earlier today. Nico has taken Sofia to her room."

"I bet he has," snapped Riccardo, taking the stairs two at a time.

Riccardo reached the landing as a door opened. Nico stepped out wearing only his boxers. "What's going on?" he asked.

Riccardo hurled himself at his cousin, rage exploding throughout his body. He pinned Nico against the wall and raised his fist.

"No, Riccardo, don't," pleaded Ariana, grabbing his forearm. "Please, let Nico explain. It might not be as you think."

The woman called Roberta also latched on to Riccardo, anchoring his other arm. Riccardo let out an aggressive growl. "If it wasn't for your mother, I'd smash your face."

Nico looked from one to the other. "Would someone explain what's going on?"

Ariana yanked on Riccardo's arm then forced her way between them. "Nico, we thought Sofia was with Carolina today, but then Carolina arrived home and declared the two of you had come to Lucca and were staying the night. We got here as fast as we could. Where is Sofia?"

Nico's eyes narrowed. "You know I wouldn't let anything happen to Sofia. She's perfectly safe in bed. Why are you really here?"

Riccardo snarled. "If you've laid one finger on her, I'll break your neck."

Ariana gasped. "Nico, please tell us you haven't... That you and Sofia haven't..."

Nico started laughing, which earned him another slam against the wall. "Okay, enough Riccardo. I haven't touched Sofia, so back off."

Riccardo released him, but stood fists clenched, ready to take a swing.

Nico sighed. "We came to Lucca to investigate something, then I thought Sofia would like to see through the *villa* and have lunch here. It seemed a good opportunity to take her sight seeing which took longer than I realized, so we decided to stay the night. Carolina said she'd tell you we were staying, so would one of you explain why you didn't trust me to look after my little sister?"

Riccardo stilled. "What the hell are you talking about?"

Ariana clutched Nico's arm. "Oh, Nico, how long have you known?"

"I've suspected since I was seventeen. Five years ago I met Sofia and discovered she was Giuseppe DeRosa's daughter. Then Dante turned up and I couldn't decide if I wanted to know or not. I feared coming face to face with him would prove I really was Giuseppe DeRosa's son." He met Riccardo's gaze. "I preferred the family think me a coward than shun my mother."

"Oh, Nico," cried Ariana. "I've wanted to tell you so many times, but then I'd lose my nerve. I've been so worried since Sofia arrived. I relaxed when I thought she and Riccardo were attracted to each other, but over the last few days I've watched the two of you together and when Carolina said you had come here, I feared the worst."

Riccardo shook his head in bewilderment. "I had no idea, and to think I accused Sofia of having an affair with you. You should have come to me, Nico. We are family and none of us would ever shun you or your mother." He looked up at the ceiling for a moment then took a deep breath. "This damned feud has hurt so many people. I dread to think how Giuseppe DeRosa's going to react with this news."

Ariana let out a shaky breath. "I will tell Giuseppe. It must come from me. We have a few more days before Dante arrives. The bad weather in America has grounded planes. Now, I am exhausted, so I'm going to bed. *Buonanotte,* my dears."

Nico turned to Riccardo. "Me too, it's been a hell of a day. I'll see you in the morning." He smiled at the woman hovering by Riccardo. "Roberta, please show Riccardo to one of the guest rooms."

"*Si*, Nico."

Nico opened the door beside him, entered and closed it firmly, leaving Riccardo alone with Roberta. He gave her his most charming smile. "*Signora*, Sofia is my fiancée and I would like to say goodnight to her before I go to bed. Which room is she in?"

Roberta beamed at him. "Ah, now I understand. You are engaged to Sofia? I did not know, *signore*. Come I will show you your room and then Sofia's. I'm sure she'll be delighted to see you." She smirked and led the way along the landing.

Sofia was sound asleep when Riccardo entered her room. She'd left the shutters open and lay in a pool of moonlight. He slid in beside her and spooned himself around her body, breathing in her heavenly scent. He'd planned to do no more than hold her, but the temptation to kiss her was too great to resist. He gently drew the silky curtain of hair off her face and out of his way, then dropped light kisses down her neck and shoulder, he ran his fingertips up her bare thigh, caught the edge of her cotton negligée and drew it up over her hip.

When a soft murmur escaped her lips, he moved his hand around to her flat belly and down across her bed of curls.

Sofia tensed then sighed and relaxed back against the warm, hard, muscled body behind her, enjoying the tingling sensations streaming through her as magic fingers trailed sensually across her belly and tantalizing lips moved slowly up and down her neck. It was the most realistic dream she'd ever had and when one hand closed over her breast and the other came to rest between her legs, she moaned, parting her legs wantonly. She could even smell the aromatic spicy cologne he always wore and feel his warm breath tickling her ear, and the hard pressure against her bottom where his…

Sofia stiffened, her eyes flying open as she registered what was pressing against her.

"Relax, Sofia," whispered Riccardo in her ear. "It's me."

She rolled over. "What are you doing here? I thought… I thought I was dreaming."

Riccardo chuckled. "I like that you dream about me, Sofia, but I assure you, I am real and at the moment very hard."

Sofia cheeks heated with the realization that the nightie she'd borrowed was up around her waist, and that Riccardo's erection now pressed into her belly. She cleared her throat, then cleared it again, staring at her hands spread over his hard chest. "Riccardo…what are you doing here?"

He drew her closer. "Carolina led me to believe you were with her at the jewelers and when she arrived home this evening I discovered you were here with Nico. Ariana and I decided it was in your best interest that we get here as quickly as possible."

"Why?"

Riccardo kissed her nose. "We were concerned Nico had ulterior motives for bringing you here. We thought he might intend on seducing you. Ariana was frantic you and Nico had run off together and were about to embark on an affair."

Ariana or you?

Sofia scoffed. "Oh, Riccardo...we came here to find out if Nico is my brother. We didn't run away together, and he's never tried to seduce me. We went to a place that used to be a home for unmarried mothers and spoke to the head nun. It's true. He suspected it, but thought your family would reject him and Ariana."

"It wouldn't have happened. Although Nico, Giovanni, and I are rivals in many things, we are very close. Being Giuseppe's son will make no difference to us."

"You don't sound surprised," accused Sofia.

"That's because Ariana and I have already spoken to Nico. He explained everything. Now, why don't you let me show you how much I missed you?" he murmured, running a finger slowly down her arm.

Sofia shivered. "You can't climb into bed and touch me like that. It's not fair. I'm not like the women you hook up with. I'm a virgin and I want a proper long term relationship."

Riccardo held in his groan. He'd suspected, but to have it confirmed. He wanted to seduce her and she was throwing reason at him. Well, he could be reasonable.

"I'm not into self-denial either, *cara mia*. If I want something, I go after it." He ran his finger from her shoulder, around the edge of her breast, then down her rib cage and across her belly, smiling when a quiver rippled through her. He drew her closer and planted kisses along her jaw and down the soft curve of her neck. He caressed her hip then slid his hand across her smooth thigh to her moist center, unashamedly coaxing her body into a state of liquid fire.

When Sofia arched into him, pressing her breasts into his chest and pulled his head down to kiss him, Riccardo was momentarily stunned. This time a groan did escaped. Was she aware of the effect she had on him, or the self-control he exerted to hold back from taking her hard and fast?

Something primal came over him, knowing she was his for the taking, but then his conscience kicked in. She wanted long term. Her heartfelt words prevented him taking advantage of her. Instead, he reined in his desire and set out to give her a taste of the pleasure available on the way to the ultimate goal.

Riccardo thrilled at the way Sofia responded to his touch. He deepened the kiss, parting her lips with his tongue and sweeping in. She gamely met him, her arms tightening around his shoulders, wrapping one leg over his thigh and opening herself wider to his probing fingers.

Groaning, Riccardo drew back, then chuckled at her murmur of disappointment and her attempt to drag him back. He positioned himself more comfortably and lowered his head to her throat licking, sucking and nipping gently across to her shoulder, then down to her breast. He took her sighs as encouragement and moved lower, capturing her nipple in his mouth and sucking deeply. He cupped her other breast and rolled her hardened nipple between his fingers until she was panting and writhing for more.

"Do you like this?" he murmured against her silky smooth skin.

"Yeees."

Riccardo smiled and nudged her further onto her back, using his knees to part her legs so he could move lower between them. With his lips, he skimmed her ribcage and belly, taking his time and using his tongue he circled her belly button.

She reached for his hair, her fingers tangling in its thickness. Wanton and alive, and not the least inhibited that her legs were spread-eagled, or that each touch of his lips had her moaning in pleasure. He slid lower, kissing her hip, then one thigh. He used his shoulders to push her legs further apart, exposing her as she'd never been exposed to any other man. The thought was enough to strengthen his resolve to take this slowly.

"Riccardo...we mustn't."

"Shush, *cara mia*. If I promise to leave you a virgin, will you let me give you a little more pleasure?"

She nodded, her beautiful green orbs focused on him as her breasts rose and fell with each panting breath.

Riccardo repositioned himself. The thought of what he was about to do sent wild anticipation and mounting lust racing through him. This was all for her pleasure.

He lifted her knees and dropped his shoulders under them, then slid his hands under her backside and lifted her. He glanced up, thrilled to see her eyes widen in absolute enthrallment. She choked out something unrecognizable as his mouth closed over her succulent bounty. Then he settled to feast, swirling his tongue around her clit, savoring the taste of her, thrusting his tongue into her moist haven.

She came up off the bed in response and shrieked. "Holy cow, Riccardo." Her hands clawed at the sheets beside him. "That's...that's...far out."

Riccardo chuckled again, and went to work sipping, licking, nipping, sucking, and thrusting his tongue deeply into her honeyed center until she was meeting his thrusts and crying out his name. He only just managed to get a hand free and muffle her scream as she climaxed and her body shuddered and stiffened under him.

She eventually floated back to earth and Riccardo leaned on his elbow, watching her intently, a smile hovering on his lips at the bemusement on her face. She lay boneless, sated, and he'd never seen anything quite so beautiful as Sofia in the aftermath of an orgasm.

She opened her eyes and beamed at him.

"I take it, you enjoyed that, *cara mia*?"

She blushed and lowered her gaze to his chest, then back again as if that was too distracting.

"What about you? If we're not going to...you know. You must be feeling..."

Riccardo rolled onto his back pulling her with him. "Straddle me."

"Why? I want to give you the same pleasure you gave me, without making love." She pulled away.

Riccardo laughed and drew her over him, separating her knees and positioning her across his thighs. "I'm going to show you how, *tesoro*."

She didn't resist as he closed her fingers around his erection and slowly drew her hand up then down. Her touch felt so good his breath caught.

"You're much bigger than I imagined." Her blush deepened, her gaze locked on his cock. "It's like velvet-covered steel. She swallowed. "You're so hard," she whispered, not taking her eyes off his manhood.

Riccardo grimaced. "It's been a common state since I met you."

She smiled, her gaze finally meeting his. "Yet you are so smooth and soft." She slid her hand up and down the full length of him.

"*Cara mia,* a man does not like to be told he's soft. Hard yes, but not soft."

Giggling, she stroked him again. "You are very hard, but you do feel like velvet... Oh, you're getting bigger. How can you possibly put that into...into?" She pulled her hand away.

"Don't think, just keep rubbing me." He drew her fingers back around him. With his other hand he caressed her breast.

She continued to stroke him, then cupped his testicles, and when he gave a low growl of pleasure, she became more adventurous, circling the tip of him and using the moisture there to rub him faster, then slower.

Riccardo clamped his hand over hers and dragged her down on top of him, rolling until she was under him. "*Merci.*" He made a guttural sound and came over her belly.

He relaxed, liking the feel of her softness beneath him. Her body fitted his perfectly and her response and enthusiasm spoke well for a physical relationship between them. The desire she evoked had almost ended in him forgoing his promise for the sheer pleasure of thrusting deep inside her. He finally lifted off her and reached for the box of tissues on the bedside table, taking his time he wiped his seed from her hand and belly.

Sofia basked in Riccardo's attention and the sensual feel of his touch, knowing full well he was taking a lot longer than necessary, but loving the fact he seemed as captivated as she. When he placed the tissues back on the bedside table and made to get up she reached for his hand. "Where are you going?"

Riccardo's lips twitched. "I never spend the night with a woman once we've..."

Sofia dropped his hand and recoiled against the pillows, dragging the sheet up to cover herself. She bit her lip to stop it trembling and turned away, shimmying down under the covers to hide her tears. She had apparently joined the ranks of his used and discarded women. She had to be the biggest fool alive.

Happy-ever-after. Not with this man. *I'm such an idiot.*

"Shit. I didn't mean that the way it sounded." He knelt at her back, caressing her hip. "Sofia, I didn't mean to hurt you. You misunderstand."

"Go away." She sniffed. "Leave me alone. I don't want to speak to you."

He pulled the covers back and slid in behind her. "Sofia, *tesoro*, come here," he coaxed, wrapping his arm around her and trying to draw her closer.

"Don't touch me. I'm not your treasure. I hate you."

"No, you don't." Riccardo hauled her around and into his arms, capturing her hands when she tried to strike out at him.

"Listen to me, *cara mia*." He pushed her down and leaned over her, holding her hands above her head. "Until I met you, I've never spent the whole night with any woman. We'd have sex, I'd leave, and that's the way I liked it. Since meeting you, all I've wanted is to spend the whole night with you. I was leaving because Nico is acting the protective brother and wants us in separate rooms."

Sofia snuffled. "Oh."

Riccardo scowled at her. "Is that all you've got to say?"

"Oh, I see."

"You're a bewitching damn woman." He looked so put out, Sofia almost laughed.

He exclaimed loudly then threw himself on his back to stare at the ceiling.

Sofia blinked several times then rolled on her side and slid closer. When he didn't react she moved the last couple of inches and placed her hand on the middle of his chest.

"I'm sorry, Riccardo. After what we did I expected you to stay and cuddle me. I should have realized you're only interested in sex, whereas I want it all. Perhaps it's good this happened. I promise I'll stay out of your way from now on. I'll get Nico to help me find the evidence. You don't have to spend any more time with me."

Riccardo swore in Italian and grabbed her, hauling her onto his chest. He wrapped his arms around her. "You don't understand, Sofia. I want to cuddle you and kiss you, and touch you, but when I do it makes me want more. I can't even get through a business meeting without wondering where you are, or what you're doing, and if you're safe. I look forward to seeing you each morning and I want nothing more than to have you fall asleep in my arms each night."

Sofia smiled. "Why, Riccardo Santini, I think you like me."

Riccardo grunted. "You think?"

"Yes, I think you like me a lot."

"Mmm...now that we've sorted that out, you can go to sleep." He tucked her into his side. "I will stay here, holding you in my frustrated state until morning, then I will sneak back to my room, rumple the bed and have a cold shower, leaving your reputation intact."

"Okay." Sofia hid her grin as she wriggled closer then rested her hand over his heart.

Riccardo gave a sigh of mocked exasperation. "I'm glad my state of frustration won't cause you any loss of sleep."

"It won't," murmured Sofia, closing her eyes happily.

Chapter Sixteen

Her heart almost bursting with happiness and having slept extremely well, Sofia almost skipped onto the terrace of *villa di tranquillità*. She found Riccardo and Nico sitting at a small round table reading their papers and drinking coffee. They looked up and smiled as she sat in the vacant chair. "What a beautiful day," she exclaimed.

Nico gave her a wink. "It is indeed, Sofia, and according to the paper, New York's airport has been shut down due to a bomb threat. You have at least another day before your brother arrives."

"Our brother," she corrected him. "And that gives us another whole day to investigate Renzina's accident and clear *Papà*."

Riccardo lowered his paper. "Sofia, you need to tell me what you're planning, where you're going, and anything you find out. If you need to go somewhere, I will take you and if you can't reach me, call Giovanni or Nico."

Sofia smiled at each of them and reached for some orange juice and a croissant. "In that case, I would like one of you to take me to a hotel called Luna Verde in Bologna, if it still exists. Then I wish to visit my grandparents and *Signora* Rinaldi."

"Why?" they asked instantaneously.

"That's the hotel where my father is supposed to have hooked up with two prostitutes. I want to interview the manager and find out if he owned the hotel back then or who did, and I intend to track down the prostitutes and interview them."

"You're not serious?" exclaimed Nico.

Riccardo's lips twitched. "Oh, I think she is."

Nico stared at Sofia. "I can't take you today. I need to spend the day with *Mamma* and sort out what we intend to do about my paternity."

Riccardo put down his paper. "That's okay, Nico, I have to be back in Bologna today so I will have my people check if the Luna Verde still exists and take Sofia there myself. Thirty years is a long time and I doubt it is still owned by the same people."

"If you have a meeting, I can always ask Giovanni," suggested Sofia.

"No, you can't. He's gone to England to speak with the couple who witnessed your aunt's accident. I tried to ring them and discovered they'd moved. It took some major favors to track them down."

Sofia jumped up and hugged him. "You did that for me?"

Riccardo glanced at Nico and gently unhooked Sofia's arms and set her away from him. "I also did it for the Santinis, Sofia. We want to know the truth too."

"Of course," she assured him, smiling. "When do we leave?"

Nico came to his feet. "My mother is having a sleep-in, so you might as well leave as soon as you like." He caught Sofia's hand. "Don't be surprised if you can't find the information you seek. It was a long time ago."

Sofia rushed her breakfast, then unable to hide her excitement, hassled Riccardo out the front door. She came to an abrupt halt upon seeing a sleek silver car parked behind Nico's Audi. "You drive an Aston Martin?" She ran down the steps and glided her hand over the bonnet. "Dante is going to be so jealous. It's his favorite car."

"It's not showy or pretentious. I'm drawn to its classic beauty in the same way I'm drawn to you." He pulled her into his arms and kissed her lightly.

Sofia stretched up for a deeper kiss and when he released her she smiled, brimming with happiness. "I have a good feeling about today, Riccardo, and if you let me drive your Aston Martin, it will make the day perfect."

Other than a smile, he made no comment as he opened the passenger door for her, then once inside, he closed the door and walked around the car.

Sofia chuckled then glanced down the drive as a man with a camera ducked beyond the entrance gates. *What is he up to?* She kept her eyes on the gates as Riccardo climbed in and started the purring engine.

"I just saw a man at the gates with a camera, and I think he took a photo."

"It's not uncommon. *La villa di tranquillità* is impressive." Riccardo engaged first gear and drove along the drive and through the gates.

Sofia couldn't see anyone acting suspiciously among the many pedestrians and bicycle riders. *It could be a tourist taking photos of a stunning villa, nothing more.*

Riccardo turned right, then made a call to his office to ask his secretary to check out the Hotel Luna Verde and its owner. By the time they drove off the *autostrada* for Bologna, they had an address, and to their amazement, Riccardo's secretary assured them the hotel was still owned by the original family.

"It doesn't mean they will remember your father, Sofia."

"No, but after that fight and our fathers being dragged off by police, they might."

"The evidence is hard to refute, *cara mia*. Your father was on his back, naked with two prostitutes on top of him."

Sofia grimaced. "I can accept it seems that way, but my father is an honest man, and he's adamant he was set up. If I can't prove that part of the conspiracy, at least I can try to prove he didn't rob his father's safe or start the fires."

"Very well." Riccardo made a tight turn into a narrow, dilapidated street then parked outside a run-down hotel with a sign declaring it to be La Luna Verde.

Sofia's optimism took a dive as she stared at the dismal premises. She doubted it looked much better thirty years ago. Why would her father have come here?"

As they approached the entrance, Riccardo took Sofia's hand. "Promise me that if I'm ever accused of anything immoral you'll give me a chance to defend myself."

Sofia stopped, alarmed by his seriousness. "Is there something I should know?"

"Only that I admire your loyalty and faith in your father's innocence. I can only hope you will afford me the same trust one day."

She kissed his cheek. "I will as long as you're always honest with me."

They entered the dimly lit reception area where a grey-headed man sat behind the counter preoccupied with a football game on the television.

"*Scusi, signore.*"

The man jumped, nearly falling off his stool.

Sofia smiled. "*Parla inglese?*"

"*Sì*, I speak English, *signorina*. How can I help you?"

"This may seem a little strange, but there was an incident at this hotel thirty years ago. It involved my father and two women. I'm trying to discover what happened."

The man looked from Sofia to Riccardo and started shaking his head then stopped. "Someone rang here earlier asking if we'd been the owners, thirty years ago. Was that you?"

"*Sì*," replied Riccardo. "My secretary rang you. Perhaps you remember a fight. The police were called and the two men involved carted away."

"I can't help you. I would have been working in London then, but maybe my mother remembers. Wait, I will check." He hurried away.

Sofia looked apprehensively at Riccardo. "His mother would have to be in her eighties."

Several minutes passed, then an elderly lady with a walking stick hobbled through the door behind the counter followed by her son. "My *Mamma* doesn't speak English," he informed them.

"*Va bene,*" replied Riccardo. "My fiancée will ask questions and I will translate them for your mother." He repeated himself in Italian for the old lady.

"*Sì, va bene,*" she answered.

Sofia smiled at the woman. "Do you remember a fight between two men in this hotel thirty years ago? They smashed up a room and the police were called to take them away. There may have been two women involved as well."

Riccardo translated and the woman listened then turned to Sofia. "*Sì, mi ricordo.*"

"She remembers." Sofia's heart sank. "Okay, ask her, who made the booking and did the man arrive with the two women or did they arrive separately, and ask her if she remembers anything unusual."

Riccardo translated then listened as the old lady spoke. In the middle of her reply she sent her son off. He returned with an old ledger and placed it on the counter. The old woman rifled through it until she found what she was looking for and turned it to show them.

Sofia leaned over to see what she was pointing at. It clearly said DeRosa, but the old lady was pointing to another name as she spoke.

Riccardo took a deep breath and turned to Sofia. "The *signora* said a man rang and booked two rooms next to each other, one in the name of DeRosa, and one in the name of Rossini. He told her two women would be arriving first and she was to give them both room keys. The women arrived and shortly after a handsome young man arrived. He seemed a little uncertain, but asked if there was a room booked in the name of DeRosa. She told him yes and sent him upstairs. About ten minutes later another man arrived, asking if a friend of his had booked in under the name DeRosa. She said yes and gave him the room number. He went tearing up the stairs and within a minute all hell broke loose. The two women came scrambling down the stairs, pulling on clothes as they ran. When it became clear the two men were trashing the room, the *signora* rang the police."

"So it did happen." Sofia hopes sank lower as she tried to come to terms with this latest information. She thought of her hard working, honest, and loving father. It didn't make sense. "Ask the *signora* if she's sure the first man seemed uncertain about the booking, and if she has any idea who the women were."

Riccardo repeated the question and the old lady went into a fit of angry screeching, surprising them. Riccardo listened then asked several questions before turning to Sofia.

"She definitely remembers him being uncertain, as if he was in the wrong place. As for the women...she claims she didn't know they were whores when they came in, but when they ran out, they were in the process of putting on coats. All they wore underneath was stockings and shameless scraps of underwear. She sees one of the women regularly about here."

The old woman spoke rapidly again, gesturing out the door. Riccardo turned to look in the direction she was pointing. So did Sofia, but she couldn't see anything.

"What is it, Riccardo?"

"The *signora* said one of the women lives on this street and works at the tile factory."

Sofia dug her fingers into his arm. "We have to speak to her."

Riccardo handed the woman money then thanked them. "*Andiamo*, let's go." He grasped Sofia's hand and they walked out of the hotel.

"Riccardo, we need to go to the factory."

"We don't have to go to the factory. Come, I have the woman's address."

"That's great."

Halfway down the ramshackle street, Riccardo hammered on a grimy door, loud enough to wake the dead.

Shuffling sounded then the door cracked open. A woman peered at them. "*Sì.*"

As Riccardo spoke to the woman in Italian, Sofia observed her expression go from surprise to suspicion. When Riccardo pulled out his wallet, the woman opened the door wider, her greedy eyes fastened on the notes he removed.

Sofia shot a glance at Riccardo. "Is that wise."

"No, but necessary if you want information." He spoke to the woman and listened to her, refusing to hand over the money until she'd answered every question. Then he paid her and took Sofia's arm, guiding her back to the car.

Stifling her curiosity, Sofia waited as Riccardo calmly put his car into gear and drove away from La Luna Verde Hotel. Once they were on the road leading into the city center he glanced at her. "You were right. Your father was set up."

"Really?" Relief surged through her body. "Tell me what she said?"

Riccardo ran his hand through his hair as his attention returned to the road. "A man in his mid-twenties to thirties wearing a suit approached that woman. He hired her and a friend to be caught in bed with a man at the Luna Verde hotel."

"Why?"

"He told them his sister was engaged to this jerk who was forever cheating on her. The man said he needed his sister to catch her fiancé in the act."

"Lies." Sofia closed her eyes with relief and then opened them as the truth hit her along with disappointment. She dropped her hand to Riccardo's knee. "Your father set up *Papà*?"

"Someone set up Giuseppe, but I'm yet to be convinced it's my father. That woman said they went to the hotel, picked up the key to their room and the one next door. Their instructions were to go into room twenty and leave an envelope on the bed, then they were to get undressed in their own room and wait by the window for a signal. As soon as they got it, they were to go into the other room where they would find a man lying naked on the bed. They were to throw themselves on him and hold him down until his fiancée arrived. They were also told to get the letter if anything went wrong."

"I see." She idly traced patterns on Riccardo's thigh, aware of his swift glances and clenched jaw. She figured he was concerned over his father's alleged involvement, but what would he do about it? Another thought struck. "But it wasn't Ariana who arrived. It was your father."

"Exactly. And when the men got into a fight the women took off, taking the letter with them. They ran around the corner to where they'd agreed to meet the man who hired them. He took the letter, gave them their money, and that was that."

"Who was he?" asked Sofia angrily.

"She didn't know him. Your father may have been set up at the hotel, but that doesn't mean he didn't start the fires in retaliation, or to cover the robbery."

"He didn't, and I'm going to prove it. Some one started the rumors, and I plan to speak to the witness who identified *Papà* running from a fire."

Deep in thought, she continued to trace her fingers along his thigh until his leg stiffened under her touch. "Sofia, if you don't want a repeat performance of last night then I suggest you remove your hand now."

"My hand?" She looked across to where her fingers lay, almost touching his crotch. She snatched her hand away as heat rushed into her face. "Sorry, I didn't realize."

Riccardo laughed and reached for her hand, returning it to just above his knee.

"I can handle it there." He grinned at her then returned his attention to the road. "I need to be at the office for a teleconference with the owners of a hotel in *Venezia* that we are negotiating to buy.

So I'll deliver you to Carolina at her shop, where I want you to stay until I pick you up."

"But I promised to visit *Signora* Rinaldi today in Ravenna. She has an envelope for me and it could be important, and I want to see my grandparents."

"Not today, Sofia."

"Riccardo, I'm running out of time. What if I take Carolina with me?"

"Not without me to protect you."

"There must be someone—what about your father? This is in his interest too." *And, if he did set up Papà then he's hardly going to do anything while Carolina's with me.*

"All right, I'll speak to my father, but I want your promise you will stay with Carolina."

"Fine," muttered Sofia grudgingly. "If your father can take us to Ravenna, he'll have to wait at a café while I'm visiting my grandparents."

"As long as Carolina is with you at all times." He glanced at her. "I won't negotiate on this, Sofia. Take it or leave it."

"*Va bene,*" she muttered.

Riccardo pulled up outside the Hotel Emilia Romagna and, as promised, walked Sofia into reception and then across to Carolina's jewelry boutique. As soon as she saw them she rushed to hug Sofia.

"*Ciao, bella.* Tell me everything and don't leave anything out."

With a farewell, Riccardo left them to it.

Sofia spent the next hour helping Carolina dress her window, and sort through a delivery of new stock while telling her what had transpired. She didn't mention anything about her night with Riccardo or what they'd done. It was too special.

Sofia had accepted she wouldn't be visiting *Signora* Rinaldi today when Carolina brought out a small tray of engagement rings.

"Wow, Caro. These rings are magnificent."

"And expensive. Our guests and customers expect superior quality. Which one do you like best?"

Sofia stared in awe at the beautiful rings, all unique and exquisite. "They're lovely, but I like this one." She picked up a solitaire diamond with an intricate filigree design up either side. "Oh yes, definitely this one." She placed it on her finger and admired it. "I think I might keep it."

Carolina chuckled. "It is also the most expensive. You have excellent taste, *amici*."

Angelo Santini strolled through the door. "*Ciao,* ladies. I am here to escort you to Ravenna?"

"*Signor* Santini, you're here." Sofia clasped her hands together. "I'm sorry to take up your time, but it's important."

"Please, call me Angelo, Sofia, and it is not a problem. I will drive you to Ravenna and wait while you visit your grandparents. Let's go. I have to be back for a meeting at five."

"*Va bene, Papà.* I'm coming too. Just let me leave some last minute instructions for my assistant and I'll meet you at the car. Get Sofia to tell you what she and Ricardo learned while you wait for me."

Sofia walked with Angelo Santini out of the hotel. Gauging his reaction, she told him about the Hotel Luna Verde and what they'd discovered. She didn't mention Nico or Ariana.

"Unbelievable," he exclaimed. "I did not hire those women, or set your father up, or spread the rumors. It wasn't me." He rubbed his jaw distractedly. "I should have known Giuseppe wouldn't betray Ariana, but I caught him with those women." He shook his head. "It is no wonder he hates my family and refuses to come back to Italia. I am sorry."

Sofia touched his arm. "There is still time to fix things."

His expression darkened. "Giovanni rang from Plymouth, in England, where he spoke with the couple who witnessed your aunt's accident."

Sofia stopped. "What did they say?"

Angelo grimaced. "There was a large, dark blue car tailgating your aunt. It kept ramming her car until it literally pushed her off the road and over the edge. They tried to explain this to the police at the time, but the language barrier was problematic. They described the driver of the car as Italian, dark haired, and wearing sunglasses."

"It could be the same man who set up my father with the prostitutes," Sofia suggested. "Did they get the number plate?"

"Giovanni did not say, but I am alarmed with the description of the car used."

"Why?"

"At the time of your aunt's accident, the Santinis and DeRosas had large dark blue vehicles. So did many of our friends and relatives."

Sofia mulled that over. Large dark blue cars were probably common back then, but what a coincidence. "At least we've discovered my father was set up at the hotel, and my aunt really was run off the road. It's coming together. I just need to collect the evidence my aunt hid before Dante arrives. Then we'll know who's responsible."

Angelo opened the front passenger door of a Mercedes and when she was seated, he squatted down beside her on the footpath. "Sofia, the closer you get to solving this matter will also mean you are more of a threat to the person behind the attacks. That worries me."

"I know, Angelo, but I have to do this for *Papà*."

"It is still possible your father set the fires as payback for what he thought I did to him. Perhaps the attacks on you are another attempt to lay a trail of blame at my feet."

Sofia fisted her hands as the need to lash out consumed her. "My father would never hire men to hurt me."

"What if he didn't intend to hurt you? We don't know that the man who drugged you was actually going to hurt you, and you weren't there when your room was ransacked. It could have been misjudgment that you were knocked down when the man on the motorcycle snatched your purse."

"What about the man who suffocated me," she asked sarcastically.

"Maybe he was only meant to scare you and his intention was to make us Santinis look like the perpetrators."

"And the cut brake lines on Carolina's car, what about them?"

Angelo raked his hands through his greying hair. "I wonder if his intention was to hurt Carolina, and you were not supposed to be in the car."

"No. *Papà* would never hurt Carolina. It's someone else." She frowned. "Who had the most to gain if the DeRosa vineyard went under?"

"We were the DeRosa's biggest competitor, and when your grandfather sold off his land, it was my father who bought it, but we did not conspire to destroy your father."

Sofia's eyes narrowed. "Would you agree that the grapes from the DeRosa vineyard were superior to those of the Santini's, and since taking over the DeRosa vines, your wines are now amongst the best in the world?"

A slow flush crept into Angelo's checks. "Yes, who told you this?"

"Several people." Sofia clenched her hands in her lap. "If it's the last thing I do, Angelo, I will uncover the truth."

"You must do what you think best, Sofia, but sometimes it's wise to let sleeping dragons lie. In discovering the truth, you may unleash more destruction than it's worth."

CHAPTER SEVENTEEN

Angelo parked near a café outside the city wall of Ravenna. Sofia climbed out, shut her door, and looked across the Mercedes' roof at him. "My grandparents live a few minutes away. So, if you don't mind waiting in that café, I will assure my grandparents I'm fine, talk to *Signora* Rinaldi, then come straight back."

"*Va bene*," said Angelo.

"*Ciao, Papà*." Carolina kissed him. "We will be back in one hour."

He hesitated as if of two minds to let them go. "Be careful." He waved them off and strolled into the café.

Most of the narrow streets in the center of Ravenna were zoned pedestrian and bicycle only. Sofia and Carolina wove their way through several of these cobbled passageways, crossed Piazza del Popolo, then wound their way to Sofia's grandparents' house.

She pressed the buzzer twice as she glanced at the passers by. It was a busy thoroughfare for shoppers and tourists and maybe someone with murder on their agenda.

The bolt slid free on the other side of the door and it opened to reveal her grandmother, Elena DeRosa. She looked at Sofia with mild interest then her eyes widened. "Sofia!"

"*Ciao, Nonna*."

"*Nipotina mia*. You come to see your *Nonna*, at last. Come, give me a hug."

Sofia hugged her grandmother then waved Carolina closer. "*Nonna*, this is my friend, Carolina Santini. Please, may she come in?"

Elena DeRosa's smile dimmed. "*Si*, if you wish."

Once they were in the huge kitchen, Sofia gathered her courage. "I didn't tell you I was coming to Italy, Nonna, because I'm here to clear *Papà's* name, and I knew you would tell him what I was up to, which would result in Dante coming to stop me. The Santinis want to end the feud and have been helping me unearth the truth."

Sofia's grandmother stared at Carolina for a moment, then looked at Sofia. "Forgive me, but I find that hard to believe. There is a lot of bad blood between our families."

"I know, but please hear us out."

"*Va bene.* We shall go into the garden. *Signora* Rinaldi is staying here while she recovers from her fall."

"How is she?" asked Sofia.

"*Cosi, cosi.* They put a pin in her arm and she needs help with dressing and washing. I am expecting your brother to arrive in the next day or so." She grimaced. "When Enrico Santini rang to tell me you were staying with them and engaged to Riccardo, I didn't ring your father for fear he might do something idiotic." She led them down the hall and into the courtyard.

Signora Rinaldi was sitting in the sun, her leg raised on a padded footstool.

Sofia smiled. "*Ciao, Signora* Rinaldi. How are you feeling?"

"*Bene, grazie,* Sofia. Please call me Donatella."

Sofia's grandmother gripped the back of a chair, her gnarled knuckles white. "*Signora* Rinaldi is here because she is fearful to go home."

"Why?" Sofia stomach clenched. "I thought the fall was an accident?"

"No. Your grandfather went to feed the cats. Donatella's home was burgled and a slimy liquid that smelt like dishwashing detergent had been poured over the back steps. That is why she fell and broke her arm. Who would do such a thing? The police have no answers." She huffed. "You sit and talk to Donatella. I will make us lunch."

Sofia looked at Carolina then pulled out a chair and sat opposite *Signora* Rinaldi. "Tell me exactly what happened, *signora.*"

"I didn't get home until late, after visiting you, and then your grandparents. My cats were hungry so I stepped out on my back steps to feed them. My feet shot from under me and I fell. It is lucky I didn't break my neck."

"What happened then?" asked Carolina.

"I called out to my neighbor. While we waited for the ambulance she packed some things for me to take to the hospital."

"And while you were in the hospital, some one burgled your house?" Sofia wrung her hands, fearing the worst. "Did they take anything important?"

"I don't think so. Your grandfather said they made a terrible mess, but nothing of value appears to be missing."

"What do you think, *signora*?" asked Sofia quietly.

"I think it is better I stay here for a while, and I think I was wise to give that envelope to my neighbor for safe keeping. You two are the only people who knew about the envelope." She cast wary eyes at Carolina.

Sofia rested her chin on her hands as doubts began to fill her mind. She'd told Salvatore Bondini, the night of the accident, and Riccardo. Who had Carolina told?

"Does your neighbor still have the envelope, *signora*?"

"No, she brought it to me this morning with some more clothes. I will get it."

Sofia and Carolina watched *Signora* Rinaldi limp from the courtyard, then turned to each other with raised eyebrows.

"Another coincidence?" said Carolina.

"Not on your life. Somebody wants *Signora* Rinaldi out of the way. They must know about the envelope and her visit. Did you mention it to anyone?"

Carolina bit her lip. "*Papà* and *Nonno*. You?"

"Ricardo and Salvatore Bondini. Do you think my grandparents are in danger?" whispered Sofia.

"I don't know, but I'm going to ring *Papà* and tell him we're staying for lunch, before he comes banging on the door."

"Okay, I'll go and help my grandmother."

Sofia entered to the kitchen to find her grandmother humming as she piled a large bowl with spaghetti. "You sound happy, *Nonna*."

"Ah, Sofia, in a couple of days I will have my two beautiful grandchildren here in *Italia*. You have no idea how I have longed for this."

Sofia took a deep breath. *In for dollar, in for a dime.* "*Nonna*, you have three grandchildren, but you know that, don't you?"

Her grandmother looked at her blankly. "I don't know what you are saying, Sofia. I only have two grandchildren."

Sofia fidgeted with a hand-towel. "Michele Bondini said you and *Nonno* left your three grandchildren an equal share of your liquidated assets. So when I discovered Ariana Santini was pregnant with my father's baby. I assumed you knew."

Her grandmother's face drained of color and she sank into a chair. "No. Tell me."

Sofia's breath caught at the sight of her grandmother's anguished face. "I'm so sorry, Nonna. I thought you must know. Ariana told me her heart was broken after discovering *Papà* had moved in with another woman, so she ran away and then married Luciano Lombardi. She gave birth to a boy. His name is Nicolas, and he is the spitting image of Dante. I met him five years ago, and he is the reason *Papà* demanded I come home. We were suspicious, so me and Nico did a little digging."

Her grandmother wiped a tear away. "Was Nicolas the young man your grandfather saw you with in Piazza Del Popolo five years ago?"

"Si."

"Poor Ariana. You know she didn't speak to her parents for years, but I had no idea. Your *Papà* is going to be very angry when he finds out. You say the will is divided between you and our *two* grandsons."

"Yes. It must have been a mistake."

"Perhaps your Nonno discovered the truth but couldn't tell me."

"There's more, *Nonna*. I've discovered *Papà was* set up. Someone convinced him to go to that hotel for a reason I haven't figured out yet. That person paid two prostitutes to wait until *Papà* was in the room then they barged in and threw themselves on him seconds before Angelo Santini burst into the room. It was set up. I spoke to one of the prostitutes and the people who own the hotel."

Her grandmother shakily reached for Sofia's hand. "Giuseppe insisted he was innocent, but people kept contacting us about money he owed them, and there were so many rumors, and the fires."

"I think Renzina died because she discovered the identity of the person who set *Papà* up for the robbery and fires. Giovanni Santini went to England and interviewed witnesses who saw a man in a dark sedan force Renzina's car off the road."

Her grandmother pressed her hand against her mouth. "Who would do this?"

"*Nonna*, that's what I'm trying to discover before Dante arrives. I have to clear *Papà's* name and find the person who set him up. Until then I'm not going anywhere."

"Of course you cannot go back to Australia, *cara mia*. You are engaged and you are having a *bambino*."

Carolina and *Signora* Rinaldi stepped into the kitchen in time to hear these words. They looked at Sofia in surprise.

"No, *Nonna*, I'm not pregnant. Enrico Santini misunderstood and jumped to conclusions and as for being engaged..."

Sofia's grandmother smiled at her. "It is a beautiful ring, Sofia. Riccardo Santini must love you very much."

"Pardon?" Sofia looked at her grandmother in confusion.

"Your ring. It is lovely." Her grandmother picked up Sofia's hand for everyone to see the sparkling solitaire.

Sofia gasped, her gaze going to the ring and then Carolina's wide eyes. "I'm so sorry, I didn't realize I still had it on. Here, Carolina, take it."

"What are you going on about?" Carolina nudged Sofia. "You're not still scared of losing the ring are you?" She gave a pointed look then turned to Sofia's grandmother. *Signora,* your granddaughter is so scared of losing the ring she wants me to lock it up. I keep telling her, it is perfectly safe on her finger. Don't you agree?"

Sofia's grandmother beamed. "Yes, I do, now let's have lunch and we shall discuss these things. Your grandfather is out with friends, so you will miss him, which is probably best for now." She glanced apologetically at Carolina.

Sofia squeezed her grandmother's hand. "*Nonna*, can I ask you something?"

"Of course, *nipotina mia*."

"You don't seem shocked that Renzina was run off the road."

"Those rumors have been around for years. If it is true then you should leave it to the police to find those responsible."

Sofia stared at her grandmother, then decided to let it go for the moment. "I had better see what *Signora* Rinaldi has for me, if you don't mind."

"No, of course not. Go ahead."

They returned to the garden and *Signora* Rinaldi passed the envelope to Sofia. She tore the end off and up-ended it. A large, antique key fell into her hand, and a piece of paper floated to the floor. Sofia picked it up.

"It's the poem again and now we have a key. Carolina, they must be connected."

"Let's have lunch. We will figure it out later."

Sofia slid the key and poem in the pocket of her jacket then went to help her grandmother finish preparing lunch. They ate while Sofia and Carolina told them everything that had happened since Sofia arrived in Italy. They played down the personal attacks on Sofia, but even so it upset her grandmother to discover Sofia's life had been in danger. She insisted that Sofia let Dante take over the investigation when he arrived.

Would he?

Sofia didn't comment on the person behind *Signora* Rinaldi's broken arm and break-in. He was probably the same person who'd cut Carolina's brake lines and tried to suffocate Sofia. Instead she kept the conversation light.

After lunch, Sofia and Carolina left the two ladies drinking coffee in the pretty courtyard. It may be siesta time, but they didn't have the luxury of sitting around talking.

The narrow street was empty of people, everything closed at this time of day. Sofia had barely stepped away from the gate when clunking had her looking over her shoulder.

"Shit!" She threw herself at Carolina, knocking her out of the path of the large dumpster bin bearing down on them. It ploughed into the gutter where they'd been standing then veered to the other side of the street, crashing into the centuries old wall of the house opposite.

"*Santa* Maria." Carolina sat on the cobbled surface rubbing her hip. "Are you hurt?"

"Another few scrapes and bruises." Sofia scrambled to her feet, looking in the direction the dumpster had come from. The road was empty; not a soul about. She held out a trembling hand and pulled Carolina to her feet. "Where did it come from?"

"Your guess is as good as mine." Carolina frowned. "Those things have locks on the wheels to stop this sort of thing happening."

"Yes, I know."

Sofia looked back toward her grandparents' home. "Another coincidence."

"We don't believe in coincidences, remember."

"Who knew we were going to be here today besides us, Riccardo and—" she swallowed "—your father?"

"I don't know. Maybe someone's watching your grandparents' house."

Sofia shivered. "It's possible, but why didn't they just shoot us?"

"Too messy. This way, it looks like an accident. What worries me is it could have been your *Nonna* or *Signora* Rinaldi on the street. They might not have heard it, and even if they did, they aren't agile enough to get out of the way. As it is, I would be dead if you hadn't crash tackled me."

Sofia continued to stare at her grandparents' house. "How can we protect them?"

"I will ask *Papà*. He will know of a security service that can safeguard your grandparents and *Signora* Rinaldi from this madman."

Do I dare trust him though? Maybe my feelings for Riccardo are clouding my judgment.

They sprinted through the cobbled streets as if chased by a pack of hungry wolves, arriving at the café as Angelo rose from his table. His smile vanished within seconds of seeing them.

"What's happened?"

"It's okay, *Papà*," Carolina assured him. "We've had a fright, but we're fine and we want to go home now."

Angelo looked from one to the other. "I am happy to take you home, but not until you tell me what has happened."

Sofia caught hold of Angelo's muscled arm and ushered him toward the car. "We'll tell you on the way home. First, I need your advice about hiring security people to keep my grandparents and *Signora* Rinaldi safe."

"From what?" His voice deepened as he frowned.

"From whoever tried to run us down with a dumpster," said Carolina.

"What!"

"We'll tell you in the car," said Sofia. "Then I want to visit Villa DeRosa and see if this key fits anything."

"We don't have time to—what key?"

Sofia and Carolina urged him to the car and once they were on their way, told him how *Signora* Rinaldi's back step had been doused in detergent, guaranteeing her feet would shoot from under her. They also told him about her burglary, the key, and the dumpster.

"We think *Signora* Rinaldi is in danger and we want to hire someone to protect her and my grandparents," announced Sofia. "We also need to stop at Villa DeRosa because if we can find the door that this key fits, then we might find the evidence to put a criminal away."

"This is ridiculous," argued Angelo. "You should reconsider going home or at least inform your father. He should know what you're doing."

"I will, but not yet."

Angelo sighed. "I am not happy about taking you to Villa DeRosa. We should wait for Riccardo and Giovanni."

Carolina shook her head. "Riccardo is busy and Giovanni is on his way back from England. And, I know he won't want to come as he has a date with a nurse called Harriet."

"I thought he was seeing the air hostess?" Sofia said, checking the road behind.

Carolina laughed. "That was yesterday. My brothers are not interested in long-term relationships, Sofia. They are players. Isn't that right, *Papà*?"

"They certainly steer clear of anything serious. Although to be fair, after Giovanni's close call, I can understand why he avoids marriage."

Carolina snorted and turned to Sofia. "Marianna was beautiful, but she was a manipulative piece of work. When she couldn't get Riccardo to date her, she went after Giovanni then announced she was pregnant. A week before the wedding, Riccardo hit on her. He told her he'd made a mistake and wanted her for himself. That's when she admitted there was no baby. It was a lucky escape for Giovanni."

Shock hit Sofia like a physical blow. "You make it sound like Riccardo is a hero. Wasn't Giovanni upset that his brother hit on his fiancée?"

Carolina laughed. "No, he was relieved. No baby meant, no wedding. Riccardo gave Marianna the flick and we haven't seen her since."

Sofia looked from Carolina to Angelo. "Even so, I can't believe Riccardo would come on to his brother's fiancée, especially as she was supposed to be pregnant."

Carolina swiveled round. "Riccardo has always been a player. He has a cynical view of marriage and monogamous relationships. He didn't believe Marianna would allow herself to fall pregnant. He has a friend who dated her and swore she was selfish, spiteful and hated the thought of ruining her body for the sake of a child. Giovanni swore he'd used protection, but accepted Marianna's word as he didn't want to attract unnecessary gossip."

Sofia stared hard at Carolina. "If Riccardo is a...player, then why go along with this engagement? Do you want him to break my heart, like Ariana broke my father's heart? I should have guessed Riccardo would resort to such underhanded behavior."

Carolina gasped. "We'd never hurt you, Sofia. Riccardo had a good reason for what he did to Marianna, but he genuinely likes you."

Turning to the window, Sofia avoided their eyes as she regained her composure.

"It's true," said Angelo. "Giovanni told me that Riccardo hasn't looked at another woman since he met you. We've never seen him so protective or possessive as he is with you. It is unfortunate you are Giuseppe's daughter, but Riccardo needs someone like you."

"You mean a gullible fool," muttered Sofia.

"No, I mean a caring, beautiful young woman who is slowly peeling away Riccardo's cynical layers and giving him something to care about, other than business."

Turning from the window, Sofia met Angelo's gaze in the mirror. "It wouldn't work, Angelo. Aside from the feud, our ethics differ considerably."

Angelo and Carolina exchanged glances but refrained from commenting. There wasn't anything they could say. The rest of the journey continued in silence until Angelo pulled up at the gates of Villa DeRosa. He turned off the engine then looked over his shoulder.

"We can stay for half an hour, then I must get back to Bologna for my meeting."

"No, you go. I want to look around on my own, then I'll walk back through the vines."

Carolina and Angelo started arguing with her.

Sofia opened her door. "I don't know how I feel about the Santinis at the moment, but I need time on my own to think. Please, go." She climbed out and shut the door.

Carolina lowered her window. "At least let me ring Nico? Someone should be with you.

"Fine." Sofia watched them drive away, then she unwound the chain from the old gates. After slipping through, she ambled up the weed-infested drive. This magnificent *villa* was hers, but how could she stay to restore it?

Her heart was heavy. Her dreams lay in tatters.

Closing the heavy front door, Sofia wandered round the old *villa* and tried to imagine what it must have been like forty or fifty years ago when her father and aunt were small. She turned in a slow circle, her gaze taking in the ornate ceilings and staircase, the large rooms that were now full of light. It would have been a wonderful home for children to grow up in. She threw the set of keys and her bag on the bottom step, then taking the key Signora Rinaldi had given her. A key that might well be at the heart of her conspiracy, Sofia wandered into the large drawing room to start her search.

CHAPTER EIGHTEEN

After some intense negotiating to buy the hotel in *Venezia*, Riccardo arrived home to find Nico and Carolina having a heated argument in the study. He pulled off his tie and tossed it on the desk. "What's going on?"

Neither spoke.

Riccardo stilled. "Where's Sofia?"

"She wanted to be alone. I may have said the wrong thing to her," mumbled Carolina.

"You think!" Nico almost spat the words out."

Riccardo raised an eyebrow. "What exactly did you say, Carolina?"

"I told her you're not into long term relationships, and *Papà* backed me up."

Riccardo exhaled and strolled round his desk. "I will speak to her."

"There's more." Nico threw himself into an armchair, his expression thunderous.

Riccardo sat and glanced at Carolina. "Go on."

"I told Sofia about Marianna. Sofia couldn't believe you would do that to your brother."

Riccardo looked at her in amazement. "You told Sofia about Marianna? Are you mad?"

"I also mentioned your cynical view of marriage and monogamous relationships."

A chill ran down Riccardo's spine. "How did Sofia react to this information?" He could barely contain his anger.

"Not good." Carolina swallowed. "I'm sorry."

Jaw clenched, Riccardo stared at her. "Is there anything else I should know?"

Carolina nodded. "Sofia wanted to know if we wanted to break her heart, like Ariana broke Guiseppe's heart—"

"And what?" roared Riccardo, his temper igniting.

Carolina flinched. "Sofia said she should have guessed you would resort to such underhanded behavior and a relationship with you wouldn't work because of your ethics."

Riccardo stood then rubbed his forehead as he tried to think of a way to mend things with Sofia. "Where is she now?"

Carolina looked down at her feet. "At Villa DeRosa. She said she wanted to be on her own for a while, and she'd walk back through the vines."

Riccardo opened his mouth then shut it again as icy fear speed through his veins. He focused on Carolina. "After everything that's happened, you left her there, alone? *Santa Maria*, are you serious?"

When Carolina didn't answer, he swore. "*Merde.* How long ago did you leave her?"

"A couple of hours," mumbled Carolina.

Shrugging out of his jacket, Riccardo dropped it on the chair. "Ring Giovanni; he's on his way here. Tell him to meet me at Villa DeRosa." He stalked to the door, wrenched it open, then stopped and looked over his shoulder. "The way things keep happening to Sofia, you'd better pray she's okay, for all our sakes."

Two hours of searching from the cellar to the attics failed to produce a door the key would fit and Sofia conceded defeat. Out of ideas and disheartened, she stood in the attic wondering if perhaps one of the many tenants had found her prize. Thirty years was a long time. She was staring out over the gnarled vines when creaking from a lower floor impinged on her thoughts. Figuring Carolina had come looking for her, Sofia went to meet her.

She stopped at the second floor landing and peered over the banister to the entrance foyer below. The front door stood wide open but there was no sign of Carolina.

"Hello?" She leaned over the railing then waited, listening.

Nothing. Somebody had to have opened the door, why weren't they responding?

A shiver of unease ran down her spine and the hair at the back of her neck stood on end. Backing away from the banister, her uneasiness grew.

A soft creak sounded behind her.

Sofia reeled and collided with a large man in black.

He shoved her and she slammed into the banister, jarring her whole body. Panic surged as a man in a balaclava reached for her throat. Sofia knocked his hands away, kicked out hard, and tried to push past him.

He snarled, caught her by the hair, and hauled her back. She cried out at the searing pain. Terror replaced her pain as his arm locked around her throat. She swung her elbow as hard as she could into his stomach and smashed her heel into his instep just as Dante had taught her. Her attacker howled and his hold slipped enough for Sofia to twist around and hit him in the face with the key.

The man pushed her back against the banister. He was strong. She screamed for all she was worth, lashing out with her right hand, backhanding him across the cheek. He roared as the ring dug into his cheek and drew blood. He had her pinned between him and the banister. Her fury gave her strength. She screamed her rage and gouged at his eyes with the key and her fingers.

Her assailant yelled then hit her in the side of the head, stunning her. His hands engulfed her neck. She clawed at his fingers, fighting for her life.

The man's hands eased, but her moment of relief was short lived. She screamed for all she was worth.

Sofia's scream had Riccardo sprinting up the steps of the old villa. He exploded into the foyer to witness a man trying to strangle Sofia.

"No!" Riccardo roared and mounted the stairs.

The assailant lifted Sofia, his intention clear.

A bolt like lightning pierced Riccardo. He hurtled back down, the adrenaline pumping as he leapt the bannister to break her fall. Her weight knocked them to marble floor in a tangle of legs and arms.

"Sofia." He clutched her trembling body to his chest.

"Riccardo," Sofia sobbed, her fingernails digging into his skin.

"I have you." Riccardo wrapped his arms around her, stroking her back as his gaze searched the upper level. It was empty.

Running footsteps drew his attention to the front door. Giovanni bounded up the steps and into the foyer. "*Santa Maria*, what's happened?" he knelt beside them.

Fear swept Sofia face before she pushed Riccardo away and threw herself at Giovanni, sobbing into his chest.

Riccardo closed his eyes. For the first time in his life he didn't know what to do. "Sofia, talk to me."

"Go away."

Riccardo met Giovanni's gaze. "A man was on the landing trying to strangle Sofia. When I yelled and started up the stairs, he picked her up and threw her over. I broke her fall."

Giovanni looked up at the landing then back to Riccardo in astonishment. "Did you recognize him?"

"No, he wore a balaclava. I couldn't go after him and leave Sofia alone, but I'd like to kill him when I find him."

Giovanni nodded. "You take Sofia and I'll search upstairs. He's probably gone, but we should still check."

Sofia shook her head and clung to Giovanni. "No, I don't want him to touch me."

Standing, Riccardo met Giovanni's gaze over Sofia's head. It was bad enough that someone wanted her dead, but to lose Sofia's respect because of a bitch like Marianna was incomprehensible. "You stay with Sofia while I look around."

He did a thorough search, finding nothing but an open upstairs window. When he leaned out he could see the broken bougainvillea where someone had descended in a hurry. He supposed it was one consolation. The attacker's hands would be cut to pieces from the thorns. He searched the garden and nearby vineyard and found no trace of the man.

When he returned to the foyer, Sofia was sitting on the bottom step with Giovanni and wouldn't meet his eyes. "I'll take you home, *cara mia*," he said quietly.

She kept her eyes on the floor and shook her head. "I'm going back with Giovanni, and tomorrow I'm moving to my grandparents' house in Ravenna. I don't want to be engaged to you anymore."

Riccardo almost growled in frustration. "Sofia, I know you've had a shock this afternoon, and you're angry because of what Carolina told you, but they don't know the whole story. You promised me, if you ever heard anything terrible about me, you would give me the chance to explain. You promised not to judge me like everyone judged your father."

Sofia was torn. She had promised, but Riccardo could seduce her into believing anything. She was so weak when it came to him, and even with everything that had happened, she still wanted to run into his arms. *I love him.*

Realizing he was waiting for her to answer, Sofia stood. "I'm going back with Giovanni. If you want to talk to me, then it will have to be tomorrow before I leave."

Giovanni put his hand on Riccardo's shoulder. "Let it go for now, bro. I'll take Sofia home while you contact the police. She can tell us what she knows later."

Sofia huffed. "I know plenty." She lifted her chin defiantly. "Someone I was beginning to care for isn't the man I thought him. *Signora* Rinaldi's accident was a deliberate attack, and her house was burgled while she was in hospital. Oh, and Carolina and I were nearly run down by a dumpster bin as we left my grandparents' house.

Riccardo and Giovanni began speaking in Italian.

Sofia held up her hand. "Ask your father or Carolina. They will tell you what happened. I just want to be left alone. I would appreciate it if one of you could organize security for my grandparents and *Signora* Rinaldi until Dante arrives. May we please leave now?"

Giovanni raised an eyebrow at Riccardo then followed Sofia to his car. They left Riccardo to lock the front door and follow.

As they approached the gate of the Santini vineyard, a police car turned in ahead of them. Coincidentally they'd come to speak to Sofia about her earlier attack. After giving a statement, Sofia escaped to Riccardo's room where she found Carolina waiting.

"I'm sorry. I didn't mean to upset you. Riccardo does care for you..." She leaned closer, staring at Sofia's neck. "Are they bruises?"

Sofia nodded. "It's a long story. Riccardo can tell you what happened and you can tell him about our visit to Ravenna. I'm moving into a guestroom and I'd like to be left alone."

"If that's what you want." Carolina was nearly to the door when Sofia called out. "It wasn't the same man as the one at the hospital. This one didn't have tattoos on his knuckles. Oh, and here's your ring." Sofia held out the ring to Carolina.

Taking it, Carolina blinked. "What's this stuck on it?"

Sofia shrugged. "It could be dried blood. A man attacked me, and I tried to defend myself by gouging him with the ring."

"What!"

"Please, Carolina, I'm tired. Ask Riccardo or Giovanni."

"Sure. You rest and I'll see you in the morning. I'll give this ring to the police. They may be able to get DNA off it." She hesitated. "I am sorry about what I said. Riccardo is a good man and he does care for you."

Sofia didn't answer; instead she turned to the chest of drawers and began pulling out her clothes. She heard the door shut as Carolina left the room. *Riccardo may care, but a leopard doesn't change his spots.*

Standing with his back to Giovanni and Nico, Riccardo stared out the French doors. His temper hung by a thread. Panic he'd never experienced seared his soul at the thought of Sofia's close call and then her rejection. Fear of what she might do now clung like a heavy fog. How could he keep her safe?

What can I do to stop her leaving?

The door opened and Riccardo turned to see Carolina hovering, a worried expression on her face. She bit her lip and stepped into the room. "Someone deliberately poured detergent on *Signora* Rinaldi's back steps, which is why she fell, and while she was in the hospital her house was burgled." She hesitated as if deciding what to divulge. "They may have been looking for the contents of an envelope *Signora* Rinaldi gave Sofia."

Riccardo's gaze shot to Giovanni and Nico whose eyes mirrored his own alarm. "How many attempts on her life before he succeeds? I want this madman caught?"

No one answered. He ran his hands through his hair then glanced at Carolina. "What was in the envelope?"

"An old fashioned key and a poem, but there's more. After we left Sofia's grandparents' house, a huge dumpster came out of nowhere and nearly ran us down."

Riccardo's head snapped up. "How is that possible?"

"Her grandparents live on a street that isn't completely level."

Riccardo cursed. "I meant, how did it happen? Did you see anyone lurking around?

"No, there was no one."

Riccardo picked up the key he'd found at the old villa. "Is this the key?"

"*Sì.*"

Giovanni came over to examine it. "It's too big to fit a normal door. I'd say it opens a gate, like the ones leading into mausoleums."

Carolina's eyes lit. "Maybe Sofia's aunt hid the evidence in the family mausoleum."

"It's worth checking," agreed Riccardo. "But first, tell me exactly what you said to Sofia, then Giovanni can tell you about the latest attack while I speak to the police. I need to organize security for Sofia's grandparents as I'm away on business tomorrow."

"Wait!" Carolina leapt forward, holding a ring between her finger and thumb. "Sofia was wearing this when she was attacked, and there's blood on it."

Riccardo reached for the ring, careful to avoid touching the setting. He, Giovanni, and Nico examined it closely.

"Where did she get a ring like this?" asked Giovanni. "It's got to be worth a fortune."

"Of course it's worth a fortune. It belongs to an order I received yesterday. She liked this one best and was trying it on when *Papà* arrived. We got side-tracked and Sofia forgot to take it off."

Riccardo examined the ring again. "She liked this one the best, you say?"

"Yes, and we didn't realize she still had it on until her grandmother spied it and said you must love her very much to buy her such an expensive ring."

The room went oddly quiet then Giovanni turned to Riccardo. "There's skin tissue on the ring. It will make it easier to identify Sofia's attacker."

Carolina sniffed. "Sofia said it was a different man. He didn't have tattoos on his knuckles."

Giovanni looked to Riccardo. "That's three men that we know of."

A cry escaped Carolina. "The bruises on her neck are awful and it's my fault. If I hadn't said anything about Marianna, none of this would have happened."

Nico put his arm around her shoulders. "It's done, Caro, and it's best if everything is out in the open. Don't worry about Riccardo, he can smooth talk his way out of anything."

Riccardo's gut twisted. Smooth talking would not work this time. Not with Sofia.

"Are you all right?" Giovanni was frowning at him.

"I'm fine. Before I speak to the police, bring us up to date on your visit to Plymouth."

Giovanni opened a notebook. "The couple who witnessed Renzina DeRosa's accident are English and were on their honeymoon. They'd stopped for a picnic at a lookout and were admiring the view below when they saw a dark blue Mercedes chasing a pale colored Fiat and ramming it. They claim they watched him make numerous attempts to force the Fiat off the road and when he finally did, he drove away."

Silence filled the room as they stared at each other, then Riccardo paced to his chair and sat. "We need to know who in this area drove a dark blue Mercedes around that time and whether any such vehicle was repaired due to a frontal collision with a pale Fiat."

"I'll take care of that." Nico picked up his jacket and left the study.

Riccardo looked at Carolina. "It is probably best if we give Sofia a little time to herself. If she doesn't come down to dinner, take a tray up to her, and give her back this key." He stood and passed it to Carolina. "Let me know how she is."

"*Sì.*" She hurried out.

Giovanni moved to sit in the armchair opposite the desk. "You obviously care for Sofia. How are you going to get around her father and brother?"

Grimacing, Riccardo stood and paced. "I have to get around Sofia first. Thanks to Carolina's efforts, I'm now on the back foot." He sighed. "If I can repair the damage, I will then decide how to tackle Sofia's father and brother."

"All right. Let me know if I can do anything to help. I'm staying here tonight, but I'm happy to speak to Sofia about Marianna for you."

"Thanks." Riccardo rubbed his eyes. "I'll speak to the police now."

Once the police left, Riccardo spent the evening formatting a plan. He would take Sofia with him to *Venezia*, where she'd be safe, and he could explain about Marianna.

It was late by the time Riccardo caught up on emails and dealt with any urgent matters. He closed his diary then swivelled the chair to stare out into the darkness, considering his next move. A soft click had him glancing at the door, hoping.

Carolina crossed the room and gave him a tentative smile. "You look disappointed to see me." She perched on the desk beside him. "I saw you talking to *Papà* in the garden earlier. Is everything all right?"

"When *Papà* didn't turn up for dinner, I went searching for him. He was down in the rose garden pruning and had forgotten the time. I was looking for him because I wanted to check his arms and hands. They were covered in scratches."

"*Papà's* hands are always covered in scratches, Riccardo."

He grimaced. "I can't figure out who would do these atrocious deeds, and now I'm reduced to suspecting my own father."

Carolina rubbed his shoulder. "This is what it must have been like thirty years ago. *Papà* unable to believe Giuseppe DeRosa was gambling and whoring, and Giuseppe thinking *Papà* had set him up. No one, not even his parents, believed in his innocence."

"Exactly." Riccardo sighed. "It's like someone's trying to set us up this time. The rumors about our money problems are growing and every time something happens to Sofia, she is in our care. It's frustrating the hell out of me. What if I fail to protect her?"

Carolina bit her lip. "Sofia's suitcase is packed. There was a notepad on the bed and she'd made lots of notes. I think she plans to sneak away tonight or tomorrow morning and I'm scared something will happen to her."

Riccardo leaned his head back against the chair. "I'll talk to her again when I go up."

"I don't know how. She's moved into the guestroom and the door is locked."

"What?" He bounded out of his chair, brushing past Carolina on the way to the door.

"Riccardo, you can't go waking the whole house when she refuses to open the door."

He stopped, his lips twitched. "There is another way."

"What are you planning, Riccardo?"

"Where are the keys to the upstairs terrace doors?"

Her eyes widened. "You wouldn't?"

"Yes, I would, Carolina. Weren't you the one who told Sofia I will do whatever it takes to protect our family and our name?"

"Yes, but what has that to do with gaining entry to Sofia's room?"

"I plan to make Sofia part of this family."

Carolina stared at him. "You're going to ask her to marry you, for real?" She slid off the desk and began jigging on the spot, then stopped and frowned. "But how? She's not happy with you at the moment, and I thought you had to go to *Venezia* tomorrow?"

"She's coming with me. I expect her brother to arrive within the next twenty-four hours, so I need the right setting to fix things with Sofia."

"What if she refuses to go with you?"

"Then I will kidnap her. I need you to pack her overnight bag with enough clothes to get her through a couple of days, and do it without her knowledge."

"How am I supposed to do that, Riccardo? She's not likely to leave her room, is she?"

"Give me fifteen minutes. I will convince Sofia to return to my room. Then you can go in and throw some things together and leave them in the study. It's very important you don't tell anyone where I've taken her."

"What if she refuses to go to your room? You can't drag her there."

"I will carry her, kicking and screaming, if necessary. Where are the keys kept?"

CHAPTER NINETEEN

Gritty-eyed from lack of sleep and tears, Sofia rolled over and dragged a pillow to her chest. She couldn't stop her racing mind, but at least she had a new strategy. Come dawn she would ring for a taxi, then take her suitcase and sneak through the vineyard, avoiding the security guard at the gates. Pick up point would be Villa DeRosa. She would leave a note implying she was going home and thanking the Santinis for their hospitality. Then she would hunt down the supposed witnesses who claimed her father owed them money.

A soft squeak impinged on Sofia's thoughts. She squinted across the dark bedroom at the locked door, barely breathing.

A rustle from behind set her pulse pounding loudly in her head. Heat flooded her body. Her breath came in shallow gasps. Someone had entered her room via the French doors, which could only mean one thing.

With her heart in her mouth, Sofia twisted onto her knees. *Shit.*

A shadowy figure loomed over her. She tried to scream but only managed a strangled croak as she fell off the bed.

The silhouette leapt after her, his large body pining her to the floor. Sofia clawed at her attacker, but he managed to capture her hands and force them back beside her shoulders.

"Shush, it's me, Riccardo."

Sofia stilled at the sound of his voice, drew in a shaky breath, and was assailed by his cologne. Her body calmed at the familiar tingle of his touch. "You scared me."

"I didn't think you'd open the door to me, and I needed to know you were all right."

Sofia squirmed. They were joined much too intimately. "I'm fine. Now, if there's nothing else you need, I'd like you to leave."

"Oh, but there is." His lips captured hers, taking her breath, sending her wits into a spin and her treacherous body dancing in jubilation. This was why she'd locked the door.

Riccardo kept kissing Sofia until she softened and molded to him. It humbled him that she still desired him, even in such a panicked state. He released her wrists as he brushed kisses across her face then down the length of her neck. When he heard her soft moan he exulted. "I was worried about you, *cara mia*. Why aren't you in my room? You know that's where you belong."

She flinched and Riccardo cursed himself for his wording.

"Get off me. I don't want you."

"That isn't true. Are you coming back to my bed of your own free will or not?"

"No, I'm not."

"Very well." Riccardo climbed off her then pulled her to her feet and paced to the door.

"You're really going?" she sounded suspicious.

Flicking the light switch, Riccardo unlocked the door and glanced back. The sight of her in her short silky negligée sent his blood in one direction. Her nipples strained against the silky fabric and aside from her bruises, her skin was flushed delicately. Another indication she was lying.

She eyed him warily then turned to the bed. "Please switch the light off as you leave."

She'd lifted one knee onto the bed by the time Riccardo crossed the room and locked an arm around her.

"What are—"

He clamped a hand over her mouth then touched his lips to her ear. "You will come to my room, Sofia. I refuse to leave you alone when there's a lunatic out there trying to kill you. Now stop struggling and be a good girl."

She tried to shove her elbows into him and kick at him with her bare feet. He neatly hauled her off the floor and more firmly against him then strode to his room.

Closing the door with his foot, he carried her to the bed and fell across it. "You have two choices, *tesoro*. *Numero uno*, you can behave and we will get a good night's sleep. Or, *numero due,* you can fight, rant and rave, in which case I will have to take measures to ensure you have other things to think about, which will also result in us eventually sleeping. It is your choice. What will it be?"

Sofia glared then slowly nodded her head. Riccardo pulled his hand away from her mouth. "Number one," she muttered.

Riccardo chuckled. "*Numero uno* it is. But if you change your mind, please let me know." He climbed off the bed, pulled his shirt out and unbuttoned it.

Sofia pushed herself up on her elbows, her beautiful eyes following his every move.

He dropped his shirt over the chair, then looked up to find her eyes downcast and shoulders hunched.

"Sofia, *cara mia*. This is for your protection."

She drew in a deep breath and released it just as slowly before raising her eyes. "In that case, can I have my toiletry bag from the guest room?" Her voice had a flat, forlorn ring to it.

His bullying tactics weren't doing him any favors, but this was where she was safest. "Do you need it right now?"

"Yes, if it's no trouble?"

Unsettled, Riccardo left the bedroom. He'd only taken a couple of steps down the hall when he heard the key turn in the lock behind him. "What the—"

"I hope that teaches you a lesson, you egotistical, fiancée stealer," Sofia yelled through the door.

Riccardo tried the handle. "Sofia, open this door."

"No," came the muffled reply. "Go to the guest room. You're not sleeping with me."

Riccardo hammered on the door. "If you know what's good for you, Sofia, you will open this door immediately. I will not be locked out of my own room."

"Go away. I'm not sleeping with you ever again."

"The hell you're not. If you don't open this door now, I'm going to—"

"Riccardo, what in heaven's name is going on?"

He swung around to see his mother and father emerging from

their bedroom at the end of the hall. Two more doors opened then Nico and Giovanni stepped into the hall.

"What's all the noise?" called Nico.

Riccardo let out a frustrated growl. "Sofia's locked me out of my room. She told me to sleep in the guest room."

His mother laughed. "Then I suggest you do as she says and stop pounding on the door. We would like to get some sleep."

Riccardo clenched his fists as his parents returned to their room. He heard Nico laughing as he too closed his door.

"Like hell." Riccardo stalked past Giovanni to the guest room. He snatched up the keys he'd used to enter Sofia's room, then as an afterthought went into the bathroom and picked up her toiletry bag. "Two can play this game, *cara mia.*"

Sofia climbed back into Riccardo's huge bed and snuggled down amongst the pillows, smiling in satisfaction. "That will teach you, Riccardo Santini."

She was still congratulating herself when she heard a key inserted into the terrace doors. "Oh no you don't." She leapt out of bed, but before she reached the doors, they opened and she found herself captured in strong, unyielding arms.

Riccardo tossed her over his shoulder. "I will not be locked out of my own room, my little actress." He chuckled. "Plus, I need to keep you close so I can protect you."

"Fine, sleep here, and just so you know, I don't want you."

"Is that so? Tell me why?"

Sofia thumped his back, blinking rapidly to ward off her stupid tears. "Because I can't give myself to you and then watch you walk away. Please, let me go before I...before I start caring too much."

Riccardo gently lowered her to the floor. "I think it's a bit late for that, *cara mia.* You already care for me very much."

Sofia bit her lip and this time the tears welled and spilled onto her cheeks. "I can't believe I have this much water inside my body." She looked away.

Riccardo softly gripped her chin and turned her face to him. He wiped the tears away then kissed her eyelids. "I didn't sleep with Marianna. However, I did infer she should be marrying me. Marianna immediately offered to drop Giovanni and confessed there was no baby. Giovanni heard every word so he called the wedding off. It may have been underhanded, but she was a gold digger and would have hurt my brother."

Sofia chewed her lip. "How do I know you're telling me the truth?"

"You don't. I can only ask you to believe me, like you believe your father, or you can ask Giovanni. Now, let's get some sleep. I have a meeting in *Venezia* tomorrow and you are coming with me. It will be necessary for us to leave early."

I love Venice. She pouted. "Fine, but don't think for one moment I'm happy about this."

Riccardo shrugged off the rest of his clothes. When he turned back to the bed he couldn't help but grin. Sofia lay under the covers on the far side of the bed. He picked up the sheet, then slid to the middle and reached out, drawing her against his chest. "I'll sleep much better now, *cara mia.*"

Sofia huffed. "Stop calling me that. I want you to sleep on the other side of the bed."

"It's not about what you want, *tesoro.* It's about what I want, and I always get what I want. Now, you can give in and sleep or let me teach you some more about the pleasures available to us."

"I'm going to sleep. Goodnight."

"*Buonanotte, cara mia. Sogni d'oro*, which means dreams of gold, or as you would say sweet dreams."

Sofia huffed and closed her eyes. It had been a day of highs and lows. She was bruised physically and mentally, and didn't know how much more she could endure.

Riccardo's powerful arms gentled around her and Sofia began to relax as a sense of safety enveloped her. *I am such an idiot. He will break my heart.*

She awoke to find Riccardo gone, and the clothes she'd laid out in the guest room on the armchair beside her. He wasn't joking when he said he planned to leave early. Sofia threw the covers back and stretched her sore body, then slid off the bed and padded into the bathroom.

After attending to nature's call, she glanced at her reflection in the mirror and gasped at the angry bruises around her throat. Dropping her thin straps off her shoulders, she let her chemise slip to the floor and raised her eyes to the mirror again. She had yellowing bruises down her side and over her knee. If Dante saw them he would go berserk.

Turning on the shower, she stepped under the warm water, closing her eyes as it soothed her sore body. She had just turned off the shower and was reaching for a towel as the door opened. Sofia screeched and pulled, but the towel caught on the hook. Naked and hot with embarrassment, she tugged on the towel as she looked over her shoulder.

Riccardo stood in the doorway fully dressed with one eyebrow raised. "Do you need help, *cara mia*?"

"No." She yanked the towel again.

Riccardo reached out as if to unhook it then stilled. "*Merde.*" His hands fisted as his furious gaze skimmed her body. "When I find the man responsible for those bruises, I will beat the bastard to a pulp then string him by his balls." He drew her into his arms.

"I'm soaking, Riccardo. I'll ruin your suit."

He lifted her mass of wet hair aside then kissed her neck and shoulder. Sofia shivered and arched her neck, giving him better access. His chuckle tickled her as he kissed his way down further, then across her breast to the nipple, closing his mouth around it and sucking gently.

Sofia moaned. She was caught in an emotional whiplash warp. One minute she hated him, then wanted him. At this very moment she needed his hands and lips on her. She thrust her breasts further toward him. "Don't stop."

He pulled away, stared at her for several seconds, then scooped her into his arms and paced to the bed. A thrill raced through Sofia as he laid her down then shrugged out of his suit jacket and threw it, uncaring of where it landed. He clasped her ankles and dragged her closer.

"I want to taste you again, *tesoro.*"

Sofia swallowed. "I don't think that's a good idea."

A slow smile spread across his face. "I think it's one of the best ideas I've ever had." He pushed her thighs wide and, before she could react, dropped to his knees.

The impact of his mouth closing over her ripped a cry of pleasure from Sofia's throat. He probed and tormented with his tongue then pushed a finger deep inside her, retreated then pushed back harder and faster. He added another finger and increased the momentum as he licked and suckled. Lifting her hips to meet him, she shuddered as an inferno of desperation built inside her.

"Riccardo, I'm…"

"Let go." Riccardo's breath tickled her already inflamed body. "You are so wet, *cara mia*." He sucked hard and Sofia cried out as ecstasy flooded her veins. She jerked then stiffened, tremors running from where his tongue still circled, all the way down her legs. He continued to thrust his fingers inside her and she cried out again as another orgasm hit.

Riccardo smiled, crawled onto the bed, and pulled her boneless body into his arms. He kissed her lips, giving her a taste of her own essence.

"I want to do much more to you, *tesoro*, but not here, not now. Get dressed, you have twenty minutes."

"Twenty minutes," mumbled Sofia against his chest. "Not after that." She shook her head. "I'm lethargic and it's your fault."

"Come, Sofia, move your pretty ass. I'll use the guest bathroom." He pulled her to the side of the bed. "Nineteen minutes and counting."

"My hair's wet."

Riccardo stepped away, picked up his jacket, and headed for the door. "Eighteen minutes," he called closing the door behind him.

"Arrrgh." Sofia jumped to her feet, grabbed her clothes, and ran to the bathroom. She had another quick shower to revive. She was dressed and tying her hair in a band when Riccardo entered the bedroom, looking less strained than when he'd left.

Sofia adjusted her skirt slightly and brushed past him. "I'm ready except for cleaning my teeth," she called and returned to the bathroom.

Riccardo chuckled. "I was teasing about the twenty minutes, but it's good to know you're a woman who doesn't take forever to get ready." He looked at his watch. "Ten minutes. I'm impressed."

They left the house before anyone was about and Sofia's spirits lifted higher when Riccardo opened the garage door, revealing his Aston Martin.

"Can I drive?" She ran her fingers lovingly over the boot.

"No, you may not." Riccardo held the passenger door open for her.

Sofia huffed and sat. "How long will it take to get to Venice?"

"Most of the morning. I am taking you via the scenic route with a stop for breakfast and lunch along the way." He expelled a breath. "The negotiations for the hotel we are trying to buy have hit a snag, so the meeting may last several hours."

Riccardo shut the door and walked around to his side. Sofia waited until he was backing out of the garage, before she asked her next question. "What am I expected to do while you are in your meeting?"

Riccardo smiled. "Wait for me in a stunning room overlooking the Grand Canal. You will not be bored."

She watched the scenery rush past for a little while then turned her attention to Riccardo and his very capable hands. "You drive well. A little fast, but well."

"Thank you, *cara mia*. Giovanni, Nico, and I belong to the Italian Car Club and a couple of times a year we go to the national autodrome at Monza to race each other."

"You race cars, like the ones in the Grand Prix?"

He laughed. "No. We drive our own cars and we race each other's times."

Sofia eased back in her seat. "What else do you do for fun, jump out of planes?"

"I have jumped out of planes, although not recently. These days I'm too busy running the company with Giovanni. As for fun... I am *Italiano*. I love football. I ski in winter and sail in summer. I like to work out, but with business commitments and the responsibility of running the vineyards and hotels, that's really all I have time for. What about you, Sofia? What do you do back in Australia?"

"I'm the office manager for our vineyard in Victoria. Like you, I ski in winter, and I spend a lot of time at a riding stable close by. I used to have a part time job there when I was younger, teaching children to ride or minding babies while their mothers rode."

He smiled. "That explains why you were so good with the baby at the airport."

"Oh, he was just cranky. I think his big sisters were giving him a headache."

Riccardo glanced at her. "Why are you not married with babies of your own?"

"If you knew my father and brother you wouldn't ask that question. Men don't stick around once they've been read the riot act. *Papà* is bad enough, but Dante is a force to be reckoned with. Their favorite saying is *'la mia famiglia è tutto.'*"

Riccardo translated. "My family is everything. I can't blame them for wanting to keep the wolves away from you, Sofia. They have my gratitude."

"Oh," was all Sofia could think to say. She studied his profile. If anyone was a wolf, it was Riccardo Santini. Even now he looked like he was planning his next meal. *And I'm it.*

After croissants and coffee at a café on the outskirts of Bologna, Riccardo bypassed the autostrada and took Sofia on a leisurely drive through country roads, and small towns, eventually stopping at Vincenza. They strolled the old quarter as he told her a little of the city's history before turning into Corso Palladio, a street of boutiques and street cafés. Sofia chose a quaint little café run by a ruddy faced, rotund Italian, where they ordered a simple meal of cheeses, grilled vegetables, and polenta—dishes famous in this region.

Sofia was people watching when Riccardo reached across and brushed a loose curl behind her ear. "It doesn't take much to make you happy, does it, *tesoro*?"

She shrugged. "Bringing me on this scenic route and showing me round Vicenza was very nice of you, Riccardo. You've given me a lot of pleasure today and I've thoroughly enjoyed it." She leaned over and kissed his cheek.

Riccardo pulled her back for a real kiss, leaving her breathless. "So, you enjoyed *everything* I've done for you today?" One eyebrow rose.

Heat rushed into her cheeks and she glanced around quickly. "Yes, even that."

Laughing, Riccardo stood and extended his hand. "Come, *cara mia*, it is time we left."

With a sigh, Sofia gave him her hand. "Very well. Thank you again for such a lovely morning and that delicious lunch."

"It is my pleasure, Sofia. The day is young, I wonder what other delights I can come up with?"

Chapter Twenty

Sofia arrived in Venice or *Venezia* as preferred by Italians, much more stylishly than her previous visit five years ago. Riccardo parked the Aston Martin in a secure parking station then surprised Sofia by leaving his keys with the attendant.

"Isn't that a bit risky?" she asked, eyeing his beautiful car.

"No, and I want it washed."

Sofia glanced back. "It's not dirty, Riccardo."

"Come, Sofia, you worry too much." He hailed a water taxi and reached for her hand. "The best way to see *Venezia* is via the Grand Canal. Would you agree?"

"Oh yes." Sofia knew she was grinning from ear to ear, but she could scarcely believe she was in Venice, and in the company of a sexy man like Riccardo. *A Santini.* She pushed the unsettling thought away, sat back, and absorbed the water traffic and elaborate architecture of the buildings along the Canal.

The taxi drew in beside a set of worn steps at *Piazza San Marco*, and, after paying the fare, Riccardo took Sofia's hand again as they strolled across the square.

He indicated an empty table at an outdoor cafe. "We have time for coffee if you would like to soak up the atmosphere and watch dozens of pigeons descend on unwary tourists.

"Sure." Having previously been to *Piazza San Marco* with Carolina, Sofia knew first hand what it was like to be on the receiving end of those fat little pigeons, but she didn't want to lose Riccardo's company just yet. For the first time in a week she felt safe and although that had a lot to do with Riccardo's company, she knew they hadn't been followed. Perhaps due to the fact, he'd taken such a roundabout way of getting here. They would have noticed if someone was tailing them.

After finishing their coffees, they strolled through the twisting alleys and over quaint little bridges until they came to the Rialto Bridge, which they crossed, then ambled along the other side of the Grand Canal.

Smiling serenely, Sofia studied Riccardo covertly every chance she got. He seemed to enjoy playing the role of tourist guide as he held her hand and gave her a running commentary on the city of canals and its history.

Glancing at his watch, Riccardo relinquished Sofia's hand and pointed to the magnificent hotel in front of them. "That is the hotel we are negotiating to buy. It is owned by the Bocellis who would like nothing better than to sell it to my family."

"So what's the stumbling block?" Sofia's gaze drifted over the gorgeous building.

"The ownership of the hotel is divided between several parties. Two are keen to sell, but the one with the controlling share isn't. She is the widow of the Bocellis' eldest son."

"Maybe she wants to pass it on to her children."

"They didn't have children. I have been told she is stubborn, strong willed, and Australian. Several traits you have in common with her."

"Ha, ha." Sofia punched him lightly in the chest. "I bet she's a sensible and intelligent woman who knows exactly what she wants."

"Giovanni is taking over the negotiations and will attempt to change her mind. She has agreed to come to Italy in the near future for a family board meeting of which he will attend."

Sofia laughed. "Ah yes. Giovanni is the diplomat of the family. I hope she gives him a run for his money."

Riccardo's lips twitched. "While I am in the meeting I would like you to stay in the hotel. I will give you my cell number in case you need me."

Sofia looked longingly down the canal. "Can't I explore a little? I won't go far and it's not like anyone knows I'm here with you."

"That is true. Other than Carolina, who I have sworn to secrecy, no one knows we are in *Venezia together*, yet the risk is too great. I'm sorry, Sofia, it's—"

"Please? I love this city and I missed seeing a couple of places last time. I promise not to go anywhere lonely."

He sighed. "What do you wish to see?"

"Giardini Papadopoli. I've never been to *Venenzia's* Botanical gardens, and I can take a water taxi there and back."

"On one condition. You let me organize for a porter to shadow you?"

"Riccardo."

"My phone is off, so if you notice anyone suspicious ask the porter to ring the hotel straight away."

"Fine."

"Do you need cash for the taxi?"

Sofia shook her head. "I have money, Riccardo. Now you go to your meeting or you'll be late, and don't worry about me. I know my way around *Venezia* better than you think."

He smiled. "That's right, this was your hideout wasn't it? Very well, give me a minute to find a porter, and don't forget six o'clock in the hotel foyer."

"Va bene." Sofia waited in the elaborate foyer of the grand old hotel while Riccardo spoke to the concierge. Soon after, a burly middle-aged man who looked more like a security guard than a porter joined her.

"Buongiorno, signorina. Mi chiamo Alfredo.

"Buongiorno, Alfredo. Mi chiamo Sofia. Let's go. *Andiamo."* She waved to Riccardo then led the way to the nearest water taxi where she found a Venetian man only too happy to take her to the Botanical Gardens.

Sofia leaned on the boats edge and watched the activity along the Grand Canal. She would have loved an evening jaunt in a gondola, serenaded by a *gondoliere.* Perhaps when all this was over Carolina would come here with her, if things worked out.

After spending a couple of hours in Giardini Papadopoli, either walking or sitting on the grass, watching life on the Canal, Sofia decided to walk back to the hotel. Alfredo insisted on staying several meters behind her. Twice she heard him speaking on his phone in a businesslike tone and surmised it was with Riccardo.

Sofia grabbed a map of *Venezia* from the ferry terminal and set off exploring, counting the bridges as she crossed them until she came out on the Grand Canal close to the *Rialto* Bridge. She crossed it and waved to Alfredo as she entered the hotel the Santinis were planning to buy.

As she walked into the hotel's foyer, a smartly dressed man stepped from behind the concierge desk. "*Scusi, signorina, è il suo nome è* Sofia DeRosa?"

Sofia smiled. *I bet Riccardo told this man to look out for a redhead.* "*Sì, signore, sono qui per incontrare il Signor* Santini."

An arm suddenly encircled her from behind and she felt a warm breath close to her ear. "You are a dark horse, Sofia DeRosa. You know more Italian than you let on."

"Telling the concierge I am here to meet you isn't difficult and I can understand more than I speak, as long as people speak slowly."

"I see." He turned her to face him, a smile spread across his handsome face. "I have organized a suite, so you can rest before dinner and freshen up. I still have a couple of things to do then I will take you to a restaurant where they serve a delicious *melanzane parmigiana* with veal *scaloppine.*

Sofia licked her lips. "Yum. Can we please take a gondola?"

"If you wish to take a gondola, who am I to deny you? We shall walk to the restaurant and you can have your ride in a gondola on the way back. And to be safe, I will organize for Alfredo to tail us."

He led her to the staircase and handed her a key. "The suite is on the third floor. I will join you when I'm finished." He gave her a wink and strolled away.

Butterflies fluttered in Sofia's stomach. *He's doing it again, seducing me without even touching me.* She shook her head and climbed the wide stairs.

Sofia opened the suite door and gaped at the sheer size and opulence of the suite. Ornately curtained French doors went from floor to ceiling and opened onto a balcony. A magnificent Venetian glass chandelier hung from a ceiling covered in frescos of maidens barely covered in veils. Two luxurious sofas took up the center of the room with an exquisite parquetry inlaid coffee table between them. Her gaze skimmed over the delicate corner lamps, thick rugs, and artwork depicting everyday life on the Grand Canal before coming to rest on double doors to her left.

She walked over and pushed them open to find an enormous four-poster bed covered in a glorious golden quilt. Delicate white organza hung from the framework, held against the posts with golden ties. Looking up, she found another ornate chandelier and more frescos. Sofia slowly took in the whole room, speechless at the splendor surrounding her.

Her gaze fell on two carry bags sitting on an ottoman by the wall. One looked like hers. She wandered over and unzipped it. The toiletry bag and her emerald cocktail dress confirmed it.

Sofia was still mulling this over as she strolled through the French doors onto the balcony. She came to an abrupt halt, transfixed. Below her was the promenade where people were strolling, enjoying the cool evening. *Gondolieri* sat in their gondolas chatting as they waited for tourists eager to hand over their euros for a romantic cruise through the narrow canals.

Further out, ferries, water taxis, sleek high-powered craft, and barges merged with the *traghetti,* the gondola used by the locals to cross the canal.

It would cost a fortune to stay in a hotel like this. A hotel the Santinis planned to buy. She knew they were wealthy, but had no idea they were *this* wealthy.

She was considering the marvel of *Venezia* and its wonderful buildings, canals, and bridges when a call drew her attention back to the promenade. Three *Gondolieri* were waving and blowing kisses up at her. Sofia laughed, waved back, and then returned to the bedroom. If they weren't staying the night, it seemed silly to take a nap and mess up the bed.

Picking up her emerald dress, underwear, and her toiletry bag, Sofia wandered into the bathroom. It was bigger than her bedroom back home. The walls and floor were lined with marble in a soft shade of green. A large bath took up the center of one wall, and a toilet and glassed shower graced one end. The vanity held an assortment of lotions and toiletries far better in quality than found in the average hotel.

Leaving the door open, Sofia padded across to the vanity. This was seriously beyond anything she'd ever seen in her life. Her gaze returned to the bath. If she had this sort of luxury at her disposal then she might as well make the most of it.

She turned on the taps and poured a delectable smelling concoction into the water. Frothy bubbles instantly formed. "Whoops, that might have been a little too much."

Once the bath was full, Sofia climbed in and relaxed amongst the bubbles. She closed her eyes and dozed lightly, enjoying the sounds of the canal through the open doors. With a shifting of air she sensed another presence and stiffened. Opening her eyes, she gasped as Riccardo, naked, magnificent, and fully aroused sank into the bath.

Sofia grinned as frothy white bubbles formed a beard on his chin.

"Ah, Sofia. How inspiring of you to organize a bath for me."

"I didn't do this for you. I wasn't tired so I decided to enjoy the amenities."

"If you weren't tired why were you asleep?"

"I wasn't asleep, just very relaxed."

He leaned over her until his chest skimmed her breasts, then kissed the corner of her mouth, smiling when she turned her face to chase his lips. "Sofia, you are a dream come true." He evaded her lips by moving to her throat.

A tremor ran through Sofia when his body pressed harder into hers and he feathered light kisses down her neck to her collarbone. His thighs weighed her down, his erection rubbing against her belly as he slid his arms around her waist. Suddenly she was lifted as Riccardo rolled, reversing their positions. Water gushed over the sides and she only just got her mouth closed before he pulled her underwater with him.

Sofia resurfaced with his legs wrapped around hers, holding her captive. She pushed against his chest, gulping in air. "Riccardo, what are you doing?"

"Getting comfortable." He edged back until he was leaning against the end of the bath and gave a sigh of contentment. "What more could a man want than to have a vibrant, beautiful woman with a sinfully seductive body naked and on top of him?"

Sofia was about to argue the danger of being in such a position when he ducked his head and closed his mouth over her nipple. She cried out in rapture and arched her back, pressing her breasts closer. She cried out again when his hand closed over her other breast and molded. Placing her knees either side of his body she eased up, stopping when his erection pressed against the apex of her thighs. Tremors shot through her.

Riccardo eased her back a little and traced her inner thigh from her knee to her curls and cupped her intimately. Sofia moaned and pressed into his hand, rocking against him. He pushed a finger inside her and began stroking. Ecstasy exploded. She writhed and trembled. Her body tightened. He moved his mouth to her other nipple and sucked hard. Sofia cried his name, stiffened, and shuddered violently, climaxing around his fingers.

Several minutes passed as Sofia lay limp against Riccardo's chest, enclosed within his arms. She had neither the desire nor the energy to move. She planned to stay just like this for the rest of her life.

He caressed her lower back in slow circles. "The water is cold, *cara mia*. We should adjourn to the bedroom."

"Hmm."

He chuckled then maneuvered her in his arms, lifting her as he stood, then stepped out of the bath. "I can't let you get a chill, *tesoro*."

"No." Sofia smiled into his shoulder as he carried her to the bedroom, then yanked the covers back and toppled her onto the bed. She licked her lips as life infused her limbs. Her breath caught when he pushed her legs apart and leaned into her. The touch of his hard, lean body molded to her softness was empowering. He wanted her. He really wanted her.

Yes.

His mouth came down hard, capturing her lips in a long thorough kiss. Sofia wrapped her arms around his strong muscled back and ran her hands down smooth skin to his firm butt, then back to his broad shoulders, not caring any longer that she shouldn't let him seduce her. She was in love with Riccardo and if he didn't make love to her now she would surely die. He moved and the thick head of his erection nudge her between the thighs, the contact igniting flames where their body's intimately touched. It was scandalous and she wanted more.

Riccardo deepened the kiss, running his hands down her body to grip her hips. Sofia held her breath. *Yes.* He pressed closer, rubbing his length against her wetness. She moaned and wrapped her legs around him. He lifted slightly and Sofia observed strain on his face, sensed the tension holding him. *What on earth is he worried about? I'm the one that's never done this before.* He pulled further back.

"No." She tried to bring him back.

"Sofia, I'm dangerously close to losing control. You don't want that for your first time."

"No, please, feel free to lose control."

He traced one hand down her outer thigh then back up the inner side and cupped her. Sofia drew in a shuddering breath, shifting restlessly beneath him. She lifted herself, pressing into his hand, and gasped as he thrust a finger inside her, then withdrew it and thrust in again and again. He released her lips and captured a nipple, gently nipping and suckling until Sofia's breast felt heavy and swollen. It was a relief when his hand closed over her other breast, but it wasn't enough.

She cried out in frustration and tightened her legs around him, drunk with passion. A whispered plea escaped her lips. "I really need you to make love to me now, Riccardo."

"Shush, *tesoro,* I don't want to hurt you." He brushed her center with his fingers. "I'll give you what you want soon." He slid his hands beneath her, cupped her bottom and kneaded. His hard, solid length pressed against her.

Desire flowed rich in Sofia's veins, her blood heating as she melted against him, her frustration mounting at his chivalry. "Please, Riccardo, I want you inside me."

She could feel the rigid length of him pressing against her and instinctively pressed closer in utter abandon, her thighs tense and quivering.

"Sofia, you're not helping. Once I take you, there will be no turning back. You will be mine. Do you understand what I'm saying?"

"Yes, stop teasing me. I'm yours, take me." Sofia felt the change in his body, his muscles tightening, and a quiver of excitement raced through her. His lips reclaimed hers in a kiss more ravaging and more demanding than any he'd given her before. She ran her hands over his naked chest, greedily exploring his hard nipples and the muscled plains of his chest.

He raised his head. "Are you sure?"

"Yes," whispered Sofia. "Please."

Riccardo escaped her hold and reached for the condom he'd left on the nightstand, covered his length, then claimed her mouth again. God, how he'd like to take her, skin to skin, but he couldn't risk it, yet. Not until he had her right where he wanted her. He ran his fingers over her smooth hip and thigh, then down over the curls at the junction of her legs. Inserting two fingers, he gently stretched her. She gasped and pushed against his fingers. Riccardo mentally swore. He needed to join with her, now. He withdrew his fingers, pushed her thighs wider, and pressed his cock against her cleft. She trembled under him. He pushed further and she stiffened.

"Riccardo, you're not going to fit."

Clenching his jaw, Riccardo withdrew slightly, exerting extreme effort to harness his desire. "I'll fit, Sofia, just relax." He pressed in again, her honeyed juices helping his progress a little further until he met with her barrier and she tensed again. "Relax, *tesoro*. Trust me."

Sofia's stunning eyes locked with his. "I do trust you." Her gaze fell to his lips. "But if I say stop, you have to stop, *caro mio*?"

Riccardo captured her lips savagely, his self-control waning. He didn't think he would last much longer. Her endearment, the first one she'd uttered, didn't help matters. He pushed in a little further then withdrew slightly and pushed in again. Her sheath closed tightly around him as he moved slowly, back then forward, struggling to stay in control. He deepened the kiss, parting her lips to probe inside her mouth. Her body relaxed and she wrapped her legs around his, pulling him closer to her own body as she met him kiss for kiss.

He began to ease out and she clutched his shoulders. "No, no, Riccardo, don't stop."

His lips twitched. "I'm not stopping *cara mia*. I'm just getting started."

Her bemused eyes met his. Before she could ask her question he thrust back into her haven.

She yelped, her fingernails digging into his shoulders.

Riccardo stilled, the effort nearly killing him. "Are you all right, *cara mia*?"

She nodded, her body tense. He caressed her arm and showered her neck and shoulder with kisses as perspiration gathered on his forehead. She relaxed again, her gaze curious then she wiggled. He needed to think about shares and mergers. *Shit no, not mergers.*

She arched her body into him, her hands sliding down to caress his backside.

Hanging on to his control by a thread, Riccardo dragged in a breath. The little temptress was slaying him and had no idea. He slowly withdrew his throbbing cock from her tight sheath then slid in again. She shuddered under him then met his next thrust. His control snapped. Letting the forces of nature take over, he thrust deep within her slick sheath.

She lifted her hips to meet Riccardo's thrusts. Her breathing was as ragged as his as the crescendo built inside him. She began to tremble. He thrust again and she screamed, her sheath contracting. He thrust again and roared his own climax.

Several minutes passed before Riccardo had the energy to lift off Sofia. He collapsed by her side and pulled her into his arms, sated, complete, and at a loss to rationalize what he felt.

"*Tesoro*," he whispered against her silky hair.

Sofia cuddled closer. "*Ti amo,* Riccardo."

Riccardo blinked several times then raised Sofia's chin so he could see her eyes. "Do you know what *ti amo* means, *cara mia*?"

"Of course. I said I love you, Riccardo."

He wound a long, thick, escaped curl around his finger. "We had a passionate encounter, Sofia. That doesn't mean you love me."

"Nonsense. I let you make love to me because I'm in love with you. But don't panic, I'm not going to stalk you. I know this thing between us is only temporary."

Riccardo hugged her. "I told you before I made love to you, Sofia, that you were mine and there'd be no turning back once I took your virginity. I have no intention of letting you go. It is not temporary. You...are...mine."

Sofia smiled serenely.

Riccardo kissed her nose. "It seems your grandfather was right. You are my *tesoro,* my treasure, and together we will repair the rift between our families."

"What are you talking about, Riccardo?"

"I met your grandfather once. He intentionally waylaid me to insist I keep you and Nico apart. He must have guessed Nico was Giuseppe's son. Strange he never informed your grandmother or Giuseppe. At the time I assured him that it had been taken care of, and Nico would forget you. Your grandfather said I had obviously never met you, or I would see the treasure you are. Then he patted my arm and said, 'Perhaps if we were to meet, the rift between the DeRosas and Santinis could be repaired.'"

Sofia gasped. "Riccardo, it was my grandfather who caught me walking through the *piazza* with Nico. I've been thinking the same thing. He must have realized then that Nico was his grandson. But he never said a word to me or *Nonna* or *Papà*. That is why he wanted to keep me and Nico apart."

"Yes, Sofia, and now I suggest you get dressed, so I can take you to dinner."

"Great, I'm starving." Sofia slid out of his arms and padded into the bathroom.

Riccardo lay frowning at the ornate ceiling. Sofia might be inexperienced in the art of making love, but he wasn't. Why then was that the most enthralling, sensual encounter he'd ever experienced?

Chapter Twenty-One

Strolling hand in hand with Riccardo, Sofia opened her senses to the nightlife of *Venezia*. Couples and groups sat at tables in restaurants. Boats and gondolas cruised up the middle of the canal. Other couples promenaded, absorbing the atmosphere.

After crossing a couple of pretty bridges, Riccardo ushered her into a small restaurant. It had a cozy, romantic atmosphere. Aromas of roasting garlic and baked bread wafted from the kitchen, making her mouth water. She glanced behind, searching for Alfredo.

"He's sitting at the café` opposite," Riccardo whispered in her ear.

After being seated, the waitress attempted to explain each of the dishes in broken English. Taking pity on her, Sofia left it to Riccardo to order while she relaxed and observed the handsome and charismatic man opposite.

Who would have guessed I'd fall in love with a Santini.

Her mind drifted back to the hotel and the kisses they'd shared, the places he'd touched her, the things he'd done to her. Heat blossomed in her cheeks and between her thighs. *Get a grip, Sofia, Riccardo might have declared you're his, but what exactly does that mean? He didn't say he loved you.*

Riccardo handed the menus to the waitress and smiled at Sofia. "The food here is superb and whenever I'm in *Venezia*, I make a point of eating here."

The waiter brought their wine and poured a little in each of their glasses. Sofia tasted hers and smiled. "*Il vino è delizioso, grazie.*"

Returning her smile, the waiter filled their glasses then placed the bottle in an ice bucket beside the table with the label facing her.

"*Santini il Vino Scintillante.*" Sofia raised her eyebrows. "This is from your vineyard?"

"*Sì*, Sofia, and it's one of our most popular wines. The grapes were planted by your grandfather and were part of the old DeRosa vineyard before it was broken up and sold."

Sofia looked him straight in the eye and took a deep breath. "What are we going to do, Riccardo? I don't want to hurt or embarrass your family, but I need to prove my father was set up, and it still could be someone from within your family."

Reaching across the table, his fingers curled around her hand. "I have Nico looking into the gambling rumors and Giovanni spreading the word that we're searching for someone with a cut face and hands. Carolina is checking to see if your key fits the DeRosa mausoleum."

She watched his thumb as he stroked the back of her hand, sending delightful shivers up and down her arm. Her mind again drifted to the intimacies they'd shared earlier and she lifted her gaze to find him watching her. She was relieved the waitress arrived at that moment with their stuffed cannelloni, giving Sofia a chance to compose herself.

Over the next couple of hours, Riccardo opened up. They discussed their families, their interests, and their childhoods. They laughed, drank the wine, and ate a variety of Venetian dishes. He even admitted to her that he was surprised to feel so comfortable talking to her. He flirted with her and told her she was desirable, interesting and funny, and the more time he spent with her the more certain he was that they belonged together. Sofia didn't need wings to fly, she was floating on happiness.

As they left the restaurant Riccardo commandeered Sofia's hand and they strolled along the cobbled lanes until they came to a canal where a couple of *Gondolieri* sat in their gondolas chatting.

Sofia looked at him hopefully. "Could we?"

"Not these. They have too many seats in them."

They crossed the bridge and strolled along a *callè* until they came to another canal with a lot more activity and small gondolas. Sofia pointed. "That one has only two seats and would be cozy."

He laughed and negotiated a price, then called out to Alfredo who sauntered over.

"*Si, Signor* Santini?"

Riccardo handed him a generous tip. "*Grazie*, Alfredo. *Si puo` andare a casa ora.*"

"*Grazie mille`, signore.*" Alfredo gave a wave and walked away.

Riccardo helped Sofia into the gondola and waited until she was seated before he joined her. "We don't need Alfredo any longer. I've sent him home."

The *gondolier* stood behind them and as soon as they were settled, pushed out into the canal. An unexpected pleasure filled her when Riccardo put his arm around her then kissed her. Happy?"

"Yes." She rested her head against his shoulder, and wrapped an arm around his waist. *Perhaps this is what I have been looking for.*

Sofia knew her grin stretched from ear to ear and didn't care. When they'd set out this morning she'd never dreamed they'd end up in a beautiful hotel in *Venezia* making love, or that they'd share an intimate dinner in a lovely restaurant, enjoying each other's company. Since coming to *Venezia* five years ago, she'd dreamed of gliding along its canals in a gondola and being held in the arms of a man she loved, and here she was doing exactly that. She raised her eyes to meet Riccardo's. "Thank you for the most romantic night of my life."

"This is only the beginning, Sofia. I plan to give you a lifetime of romantic nights."

Drawing back, Sofia met his gaze. "A lifetime?"

Riccardo shook his head. "You still don't get it, do you?" He reached into his pocket, withdrew a small velvet pouch, and handed it to her. "This is for you, *tesoro.*"

Sofia held the pouch in her palm. "What is it?"

"Open it."

Her heart in her mouth, Sofia pulled the tiny drawstrings apart, then upended the pouch. Out fell the beautiful ring she'd taken off yesterday and given back to Carolina.

"This isn't mine, Riccardo, it's from Carolina's latest collection."

He smiled. "Carolina told me it is your favorite, that you loved it."

"It is and I do, but I can't accept this ring. It's horrendously expensive."

"You need an engagement ring, and I want you to have this one."

Totally confused, Sofia stared at him. "But our engagement isn't real. I can't accept this." She held up the sparkling ring and studied it. "It's been cleaned. You were supposed to give it to the police."

Riccardo took the ring and lifted her left hand. "After you gave the police your statement yesterday, they took the ring and had the skin samples removed then returned it to me late last night."

"But our engagement isn't real."

He slid the ring onto her finger. "Did we, or did we not make love this evening, Sofia?"

"We did," whispered Sofia, her cheeks heating.

"And did I inform you that I have no intention of letting you go?"

"Yes, but you didn't mean it...not like forever. Because if you did, that would mean...that would mean you want to marry me and we both know that's not true."

Riccardo muttered and pulled her into his arms. "Why is it so hard to believe I want to marry you, Sofia? Tell me that."

She leaned back, momentarily lost for words, then cleared her throat. "Riccardo, you've only known me a little over a week, and I can't recall you asking me to marry you. That might have given me an indication of your feelings."

Riccardo drew her closer. "You're right. Sofia, would you please do me the honor of becoming my wife?"

She squirmed until he released her enough that she could look up at him again. "But why do you want to marry me? Are you prepared to give up other women for ever?"

"Sofia, we are well suited. We enjoy each other's company and you can't deny we have a strong attraction to each other. You will never bore me and you will make a wonderful mother to our children. By marrying me you will have everything money can buy. And, you have my word; there will be no other women. So you will marry me, *sì*?"

Sofia stared, stunned to silence as she replayed his words. "That has got to be one of the most unromantic proposals in history. I don't care if we're well suited, or that we have a strong attraction. I certainly don't care that you can give me everything money can buy. There is something I want much more than those things and if you can't provide it then I won't marry you."

Riccardo couldn't believe what he was hearing. Sofia was refusing to marry him because he hadn't offered her enough. Over dinner he'd opened up more to her than any other woman. He'd fantasized about her holding his child to her breast. Welcoming him into her arms every night. *Santa Maria*, he was crazy about her. *What the hell more does she want?*

Before he could put that question to her she was squirming in his arms again, twisting round toward the *gondolier*.

"I thought they were supposed to serenade us. Not that I'm complaining, I just thought it was part of the package and it's something I always wanted to experience."

Riccardo muttered an oath under his breath at her purposely-swift change of subject. "*Gondoliers* don't serenade the tourists, Sofia. You might find a few that like to sing while they work, but most do not. They are here earning a living."

"Oh." Sofia smiled at the *gondolier* then leaned back against Riccardo's shoulder and sighed. "It's still romantic even without the serenading."

Riccardo kissed the top of her head. "Is that what you want, Sofia, a romantic proposal?"

She edged away until they were looking into each other's eyes. "Yes, Riccardo, I want a romantic proposal but it's not the reason I won't marry you."

He gently brushed an escaped curl off Sofia's face then lowered his head and kissed her pretty lips. "How will I know what you want, if you don't tell me, *tesoro*?"

She smiled. "I shouldn't have to tell you, *caro mio*. You should know."

Riccardo growled in frustration. "You want to drive my Aston Martin?"

"Yes, but that goes without saying."

"You want me to ask your father for your hand?"

"Yes, but I'd rather you alive than dead, so I'll give you a pass on that one."

"Do you want me to make love to you again, *tesoro*?"

Sofia snuggled closer. "Yes, but that's not what's stopping me from marrying you and I'm not saying any more. You have to figure it out on your own, *caro mio*."

"I can always torture it out of you."

"You can try, but I might do a little torturing of my own."

Riccardo met her challenging eyes and a thrill raced through him. The little minx was attempting to seduce him. Voices drew his attention to the sidewalk where people were seated at a restaurant. He realized they were almost back at their hotel so he kissed her fleetingly.

"You're in big trouble sweetheart and as soon as I get you back to our room, I intend to deal with you properly."

Sofia giggled. "You promise?"

What have I created? My innocent angel has become a seductress. "I promise."

Sofia straightened as the *gondolier* guided them in against a set of old steps and held the gondola steady so Riccardo could help her out.

She turned to the *gondolier* and smiled at him. "*Buonanotte, signore è grazie.*"

"*Prego, signorina, buonanotte.*"

Riccardo took her hand and they were about to walk away when the *gondolier* called after her. "*Signorina, lei dovrebbe sposare quell'uomo.*"

Sofia frowned at Riccardo. "I'm not certain, but did he tell me I should marry you?"

Riccardo laughed. "He said you should marry that man. I assume he's referring to me."

Sofia waved to the *gondolier*. "I will if he gives me what I want."

They walked a little further along the promenade to their hotel, then took the stairs to the third floor. As soon as Riccardo had Sofia inside their suite, he locked the door then swept off her feet.

"Riccardo, what are you doing?"

"What I promised, *tesoro*. You are about to get what you deserve."

Sofia trembled, anticipation glowing in her eyes. He carried her through to the bedroom where he halted beside the bed and let her slide slowly down his body until her heels touched the carpet. He held her captive, her pulse racing under his fingers as he decided on her punishment.

She squirmed, pressing closer.

Riccardo held her still, savoring the feel of her fingernails digging into his arms, her ripe breasts against his ribs, and her firm belly pressed to his erection. He might have experience over her, but she definitely had an abundance of curiosity and was quick to put into practice what she learned. He knew she was wriggling against him in order to excite him, but he was determined to draw out her punishment.

"It won't work, Sofia. I am not going to rush this. By the time I have finished with you, you will have begged, cried, and screamed."

Sofia shrugged. "I'm not the least bit worried. Do your worst, *tesoro*. I can take anything you dish out."

He laughed loudly. His angel had no idea what she was in for and was still challenging him at every opportunity. "Very well, *cara mia*. It shall be as you wish." Riccardo released Sofia's hips and went down on his haunches in front of her. He picked up her left foot and slipped the high heel off then pressed his mouth to her instep, smiling when she gasped. He followed with a kiss to her ankle, her calf, and knee.

Sofia held her breath as Riccardo put her foot down gently and turned his attention to her right foot. She watched him glide his fingers slowly down her calf, catch her heel strap in his fingers, and slide her shoe off, then press another warm, opened-mouthed kiss to that instep, ankle, calf and knee. *Lord, if he's going to go this slowly, I will beg.*

Riccardo came up on his knees and ran his hands slowly up the back of Sofia's calves and thighs, stopping when he reached her bottom. She made another strangled gasp as he hooked two fingers into her panties and slowly peeled them away from her, then all the way down to her ankles.

She ran her fingers through his tousled, thick hair, trying to remain standing as he caressed the back up her thighs then bottom and gently kneaded. It was almost a relief when he moved away. She opened her eyes to discover him smiling wickedly.

"You call this torture?" she asked bravely.

Riccardo's lips twitched. He pulled her gently astride his lap then planted soft kisses on her forehead, eyelids, nose, cheeks, and chin.

Sofia grumbled, frustrated that he wouldn't kiss her properly. Her grumble turned to a moan as he feathered kisses down her neck and across her collarbone. She moaned again when he closed a hand over her breast, molding. His fingertips rolled her sensitive nipple, giving her some little relief.

"More. I want more."

He chuckled, his warm breath tickling her neck. "You're not even close to desperate yet, Sofia." He sat back a little and reached out, rubbing the palms of his hands over and around her swollen breasts, pressing a little harder against her nipples and chuckling when she closed her eyes, arched her back, and pressed her breasts harder into his palms. He slid his fingers down and around, touching her moist center.

Sofia jerked at the contact. Hot need consumed her. She pressed herself into his hand and moaned when he pushed a finger inside her to massage that incredibly sensitive spot. Her lips parted in a cry, but Riccardo claimed her lips, cutting off the sound. He deepened the kiss, darting his tongue into her mouth, imitating his finger.

Sofia clung to his shoulders, thrusting her pelvis against his finger as a desperate need built inside her. She nearly screamed in frustration when Riccardo removed his finger and stopped kissing her.

"Please, I was so close."

"You're still not desperate enough, *cara mia*. I said begging, remember." He laughed at her frustrated groan and ran his hands up her arms, over her shoulders, and behind her neck, unclipping the catch that held the top of her dress.

Sofia felt his erection jolt as he peeled down her bodice, exposing her lace bra and breasts straining to be free of the constricting material.

He smiled again, and reached behind her to unhook the offending piece of clothing. As her bra fell away, Sofia felt instant relief and managed to capture one of his hands and bring it to her aching breast. Pleasure surged through her when he complied and closed his hand, pushing her gently against the bed and lowering his mouth to take her other aching nipple in his mouth.

"Yes."

He rolled his tongue around her areola and mimicked it with his fingers on her other breast. His free hand slid between her legs to caress her heated skin.

She pressed into his hand as he pushed two fingers inside her, slowly drawing them out then back in until she was moaning and undulating. He withdrew his fingers and lips, then raised an eyebrow.

She cried out in frustration. "No, Riccardo, please...I'm begging. Don't stop."

He chuckled and stood, pulling her up with him, then he reached behind her and pulled down the zip, letting the dress fall to the carpet. His gaze roved leisurely from the top of her head to the tips of her toes and back again.

"Riccardo, please, I want you."

He stepped closer and pulled the clip from her hair, seemingly mesmerized as it cascaded down her back. He raked his fingers through it, then steadily looked into her eyes.

"You are mine, *tesoro*."

Placing his hands around her waist, he lifted her onto the bed, then kept his gaze locked with hers as he shrugged out of his jacket and kicked off his shoes.

She licked her lips. "I thought you were supposed to be torturing me."

"Your torture is far from over, sweetheart."

Sofia squirmed in anticipation and watched him undo his buttons then peel off his shirt, revealing his beautifully broad, muscled shoulders and chest. She was giddy with desire as his fingers went to his belt, then flicked his trouser button undone and eased the zip down, painstakingly slowly. Her gaze fell on the large bulge in his jocks. It seemed he was as desperate for her as she was for him.

Riccardo stepped closer to the bed, his gaze running over her. Sofia stretched, thrilled to see the burning desire in his eyes. He placed a hand under each of her knees and drew them up, pushed them wide, then lowered his shoulders between them.

"Now I'll give you your reward, *tesoro*."

Sofia gasped as his mouth closed over her and he thrust his tongue inside her heat, stroking and sucking. His shoulders wedged in under her thighs, spreading her wider as his hands cupped her bottom, lifting her so he could openly feast on her.

She cried out as molten streaks of liquid fire shot through her, leaving her weak and trembling. He pushed a finger inside her and thrust until she was squirming and clawing at the sheets, defenseless, completely at his mercy. "Riccardo, don't you dare stop this time."

His chuckle vibrated against her sensitive skin then he lifted his shoulders slightly, bringing her higher off the bed and sucked hard, thrusting his fingers into her.

She exploded, screaming as a violent shudder racked her body. She went rigid, climaxing around his fingers, yet he continued to stroke and suck, extending her climax until she was shaking uncontrollably. "No more," she begged

He released her and moved away. She heard a drawer open and close.

Sofia slumped back against the bed, exposed and uncaring, completely wiped out by what he'd done. His idea of torturing might well work. She opened her eyes.

He lay beside her, supported by his elbow, smiling. "Now *cara mia*, your torture continues."

"I can't take anymore."

He laughed, deep and sensual. "Marry me, Sofia?"

She moaned and closed her eyes. "No, not until you give me what I want."

Riccardo lowered himself slowly until she was pinned beneath him. "Very well, *cara mia*. I was going to give you a reprieve, but you give me no choice." He pushed his knees between her legs until they cradled his body and she lay open to him.

"Liar," whispered Sofia, her libido reignited as he nudged into her. "You wouldn't know the meaning of reprieve, and if you think this is torture then I say, bring it on."

Riccardo laughed. "You never cease to delight me, *tesoro*. I must kiss those beautiful lips before they get you into any more trouble."

He took her mouth in a sensual demanding kiss, his tongue tangling with hers as he nudged against her wet center. She moaned against his lips.

Riccardo thrust deep. She gasped, her fingernails digging in, her legs wrapping around him. He withdrew and thrust again, all the way to the hilt, slamming her into the mattress and pillows. He kept thrusting and she met each one with cries of abandon as the crescendo built.

Suddenly he pulled out and sat back on his ankles. Before Sofia could screech in frustration, he lifted her up over his hard thighs.

"Riccardo, no... You beast." She attempted to pull him back down but he held strong, gathered her closer, and took her mouth in another searing kiss. Sofia fell into the kiss, her hands seeking out the hard length pressed against her belly. She closed one hand around its thickness and began stroking, like he'd shown her. Her other hand found a firm testicle and she squeezed gently, drawing a low groan from him.

"Was that a sound of pleasure or pain, *caro mio*?" she whispered.

"Imp." He brushed her hands away. Before she could reach for him again, he grabbed her by the waist and spun her round until her back was against his chest.

"Lean forward and put your hands out to support you." He placed a hand in the middle of her back then with his other hand, soothingly caressed the heated skin of her backside, dipping his fingers to brush between her legs, wringing another moan from her.

After a kiss at the base of her spine, he placed his hands on her hips and moved up behind her, pushing her knees apart until she could feel his hard length cradled between her legs. He released one hip to cup her breast. Sofia moaned and pushed back against him.

Riccardo gripped her hips again. "What do you want from me, *tesoro*?"

"I want you inside me."

He held her steady and eased into her from behind.

Sofia gasped, her wits scattering as he drew out and forged back in, then again faster. "This is incredible, amazing." She rocked back into him, meeting his thrusts and pushing him to go faster. She could feel another climax building as her body tightened. He released one hip and reached between her legs to rub her until she cried out, trembling uncontrollably.

Her body tightened with anticipation. He thrust harder and deeper, continuing to rub her intimately with his fingers. Sofia arched as white light erupted and every cell in her body exploded. She screamed and shattered with Riccardo deep inside her. He thrust hard once more then let out a guttural roar.

Sofia's arms collapsed under her and they fell to the bed,

boneless. She was aware of Riccardo pulling her hair back, then the touch of his lips as they grazed her shoulder, but she couldn't raise the energy to respond, so lost was she in euphoric stupor, thunderstruck by the carnality of what they'd done and the sensual pleasure of it.

Riccardo rolled to the side and pulled her unresisting body into his arms.

She placed her hand over his heart and mumbled.

"I didn't understand, Sofia. Say again."

Sofia eyelids lifted fractionally. "I love you, Riccardo. *Ti amo.*"

He smiled and kissed her forehead. "So you *will* marry me?"

"Not until you give me what I want."

Riccardo wanted to shake her. "And that is?"

Her eyelids fluttered closed, her body softened in his arms, and her gentle breath puffed against his chest. He gazed down at her long, red-tinted lashes resting against her fair cheeks, her kiss swollen lips, her fiery curls spread out over the pillow, and her small hand lying on his chest. He shook his head in frustration, removed her hand, and slid out of the bed.

After returning from the bathroom, Riccardo climbed back in beside her and reached for the lamp, throwing the room into complete darkness. He lay in a state of frustration, stewing over what she could possibly want.

His eyelids drooped. Her declaration of love brought a smile to his lips. If she were so sure she loved him then why wouldn't she marry him?

Riccardo's eyelids sprang open.

"*Stupido idiota,*" he cursed softly, slapping his forehead as the puzzle fell into place. Of course she didn't want anything of material value. Giuseppe DeRosa and his son ran a successful vineyard, their wines making a name for themselves in Australia, New Zealand, and America. She could afford anything she wanted. Her price for marriage was much higher.

He lay there thinking. Sofia had beauty, intelligence, passion, and a caring and loyal nature. She would stand up for what she believed in and undoubtedly make a wonderful mother and partner. His desire for her was insatiable and mounting by the minute.

Riccardo smiled at the memory of her shocked expression when she realized he was going to take her from behind, and her screams of pleasure when he did.

But do I love her?

Chapter Twenty-Two

The thrill of driving the Aston Martin far outweighed the fear of being in charge of such an expensive vehicle, but it literally purred under Sofia's hands. She put the indicator on and carefully merged with the traffic, then shot an anxious glance at her passenger. He'd gone awfully quiet, which was odd after the way he'd woken her this morning.

Her cheeks heated at the memory of him spooned around her, his fingers caressing her thigh, his lips feathering kisses along her neck and shoulder. Her cheeks grew hotter at the thought of what else he'd done and an excited shiver ran through her. Last night he'd promised she would beg, cry, and scream, which she had. This morning he'd made her scream again as he entered her from behind, thrusting into her again and again until he'd sent her spiraling into another magnificent orgasm. Later, he'd surprised her at the parking station when he'd thrown her the keys and told her she could drive. Sofia had squealed in delight and run to open the car, leaving Riccardo to stow the bags before sliding into the passenger seat.

Now his hands were clenched on his thighs. She could sense his tension and he hadn't spoken for half an hour. She figured he didn't allow many people to drive his pride and joy, if any. Yet he was staring out the window as if deep in thought, not concentrating on her driving skills at all. Was he regretting his proposal? She could stew and worry over it all day or take the bit between her teeth and find out.

"Does my driving make you nervous or is it just that I'm driving this car?"

Riccardo's lips twitched. "Neither, Sofia, you drive well. I'm sorry if I'm distracted, I have a lot on my mind."

"Like what?"

"Convincing you to accept my proposal. Convincing your father to agree to our marriage. I turned off my phone yesterday so we wouldn't be disturbed. When I turned it on a short while ago there was a text from Giovanni. Your brother arrived this morning and sent word via your grandparents that you are to return to Australia with him."

"No. If I give in now, I'll lose the *villa* and never clear my father. We are so close."

His fingers stretched out along his jeans. "I was hoping you'd say that. At least it gives me more time to brow beat you into marrying me."

She laughed. "Brow beating won't work. Did Giovanni have any other news?"

"Yes. He's located some of the witnesses claiming your father owed them money. It appears they *were* bribed. That's the good news. The bad news is Carolina tried the key in the DeRosa mausoleum. It doesn't fit."

"My aunt left a poem. I think it's a code of some sort and the key is tied to it. I just need more time to work it out."

"They can't force you to leave, Sofia. I will talk to your brother and make him understand how important this is. I won't allow you to leave. You belong to me, remember."

Sofia glanced at the beautiful ring sparkling on her finger. "You haven't given me what I want yet, Riccardo."

"I'm working on it, sweetheart. Believe me, I'm working on it."

They arrived back at the Santini vineyard to find an assortment of cars parked in front of the *villa* steps.

Sofia bit her lip. "I wonder if Dante is already here."

Riccardo shrugged. "We'd better go in and see."

She handed Riccardo his keys and waited while he collected their bags, then they walked up the steps together, entering the foyer as Giovanni came striding out of the sitting room.

"Riccardo, Sofia, where the hell have you been?"

Sofia smiled. "We went to *Venezia*."

"*Venezia*?" He looked over Sofia's head at Riccardo. "I had made up my mind to ring the police when Carolina informed me you'd packed overnight bags. What were you doing in *Venezia*?"

A slow smile spread over Riccardo's face. "I was...wooing a reluctant bride."

Giovanni's eyebrows shot up. "And were you successful in wooing her?"

His lips twitched. "You could say we're enjoying the negotiations immensely."

Sofia rolled her eyes. "For goodness sake, will you two stop? Giovanni, why are there so many cars outside? Is my brother here or has something happened?"

He looked back over his shoulder at the closed door.

"Your brother hasn't arrived yet, but our family and most of our neighbors have. There's a rumor that Giuseppe DeRosa has taken a contract out on Riccardo's life."

"What?" Sofia stared, unable to believe her ears.

"My life?" queried Riccardo.

"Yes, your life. There's another rumor being bandied about that Sofia has disappeared and the last person she was seen with was you. When I checked with the hotel in *Venezia* they assured me you attended the meeting on your own."

"That's ridiculous," muttered Sofia. "Someone is spreading vicious rumors, trying to discredit our families, and if we aren't careful they will succeed, again."

Riccardo caught hold of Sofia's hand then glanced at Giovanni. "I think it's vital everyone continues to believe Sofia and I are engaged. We can also kill one rumor right now by walking in there and informing them we slipped off to *Venezia* for a romantic getaway."

Sofia's face flooded with warmth. "Riccardo, if Dante hears that, he'll go nuts."

"I will handle your brother, Sofia. Now take a deep breath and act natural."

Giovanni snorted. "Sofia doesn't have to act. That blush will leave no one in any doubt as to what you two have been up to."

She cringed, her face heating even more as Giovanni opened the door and Riccardo escorted her through.

Giovanni cleared his throat, drawing the entire room's attention.

"Look who I found. Apparently we've been worrying over nothing. These two love birds have been in *Venezia*."

Sofia buried her head against Riccardo's chest, mortified.

He put his arm around her. "Sorry, we wanted some time alone and after Sofia's last attack, I preferred no-one knew where we were going."

Caterina Santini came over and stroked Sofia's hair, her eyes shooting daggers at her eldest son. "Sofia, I think you need a few minutes to compose yourself after being so rudely embarrassed by my thoughtless sons. Go upstairs with Carolina. I will call you when everyone has left."

Sofia nodded and almost ran out of the room, closely followed by Carolina. She bounded up the stairs; taking them two at a time then ran down the hall to Riccardo's room and sank onto the bed still reeling with humiliation. Her brother would have to stand in line if he wanted to throttle Riccardo, because she had first dibs.

Carolina sat beside her and put her arm around her. "It's okay, Sofia, my brothers are thoughtless jerks. Tell me what really happened in *Venezia*."

In the drawing room, Riccardo studied everyone as pandemonium broke loose, some arguing they'd known all along there was nothing to the rumors, others warning Giuseppe would react badly to a romance between Sofia and Riccardo. Everyone wanted to know where the rumors were coming from. A loud commotion outside the door halted the arguing. The door burst open and the security guard normally posted at the front gate came flying across the threshold, landing in a heap on the tiles. Riccardo helped the man up and braced himself.

Dante DeRosa had arrived.

Silence filled the room as everyone's gaze went to the door. A broad shouldered, tall man stepped into the room, his face set like granite. Not a muscle moved as his eyes scanned the room. There was a collective gasp as everyone focused on his face.

Riccardo and Giovanni stepped forward, ready to intercept Sofia's brother.

Dante DeRosa moved to the side as Lorenzo and Elena DeRosa

stepped through the doorway and joined him. Sofia's grandfather glanced around the room. "We don't want any trouble. We just want Sofia and we'll leave."

Closing the gap, Riccardo shook his head. "Sofia is not leaving. She is under my protection and wishes to remain in *Italia*."

Dante DeRosa stepped forward. "Where is my sister?" His cold eyes bored into Riccardo only shifting when Riccardo's grandmother shuffled up to Dante. She lifted her hand as if to touch his face. Dante DeRosa reared back, his eyes narrowing.

Enrico Santini joined his elderly wife, leaning heavily on his walking stick as he stared at Dante. Ricardo's grandmother held a hand to her chest. "I am Louisa Santini. You are Giuseppe's son, Sofia's brother?"

Dante eyes flicked between Riccardo's grandparents. "That's right, where is Sofia?"

Riccardo's grandmother turned to Elena and Lorenzo DeRosa accusingly. "You knew?"

Elena shook her head. "Sofia told me a couple of days ago and asked me to say nothing. I suspect my husband guessed the truth when he saw Sofia with Nicolas."

Dante DeRosa looked from one to the other. "What truth?"

"That my son, Nicolas, is your half brother," said Ariana, standing.

Dante swung to face Ariana. "I beg your pardon? What half brother?"

Nico pushed himself off the couch and stood. "That would be me."

Dante DeRosa drew in a sharp gasp, his eyes narrowing as he studied Nico.

Riccardo did the same. Dante and Nico were much too alike to be anything but brothers. They shared the same height, coloring, square jaw, straight nose, and defiant stance. To Riccardo, the only differences was Dante looked heavier in the chest and shoulders, his arms more muscled, and his features hard compared to Nico.

"What's going on? Who are you?" demanded Dante.

Nico raised an eyebrow. "I believe I'm your brother." He shrugged. "It was Sofia who spotted the likeness between us. She set out to discover the truth."

Dante appeared completely bamboozled as he stared at Nico, then he pulled out his phone. "Excuse me. I need to speak to my father."

He swiped a finger across the phone, touched the screen a couple of times, then put the phone to his ear. His gaze locked on Nico as he waited for it to be answered.

"*Papà*, it's me, Dante. They're not saying where Sofia is, but there's something else you need to know. You have to see this with your own eyes or you will never believe..." Dante looked at his phone then Ariana. "He hung up, but I think he's coming."

Ariana dropped to the couch. "Giuseppe's coming to *Italia*?"

Dante gaze focused on Ariana. "My father is already in *Italia*, *signora.* He was waiting in the car as he refused to set foot inside this villa."

The front door crashed heavily against a wall and everyone jumped.

"*Santa Maria*," exclaimed Caterina.

A collective gasp went through the room as another man appeared in the doorway, his dark eyes boring into Angelo Santini.

Riccardo squared his shoulders. Giuseppe DeRosa was an impressive man. He stood tall, broad shouldered, and imposing with hardly a grey hair and looking fitter than a lot of men half his age. Giuseppe's eyes met Dante's briefly. A movement to his left caught his attention as Nico stepped away from the couch.

Riccardo tensed as Giuseppe DeRosa's gaze flicked from Nico to Dante and back.

"Who are you?" he asked, his voice catching.

"He is our son, Giuseppe."

Giuseppe tensed then, as if in slow motion, turned to his left where Ariana sat on a couch. The silence was deafening as they stared at each other for so long people began to fidget.

Finally, Ariana stood, faltered then stepped toward Giuseppe DeRosa, her eyes filling with tears.

Riccardo felt like an interloper as his aunt searched the face of the man she'd once loved. She blinked her tears away. "I named him Nicolas because it's your middle name."

Giuseppe DeRosa looked ashen, like his world had crashed. His eyes never left Ariana's face. She placed her hands on his chest as if it were the most natural thing to do, tears streaming down her face.

Giuseppe made a choking sound and pulled her into his arms, stroking her back soothingly. Ariana began sobbing.

Riccardo's mother threw open the terrace doors, drawing everyone's attention. She wiped tears from her face then cleared her throat. "Except for my immediate family, Salvatore and the DeRosas, I would like everyone else to go home and let us sort this out privately."

Giovanni and Nico helped encourage relatives, friends, and neighbors to leave. Everyone else seemed uncertain what to do as Giuseppe continued to hold a sobbing Ariana in his arms while he stared at Nico. After several minutes, Giuseppe guided Ariana to one of the lounges then sat beside her. "Why have you kept my son from me?"

She shook her head. "It wasn't like that, Giuseppe. When I got back you were gone and I couldn't find you. Renzina and I hired an investigator to search for you and when he found you..." Ariana put her hand over her mouth to hold back a sob, then took a breath. "He told us you were living with another woman, but I didn't believe him. I came to your house and she answered the door. She begged me to go away because she was pregnant and you were all she had in the world. I told her you had a right to know about our baby and she promised to tell you." Tears rolled down Ariana's cheek again. "You didn't contact me so I ran away."

Giuseppe went to pull her back into his arms but Ariana resisted. "When Nico was six months old, I tried to see you again, but you weren't there and Renzina had died. I hired another investigator and he discovered you'd immigrated to Australia." Ariana collapsed against Giuseppe's chest.

Riccardo tensed as Dante turned toward Nico. "So we are half-brothers."

Nico's lips twitched. "Seems that way."

Dante didn't smile. "What was between you and Sofia five years ago?"

"Nothing. I suspected I might be Giuseppe's son, and when Sofia first met me she said I reminded her of you. It fitted."

Dante glanced at Riccardo, narrowed his eyes, then pulled a folded piece of paper out of his shirt pocket. "Perhaps you would be good enough to explain this?" Anger radiated off him as he thrust the paper at Riccardo.

What now. Riccardo unfolded the paper and glanced down. It was a photo of him holding Sofia in his arms. They were standing near his Aston Martin in front of Nico's villa. Riccardo's heart constricted at the sight of Sofia smiling up into his face, her hands resting on his chest, her body molded to his. There could be no doubt to her infatuation. Across the bottom, someone had written, *Riccardo Santini is about to add another notch to his belt.*

Riccardo met Dante's hostile eyes. "Where did you get this photo? Who sent it to you?"

"It was emailed to our vineyard office in Australia from the Emilia Romagna Hotel in Bologna. Is it true? Have you seduced my sister?"

Riccardo was saved from answering by the sound of two sets of heels clattering down the stairs. He turned as Carolina burst through the open doorway.

"We saw the cars leaving. How did you get rid of everyone so—" Carolina stopped abruptly as she came face to face with Dante DeRosa.

Sofia slammed into her, knocking Carolina into Dante's chest.

"Ow, Carolina. You don't just stop in the middle of the...Dante." Sofia gasped, her eyes darting from Dante to Riccardo.

Thunderstruck, Sofia's gaze fell on Carolina's wriggling in Dante's arms. It surprised her to see panic in her friend's eyes. Sofia unconsciously took a step closer to Riccardo, reassured when he put a protective arm around her, not in the least intimidated by Dante's cold stare as he held Carolina captive.

Dante's gaze dropped to Carolina now wriggling in earnest. He released her and she stumbled across the room to stand between Giovanni and Nico.

The atmosphere in the room had a definite chill as a man came to his feet, the movement drawing Sofia's attention. "*Papà.*" She broke away from Riccardo and ran into her father's arms. "You're here...in *Italia*... I can't believe it."

Her father hugged her then he turned hostile eyes, identical to Dante on Riccardo. "I came to *Italia* because I have been hearing worrying things. My daughter was supposed to be on a holiday in Australia and yet she is here. I have been told she has been drugged, robbed, and involved in a car accident. I have been told she is engaged to a Santini, which I know cannot be true."

Sofia stepped back. "Who told you these things, *Papà*?"

"It doesn't matter who told me, Sofia. I want to know what is going on."

Sofia glanced around the room at her grandparents who were now standing with Riccardo's grandparents and Salvatore Bondini. Her gaze moved to Giovanni, Carolina, and their parents standing near the terrace windows, and Nico who strode across the room to sit with his teary mother. Sofia's gaze moved to Dante standing near the door, then Riccardo who was watching her carefully. Finally she looked back up at her father.

"It's true, *Papà*, Carolina and I were drugged by a man who also broke into my hotel room and who knocked me down with a motorcycle. He was trying to get hold of letters I was sent anonymously and now he's dead. We think he was given an overdose by the same person who set you up thirty years ago."

Dante swore.

Her father looked shocked, then his gaze locked with Angelo Santini's. "If I find you are responsible for hurting my daughter."

"No, *Papà*," cried Sofia. "It wasn't Angelo. We've proven you were set up at the hotel and Nico has spoken to most of the so-called witnesses. They were bribed to lie about your gambling and the prostitutes. Giovanni tracked down witnesses that swear they saw a car force Renzina off the road and we believe the same person may have killed her because she was about to expose them for setting you up."

Shocked cries came from the other side of the room and Sofia silently cursed her big mouth. She hurried over to her grandfather and hugged him. "*Nonno*, I'm sorry you have to hear this, but it's true. Somebody did run Renzina off the road and we think that person is behind the drugging, robberies, and Carolina's cut brake lines. He could even be the man who suffocated me and then tried to strangle me."

"What!" her father and Dante roared in unison.

Sofia whirled back to face her furious father and brother. "It's true. Some person cut Carolina's brake lines and if it hadn't been for her incredible driving we would be dead, and when I was in hospital a man suffocated me with a pillow. Riccardo resuscitated me then a couple of days ago a man tried to strangle me. It was Riccardo who rescued me again." Sofia could see she'd shocked her father and Dante.

"It's because I'm close to exposing him. If it weren't for the Santinis, he would have succeeded in killing me."

Dante stalked across the room and grabbed hold of her arm. "It's not worth your life, Sofia. You are coming home with us, now."

The room erupted as everyone voiced their objections and opinions. Sofia wondered how anyone could understand anything.

Carolina stepped up to Dante and pulled his hand away from Sofia. "No, you can't take her. We are going to find this madman and clear your father's name. It is the only way our parents and grandparents can be friends again. Don't you want to clear your father? Don't you want to know who's responsible for wrecking so many lives?"

Sofia watched as Dante looked into Carolina's big brown pleading eyes, then down to the hand she was gripping his with. He turned his fingers and caught her hand in his.

"Do you remember our conversation five years ago, *bella*?"

Carolina tried to pull her hand away, looking desperate when Dante refused to release her. Sofia went to rush forward. Giovanni, Nico, and Riccardo beat her to it.

Sofia's father held up his hand. "Let her go, Dante." He turned back to Sofia. "*Tesoro*, we are leaving, get your things."

"*Papà*, I can't leave. I have to solve this and it would help if I knew who told you about the drugging, the robbery, the car accident, and my engagement, which is also true. Riccardo and I are engaged."

Sofia moved to stand beside Riccardo in defiance. Her father swore and lunged toward them, his hands fisted. Riccardo pressed Sofia behind him as Giovanni stepped into her father's path.

Sofia's father turned and directed his wrath at Angelo Santini. "Isn't it enough that you took everything from me thirty years ago and turned my family and friends against me? Isn't it enough that you made me out to be a filthy, cheating swine, willing to rob my own parents and set fire to the vineyard I loved? Isn't it enough you deprived me of Ariana and a son I didn't know about? Must you take Sofia too?"

Sofia pulled away from Riccardo, pushed past Giovanni, and confronted her father. "*Papà*, you've got it wrong. They didn't do it. You were set up. Please, *Papà*." Tears streamed down her face.

Her father's face softened slightly. "Sofia, *tesoro*. Forget about clearing my name. It is enough that I know I didn't do those things and that's all that matters. Come back to Australia with us now and we will never mention this business again. If you are worried about Nicolas then don't be. He and Ariana can come visit us whenever they want."

Sofia clutched her father's hands. "No, *Papà*. I can't."

Her father pulled away. "We're leaving in the morning, Sofia. If you choose to stay with him—" Giuseppe glowered at Riccardo "—you will be lost to me forever."

Sofia looked around the room at the Santinis and DeRosas who had come to mean so much to her and with tears still pouring down her face, she ran out through the terrace doors into the garden.

Riccardo shook his head in disgust. He wanted to go after Sofia, but that would have to wait. "You are a fool, *Signor* DeRosa, and you've just broken your daughter's heart."

Giuseppe's shoulders stiffened. He leveled his furious gaze on Riccardo. "If anything happens to Sofia, I will kill you." Giuseppe gave a nod to Dante then started toward the door.

Ariana ran after him. "Giuseppe, wait. You have to go after Sofia and tell her you didn't mean it. Please don't let history repeat itself. Haven't we been through enough? Can't we please mend our broken bridges?"

Giuseppe stopped, turned, and looked at Ariana. "I wasn't the one to break them, *cara mia*." He turned back to the door only to be blocked by Riccardo's father.

"Giuseppe, we need to calm down and talk. I'm sorry I didn't believe you, but when I found you with those women, what was I to think? I am truly sorry. We need to end this feud and find out who set you up. I swear it wasn't me, but whoever it was, he is still out there, and still spreading rumors, and your daughter's life hangs in the balance."

Ariana squeezed Giuseppe's arm. "Help us figure it out, my love, then Sofia can go home with you."

Anger consumed Riccardo, but he held his tongue. *I will not lose her.*

Giuseppe glanced out through the terrace doors. "What about this engagement?"

Angelo shrugged. "It isn't binding. They're not really engaged."

"Like hell they're not," snapped Giovanni. "It might have started out that way, but Riccardo will be marrying Sofia." He turned and stalked over to the bureau to pour a drink.

Riccardo's attention focused on Dante DeRosa who was glowering at Carolina. She blushed and turned away. Eyes narrowing, Riccardo watched his sister edge toward the terrace doors, avoiding eye contact with everyone. The tension in Riccardo's shoulders eased when Carolina sent him a hesitant smile then disappeared through the doors. He hoped she'd be of some comfort to Sofia. In the meantime he would try to make Giuseppe DeRosa see reason.

Riccardo's father placed a hand on Giuseppe's shoulder. "My friend, we need your help to find the person behind these attacks. My daughter and *Signora* Rinaldi could have been killed along with Sofia. Please help us."

Hope grew in Riccardo's chest as Giuseppe looked to his son, but Dante's attention was centered on the terrace and Carolina's fleeing figure.

Giuseppe drew in a deep breath. "I will do anything to protect Sofia, but I don't know how I can help you. If, as you say, you're not responsible then I have no idea who else it could be."

"It would help, *Signor* DeRosa, if we knew who you have been talking to."

Giuseppe's gaze moved beyond them, then quickly returned. "No, that person has nothing to do with any of this."

Salvatore Bondini crossed the room and stopped before them. "Giuseppe, you can tell them it was me." He turned to face the rest of the room. "I never believed Giuseppe did the things he was accused of. He may have been a little wild, but he had a good heart. His family, the vineyard, Angelo, and particularly Ariana were everything to him."

Riccardo's grandmother clapped her hands. "Enough. I'm going to get Maria to serve lunch. I want us to sit down around the table and go over everything. It is what we should have done thirty years ago. We have a lot to make up for."

Chapter Twenty-three

Sofia sat cross-legged on the soft grass, hidden from anyone approaching by a heavily planted garden of rose bushes. She hung her head, holding back tears. They were so close to discovering the truth. She loved her father, but wanted to stay with Riccardo.

It's not fair.

She lifted her head, swallowed, and swiped the tears away. "I'm not going home." She threw herself back and stared at the clear blue sky. "This is my home now."

Heels clicking on the terrace drew Sofia to her knees. Carolina stood at the top step, searching. Sofia didn't move. She loved Carolina, but right now she didn't want company.

Carolina ran down the steps and was half across the lawn when Dante stepped through the terrace doors, looked about, then with determined strides, followed Carolina.

Sofia huffed. "I don't want to talk to him either." She sat back on her heels, wishing they'd give up and leave her alone.

Carolina was almost to the rose garden when Dante caught her from behind and lifted her off her feet. Sofia blinked. *What on earth?*

"Let me go, you brute." Carolina struggled in vain against his muscle-bound arms as he carried her around the garden toward Sofia's hiding place.

"Let me go or...or I'll scream."

Dante dropped Carolina, spun her round, and backed her up against a garden wall. Sofia, stunned, watched as her brother raised one hand and ran a finger down Carolina's cheek, along her jaw, and across her lips.

"Such tempting lips, *bella*, even after five years." He smiled.

A shiver ran through Sofia. She'd never heard her brother's voice sound so sensual, and what did he mean? What had happened between them five years ago?

Carolina pushed against his chest. "I only have to scream and my brothers will be here in seconds."

Dante chuckled. "Go ahead, scream." He raised his other hand to Carolina's hair and opened the clip, releasing the perfectly twisted French braid. It cascaded down around her shoulders, then he lowered his head and captured Carolina's mouth in a kiss that left Sofia gob smacked. She'd never seen her brother ever act like this.

Carolina moaned and slid her hands up Dante's chest and around his neck, blatantly returning his kisses. Dante cursed, gripped Carolina's hips, and dragged her against him.

Sofia clasped her hand over her mouth and sank back on her heels. *I don't believe this. Dante and Carolina.* Her head swam. *What happened five years?*

"Carolina, where are you?" Caterina's voice carried clearly across the lawn as she stepped onto the terrace.

"Oh God." Sofia came up on her knees again and peeped through the roses. Caterina stood on the top step, her hand up blocking the sun's rays.

"Carolina, Sofia, where are you?"

Sofia sagged in relief. The sun was in Caterina's eyes. She couldn't see Dante and Carolina against the wall, their eyes locked, their breathing ragged.

Caterina turned back inside. Dante took Carolina's hand and pulled her after him, away from the rose garden. Carolina stumbled and he had to steady her. Even from this distance, Sofia could see Carolina's eyes were glazed, her lips swollen, her face flushed. If anyone saw her, they would be left in no doubt as to what Carolina and Dante had been doing.

Dante cursed. "Come with me."

Carolina didn't put up any objection as Dante dragged her deeper into the gardens.

Sofia slowly climbed to her feet. If she hadn't just witnessed the chemistry between those two, she'd never have believed it. Dante had always been a lone wolf, contained, unbending, detached, and impenetrable. Carolina was outgoing, poised, serene, and giving.

They were nothing alike. Sofia cursed. *I have to stop Dante before he punishes Carolina because of me.* She straightened her shoulders and set out after them.

"Sofia." Riccardo ran down the steps, then leapt over a low hedge and jogged around the rose garden. "Are you all right?"

"Not really. I need to..."

He hugged her. "Your father and I believe the same thing, Sofia. *Famiglia è tutto.* Family is everything. He could never disown you because he loves you, as do I."

Sofia sucked in a sob, hardly daring to believe it. She pulled away and looked into Riccardo's beautiful dark eyes. "You love me?"

"*Sì, t'amo, tesoro mio.*" Dropping to his knees, Riccardo took her hands in his. "Sofia, my love. Everything I own is yours. My heart belongs only to you. Will you marry me?"

Sofia's heart swelled. "Oh, Riccardo. I love you so much. Yes, yes, yes."

He rose to his feet, slid his hands down her backside, and hauled her against him.

Sofia gasped then gasped again as his hands slid under her bottom to her thighs, gripped them firmly, and pulled her legs around him. She shrieked and grabbed his shoulders, holding on tight. "Riccardo, someone might see us."

He brought his mouth down hard on hers, cutting off the rest of her objection. As she returned his kisses the pressure of his lips softened, still demanding but warm, enticing, persuasive. The tip of his tongue traced her lips in an intimate caress and the last of Sofia's resistance fled. She wrapped her arms around his neck then parted her lips welcoming his tongue as he deepened the kiss, demanding everything she had. A frisson of pure excitement ran through her as she met his demands with her own. He shifted, took several steps, and sat Sofia on the edge of a marble table, one of his hands supporting her as he devoured her mouth. His other hand closed over her breast. Shock waves raced through her. She pressed closer.

Riccardo put aside all restraint and kissed her deeply, ravenously, searching for appeasement, assuaging a craving that had plagued him all day—a craving that no other woman would ever satisfy. He slid his hand under her top and pulled her bra aside then captured her nipple with his fingers, rolling it to a hard bud. Sofia's legs tightened round his waist, locking his hard length against her. Between them hunger surged, desire flared, then exploded.

Someone swore loudly.

Riccardo jerked away from Sofia, still in a haze of passion. He turned to see Dante striding toward them, dragging a disheveled Carolina after him.

Sofia dropped her legs and slid her hands down to Riccardo's forearms.

He moved his hand from under her blouse but only to place it on her thigh. His eyes narrowed at the sight of his normally immaculate sister who wouldn't be caught dead with a hair out of place. Her face was flushed, her lips swollen, her dress rumpled, and her hair falling loosely around her shoulders. She looked like Sofia did when she'd been thoroughly kissed. His eyes swept back to Sofia then to his sister again. They shared the same starry-eyed enthralled expression.

He bristled, turning hostile eyes on Dante. "Take your hands off my sister or it's the last thing you will ever do." Sofia's gaze shot to his face, obviously undoubtedly because of his cold, blunt voice.

Dante returned the look of hostility. "You take your hands off my sister or it's the last thing *you'll* ever do."

"*Merde.*" Sofia slid off the table and stepped between them, colliding with Carolina. For a moment the four of them were compacted like a can of sardines, Sofia and Carolina facing each other as they tried to hold Ricardo and Dante apart.

Riccardo almost laughed.

Sofia glared at Dante and then Riccardo. "We do not need you two going at each other like bulls. You are repeating history, misconstruing things that aren't what they seem."

Riccardo continued to glower at Dante DeRosa.

Sofia threw up her hands, causing everyone to flinch. "Fine, go ahead and throttle each other. Carolina and I will be the mature ones here and solve this thing without you." She gave them both a shove, not that it had any impact. "Argh." She clutched Carolina's hand and they stalked off toward the villa.

Riccardo watched them disappear into the house then turned to

Dante who was raking his hands through his hair, calming it back into place.

"Well?" asked Riccardo.

Dante eyed him coldly. "What are your intentions toward Sofia?"

"I'm going to marry her. What are your intentions toward Carolina?"

Dante sighed. "I've got no idea. I've never met a woman who distracts or frustrates me to such a degree. Do you love Sofia?"

"Yes. How can Carolina distract you, when you've never met before?"

"We met five years ago when she acted as a decoy to prevent me finding Sofia. She was determined to thwart my every move."

Riccardo huffed. "I know the feeling. Ever since Sofia stepped foot in *Italia*, I have been in a state of perpetual frustration."

They glanced toward the villa, then as if by mutual consent strolled toward it. As they reached the terrace Riccardo turned to Dante. "Carolina may act worldly and sophisticated, but she isn't. She has a soft nature and is normally very restrained; at least she is until she gets behind a steering wheel."

Dante grunted. "Or unless it concerns Sofia, then she becomes determined and crafty."

Riccardo nodded. "You can also add defiant, rebellious, and secretive if it involves Sofia. My point is, I don't want her left devastated when you return to Australia."

Dante nodded. "I don't want Sofia hurt either."

The terrace doors leading into the dining room opened and Nico called out, "There you are. Lunch is ready and we want to get started."

Ariana stepped around Nico and scowled at Riccardo and Dante. "Sofia and Carolina have gone to put cool water on their faces after a little *too much* sun. I think it is not the sun they should be wary of." She sent another scowl shooting across the terrace before turning on her heel. "I will be watching you two."

Dante grinned sheepishly at Nico. "Your mother is a very wise and beautiful woman."

Nico grinned back. "Yes, and *our father* hasn't a hope of escaping her this time."

"I assure you, *our father* won't be leaving without the woman he never stopped loving."

Riccardo shook his head as identical ironic smiles spread over Dante and Nico's faces, a dimple appearing in their cheeks, before they each raised an eyebrow at him. The likeness was astounding.

Sofia observed the two families and Salvatore Bondini over the next couple of hours as they went over the attacks on her and every detail they could remember from thirty years ago. By afternoon tea, they were no nearer to discovering who had set up Giuseppe or the reason behind it. It unsettled Sofia that at the time of Renzina's car accident, Enrico Santini, Lorenzo DeRosa, and Salvatore Bondini owned dark blue Mercedes, as did several other families and relatives in the area.

Salvatore Bondini looked exasperated. He turned to Sofia's father. "It makes no sense. Who could possibly hate you this much? The other thing I don't understand is why you went to the hotel in the first place?"

Giuseppe glanced at Ariana then turned to Salvatore. "I received a note on the same scented paper Ariana always sent me, instructing me to meet her at that hotel...and to be waiting naked on the bed. She'd never suggested anything like that before, but we'd just spent a weekend in Lucca and I was desperate to be with her again."

He drew in a deep breath. "I was on the bed, when two women in lingerie burst in and jumped on top of me. I was trying to get them off me when Angelo opened the door and started roaring at me. The rest is history."

Ariana put her hand over his. "Giuseppe, are you sure it was the same paper? I order it from England. For it to be mine, someone had to have taken it from my room."

Giuseppe nodded. "It was yours, Ariana, right down to the monogram. That's why I went to the hotel and that's why later, I assumed Angelo or your father had set me up."

Both men shook their heads.

Caterina threw up her hands in disgust. "It's obviously someone who knew Ariana used that paper. I suggest we take a break and look at it tomorrow. I've had an invitation to go to the opening of Bologna's latest gallery this afternoon, so any ladies who would like to come are welcome to join me. You men will have to do without us."

Nico rounded the table and stopped in front of Sofia. "Before you go, I have something important to tell you."

"Okay." Sofia held her breath. She didn't think she could handle too many more revelations.

Nico squatted beside her. "I have been talking to my mother, and she backed up Sister Augusta's claim. It was my...stepfather's wish that I be told the truth then take my rightful place amongst the DeRosa family. So I have decided to honor his wish and change my name from Lombardi to DeRosa."

Sofia hugged him. "That's so nice. Just don't try bossing me around."

"I wouldn't dare." He winked and strolled over to speak with Dante.

Sofia turned to Carolina as they moved toward the door. "I'm not going to the art gallery. There has to be a clue between the key, the poem, and the photo album. Why else would my aunt hide them like that? I'm going upstairs to have another look at them."

"All right, but here, take my phone, and ring my mother if you discover anything."

"I don't need your phone. I can use the landline."

Carolina rolled her eyes. "Take it, Sofia. Last time I left you alone, you were attacked."

At the sound of high heels and a female voice with an English accent, Sofia looked toward the hall. Carolina laughed at the recognition and confusion on Sofia's face.

"Hannah is Salvatore's granddaughter; she's probably here to pick him up as Michele is in *Milano* on business."

Sofia stayed where she was as the English girl walked through the door, smiled at everyone, then strolled over to Salvatore Bondini and kissed his cheek. "*Ciao, Nonno, ciao tutti.* Can I take my grandfather home now?"

"*Sì, sì,*" came a chorus of voices.

Sofia lowered her voice. "Why was Hannah raised in England and not here?"

"It's a long story." Carolina took hold of Sofia's elbow and urged her out into the hall. "Hannah's mother was English and died two years ago, leaving Hannah without a single relative. After the funeral, Hannah went through her mother's personal papers. She discovered her father was an Italian solicitor by the name of Michele Bondini and he worked with his father, Salvatore Bondini."

Sofia glanced toward the dining room. "So why does she work for the Santinis?"

Carolina's eyes sparkled and she rubbed her hands together in glee. "That's the best bit of the whole story. Hannah arrived on Salvatore's doorstep announcing she was his granddaughter, but Michele denied parentage. Is that a real word? Anyway, Salvatore insisted on blood tests, which confirmed Michele is Hannah's father. He had no choice but to accept the fact, although he swears he doesn't remember her mother."

"But surely he'd remember..."

"Exactly," cried Carolina bounding past Sofia. "Michele didn't want Salvatore to think badly of him, so he has no choice but to accept the results or face Salvatore's wrath."

Sofia raised her eyebrows at Carolina. "Is that true or just your take on it?"

"It's my take, but when Hannah first arrived she knew no Italian. That's why she's working for my brothers. She handles the English correspondence and does a little work for Nico, who she has a crush on."

Sofia laughed. "You're such a romantic, which reminds me, what's going on between you and Dante?"

"Nothing."

"I saw him kiss you in the garden and it wasn't the first time. He would have ravished you if Ariana hadn't called us, and you would have let him. What happened five years ago?"

Carolina sighed. "Dante kissed me and ruined me for any other man."

Sofia gasped. "My brother had sex with you?"

"No, he kissed me."

"How does a kiss ruin you for any other man?" Sofia blinked as the truth hit her like a ton of bricks dropped from a great height. She knew the answer to that better than anyone. When such a dynamic connection of mind, body and soul took place, a chemistry and connection that left one floundering, no one else would ever be good enough.

Carolina stopped fidgeting with her bangle and looked up. "I've never been kissed like that by any other man, Sofia." She rubbed her hand across her eyes. "I'd begun to think I'd imagined it, but after today I know I didn't. When Dante kisses me, I go up in flames. I lose control and turn into someone else."

"I know how that feels." Sofia blinked. "Caro, Dante hates the Santinis. What are you going to do?"

"Avoid him, try to move on. Maybe I should sleep with him and hope it gets him out of my system."

"Bad idea. That will just make you want him more."

"Carolina, are you up there?" called Ariana.

She jumped at the sound of her aunt's voice. "*Sì, zia.*"

"Come down, your mamma wishes you to drive us to Bologna."

Carolina grimaced. "Coming, *zia.*" She hugged Sofia quickly. "I'll see you later. I suspect it's my aunt who wants me to drive them to Bologna to get me away from Dante."

As soon as Carolina disappeared from sight, Sofia continued on to Riccardo's room. She walked across to the dresser, laid down the phone, and picked up the key, poem, and album. "There has got to be a connection between you three." She sank onto the bed, opened the album, and meticulously went over each photo. By the last page she'd uncovered nothing new, but it worried her that there were two empty spaces where someone had removed photos. Next, she turned to the poem, reading it and re-reading it until she became frustrated.

"This is so annoying," she cried, bouncing on the bed. The album fell to the floor. As Sofia picked it up a photo dropped out. A photo Sofia hadn't seen before.

"Where did you come from?"

She studied the photo carefully. It was a shot of Renzina as a young girl, perhaps about twelve, and she stood beside a well in a pretty garden. Sofia frowned and picked up the album again, carefully examining the inside of the front cover. Nothing. She turned the album over and examined the inside of the back cover, excitement mounting when she discovered the corner of a photo poking out near the spine.

"Yes." Sofia pulled out the photo and checked for any others. Finding none, she turned back to examining the second photo. It was another shot of Renzina standing in front of a steel door, holding a large key in her hand, the same key that lay on the bed beside Sofia.

"Where is this door?" She thumped the bed and the poem rustled under her hand. She picked it up and starting reading.

I once had a garden, where flowers and a wishing well held center stage.

As I grew older my garden became my secret place where I could sit and dream.

Only those closest know the key will lead them to my heart and the treasure within.

"It's a secret garden. Renzina had a secret garden." Sofia picked up the photos. "This is the wishing well and it's in a secret garden." *Only those closest know the key will lead them to my heart and the treasure within.* "I have to find this garden." Sofia jumped up and paced.

"My grandparents would know." She picked up the poem and the key then ran from the room, along the hall, and down the stairs. The house seemed oddly quiet.

Sofia found her grandfather and Enrico Santini sitting out on the back terrace reminiscing about happier times.

"*Nonno*, do you know where this garden and well are?" Sofia handed the photos to her grandfather.

"*Sì.*" He passed them to Enrico.

Enrico smiled. "*Sì, sì*, Lorenzo. We built a fine well and the wall. It was a good wall."

Sofia clenched her hands impatiently. "I have a key, too." She placed the key on the table between them. "I think it might fit the door in the other photo."

Lorenzo looked at the key. "*Sì*, it is the key." He picked up the second photo. "That was a fine solid door and it stopped the boys, didn't it?"

"*Sì*, it did."

She frowned. "Stopped the boys from doing what, *Nonno*?"

"Giuseppe and Angelo used to torment Renzina something terrible. She would make gardens and they would ride their bikes through her flowers. So Enrico and I built her a garden with a wall around it. It was a good wall."

"A great wall," said Enrico.

"But where is it?" Sofia hopped from foot to foot.

Her grandfather looked at her in surprise. "Behind the *villa*, Sofia."

"Which *villa*?"

"What do you mean, which *villa*? Villa DeRosa."

"But, *Nonno*, I walked around the *villa* and I didn't see any garden walls."

Enrico put his hand on Lorenzo's shoulder. "*Sì*, it is still there, my friend, but the walls are covered in ivy so thick it's like a huge hedge."

Sofia couldn't contain her excitement. "Is there a wishing well in the garden, and does this key open the door?"

"*Sì*." Both men nodded.

Sofia chewed on her fingernail and tried to think. She looked down at the poem in her hand. "*The key will lead them to my heart and the treasure within.* What does this key have to do with Renzina's heart?"

Her grandfather smiled. "Renzina wanted her garden in the shape of a heart, so the wall is the heart, and that key opens the door."

Sofia gasped. "The wall is the heart and the key opens it and the well is in the garden. I know where the evidence is hidden, *Nonno*. Where is *Papà*? Where is Riccardo?"

"Your *papà* and Ariana went for a walk through the vineyard."

Sofia bit her lip. "Where's Riccardo?"

Enrico waved his hand back over his head. "He went with Giovanni and your brother, Dante. The police called about the partial number plates of the car that ran Renzina off the road. They have gone to deal with it."

Damn. "Has Carolina left yet?"

Enrico nodded. "*Sì*, she's gone to Bologna with Caterina, Louisa, and your *nonna*."

"What about Nico?"

Enrico and her grandfather looked at each other, then Enrico patted Sofia's hand. "He left soon after Riccardo and the boys. The police discovered a body. They think it is the man who attacked you in the hospital."

"Another body?" A chill ran through Sofia. She clenched her hands to stop them trembling and drew in a shaky breath. "How did he die?" Sofia caught the quick look between the two men. "Please, *Nonno*, tell me."

Her grandfather sighed. "He was hit by a train. The police say blood tests show high levels of alcohol in his system."

Sofia frowned. "But, *Nonno*, why do they think he's the man who attacked me?"

"He had tattoos on his fingers and matched the description of your attacker, so they went to his house and found the motor cycle that hit you. Now the police have decided your attacks are linked." He snorted. "Imbeciles. Nico has gone to the station to find out more."

This is a nightmare. Sofia straightened her shoulders. "I know where Renzina hid the evidence. I have to retrieve it before anyone else gets hurt."

Enrico and her grandfather shook their heads then her grandfather clasped Sofia's hand. "No, you wait here until Dante comes back."

"*Nonno,* that could be hours." Sofia chewed her lip. "I'm going to get help." She ran back upstairs, snatched up Caterina's phone, and called Riccardo. When he didn't answer she left a message then rang Dante, then Nico, Giovanni, and her father.

"For goodness sake, where are you all?" She selected Catarina's number and relief flooded her when Carolina answered.

"*Pronto, chi parla?*"

"Carolina, I know where the evidence is. It's in a secret garden behind the Villa DeRosa and the only way in is through a steel door that the key opens."

An excited scream on the other end made Sofia cringe. She waited while Carolina repeated her news to the others in the car.

"Carolina, the police found another body and they think it's the man who attacked me in the hospital. I need to get that evidence, but everyone's disappeared and no one is answering their phones. The only people here are our grandfathers."

"Don't you dare go on your own, Sofia. We are turning around and coming back."

"Okay, I'll wait." Sofia hung up and began pacing.

Chapter Twenty-four

Sofia was almost frantic when she heard a car. She ran to the window and peered out. *Michele.* She ran back to the terrace.

"*Nonno, Enrico*, Michele Bondini is coming up the drive."

"He's probably come to pick up his *papà*," called Enrico. "Tell him Salvatore went home with Hannah."

"Sure, *Enrico*, but I'm going to ask him to come with me to Villa DeRosa to search for the evidence." She didn't wait to hear their replies, instead, raced back through the villa, picked up the key, pocketed the phone, and swung the front door open. Michele was getting out of his car.

"Michele, I'm so glad you're here." She ran down the steps. "Your father has gone home with Hannah, but I need you to take me to Villa DeRosa."

He stood with the sun behind him and although Sofia couldn't see his face, she heard the surprise in his voice. "What's the rush? Where is everyone?"

"Who knows? They've disappeared. But I've discovered where the evidence is that's all I need to clear my father. It's hidden in a secret garden and I've got the key."

"Does Riccardo know?"

"No, he's disappeared along with my father and brothers."

"Your father is here...in *Italia*? That's unbelievable and unfortunate."

Sofia frowned. "Why unfortunate?'

"Because by coming here your father will reignite the feud between the Santinis and DeRosas. I have done my best to keep a lid on it."

"No, he won't. My father and brother arrived this morning and spent several hours with the Santinis. They're working together to discover the truth." She ran around the other side of the car. "You have to help me, Michele. The police found the body of the man who attacked me in the hospital, and Nico's gone to the police station to find out more. I'm not allowed to go anywhere on my own."

"That is unsettling. I would prefer you waited for Riccardo or your brother, but I suppose if you think this evidence will clear Guiseppe, then they won't mind if I take you." He unlocked the car.

Sofia yanked the door open. "*Grazie.*"

Michele drove the short distance to Villa DeRosa then parked around the back beside a wall of thick ivy.

Sofia climbed out and looked up. "The wall is under that ivy, and there's a secret garden behind it. We just need to find the door."

"I had no idea."

"Come on." Sofia pushed and pulled at the thick curtain of ivy. "This wall was built when my aunt was a little girl." She yanked more of the heavy foliage aside. "The door could be anywhere, help me search."

Michele hauled aside more ivy and they started working their way around the wall. They were almost back to where they'd started when Michele uncovered the steel door.

"Here it is," he called, his voice sounding as excited as Sofia.

Her hands shook as she inserted the key and turned it. There was a noisy clunk as the chamber fell. Sofia cheered and shoved. "It's stuck; you'll have to help me."

Putting his left shoulder against the door, Michele braced his feet and pushed until the door scraped against the paving. "I really am surprised. I didn't know this garden existed."

Sofia stood back, holding the ivy as he pushed. "But I thought you were friends with my father and Angelo. Didn't you play here?"

"We weren't close as young children and the only times I came here would have been with my parents for the occasional evening meal. I don't think I ever came out here."

With a final shove, Michele pushed the door wide. Sofia stepped through and stared around the overgrown, forgotten garden. "Wow."

Michele glanced sideways at her. "Are you sure it's in here?"

"I'm sure". She started toward the center of the garden, dodging round scrawny shrubs and stepping over prickly vines and long grass until she came to the unmistakable gabled roof of a wishing well.

"I found it." She glanced back.

Michele had stopped to untangle a thorny vine from his trousers, the left side of his face clearly visible. A twinge of uneasiness stole over Sofia as she stared at his cheek and the two stitches marring it. "Michele, what happened to your face?"

His gloved hand touched his cheek. "I had a cancer spot removed. I apologize if the stitches upsets you."

Dropping her gaze to his gloved hands, Sofia swallowed. Could Michele be the man who attacked her? What possible reason could he have for setting up her father?

Wiping her clammy hands on her skirt, she turned back to the well and pulled the long grass away from the bricked sides. "It doesn't bother me. When did you have it done?"

"Three days ago, while I was in *Milano*, I only got back this afternoon."

Sofia let out a breath she hadn't realized she was holding. "You've been in *Milano* for three days? So you don't know about my latest attack?"

"My father told me when I arrived home. Do you have any idea who he was?"

She shook her head, wondering if this seemingly unassuming man could be lying to her. With his weight and age, he'd never catch her if she ran.

He peered at the well. "Is there anything in it?"

Sofia peered over the edge, disappointed to find it shallow and full of weeds. "No."

Joining her, Michele glanced up under the gabled roof. "Why would you think the evidence is hidden here?"

Sofia glanced at the open door. The others shouldn't be much longer. If Michele were somehow involved then how was she to find out, without ending up dead? *Stall him.*

She handed him the poem then dropped to her haunches and ran her hands over the bricks. "*Signora* Rinaldi gave me a photo album that belonged to my aunt. I found that poem in the back along with a couple of photos of this garden. *Signora* Rinaldi also gave me the key.

I think the poem refers to this garden, and the key *did* open the door after all."

"It is just a poem. You are clutching at straws, *signorina*."

"Michele, this garden is surrounded by a wall that has been built in the shape of a heart and the key opened it." Suspicion gnawed at her. "Take your driving gloves off and help me get this plaque out. I think there's a cavity behind it." She needed to make sure his hands weren't torn to pieces.

Squatting beside her, Michele examined the plaque. "We need something to lever it off." He picked up a piece of broken roof tile and tried wedging it behind the plaque.

"Use your fingers, Michele, that's too thick. Take your gloves off or they'll get ruined." *Why won't he take his gloves off?*

"My fingers are too big. You do it and I'll wedge the tile in behind."

Sofia looked at Michele's gloved fingers again. They were rather large. Again she felt a sense of uneasiness as she raised her eyes to meet his. She drew in a deep breath. Had she just made a terrible mistake coming here? *It can't be him, it can't.*

If he was her attacker, she couldn't let him guess her suspicion. Gripping the plaque, Sofia wedged her fingernails behind it, and began to jiggle back and forth. "It's moving. Quick, stick the tile in."

Wedging the tile behind the plaque, Michele jimmied until it gave way and fell at their feet. "There is something in there!" he exclaimed.

Sofia reached in and pulled out a parcel wrapped in oilskin cloth. She unfolded the material carefully. "It's a tin box."

Michele's eyes rose from the box to Sofia's face. "Open it."

She nodded and did as he asked, prying the lid off. It fell to the ground. With shaking hands she lifted out a thin diary and some papers. "They're in Italian."

Leaning over, Michele took the papers. "These are bank bonds and—" he shuffled through the sheets, his eyes shining "—these bonds must be worth millions now." He placed them back in the box and plucked it out of Sofia's hand. "They're the missing bonds that disappeared from your grandfather's safe thirty years ago."

Sofia flicked through the diary. "It's in Italian too." She closed it and tapped the cover with her fingernails. "I think we should take these straight to my father."

"I agree." Michele reached for the diary. "Can I see it?"

Sofia held it to her chest. "My father should be the one to read it first. After all, he suffered the most from the accusations."

"*Si*, Sofia, but the sooner we know who to guard against, the better."

"We can tell you who to guard against," called a female voice from behind them.

Sofia spun around to face the newcomer. Carolina stood there with a double barrel rifle pointed directly at them. Behind her stood Hannah.

Sofia clutched the diary tighter and drew in a shaky breath. "What are you doing, Carolina?"

Michele took a step toward them. "I don't know what you think you are doing, but this is not the answer. Please put down the rifle, Carolina."

"Stay where you are Michele or I'll shoot."

Sofia glanced from Carolina, to Hannah, to Michele. "What's going on?"

Michele scowled. "I have no idea. Carolina, give me the rifle?"

She shook her head. "No, *signore*. You set up Giuseppe DeRosa, and ran his sister off the road, and you arranged the attacks on Sofia."

"Are you sure, Carolina?" Sofia clung to the diary.

"I know you'll find this hard to believe, Sofia, but since arriving in Bologna, Michele has had you followed. He even had Hannah feeding him information on your movements."

Sofia glanced at Hannah. "Is that true?"

She blushed. "I'm sorry, Sophia. At first I thought Michele just wanted to protect you, but then I caught him faxing a photo of you and Riccardo to a number in Australia, and across the bottom he'd written, *Riccardo Santini is about to add another notch to his belt.*"

Sofia gasped and looked at Michele. "Why would you do that?"

"To protect you. I thought it might motivate your brother to come and get you before somebody succeeded in killing you. I did it for your own good."

Sofia exhaled. "That's what brought my father here." She focused on Carolina and Hannah.

"Let's calm down. Michele may have faxed a photo of me and

Riccardo to *Papà*, but that doesn't mean he's behind the conspiracy, or my aunt's death and the attacks on me."

Carolina waved the rifle at Michele. "He wasn't in *Milano* the day you were attacked, Sofia. He was here." She glanced at Hannah. "Tell Sofia what you told me."

Hannah nodded. "I came home early, put my car in the garage, and went to my room. No one else was supposed to be home." She shot a quick glance at Michele. "I heard a car and looked out to see Michele's Saab coming up the drive. A few minutes later he drove off again."

Michele scoffed. "You may have seen my Saab, but I wasn't driving it. I asked my secretary to pick up some papers for me."

"There's more," blustered Hannah, her eyes on Sofia. "A short while ago, Riccardo and your brother came to speak to my grandfather. They wanted to know about a car he once owned that matches the vehicle that ran your aunt off the road. Riccardo said, whoever is attacking Sofia, knows her every movement. I sneaked into Michele's room and searched it. I found a bunch of keys with a Villa DeRosa tag and his camera. It has lots of photos of you and Riccardo on it."

Sofia recoiled. "Photos?"

"Yes," asserted Hannah, holding up a camera and bunch of keys.

Michele threw up his arms. "I told you why I took the photos."

A shudder ran through Sofia as she glanced between Michele and Hannah. They stared at each other with loathing. They obviously hated each other, but it didn't mean Michele was her attacker.

"I know how we can resolve this." Sofia pointed to Michele's hands. "Take off your driving gloves. The man who attacked me at Villa DeRosa escaped by climbing down a thorny Bougainvillea. If you're innocent then your hands won't be cut to pieces."

Michele shoved the tin box at Sofia, removed his gloves and held out his hands. They were clean and free of any cuts or scratches. "Satisfied."

Carolina looked thwarted.

Hannah frowned, her hands dropping to her sides. "I was so sure, right down to the number plates."

Sofia heaved a sigh of relief. "It's okay, Hannah. We all make mistakes and at least no one got shot. Where did you get that gun, Caro?"

"It's my father's clay pigeon rifle."

Michele walked over and took the rifle out of Carolina's hands. "That was a very foolish thing to do. You could have shot me."

"Sorry. I arrived home and couldn't find Sofia, then *Nonno* told me she'd come here with you. I was about to follow when Hannah arrived in a panic and the rifle was the only thing I could think to grab."

Sofia frowned at Hannah. "What were you saying about number plates?"

"A couple of days ago, Riccardo asked me to approach every panel beater within an hours drive and ask if they had a record of repairs to a dark blue Mercedes, thirty years ago. Most had changed hands, gone out of business, or didn't keep records that old."

"I get the feeling there's an exception," Sofia said, watching as Michele snapped the rifle open, emptied the chambers, and closed it again.

"Yes. After Riccardo and your brother left, I got a call from a man who repaired a dark blue, 1952 Mercedes Benz 300 Adenauer, thirty years ago. He recollected it clearly because the owner had paid well above the going rate. The number plates matched my grandfather's."

Sofia hugged the tin box and diary. Was Salvatore the man behind this? "Michele, do you think your father is responsible for Renzina's death?"

"I..."

"No," said Hannah. "My grandfather told Riccardo he was in America when Renzina died and they could easily check. I was about to tell Salvatore my suspicions when Michele turned up with his face stitched. I waited until he drove off again then I told Salvatore, but he said I had to be wrong."

Michele sighed. "Hannah, you are so naïve, just like your mother. At least she knew when to cut her loses and run." He lashed out, the rifle butt connecting with Hannah's head in a sickening crack. She made no sound as her legs buckled underneath her.

Sofia and Carolina screamed and dropped to their knees beside Hannah, the tin box falling to the ground and spilling its contents.

Sofia stared at Michele in disbelief. "How could you do that? What if she dies?"

He threw the rifle aside and pulled out a handgun. "I really don't care." He bent and scooped up the camera and keys.

Carolina glared at him. "You heartless pig. If you kill us, our families will hunt you down and tear you to pieces."

He sneered. "Not with what I've got planned. Now give me the box."

Sofia looked at Hannah's still face and the blood spreading over the grass under her head, then she glanced into Carolina's furious eyes and calmness settled over her. *Riccardo and Dante will save us.*

With Carolina screening her, Sofia reached into her pocket and drew out the phone. She didn't have time to call anyone but she could record the bastard. She met Carolina's gaze before looking at Michele. "If you're going to kill us, can you at least tell us why?"

"I would've thought that was obvious, *signorina*. You know too much and no matter what I did to scare you off, you wouldn't give up."

Sofia edged the phone back into her skirt then ripped the cotton frill off and wrapped it tightly around Hannah's head. "So it was *you* who set my father up and spread the rumors. Why?"

Keeping the gun trained on them, Michele shrugged his shoulders carelessly. "Giuseppe had it all—money, popularity, friends, success, women. He would see something he wanted and almost with the snap of his fingers, he had it."

"That's no reason to destroy my father. I thought your family was close to the DeRosas. What would your father say?"

Michele snarled. "My father is a stupid old man who always thought more of Giuseppe DeRosa than his own son. But, yes I had another reason to ruin your father *and* Angelo Santini. They didn't think I was good enough for Ariana."

Sofia stared at him aghast. "Nico's mother?"

"Yes. I worshipped Ariana, but they didn't want me near her. Angelo warned me off and then Giuseppe swept in and took her for himself. So I ruined Giuseppe, but then his sister Renzina stepped in and started her own investigations. Like you, she just couldn't leave it alone."

He spat on the ground. "Even after I got rid of Giuseppe, Ariana refused to go out with me. Instead she took off and married an old man. When he died, I offered to take care of her and her son, but still she refused me, because she never got over Giuseppe. And now he's back. I can't believe it."

Sofia stared at him in astonishment. "You set up my father with the prostitutes to break up his engagement to Ariana?"

"Yes, and everything worked out better than I could have hoped."

Leaning over Hannah's still body, Sofia placed her fingers against the side of her neck. *Please don't die.* Relief surged as she detected a steady pulse. *Thank God.*

"Is she dead?" asked Michele impatiently.

Sofia's gaze lifted to Carolina's stricken face and their eyes met. "I can't feel a pulse."

"Good, now get up slowly, and give me the box," ordered Michele.

Sofia swiped a tear away, leaned over, and picked up the box and its contents. *Maybe if I delay somehow we'll have a chance to get away.* She glared at him. "Wasn't it enough to break up Ariana and my father? Why set the fires and run Renzina off the road?"

He snickered. "After the threats your father made, it was an opportunity I couldn't resist, plus Angelo needed to suffer too. So I robbed your grandfather's safe, spread rumors, and bribed a couple of witnesses." He waved the gun at them. "Come, I don't have time to waste."

Carolina cast Hannah one more look then stood and walked toward the heavy door.

Sofia followed. "Why did you run my aunt off the road?"

"Renzina refused to believe her dear brother was guilty. She kept nosing around and harassing the witnesses. Then while I was out of the office she came to see me and convinced my secretary to let her wait. She found the bonds and escaped before I could stop her. She refused to tell me where she'd hidden them and told me she was going to the police. I couldn't let that happen."

Carolina and Sofia reached the door, stopped, and glanced back toward Hannah.

"Keep moving," urged Michele. "Go through then lock the door. I don't want anyone going in there until I get rid of the body."

Sofia glared at him as she dragged the door shut and locked it. "Don't you even care that Hannah is the apple of your father's eye? How can you be so cold blooded?"

He waved them in the direction of Carolina's mother's car. "I refuse to share my inheritance with that little nobody. Now bring the key and walk to the back of the car."

Sofia gripped the box in one hand and the key in the other. They were the only weapons she had, but at least this time she had time to plan and question. "Why didn't your hands get damaged by the bougainvillea?"

"I had driving gloves in my pocket. Sadly they were destroyed."

Sofia and Carolina halted by the boot of the Mercedes. Michele kept the gun trained on them as he opened the boot.

"What are you going do?" Sofia demanded. "My grandfather and Enrico Santini know you brought me here."

Michele laughed cruelly. "And so I did, but I will inform the police that you told me about Riccardo and your brother interviewing my father, so I dropped you here and raced home to see what the fuss was about." He laughed again. "I had no idea your attacker was waiting in the *villa* for you." He pointed the gun at Carolina. "Get in the boot."

She shook her head. "No, I won't let you hurt Sofia."

He swore then backhanded her across the face. She cried out, falling into the boot. Michele shoved her feet in and slammed the lid, then swung the gun on Sofia."

"No," shouted Sofia, putting her hands up to protect her.

Michele lifted the gun high then brought it crashing down on her shoulder. Sofia yelped and fell to the ground.

Carolina screamed from inside the boot.

Grabbing Sofia's arm, Michele hauled her up. "Now walk to the *villa*."

Chapter Twenty-Five

Wincing in pain, Sofia did as he asked, walking as slowly as she dared. *I have to stop him before he kills Carolina and Hannah, but how?* She swallowed. "You're a dead man when Riccardo and my brothers catch up with you."

"Brothers? You said you only have one brother?"

Climbing the terrace steps, Sofia purposely tripped on the top one and fell to her knees. She flung one hand out to save herself, deftly dropping the large key over the edge, amongst a stack of weeds. At least Michele couldn't get into the garden now. Rising to her feet again, she faced him. "Nicolas Lombardi is my half brother."

"You're lying," roared Michele, his face mottling with rage.

"No, I'm not. We found out for sure a few days ago and Nico is changing his name to DeRosa. *Papà* and Ariana are delighted."

He took a step toward her. "Inside now."

She lurched back at the venom in Michele's eyes. A cold shiver ran down her spine as she pressed up against the door. *This isn't good.* "I don't have the keys to the villa."

His lips thinned. "*Non è un problema*, I have the spare set." He threw the keys, keeping the gun pointed at her. "We are going to the front parlor."

Sofia unlocked the door and did as he'd asked; praying Riccardo and Dante had checked their messages. She stopped in the center of the parlor. Why was it the bad guys always confessed before they killed you? *He hasn't confessed to everything.*

"What happened to the two men who attacked me?" she asked.

"They were loose ends that needed tidying up."

Heart thumping, Sofia clenched her fists to stop them trembling. "And me?"

"Another loose end. I'm going to kill you too."

She shivered. "Why didn't you do it in the garden?"

"I intend to burn Villa DeRosa to the ground and when they search through the rubble, they will find your body."

Her stomach cramped. *Poor Papà.* How could she keep Michele talking?

Willing her body to calm, Sofia drew back her shoulders and inhaled deeply. "What are you planning to do with Hannah and Carolina?

"I will take them up to one of the scenic lookouts, then send their car careening off the edge. Sadly when the police find the wreckage, they will discover two bodies."

Sofia's jaw clenched as bile rose in her throat. "You've thought of everything haven't you? I suppose you're going to blame my death on the Santinis."

"Of course. Now stay where you are."

Sofia's shoulders sagged. *I need more time. They can't be that far away. Think, Sofia.*

"How will you blame the Santinis? The least you can do is tell me what you intend."

He gave an offhand shrug. "I will bring Angelo Santini here on the pretense that you are in the *villa* alone and I fear for your safety. He will see the flames and rush in to save you. I will make it look like he killed you to prevent you marrying Riccardo. Your father will retaliate by killing Angelo."

Sofia watched the gun nervously. "That won't work. My grandfather and Enrico Santini are aware you brought me here, and *Papà* is out walking with Ariana. They will know someone is trying to set both families up. *Papà* won't kill Angelo."

Michele's eyes blazed. "You are lying. I saw the women in Ariana's car. They have gone to Bologna as I organized."

"I'm not lying. It was Carolina driving the car, not Ariana, but they turned back when I rang them." Sofia watched Michele pace the floor for a couple of minutes.

He came to a stop and scowled at her. "Put the key in the box and pass it to me."

Sofia prized the lid up a little and pretended to put the key in, then closed it firmly.

At the sound of squealing tires and roaring engines, Michele whirled and ran to peer through the closed French doors. "No, this is not supposed to happen yet."

Sofia gripped the box tightly. "It appears your plan is coming unstuck, Michele."

His head snapped round. "Stay where you are and don't make a sound." He turned back to the window.

From where Sofia was standing, she couldn't see who had arrived, but she heard at least three doors slam and several male voices shouting as they ran toward the secret garden. She said a silent prayer then hurled the box as hard as she could at Michele's head.

Boom!

A gunshot echoed round the room, the bullet shattering the ornate knob holding the chandelier to the ceiling. Sofia screamed as the old chandelier shook violently then dropped several inches. She dived clear, landing hard. Her gaze swung to Michele to find him aiming the gun at her.

She threw herself toward a shrouded couch as a loud shot rang out and the wall above her exploded, showering her in bits of cement. Sofia screamed again and crawled further behind the couch, cringing as the chandelier crashed to the floor, shattering into thousand of shards

The noise was like a bomb going off. Michele cried out. She hoped a razor sharp shard had hit him fatally. Male voices shouted and someone was hammering on the front door.

Sofia dragged herself to the far end of the couch and peeped round. Michele crunched across the glass and picked up the tin box, then backed toward the French doors.

Sofia's lungs seized as he took aim at her again. She slithered back, squeezing into a ball as bullets hit the couch and wall inches above her. *Riccardo.*

Riccardo looked around desperately. "This door is never going to budge." Sweat ran down his back as he tried to shoulder-charge the door again.

Another shot rang out and another.

Swiping sweat from his eyes, Riccardo sprinted round the house to the side terrace, rage and adrenaline pumping through his veins. *Please, God, don't let me be too late.*

He skidded to a halt as a heavy-set man backed toward the French doors. The man held a gun, his arm outstretched and his profile clear. Riccardo's heart plummeted. He flinched as two more shots rang out. "Bastardo."

Riccardo launched himself through the French doors. They disintegrated on top of Michele, taking him to the ground where he lay among the shattered glass.

Bounding to his feet, Riccardo's gaze searched the room. There was no sign of Sofia. He kicked aside bits of smashed doorframe and glass to get to Michele, who scrambled to his knees, reaching for the gun.

Riccardo kicked Michele's thigh, sending him sprawling. "*Bastardo! Ti uccidero.*" He roared, grabbing Michele by the collar of his suit to haul him to his feet.

"Where is Sofia?" He slammed Michele against the wall. "Tell me, or I'll kill you?"

Michele made a choking sound. "Please, Riccardo, it wasn't me. I was trying to protect her from your father. Angelo doesn't want you to marry Sofia. He's the one who has been trying to kill her."

"Liar." Riccardo smashed his fist into Michele's jaw. "I'm going to kill you." He drew back his arm and rammed his fist into Michele's nose, shattering bone and hurting his own hand. It wasn't enough to ease the pain piercing his heart and soul. He roared in agony and smashed his fist into Michele again and again.

Sofia crawled to her knees at Riccardo's frightening roar. A shiver ran through her. She'd never heard anyone so threatening and she feared Riccardo would kill Michele. As she poked her head over the couch, she saw Dante and Nico attempting to pull Riccardo away from Michele. Giovanni stood brandishing the gun.

"Where is she?" thundered Riccardo.

"I'm here," called Sofia, shakily.

Riccardo reeled around, his wild gaze finding her. He shrugged off

Dante and Nico then strode over the broken glass, caught her under the arms then hauled her over the back of the couch into his arms.

"*Tesoro*, I thought he'd killed you."

Wrapping her arms around Riccardo's neck, Sofia hugged him. "He tried, but he missed. I was so frightened you wouldn't make it in time."

Easing her back, Riccardo's gaze searched her face. "I nearly didn't."

Sofia wiped the moisture away at the corner of his eyes then kissed him. "But you did."

Dante and Nico stepped over the glass then hugged her in turn.

As Giovanni stood over Michele, he pointed at the couch. "With all those bullet holes, I'm amazed he missed you."

Nico leaned over the back. "Santa Maria, you must have a guardian angel, Sofia. There are holes everywhere. Are you sure you're not hurt?"

"I'm fine, but Hannah's unconscious and bleeding from a head wound. She's locked in the secret garden. I dropped the key to it in the weeds beside the back steps of the villa."

Nico stared at her with disbelief. "Michele tried to kill Hannah?"

"Yes, he hit her with a rifle really hard and Carolina's locked in the boot of Ariana's car." She swallowed. "In case we were killed, I recorded everything on Carolina's phone."

Nico's fists clenched as he shot a vicious look at Michele. "I'll see to Hannah." He ran from the room.

"I'll get Carolina and ring for an ambulance and the police," called Giovanni taking the gun and running after Nico.

Dante gave Sofia a relieved look then dragged the dazed and bloodied Michele outside.

Riccardo picked Sofia up and carried her over the shattered glass to the terrace. "I love you, *cara mia*." He strode down the worn concrete steps and lowered her feet to the grass.

Sofia wrapped her arms around Riccardo's waist and looked into his face. "I love you too, darling." She was shaking so badly her teeth chattered. All strength seeped away and she sagged against him. Tears welled and spilled down her cheeks.

Riccardo squeezed her tighter. When his voice came, it sounded husky. "I thought I'd never see you alive again. I thought I'd never get the chance to tell you how much you mean to me and that you are the only woman for me." His voice cracked.

Sniffing back the tears, Sofia placed her finger against his lips. "I feel the same way about you, my love." She cleared her throat and straightened. "Everything's going to be okay, Riccardo. We've cleared my father and caught the man responsible. Our families will be friends again and I can stay here in Italy with you." She sniffed again and buried her face against his chest.

"Ah, *tesoro*, everything will be wonderful as long as we are together." Riccardo's hands stroked up and down her back, the heat of his body slowly warming her. He chuckled. "I don't think we're the only ones in love. Look."

Sofia glanced out over the bedraggled gardens to the vines in the distance and smiled. *Papà* and Ariana were some distance off, walking toward the villa, deep in conversation with their arms around each other. Sofia smiled at Riccardo. "I think you're right, and I couldn't be happier for them." She glanced at Dante standing on the tangled lawn in front of the villa, his shirt covered in Michele's blood. Michele sat in a crumpled heap at Dante's feet.

"Sofia!" Carolina hurtled round the side of the villa. She skidded to a standstill when she saw them. "Thank God, you're alive." Her gaze moved to Dante and Michele. She screeched. "Dante! You're bleeding."

He stepped away from Michele and caught Carolina in his arms as she hurled herself at him. "This is not my blood, *bella*, but I'm flattered by your concern." He pulled her close, then bent his head and kissed her.

Sofia darted an anxious glance at Riccardo. "Don't be mad. They like each other."

Riccardo sighed then raised Sofia's chin to place a chaste kiss on her lips. "Carolina will never leave Italy or our parents."

Sofia smiled. "Maybe she won't have to. I think it is Dante and Carolina who are destined to restore the Villa DeRosa and vineyard to their former glory. I also think my father will sell our vineyard in Australia and return to Italy to marry Ariana and help Dante."

"We will see."

Sofia kissed him then tapped her nose. "I think Nico is keener on

Hannah than he lets on. Did you see his face when he discovered she'd been hurt?"

"Yes, and it explains why he is always requesting her services in his office." Riccardo inhaled deeply. "As soon as the police are finished with us, I'm taking you to *Venezia*, where I intend to keep you to myself for a whole week."

Stretching up, Sofia returned his kiss. "That sounds wonderful, *caro mio*, absolutely wonderful, and I would love nothing better, but my father will never allow it. He's a bit old fashioned that way."

Riccardo groaned. "Then we shall get married as soon as possible. In the meantime, don't for one moment think you'll be sleeping anywhere but my bed. You will just have to sneak in every night."

Sofia giggled. "I wouldn't have it any other way, my love."

Nico strode around the side of the *villa* carrying Hannah in his arms, her head resting against his shoulder. She looked pale as she gave Sofia a sad smile.

Giovanni followed them, ploughing through the knee-high grass. "Everything okay?"

"*Si.*" Riccardo said. His arms tightened around Sofia. "We are getting married as soon as it can be arranged. You will have to close the deal on the hotel in *Venezia* on your own."

Giovanni gave Sofia a pained look. "To do that, I must convince a reclusive Australian lady to sell her share of the hotel, and from what I hear, she's as stubborn as you."

Riccardo chuckled. "While I was in *Venezia*, I discovered she's young and attractive, so you could try charming her into selling."

Giovanni winked at Sofia. "That won't be a problem as long as she doesn't bewitch me as you have bewitched Riccardo."

"Ha, ha, you're such a comedian." Sofia stuck her tongue out at him.

A siren sounded in the distance.

Riccardo entwined his fingers with Sofia's. "Come, the police are almost here."

"Okay." Sofia glanced at Michele's swollen and bloodied face as he sat hunched on the ground, staring mutinously at Nico and Hannah.

The police pulled up, followed by an ambulance, and two cars carrying the elderly Santinis, DeRosas, and Salvatore Bondini.

Hearing the sirens, Giuseppe and Ariana ran along the avenue of overgrown vines.

While the paramedics examined Hannah, everyone else gathered round as the police took charge of Michele.

Sofia explained how she'd figured out where the evidence was. And how she'd come to the garden with Michele and all that followed then handed the phone to the police. "It's all recorded for you."

With tears in his eyes, Salvatore Bondini looked at his son in utter bewilderment, but Michele said nothing as he stared with contempt at his father. The policemen placed him in their car then Salvatore turned and walked unsteadily to the ambulance.

Sofia frowned. "There are still two things that need answering. Michele told me my two brothers were going to receive a large amount of money each." She looked at her grandmother. "But you didn't know Nico is your grandson, so it had to be Nonno who knew." Sofia's gaze shifted to her grandfather. "Who sent Renzina's letter to my father?"

Her grandfather sighed. "When I saw you walking with Nicolas in the Piazza five years ago I knew he was Giuseppe's son. The likeness was indisputable. Recently, your Nonna and I were going through Renzina's papers and I found her diary. She mentioned several times that Ariana was carrying Giuseppe's baby, so when I decided to liquidate my assets, I had Nicolas included in the settlement. I didn't know what else to do."

Sofia nodded. "And the letter. Did you send that too?"

"No, I had no idea it existed."

"I sent the letter."

They all turned to look at Sofia's grandmother. She smiled sadly. "I didn't know about the diary, but I found Renzina's letter addressed to Giuseppe. It broke my heart to realize my son was innocent and we hadn't believed him." Tears filled her eyes as she focused on Giuseppe. "I knew you would never willingly come back to *Italia*, but I decided to post the letter anyway. I never imagined Sofia would open it and then come to *Italia* on her own. *Caro mio*, I hope you can find it in your heart to forgive us for doubting you?"

Giuseppe left Ariana's side and wrapped his arms around his mother and father. They clung to each for several minutes before regaining their composure.

Sofia fought to hold back tears as Riccardo put his arm around her. He smiled down at her. "I think everything's going to be all right."

"I think so too." She closed her eyes and rested her head against Riccardo's chest, taking a few moments to savor the sense of triumph, exhilaration, and peace she felt.

I did it.

One of the policemen strode over. "*Scuzi, signore e signori.*" He smiled at Sofia and Riccardo. "This is crime scene. You may go to the Villa Santini and your statements will be collected later."

Riccardo nodded. "*Grazie.*"

As Salvatore and Nico climbed into the ambulance with Hannah, Riccardo tucked a stray curl behind Sofia's ear. "Let's walk home through the vineyard."

"I'd like that."

They waved their families off, then Sofia slid her hand into Riccardo's and they strolled across the bedraggled gardens and along a row of lush vines, heavy with ripe grapes.

Riccardo paused and gazed into her eyes. "I love you, Sofia, more than I ever imagined possible." His eyes took on a wicked glint. "You are mine, *tesoro.*"

Sofia beamed, knowing her love shone in her eyes. "No, *tesoro,* you are mine." She reached up and stroked his cheek lovingly. "Thank you for helping me discover the truth and for protecting me and loving me. Thank you for making me part of your family."

Riccardo's strong arms tightened, drawing her intimately against him. "*La mia famiglia è tutto.*" His beautiful dark eyes radiated love and desire. "You are everything to me, *tesoro.* I will cherish and worship you for all eternity."

A single tear rolled down Sofia's cheek. "As I will you, my love."

Riccardo's hands skimmed down her back. He lowered his head, dropped a kiss on her collarbone then feathered several more kisses up her neck. Desire rippled through her.

He chuckled. "I'm afraid I may have to torture you for what you put me through today."

Sofia giggled. "Don't be afraid, *tesoro.* You know I can give as good as I get."

Riccardo laughed. "Oh my darling, what have I unleashed? Let's see if you are quite so self-assured in a couple of hours."

THE END

About The Author

Erin Moira O'Hara grew up in the Blue Mountains of Australia, with a garden backing onto native bushland, hidden caves and fabulous lookouts. Weekends were spent exploring, climbing trees and creating secret bases. Her love of reading began with visits to the local library, where she became absorbed in a world of intrigue, fantasy and action-packed adventures. The moment Erin read her first romance; she recognised the importance of finding the right man to share her life. She now lives with him close to the largest saltwater lake in Australia. Their home overlooks bushland and is surrounded by an abundance of bird life and an ever-growing garden.

Erin's writing encompasses everything she loves—intrigue, suspense, passion and romance.

If you would like to know more, please visit:
http://www.erinmoiraohara.com